THE RAI

BEING SOME PASSAGES IN THE LIFE OF JOHN FAA, LORD AND EARL OF LITTLE EGYPT

S. R. CROCKETT

First Published 1894

This Edition Published 2020

Adapted by Neil Campbell

INTRODUCTION TO THIS EDITION

The Raiders was first published by S.R. Crockett in 1894 and is generally regarded as one of the finest of his extensive body of work.

It is set in the part of Scotland I grew up in, Kirkcudbrightshire, and I have spent many days walking and climbing in the moors and mountains where much of the action occurs, and almost all of the place-names and features described can be identified today. I have walked almost every mile of the routes taken by the characters in the book and, as they discovered, it is often hard going. But there are natural features to marvel at, some of which feature in the book, the equal of anything in the Scottish Highlands.

For the telling of the tale, Crockett assembled a rich variety of characters and relationships. We are presented with the confused but brave central character, his mysterious associate, his female nemesis, the ruthless pirate, the gently bickering spinsters and the tragi-comic farmhands and many more. There are some genuinely funny scenes, but also ones of high emotion. It is one of the strengths of the novel that most of the dialogue is written in the Scots language, however, this makes it a difficult read today even for Scots, and it is almost impenetrable to non-Scots.

So, in an effort to make this excellent tale more accessible to a wider readership, I have produced this version solely in English. Some minor changes to the narrative have also been made to provide a more fluent read for modern readers. In no way should this be seen to undermine current efforts to support the Scots language, which I applaud, and the original version is still in print. Blame lockdown.

It's all about the story, who wrote it and the place in which it is set.

I also hope that this might also promote increased interest in the works of Crockett and any profits from this publication will be directed to organisations involved in that activity.

Neil Campbell
Yealmpton, Devon
December 2020

The Stewartry of Kirkcudbright

DUNGEON of the BUCHAN

Loch Enoch

Clatteringshaws

Parton

Mossdale

Dumfries

Bridge over Black Water of Dee

Clachanpluck

Cree Bridge

Bridge of Dee

Earlstoun

Kirk-cudbright

Craigdarroch

Isle of Rathan

Irish Sea

5 miles (approx)

Patrick's journeys – both started from the coast, the first going anticlockwise, the second, clockwise. ···········

The Dungeon of the Buchan

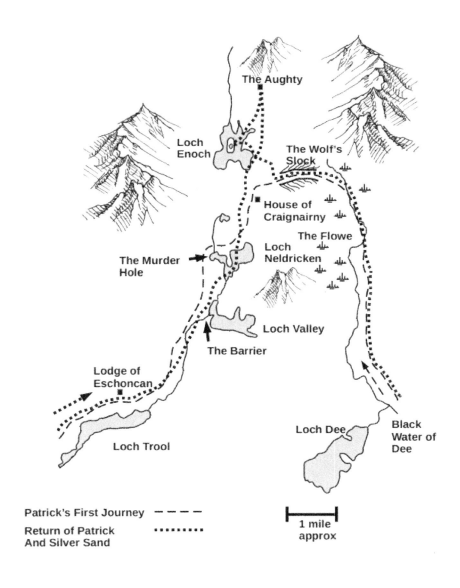

The Aughty

Loch Enoch

The Wolf's Slock

House of Craignairny

The Flowe

The Murder Hole

Loch Neldricken

Loch Valley

The Barrier

Lodge of Eschoncan

Loch Dee

Black Water of Dee

Loch Trool

Patrick's First Journey — — — —

Return of Patrick And Silver Sand ·········

1 mile approx

FOREWORD.

I, Patrick Heron of Isle Rathan in Galloway, begin the writing of my book with thanks to God, the Giver of all good, for the early and bountiful harvest which He has been pleased to give us here in little Scotland, in this year of His Grace, 17--. It is not the least of the Lord's mercies that throughout all this realm, the crops of corn, Merse wheat, Lowden oats, and Galloway barley, should be in the stockyards under thatch and rope by the second day of September.

So, with a long winter before me, the mind running easy about the corn, despite rising prices, I am not likely to get a better season of quiet to write down the things that befell us in those strange years when the hill outlaws conspired with the wild freetraders of the Holland traffic, and fell upon us to the destruction of the life of man, the carrying away of much bestial, besides the putting of many of His Majesty's lieges in fear.

Now it will appear that there are many things in this long story which I shall have to tell concerning myself which are far from doing me credit, but let it not be forgotten that it was for me the time of wild oat sowing when the blood ran warm. Also these were the graceless, unhallowed days after the Great Killing, when good Christians had been driven from the hills of Galloway and Carrick, and when the fastnesses of the utmost hills were held by a set of wild outlaws – cattle reivers and murderers, worse than the painted savages of whom navigators to the far seas bring us word.

It was with May Mischief that the terrible blast of storm began (and most storms among men do begin with a bonny lass, like that concerning Helen of Troy, which lasted ten years and of which men speak to this day). The tale began with May Mischief, as you shall hear. I still use her old name, though the years have gone by, and in talking of the old days and of all our ancient ploys, there are now children to be considered. But it is necessary that before the memory quite dies out, some one who saw these things should write them down. Some, it is true, were deeper in than I, but none saw more or clearer, being involved in both the inception and the conclusion of the matter.

CHAPTER I.

MOONLIGHT AND MAY MISCHIEF.

IT was on Rathan Head that I first heard their bridle-reins jingling. It was my custom to walk in the full moon at all times of the year. The moons of the months are wondrously different: the moon of January, serene among the stars – that of February, wading among chill cloud-banks of snow – of March, brownish-grey with the mist of burning heather – of early April, clean washed by the rains. This was now May, and the moon of May is the loveliest in all the year, for with its brightness comes the scent of flower-buds, and of young green leaves breaking from the quick and breathing earth.

So it was in the height of the moon of May, that I heard their bridle-reins jingling clear and saw the harness glisten on their backs.

"Keep well inside your own house when the Marshalls ride!" said my father, nodding his head at every third word in a way he had.

I shall never forget that night. I rowed towards the land in our little boat, which was usually drawn up in the cove on Rathan Isle, and lay a great time out on the clear, still flow of a silver tide that ran inwards, drifting slowly up with it. I was happy and at peace, and the world was at peace with me. I shipped the oars and lay back thinking. A lad's mind runs naturally towards young lasses, but as yet I had none of these to occupy me. Indeed there was only one of my own standing in the neighbourhood – one May Maxwell who was called, not without cause, May Mischief, a sister of the wild Maxwells of Craigdarroch – and I could not abide her. There was nothing in her to think about in particular, and certainly I never liked her; nevertheless, one's mind being contrary, I began to think about her as the tide swirled southward by Rathan – especially on the curious way she had of smiling when a wicked speech was brewing behind her eyes.

My skiff lay just outside the lee of the land, the black shadow of the Orraland shore was on my left; and both the boat and I were as clear in the moonlight as a fly on a sheet of white paper.

There was a brig at anchor in the bay, and it was along the cliffs towards her that I saw the horsemen ride. They were, I knew, going to stow its cargo into shelters. I thought how fine they looked, and wondered how long it would be till my father would let me have a horse and a smuggler's rope and join the Free Trade among the Manxmen, when all at once I got a sudden, horrid surprise.

I could hear the riders laughing and wagering among themselves, but I was too far away to hear what the game might be. Suddenly one of them whipped a musket to his shoulder. I was so near the shore that I saw the flash of moonlight run along the barrel as he brought it to his eye. I wondered what he could be aiming at – most likely a sea bird.

"Clip! Splash!" went something past my head and through the bow of the boat. Then after the crack of the gun came a great roar of laughter from the cliff edge

"A miss! A palpable miss!" cried some one behind.

"Hold her nose down, you fool!"

"Now, Gil, you're next. See if you can do better."

I was somewhat dazed with the suddenness of the cowardly assault, but I seized my oars by instinct and rowed shorewards. I was in the black of the shadows in three strokes, and not a moment too soon, for another ball came singing after me. It blew the blade of my left oar into splinters, just as the last silvery moonlit drops fell from it before, at last, I was submerged in the shadow. Again the laughter rang loud and clear, but heartless and hard.

"Good evening to you, fisherman." cried the man who had first spoken. "The luck's with you tonight; it's a fine night for flounders."

I could have broken his head, for I was black angry at the senseless and causeless cruelty of the shooting. My first thought was to make for home; my second to draw to shore, and find out who could send a deadly bullet with so little provocation to a harmless lad in his boat on the bay. So without pausing to consider of wisdom and folly of this (which indeed I have rarely done to my advantage in my life), I sculled softly to the mainland with the unbroken oar.

Barefoot and barelegged I got into the shallow water, taking the little hooked anchor ashore and pushing the boat out that she might ride freely, since the tide was running upwards like a mill-race.

Then I struck through the undergrowth till I came to the wall of the deserted and overgrown kirkyard of Kirk Oswald. There stands a great old tomb in the corner from which, I thought I could observe the shore and the whole route of the riders, if they were on their way to unload the brig.

There was a broad splash of moonlight on the rough grass between me and the tomb of the MacLurgs. The old tombstones reeled across it drunkenly, yet all was still and pale. I had almost got to the edge of this white patch of moon-shine which I intended to cross, when, with a rustle like a brown owl alighting swiftly and softly, someone took me by the hand, wheeled me about, and before I had time to react, carried me back again into the thickest of the wood.

I looked at my companion as I ran, as you'd expect. I saw a girl in a light dress, high-kilted – none other than May Mischief of Craigdarroch. But she pointed to her lip to show that there was to be no speech; and so we ran together, although she led, to an angle of the old wall, where, standing close in the shade, we could see without being seen.

Now I could not understand this at all, for May Mischief never had a civil word for me as far back as I remember, and made so many jibes and jeers that I never could endure the girl. Yet here we were, jinking hand in hand under the trees in the moonlight, for all the world like lad and lass playing at hide-and-seek.

Soon we heard voices, and again the bits and chains rattling as the horses, suddenly checked, tossed their heads. Then the spurs jingled as the riders dismounted, stamping their feet as they came to the ground.

Twenty yards below us a man raised his head over the wall. He whistled low and shrill.

"All clear, Malcolm?"he cried. I remember to this day the odd lilt of his voice. He was a Campbell, and gave the word Malcolm a strange twist, as if he had turned it over with his tongue in his mouth. And, indeed, to this day that is the way of a man from Kintyre.

A man stepped out of the doorway of the MacLurg tomb with a gun in his hand. May Maxwell looked up at me with a triumphant look in her eyes, which I took to mean, "Where would you be now, if it wasn't for me?" And indeed the two shots at the boat in the moonlight told me where I would have been, and that was on the ground with a gunshot through me.

A dozen or more men came swarming over the broken wall. They carried a long, black coffin among them – the coffin, as it seemed, of an extraordinarily large man. Straight across the moonlit grass they strode, stumbling on the flat tombs and cursing one another as they went. There was no solemnity as at a funeral, for the jest and laughter ran light and free.

"We are the lads," cried one. "We can bury the spirits and we can raise the dead!"

They went into the great tomb of the MacLurgs with the long, black coffin, and in a trice came out jovially, abusing one another still more loudly for useless dogs of peculiar pedigrees, and dealing great claps on each other's backs. It was a wonder to me to see these outlaws being so cruel and so merry at the same time.

Some of them went down by the corner of the kirkyard opposite to us. May Maxwell, who had kept my hand, fearing, I think, that we might have to run for it again round the circle of shade, plucked me sharply over to see what they were doing.

They were opening a grave, singing as their picks grated on the stones. I shivered a little, and a great fear of what we were about to see came over me. I think if May Maxwell had not gripped me by the hand I would have run for it.

The man we had first seen came out of the tomb and took a look at the sky. Another stretched himself till I heard his joints crack, and said, "Hey How!" as though he were sleepy. Whereat the others railed on him, calling him "lazy vagabond."

Then all of them turned their ears towards the moors as though they were listening for something of importance.

"Do the Maxwells ride to-night?" asked one.

"Shush," said another. "Listen!"

He said this in so awe-stricken a tone that I also was struck with fear, and listened till my flesh crept.

From the waste came the baying of a hound – long, fitful, and very eerie. There was a visible, uneasy stir among the men.

"We must go," said another, making for the wall; "it is the Loathly Dogs. The Black Devil himself is out tonight. I'm leaving."

"Stop!" cried one with authority (I think the man called Gil). "I'll put an ounce of lead through your vitals if you don't stand in your tracks."

"It'll be worse for you if the Ghaistly Hounds get a grip of your shins, Gil, my man. They draw men quick to hell!"

At that word the company panicked, and they took to their heels, every man hastening to the wall. Soon, from the other side of the wall came the noise of steeds being mounted, and a great clattering of stirrup-irons as they fled.

May Mischief came nearer to me, and I heard her breath come in little broken gasps, like a rabbit that is taken in a net and lies beating its life out in your hands. At which I felt like a man for the only time that night.

But not for long, for what we saw next brought us both to our knees, praying silently for mercy. Over the wall at the corner farthest from us there came a fearsome pair. First a great grey dog, that hunted with its head down and bayed as it went. Behind it lumbered a still more horrible beast, great as an ox, and as grim and shaggy, but clearly monstrous and not of this world, with broad, flat feet that made no noise, and a demon mark on its side, which showed that the Devil himself had followed the chase that night. May Mischief clung to my arm, and I thought she had swooned away. But the beasts passed some way beneath us, like spirits that flit by without noise, save for the ghostly baying which made one sweat with fear.

Whilst we remained in the graveyard, the sounds moved into the distance. The horsemen dispersed in a wild fury. We could hear them labouring their horses and riding spread out over the fields, crying tempestuously to each other as they went. And downwind the bay of the ghostly hunters died away.

May Maxwell and I stood together a long while before we could loosen from one another. We held hands and continued to look at each other, but strangely. I wanted to thank her in words but could not, for something came into my throat and dried my mouth. I dropped her hand suddenly. Yet as I searched for words, my mind switching between gratitude and bravado, I could not find any in my time of need.

For a little while, May Maxwell stood silently before me, her hands fallen at her side, looking down as though she was expecting something. I could not think what. And then she took the skirt of her dress in her hand, dusted and smoothed it a moment, and began to move slowly away. But I stood fixed like a sentry.

Then I knew by the dancing light in her eyes that something was coming that would make me like her less than ever, and I would not be able to prevent it. Because of my lonely life on Isle Rathan I was as empty of words as a drum.

"Good evening to you," she said, dropping me a curtsy; "virtue is its own reward, I know. And it's even virtuous to do a sheep a good turn, though not particularly interesting. Good evening to you, Sheep!"

With that she turned and left me speechless, remaining at the wall. Yet I have thought of many things since which I could have said – clever things at that.

May Mischief walked very stately and dignified across the moonlight, and passed the open grave which the riders had made as though she did not care a button for it. At the gap in the wall she turned (looking mighty pretty and sweet, I admit), nodded her head three times, and said solemnly, "Baa!"

As I rowed home in the gloaming of the morning, when the full flood-tide of daylight was drowning the light of the moon, I decided to myself that I hated the girl more than ever. Whatever she had done for me, I could never forgive her for mocking me.

"Sheep," she mocked, and again, "Baa!". It was unbearable. Yet I remembered how she looked as she said it, and the manner in which she nodded her head, which, I can tell you, was vastly pretty.

CHAPTER II.

JOHN HERON OF ISLE RATHAN.

JUST why my father called me Patrick I have never yet been able to understand. His own name was John, which, had he thought of it in time, was a good enough name for me. It may have been his sense of humour, for indeed he used to say, "I have little to leave you, Patrick, but this old ramshackle house on the Isle Rathan and your excellent name. You will be far on in life, my boy, before you begin to bless me for christening you Patrick Heron, but once you begin you will not cease till the day of your death."

I am now in the thirty-seventh year of my age, but have not yet begun to bless my father – at least not for the reason indicated.

My father, John Heron of Isle Rathan, on the Solway shore, was not a strong man during his life. But he married a lass from the hills who brought him no dowry, instead, what was better, a strong gift of sense and good health. She died, soon after I was born, of the plague which came to Dumfries in the Black Year, and from that day my father was left alone with me in the old house on the Isle of Rathan. John Heron was the laird of a barren heritage, for Rathan was only a small isle – in fact only an isle when the tide is flowing, except in the very slackest of the neaps. Twice a day there is a long track of shells and shingle which leads to the mainland. This track is, however, somewhat dangerous, for the Solway tide flows swift and the sands are shifting and treacherous. So we usually came and went by boat, except when I or some of the lads sought adventure, as I did later when I got well acquainted with May Maxwell, particularly during the days of mid-summer madness described herein.

Here on the Isle of Rathan my father taught me English and Latin, Euclid's science of lines and how to use them for oneself. He loved the mathematics, because he said even God Almighty works by geometry. He taught me also surveying and land measuring. "It is a good trade, and will be more in request," he used to say, "when the lairds begin to parcel out the common land and hill pastures, as they surely will. It'll be a better trade to your hand than keeping blackfaced sheep off the cliffs of Rathan."

And so it has proved; and many is the time I have talked over with my wife the strange far-seeing prophecy of my father about what the lairds would do in more settled times. Indeed, all through my tale, strange as it is, I have occasion to refer to my father's sayings. Many is the time I have benefited by remembering his words; many the time, also, that I have had a serious mishap because I have neglected to heed his warnings.

It was a black day for me when my father lay dying. I remember it was a dry day in early spring. The tide was coming up strongly with the east wind pushing against it, and making a noisy surge all about the rocks of Rathan.

"Lift me up, Patrick," said my father, "and let me see again the bonny tide breaking against the old tower. It will break there many and many a day with me not here to listen. Each time you hear it, laddie, you'll remember your father who loved to dream to the splashing of it, just because it was Solway salt water and this his own old tower of the Isle Rathan."

So I lifted him up according to his word, till through the narrow window set in the thickness of the ancient wall, he could look towards the Mull, which was clear and cold slaty blue that day – for, apart from when it brings the dirty white fog, the east wind clears all things.

As he looked, a great fishing gull turned its head as it soared, making circles in the air, and fell – a straight white streak cutting the cold blue sky of that spring day.

"So has been my life, Patrick. Mostly I have been like a great gull diving for herring on an east-windy day. Sometimes I have got a flounder for my pains, and sometimes a worthless piece of drowned sprat, but of the real herring – desperately few, man, desperately few."

"I have tried it all ways, Patrick, my man, you know," he would say, for in the long winter evenings when all was snug inside and the winds were trying the doors, he and I did little but talk. He lay many months dying. But he was patient, and most anxious that he should give me all his stores of warning and experience before he left me and Rathan.

"Not that, at the outset, you'll profit much, Patrick," he would say; "from me telling you to watch out for briars when you charge through the bushes. You'll have to get hurt and scratched, overturned and torn, till you learn as I have learned. Yes, yes, you will that!"

My father was a dark man, not like me who am fair like my mother. He had a pointed beard that he trimmed with shears, which in a time of shaven men made him conspicuous. He was very particular about his person, and used to wash his linen every second week, working like an old campaigner himself, and me helping – a job I had little stomach for. But at least he taught me to be clean by nature and habit.

"We can't judge godliness," he would often say, "Try as we may, Patrick. But cleanliness is a kindly, common virtue, and it gets you so far on the road, at any rate." That was one of his sayings.

My father was not what you would call a deeply religious man. If he was, he said little about it, though he read daily from the Scriptures, and also expected me to read a chosen part, questioning me sharply on the meaning. But he did not keep company with the lairds of the countryside, nor with the tenants. He took no part in the services which were held by the Society Men who collected in the neighbourhood, and who met piously for their diets of worship at Springholm and Crocketford. Yet his sympathies were plainly with these men and particularly with Mr. Macmillan of Balmaghie – but not with the established ministers of the parishes. On Sabbaths he always encouraged me to take the pony over in the great wide-bottomed boat to the shore, and ride on Donald to the Kirk of Dullarg or the Societies meeting.

"You see, Patrick, for myself I have tried different ways to it. I have been out with the King's riders in the bad old days. Silver Sand knows where. I have been in the peat-mosses and pits with the persecuted men. I have lain snug and cosy in Peden's cave with the old man himself at my back. So you see I have tried all ways. My advice to you, Patrick, is not to be identified with any extremes, to read your Bible strictly, and if you get a good minister to sit under, to listen carefully to the word preached. It's more than your father ever did for any length of time."

But bit and bit he grew weaker, as the days grew longer.

"Now, Patrick," he said, in the still time of one morning, at the hour of slack tide, when the watcher sitting up with the sick gets chilly and when the night lies like a solid weight on the earth and sea. This was when my father called for me.

"I'm going, Patrick," he said, just as though he were going over to the Dullarg in the boat; "it's timel was away. I wish for your sake that I had more to leave you. If I had been a better boy at your age, you could have had more; but then maybe it would have been you that would be ill now. It's better that it was me. But there'll be a some silver in Matthew Erskine's hands for you despite that. But if you can be content to be doing with so little, that would be better than leaving you in misery with the lairdship of a barony."

He was silent for a while, and then he said - "You are not afraid, Patrick? "

"Afraid, father," I said, "why would I be afraid for you?"

"Well, no," he answered, very calm, " I am not a man to make a to-do about dying. I bid you goodnight, my son Patrick." And so he passed, as one might fall to sleep.

He was a quiet man, a surprisingly humoursome man, and I believe a true Christian man, and all his deathbed testimony was as I have told.

CHAPTER III

DAWN ON RATHAN SANDS.

IF there is anything bonnier or sweeter in this world than a May morning on the Isle of Rathan by the Solway shore, I have yet to see it — except perhaps the blush that comes over a young maid's face when one that is not her lad, but who one day might be, comes knocking at the door.

Some months after my father's death I remember just such a morning. Certain other lads of my age, of good burgher families, that did not find themselves altogether comfortable at home, had settled in the house of Rathan. The house and lands with all the sheep and some six thousand pounds sterling of money were not yet in my possession. Matthew Erskine, the Dumfries lawyer, who had my father's confidence, put no barriers on my doing as I pleased; and thus carried out my father's intentions, which were that I should neither be hampered in well-doing nor even in ill-doing. For this was ever his way and custom.

"When I was a lad," he used to say, "I was not free to come and go as I pleased, and most of the evils of my life have happened to me because I was unable to choose between right and wrong early enough. So I will even leave you, Patrick, as says the catechisms, to 'the freedom of your own will.' "

The lads who had come to stay with me on Isle Rathan, at least for the summer season, were Andrew Allison, a burgher's son from Carlinwark (where there are only a few decent people, which made his father the more remarkable) and his brother, John. Also there was a cousin of the Allisons that came from the ancient town of Kilconquhar, high up on the Nith Water. There was also, to our joy, one Jerry MacWhirter, a roguish fellow that came to help me with my land-surveying, but was keener to sketch, in colour, the hues of the landscape and the sea. But he was dearest to us because of his continual merry heart, which did us good like a medicine.

So the five of us lads lived in the house, but I was the biggest and oldest. Also, since the house was mine, it was my duty to rule, otherwise we would have been an unruly crew. But in truth I enjoyed ruling, and did so with an iron hand.

With us at times there was one Silver Sand, who will receive a chapter to himself, later in this account.

Now, I must describe the house we had on the Isle Rathan. It stood in a snug angle of the bay that curved inward towards the land and looked across some mossy, boggy ground to a range of rugged, heathery mountains, on which there were very many grey boulders, about which the heath and bracken grew deep.

The ancient house of the Herons of Rathan was not large, but it was very high, with only two little doors to back and front – the front one set into the wall and bolted with great bars into the solid rock above and below, and into the thickness of the wall at either side. The back door opened into a passage which led first to a covered well in a kind of cave, where a good spring of water bubbled up with little sand grains dancing in it, and then by a branch passage to an opening among the heather. You might search for this entrance but you would never find it on your own. The windows were very far up the sides, and there were very few of them, since they were made for defence in more perilous times. Upon the roof there was a flagstaff and so strong a covering of lead and stone flags that it seemed as though another tower could have been built upon it. The Tower of Rathan stood alone, with its offices, stables, byres, and other belongings back under the cliff, the sea on one side of it, and on the other the heathery and rocky isle, with its high sheep pastures. Beneath, the sea-holly and dry salt plants bloomed blue and pink down near the edge of the sea.

Fresh air and sound appetites were more common with us lads on the isle than the wherewithal to satisfy our our belly cravings. However, to be attended by a woman was out of the question. It was not seemly that any young one should be with us, nor did we wish our wild activities to be seen by any much older than ourselves. So we had to fend for ourselves, but when it got close to the day when I received my small quantity of money from Matthew Erskine, the Dumfries lawyer, the living was very scanty on the isle.

For when I had money, it was always easily spent. But at the worst of times we had a stake salmon net which we fished every morning when the fish were clean, and there were flounders all the year round. Thus we lived, and, all in all, quite well, considering that the country was a poor one and we had no friends that bore any goodwill to help us – except May Mischief at Craigdarroch, who, for all her jeers, left a great tankard of milk aside for us every morning and night.

So on this May morning I rose long before the light and went out into the cool, damp air of the night. The tide was going back quickly, and it was this which made me rise at such an unseemly hour. It has always struck me that when the Creation was pronounced to be very good, insufficient attention was paid to the matter of the tides. But in a great job like the making of the earth, small points are apt to be overlooked. For instance, it would have been a great advantage if the tides at Rathan had been regular in the morning, leaving the nets clear at something like seven o'clock in summer and nine in winter. But I was not consulted at the time, and so it is as it is – a trifle inconvenient for all parties.

Now I am a man of my devotions, and give thanks to a kind Providence every morning for the preservation of the night. But I am well aware that the quality of my thankfulness is not what it should be at half-past two on a bleak and chill morning when the nets must be checked. So I say again that both parties suffer by the present arrangement.

But this morning there was not a great deal to complain about, apart from leaving the others snoring in their hammocks and box-beds round the chambers of dark oak where they were lodged. The thought of this annoyed me as I left.

It was still dark when I went out with only my boots over my bare feet, and the chill wind whipping about my legs. What could be seen of the sea was the colour of the inside of an oyster-shell, pearl grey and iridescent. The land loomed mistily dark, and there was a light showing at the farm-town of Craigdarroch, where the Maxwells dwelt, which made me wonder if it could be that hellcat lassie, who had called me a sheep, wandering abroad so early. For in spite of her smile she was a lass that none of us lads of the Rathan could abide. Still, I confess it was comforting to see some one else astir at that time in the morning, even across half a mile of salt water.

From Rathan Head I looked out seaward and saw one of the fast brigs of the Freetraders from the Isle of Man, or perhaps from Holland, manoeuvring outwith the tide. Little thinking how much she was to cost us, I watched her draw away from the land against the swiftly brightening sky. None of us, apart from the Preventive officers, had any ill-will with the traffic itself; though my father had taught me never to use any of the stuff, desiring that I should be hardy and endure wind and weather without it. Still, when it was carried out decently, he did not see what right the Preventatives had to keep other folk from doing what their fathers had done before them. King George, decent man, who had recently arrived from Germany, surely could not be harmed much by a poor man's whisky still in the lee of the peat-stack.

But certainly there were good and bad, decent and indecent, working in the traffic, as we were soon to learn.

It was cold and unkindly on the flats, and there was nothing except lythe and saithe in the nets – save some small red trout, which I cast over on the other side, so that they might grow large and run up the rivers in August. So little was there that I, with exceedingly cold feet and not in the best of tempers, had to proceed to the flats and tramp flounders for our breakfast. Then I wished that I had wakened two of the others, for Andrew Allison's feet were manifestly intended by nature for tramping flounders, being as broad and flat as the palm of my hand. Moreover, John his brother was quick and keen on the job – though I think chiefly because he was keen to get back to his play in the caves and on the sand with his ancient crony, Bob Nicoll.

But I was all alone on the flats, and it was sufficiently dreary work. Nevertheless, I soon had my baskets full of flapping, slippery fish, though it was none too nice a job to feel them slide between your toes and wriggle their tails under your instep. That was what gave Andrew Allison so great an advantage at the business, for he had no instep – at least not to speak of.

When I got to the shore with my breakfast ingredients I could not feel my feet at all, but I could see my legs causing them to move and in some fashion to carry me. So I returned to the house, which now stood bright in the morning sunshine.

Entering the darkened chamber out of the morning sun was startling. It greatly annoyed me to hear the others still snoring in their naked beds, with me so cold and weary from my morning's work. Moreover, the air had the closeness that comes from thick walls and many breathings.

Throwing down my fish and slipping off my damp clothes to be dried before the fire, I threw myself into the bed which Andrew Allison and I occupied together. He lay next to the wall. Without a moment's delay I placed my ice-cold feet where it would do them most good. This caused my companion to awake with so great a yell that the others tumbled instantly out of bed, thinking that, at the very least, the Freetraders must be on us. As for Andrew, he lay still and acted as a warming-pan, being, fortunately for me, between me and the wall.

As I grew warmer I issued my orders to the others.

"Lazy slug-a-beds,"ordering the youngsters about like a skipper, "get about your work! You, John Allison, get the boat and go over to Craigdarroch for the milk, and be back by breakfast-time; and if you as much as lift the lid of the can, I'll thrash you till you can't stand. Besides, you'll get no breakfast."

John got his cap, grumbling and shaking his head.

But he went.

"You, Rab, clean the fish, and you, Jerry Mac-Whirter, get a fire started, and have the breakfast on the table in an hour. Dry my clothes before the fire."

°'It's Andrew's day!"said Jerry.

"Maybe it is," said I," but for now Andrew is not ready. He was tired yesterday, and he needs a rest this morning. Get the breakfast and be nimble. It'll be better for you."

"But, Rab says -"began Jerry, who was reluctantly putting on his clothes.

"Not another word out of your mouth!" I cried, imperatively.

It is wonderful what firmness does in a household.

In this way I had a good sleep before breakfast.

When I awoke Andrew was up. He had stolen out of bed and taken a sea plunge from the southernmost rocks, drying himself on the sand by running naked in the brisk airs of the morning which drew off the sea.

There is no finer breakfast than flounders fried in oatmeal with a little salt butter as soon as they come out of the water, with their tails jerking *flip, flap*, in the frizzle of the pan.

"Gracious," said Jerry, " but it's good. I'm glad I got up out of my own free will."

Andrew and I being captain and lieutenant of the gang, had forks; the rest had none, which is an advantage to eating flounders. It is most amazing the number of bones a flounder can carry, seemingly without any trouble. Also it is a mercy that none of us choked on any of them, in our haste to eat.

CHAPTER IV

THE CAVE OF ADULLAM

RATHAN ISLAND lay in the roughest tumble of the seas. Its southern point took the full sweep of the Solway tides as they rushed and surged upwards to cover the great deadly sands of Barnhourie. From Sea Point, as we named it, the island stretched northward in many rocky cliffs riddled with caves. For at this point the softer sandstone you find on the Cumberland shore rises from under the sea. So the island was more easily worn into sea caves and strange arches, and towers and stacks sitting by themselves out in the tideway like children's playthings.

In these caves, which had many doors and entries, I had played with the tide ever since I was a boy. I knew them all as well as I knew our own back-yard under the cliff. And before long, this knowledge was to stand me in better stead than the Latin grammar I had learned from my father.

In fine weather it was pleasant to go up to the highest point of the island, which, though hardly a mountain, was called Ben Rathan, and see the surrounding country. The smoke from the many farm-towns and villages, as well as countless cot-houses, can be seen blowing the same way when the wind is light. The morning was the best time to go there. Bees hummed about among the crisp heather, which was springy just like our little Shetland pony's mane after my father had docked it. There was a great silence up there – only the sound of the sea from the south, where the tides of the Solway relentlessly chafed against the rocky end of our little Isle of Rathan.

Then, nearest to us, on the eastern shore of Barnhourie Bay, the farmhouse of Craigdarroch can be seen, with the Boreland and the Ingleston above it, which are common names in Galloway.

Wherever there is a Boreland you can be sure that there is an Ingleston not far from it. The reason for that is, according to my father, when the English came to settle in their "tons", they brought their "boors", or serfs, with them. So, boor-lands were always to be found near English towns. And also from Ben Rathan, looking to the westward, just over the cliffs, you may see White Horse Bay, much frequented lately as a convenient place of unloading by the Freetraders of Captain Yawkins' band, with whom, as my father used to say quaintly, no honest smuggler should keep company.

For in Galloway there were, as every one knows, two kinds of the lads who bring over duty free produce from Holland and the Isle of Man. There are the decent lads who run it for something honest to do in the winter and for the spice of danger, with no thought of harm to King George, worthy gentleman; and there are also the "Associated Illdoers," as my father would often call them in his joking way – the Holland rogues who got this isle its nickname of Rogues' Island by running their cargoes into our little land-locked cove which looks towards White Horse Bay. These last were fellows who would stop at nothing, and quite as often as not they would split the head of a lass from the Cumberland shore, or slit the throat of a Dumfries burgher just to see the colour of his blood. But these Black Smugglers could never have reached a stage of such daring and success unless they had made themselves friends with the disaffected of these parts. The truth of the matter was that in the wilds of Galloway on the way to Ayrshire, up by the springs of the Doon and the Dee, there is a wide expanse of incomparable wildness, occupied by all the evil gypsies of the hill – red-handed men, outlaws and aliens.

When a vessel came in, they openly marched down to the shore with guns, swords, and other weapons – Marshalls, Macatericks, and Millers, often under the leadership of Hector Faa – and escorted to their fastnesses both the smuggled and stolen goods, for there was as much acquired by rustling and theft, as of the stuff which was only honestly smuggled.

My father had fallen out with Yawkins when he began robbing men and seizing maids.

I can remember him coming to the Rathan, a thick-set, dark man, with his head very low between his shoulders. He had a black beard and there was a cast in his eye. He swore many strange oaths.

Being a Hollander, the most of his conversation seemed to be "dam," but it was clear he was trying to persuade my father to something.

"It's scandalous nonsense," said my father over and over to him;" and, more than that, it's rank black-guardism; and as for me, I shall have no dealings with the likes of you about the matter."

From which I gathered that in his wilder days my father had had his hands pretty deep in the traffic.

Across the fertile valley of the Dee, we could see from Rathan Head the blue shadowy hills, where, among the wild heather and the empty spaces where the curlews cried all summer long, the gypsies had their fastnesses. On those blue hills, to us so sweet and solemn, no king's man had been safe since the days of religious persecution by Claverhouse.

Little did I think, as I used to sit and watch them, with Andrew and young Jock Allison, Rab Nicoll, and little Jerry, on the smooth heather of Ben Rathan, that I would often tread the way up to those fastnesses about the Dungeon of Buchan before the matter was ended.

It was after breakfast when most of us were out on the cliffs, looking to seaward with my father's old prospect-glass (which was one of our choicest possessions) when little Jerry, who had been drawing the coast and hills, came up the hill in great leaps, shouting that there was a boat coming round the point running against the tide, with two men rowing.

I turned the glass on the boat as she came, and was soon able to pick her up.

"It's your mother, Andrew Allison," I said, "and yours, Jerry, my lad. They'll be getting anxious to see you!"

"Save us," said Andrew; "I'm away to hide!"

"Away with you, then," I said, "but don't tell me where, so that I can't tell more lies than are necessary."

I was well aware that there was some work for me to do during the next hour, for neither Mistress Allison, the magistrate's wife, nor even Mistress MacWhirter, were cautious with their tongues when they got a subject to do them justice.

But my father gave me advice in regard to the tongue of a scolding woman. I don't know how it would work if you always had her in the house with you, but when you have only to stand it for a short time, it is altogether infallible. My father had a great respect for Scripture, and he had Scripture to thank for this.

"Remember, Patrick," he used to say, "that the Good Book says, 'A soft answer turneth away wrath. Now keep your temper, laddie. Never quarrel with an angry person, specially a woman. Also, a quiet answer is always best. It makes them far madder than anything else you could say."

As we looked the boat sped nearer, and, peering through the prospect-glass again, I could see that it was rowed by two – a lass and a man. It was the Craigdarroch boat – white with a green stripe about it, very elegant. So I did not need to be a prophet to know that it was my daft Maxwell lass, known to us as May Mischief, that was oaring the wives across.

It made me anxious to think that she should hear all the turmoil of their ill tongues. Not that I cared for May Maxwell or any like her, only it was galling to let a lass like that, who was for ever gibing and jeering, get new ammunition for her scoffs and jeers. The last time I saw her, when I went over to Craigdarroch myself for milk – on a day that it blew hard and I would not send the younger ones – she had a new word for me.

She called me "Adullam." Well, any name was better than "Sheep".

"Now, Adullam," she cried, as soon as I could get near the farm past some barking dogs, "this is a fine business. I suppose you think that you are a great captain, like King David in the cave; and that all that are discontented and in distress will gather to you, and you'll become their captain. A bonny captain, Adullam. There's a fine big house up in Edinburgh, I hear, that's full of such captains. They put straight-jackets on them there, and tie them up with ropes." I did not answer this, remembering my father's prescription.

"O, you think you're a fine lad," said the impudent besom. "You're all fine lads, in your own opinions, but some knotty birch twigs would be more use than 'captains.' I'll speak to my father about that!" she said, pretending to leave.

Now when she spoke in this fashion I got a great deal of comfort just from saying over and over to myself, " You impudent besom! You impudent besom!" But before I knew it, the words came out and I was immediately horrified at the sound of my own voice.

I had never so spoken to a young woman before; indeed seldom to the breed at all. For my father and I kept ourselves very close to ourselves in Rathan Isle.

But instead of being offended the daft lassie threw back her head and laughed. She had close curls like a boy, and her way of laughing was strange, and struck me as though some elf were tapping down at the bottom of my throat with his forefinger.

There was something bewitching about her laughter.

"Well done, Adullam, one day you'll not be so daft, when you lose your childish ways and get your hair cut," said she.

"Leave my hair alone – it's not interfering with you!" I said, so coltish and stupid that I hated the lass for humbling me that way – me that had such a good an opinion of myself because I lived alone.

So it was no wonder that the thought of her hearing what the pair of old scolding wives had to say to me for leading their precious sons astray made me feel bitter and twisted.

CHAPTER V.

AULD WIVES' CLAVERS

THE boat was coming in quickly and I could see that Mistress Allison, who was steering, had no idea, so that in spite of the efforts of the rowers, the boat was in danger of being carried past the landing-place.

Now, though I wished the whole crew were somewhere else, I did not want anyone drowned on the Rathan cliffs, so I ran down alone, to help pilot them in. The lads had fled: and, indeed, their absence was better than their company. Only little Jerry MacWhirter sat calmly finishing his perspective drawing on the hilltop.

"Tell my mother I'll be down in a moment!" he cried after me as I ran. But I thought he was joking, and went on without reply.

At last the keel grated on the beach, and I pulled the boat ashore. Just as I did the daft Maxwell lass that I was so angry with, unshipped her oar, put her hand on my shoulder, and leaped ashore like a young goat. The two old wives were speechless with black anger.

"Good-day to you, Mistress Allison and Mistress MacWhirter, and to you, May Maxwell," I said, lifting my bonnet to each, and speaking as I ought, just to show that I was not so rough and ill-bred.

"Good-day to you, Adullam!" says May; but the two old wives said neither "Fair-good-day" far less "Fair-good-evening," but only sat and glowered. I stood at the side of the boat to offer them a hand; but Mistress Allison waved me away, and asked the great ox of a farm lad who was on the oar to jump out and help them ashore.

"No, and I won't, either!"said that youth, pleasantly. "Will Maxwell said that I was to stay with the boat – so I will. You can jump."

So he would not help, but was willing to give his reasons.

"Will is my master, and he's a man to be wary of, I can tell you!"he said, and that was all they could get out of him.

So the old wives, who could have eaten all they liked of me with pleasure and ease, had to accept my helping hand to get them out of the boat, which had grounded high on the shell-sand and now rocked upon an uneven keel.

"Think of the honour of it, Mistress Allison!" cried the belligerent lass May Maxwell, standing with her hands on her sides and her elbows crooked out in a fashion of her own. (I can't think what made me notice these things, for I disliked the girl). "Think," says she,"of the honour of being handed out by a laird on his own ground, or rather a prince in his in kingdom, for all this isle belongs to his lordship. You're a grand woman today, Mistress MacWhirter!" And she pretended to look about grandly, as though taking in a prospect of wide dominions.

But I said nothing out loud, but I kept saying to myself, "Ill-tongued hussy!" And I said that over and over.

But she was not finished, and went on, "Are you captain or a general, Adullam? – my memory's failing. I think you mentioned it the last time you were over at Craigdarroch. Or is it nothing less than to be a king that'll do for you? My faith," she added, looking round, "I'm thinking that your standing army's all run away!"

She now laughed elfishly, though I, that can appreciate humour as well as any man, could see nothing whatever to laugh at.

" Here's the standing army, Mistress May Mischief!" cried Jerry MacWhirter, standing as bold as brass on the edge of the sea cliff which rose above the white sands of the bay.

"Good morning to you, mother," he said, lifting his blue bonnet politely, "and my service to you, Mistress Allison. Your son Andrew sends his love to you."

"You impudent vagabond!"

At the word both of the women made a rush at him with so angry an expression that, even as a grown man, with (some) hair on my face, I stepped back a pace myself. But as for little Jerry, he never turned a hair, but only sat down on the edge of the cliff, looking now at the group and now at his drawing.

"Don't be in a hurry, mother," he said. "It's bad for the digestion, and this bank's too steep for someone of twenty stone, Mistress Allison. Try round to the left. There's an easier way there."

His mother's tongue got vent.

"You annoying rascal," she cried," you're a disgrace to our family, that were always decent grocers! Wait till I get you home. I'll force you home with a strong hand, my lad, and take a stout stick to you when I get you there. You shall suffer for this if there's hazel oil in Dumfries, taunting and jeering at your own blood-kin."

Little Jerry had a piece of paper on his knee, and he made marks on it with a pencil as if he were drawing a map. I greatly admired this.

"No, mother," he said," I didn't speak ill to you, or about you. I only advised you for your health not to excite or overexert yourself, because, as you know, Doctor Douglas tells you that it's bad for the bowels. But my respects to my stepfather, the Doctor. I hope you left him well."

"I tell you that as sure as my name's Sarah MacWhirter, you'll get such a licking when you come back to Dumfries you'll not get over it for a month. I'll get the burgh hangman to attend to you, if I haven't the strength to make you jump myself."

At this fearful threat I looked for Jerry to lower his colours, but he seemed more than usually calm, and turned his head sideways to look this way and that at his map, like a wild bird on a bough when it is not sure about you.

"No, mother, licking's over now! It's all over with," says he; "so it's not for me to say whether or not your real name is Sarah MacWhirter or Sarah Douglas. I wasn't at either of your weddings – not that I remember – but whether or not, strap, tawse, birch, and hazel, are all in the past; and I'll not come home again till you promise to leave me alone."

"You know full well, you vagabond, that you would be left alone. Yes, and made much of if you would consent to be a decent grocer in the Wynd, and succeed your father in the shop."

"No, mother, I'll never be grocer nor even a chandler. The provision business is a good trade, but it's not for me. I'm always so hungry that I would eat all the profits. I would rather sell the red ochre for marking sheep, mother, like Silver Sand. Can you leave me alone?"

His mother and Mistress Allison, quite aghast at the turn affairs were taking, had retreated, and were for making their way up the cliff by themselves. May Mischief had gone back again to the boat, and was lifting something heavy out of it. I went down to help her, as I never could abide to see a woman do man's work, even if I had reason to dislike her, as I had good reason to. Though, to tell the truth, I also had some good reasons to think well of her, remembering the night by the tomb of the MacLurgs in the kirkyard of Kirk Oswald.

Then I heard little Jerry say from his post on the top of the cliff, "Might I trouble you, Mistress Allison, just to stand still till I get your figure done? It doesn't look too good without the head, especially as I haven't enough paper to draw your feet."

I began to see that though Jerry might be an exceedingly useful ally with the tongue, his answers, though soft enough to satisfy Solomon himself, were not enough to restore some peace. On the contrary, if the two ladies were angry when they came seeking their sons on my island, Jerry had made them ten times worse now.

All this time I was helping May Maxwell out of the boat with something heavy, wrapped in a white cloth. Whatever it was it gave out a rare good smell to me, compared with a breakfast some hours before of plain flounders tramped on the flats at three in the morning.

Overhead the two good dames were labouring upward, Mistress Allison crying as she went-

"Andra! Jock! - wait till I catch you!"

This mode of address struck me as, to say the least of it, unwise, and as one might say injudicious.

On the hillside Mistress MacWhirter made ineffective swoops at her erring son, who evaded her as easily as a swallow gets out of the way of a cow.

"And, my faith," cried the good dame, exceedingly irate, "you are mighty wasteful, my laddie! Why are you wearing your best clothes, I'd like to know? "

"Because I have none better!" said her obedient son, was all the answer that was needed.

The reasoning was excellent. If he had better he would have worn them. He had done his best.

I came up the path in the sunlight, carrying the Maxwell lass's packet under my arm, and mighty weighty it seemed to be. It was very hot underfoot with the sun reflected from the rocks. It was clear sky overhead.

"What are you going to say to them?" May Maxwell asked, looking across at me in a way that I thought seemed to be friendlier.

"I don't know," I said, "I was thinking of letting them get it all their own way for the sake of peace."

"Man, Adullam, for a lad that longs to be a general, you have little guile about you. That's good enough for a while, especially when there's only one of them. But there's two old wives' tongues here, and it would be useless, for as soon as one of them runs out of breath, the other one will take over, and the deafening will just be eternal."

"But what will I do then, May Maxwell?" said I.

"Miscall their children to their face. Tell them that they are sponging tinkers – and the laziest , unskilled rogues in the country. If that doesn't make their mothers change their tunes, my names not May Maxwell."

"Your name's May Mischief, I know why now!" I said, roguishly.

"What, ho, Adullam!" she cried, making a pretty, mocking mouth, "this will never do. Don't try to be funny, like our dog Toss that tried to walk like a cat on the lip of the boiler and fell amongst the pig's meat. No, no, Adullam, stick to your generalling and captaining. Did you ever hear of the calf that tried to be humorous?"

"No," said I, "and none of your jibes." For this was no time for tales.

"'Well, 'said the farmer to the calf,' I intended to keep you, but a cow with a sense of humour is not something that I can have about the house. The last one ate all the wife's half-year's washing. So I'll just have to see what kind of veal you'll produce.' Upon this, the humourous calf died suddenly. It's a lesson to you," said Mistress May, coming quickly to the end of her parable.

This was always the way that she jeered at me, and I cannot think why I was not more angry. Maybe it was because she was just a little lissom thing, like my smallest finger with a string tied round the middle of it.

When we got up to the house we went directly into the kitchen. There we found the two dames standing in the middle of the floor, each turning about on her own pivot, and sniffing contemptuously. I could hardly keep from laughing out loud. I looked to May Maxwell to see if she was as well. I was sure that, as she saw humour in so many things, she would find this vastly amusing.

But I was never more mistaken. Her little nose was more in the air than usual. I always meant to tell her when she was going on to me that her nose turned up at the end. I never did, however, chiefly because I did not believe that she would have cared a pin if I *had* said it.

But her advice was worth trying.

The kitchen, which had an oak seat down one side of it, also had also box-beds let into the wall, and two hammocks hanging for those of us who preferred the swinging beds. Now none of these beds were made, but the linen was clean enough, since Silver Sand took it over to a decent wife in the village of Orraland every three weeks to be washed. The bachelor manners of the house of Rathan did not stretch to bed-making.

It was just a vanity as far as we were concerned. We rose up, and we heaved our coverings over the foot of the bed; or we left them lying on the floor beneath the hammock where they had slipped off. When we got in we drew them over us again. This was our bed-making. But in the two elder women, and even in May Mischief, this innocent practice caused new and more bitter indignation.

"And this is the place that you've lured my Andrew and my Johnnie to, poor lads!"cried Mistress Allison, her twenty stone of bulk shaking with indignation after the difficulties of the ascent.

"Will you please take seats, my ladies?" said I, standing as politely as I could with my hat in my hand, for I was in my own house.

The two dames looked at me, then at one another. Finally they agreed to sit down. This they did, each in her own manner. Mistress Allison took hold of a chair on which some books and drawings of little Jerry's were laid. As she tilted it forward these slid to the floor. The good lady let herself drop into it like a sack of flour dropping on the ground when the rope slips.

The thin, spare, irascible Mistress MacWhirter took out of her swinging under-pocket a large India-red kerchief. Then she carefully dusted the chair, turning it bottom upward in a way which betrayed a rooted distrust of everything in the Rathan. May Mischief simply took a good look at the window-sill, set the palms of her hands flat upon it at her sides, and hopped up like a bird, but backwards.

Now the lads Andrew and Johnny Allison, with Rab Nicoll, their cousin, were hidden at the end of the inner wall, where the passage led from the back door out to the moor. They were therefore perfectly within earshot.

As soon as Mrs. Allison got her breath she began,

"Now, Master Patrick Heron, could you tell me by what right you keep my laddies here, when they should be serving in their father's shop and running their mother's errands – you that call yourself a laird? A good laird, he says, who entices away decent folk's children from their own doorpost to his ramshackle house, and keeps them there – a few poor little boys to cut his firewood, and live in this fearsome-like hole."

"Yes," cried the shriller voice of Mistress MacWhirter," and there's more. It was him, nobody else, that set my Jerry, who was always a good lad, against becoming a grocer."

"Thank you, mother, your obedient servant, Jerry MacWhirter," put in the little rascal from the outside somewhere.

"You are a disrespectful hound, a black sheep in my bonny flock, a------
"

"The poor lad that you and my stepfather licked till he was black and blue, but that you'll lick no more on this side of the grave! " cried Jerry from the doorway, showing his witty, comical face round the corner.

I thought it was now time to try May Mischief's advice.

"Have you said all that you'd like to say?" I asked, looking from one to the other.

Neither spoke, knitting their brows and looking darkly past one another out at the window. May Mischief, who I glanced at before I began, to see how she was taking the matter, had her fingers plaited together over her knee, holding it a little up and dangling her foot as she listened, innocent as a kitten thinking about the cream-jug.

"Now, listen to me," I said, slowly and calmly, and speaking as English as I could; " I have a question or two to put to you both. In the first place, did I ask or invite your sons to come to this my house on the Rathan Isle? As far as I know they each came without so much as a 'By your leave!' They have been here, a pack of idle vagabonds, eating me out of house and home for the better part of two months. Is this to my benefit? They have finished a side of pig for me between them. I'll be sending you in a fine account, Mistress Allison, for they're good eaters, just like yourself."

At this Mistress Allison fidgeted in her seat as though something was making her uneasy. Things were not going so well. It was one thing for her to abuse her treasures, but quite another to sit and hear an outsider give her sons the rough side of his tongue. Mistress May Maxwell looked on from her perch on the window-sill, but never said a word. Butter would not have melted in her mouth.

"And as for your son, Mistress MacWhirter, I have had to expel him from the house for ill-bred conduct four times--"

"Five! Tell the truth when you are at it, if you are a laird!" corrected little Jerry from the door.

"I stand upon my rights. Five, by Macmillan's cup!" (A communion cup of ancient silver belonging to MacMillan of Balmaghie, the first Cameronian minister, to which a special sanctity was attached by the country folk).

"And I declare that I shall no longer harbour such a nest of rogues and vagabonds on the Isle of Rathan," said I. "There has been no peace since any of the names of Allison and MacWhirter arrived. More than that, I am fully persuaded that they are hand in glove with notorious Freetraders, such as Yawkins and Billy Marshall. For all that I know they may be art and part in supplying undutied goods to various law-breaking, king-mocking grocers and even magistrates. I am resolved to lodge information with the officers of His Majesty's Preventive forces and get the reward."

When I had finished I glimpsed at May Mischief to see how she was taking it. I was rather proud of that last bit about smuggling myself, and I thought that she would see the humour of it too, but instead I saw that her face was both pale and frowning. Then I remembered that the Maxwells of Craigdarroch, all the seven big sons of them, and even their dour Cameronian father, were said to be deeper in the Gentle Traffic, as it was called, than any others in the locality.

It was she who spoke first, and her words had a little tremor in them. "I would have you know, Laird Heron," she said, "that there are decent men who do not believe that King George has any right to say 'you shall not brew yourself a drop of comfort or bring a barrel from the Isle without my leave, as your fathers did from ancient times,' and yet who have no dealings or comradeship with Yawkins, the Marshalls, and their like."

She still sat on her perch on the window-sill, but she did not swing her feet any more. Indeed she leant forward a little anxiously.

" Mistress May," says I, "I'm obliged to you for your word. Indeed it would wrong of me to think any such thing. Far be it from me to meddle with decent folk that have to earn a living. But what I'm speaking of is a very different matter, here are four idle rogues living and sponging on me for months---------"

'Three!" put in Jerry from the door. "*I* work hard!" says he.

"Aye, so does the devil," said I, dryly, for all the work he did was painting and drawing.

The two old ladies stood up together, like when geese picking worms and beetles from the sand, stretch their necks at a sound of alarm.

"I would have you learn, you that are miscalling my sons, Andrew and John, that they are decent lads from decent people, burgher folk, and your father's son will never be like them."

"God forbid!" said I.

"None of your taunts," she said. "I'm sure none of my lads will stay a day longer in this house when

I tell them what you have said about them, pure ill-guided, innocent young things."

May Mischief seemed to incline her ear, tipping it a little to the side as if to listen. I knew well what was the matter. She was nearest to where these rascals, Andrew, John, and Rab were hid at the back of the wall. I could distinctly hear that rogue, Rab, laughing.

"There's rats in this house, I'm sure! Ouch, I see one!" she cried, following something with her eye along the dark of the passage as if terrified. "Mistress Allison, take care; I think it's run into your petticoats!" she cried, pointing at the threatened territory with her finger.

That good dame rose from her seat with greater agility than one might have expected from a twenty stone weight.

"Don't tell me lies, lassie," she cried, swishing her tails about with great fervour.

By accident she whisked a ball of grey wool, which we had for darning our stockings, out from under her. It bounded away into the dark passage. The ladies caught a glimpse of it from the corner of their eyes.

"Save us!" cried both of them together, springing upon one chair and clutching one another. "There's a nest of them."

May Mischief by this time was standing on the window-sill as terrified as the rest.

"Patrick Heron, tell me the truth," she cried, with her eyes like coals, "tell me the truth – are there really rats in this house?"

"Plenty of them," said I; "they join us on the table at supper-time."

Now this is a great mystery, for in all respects a braver lass never breathed. She gave me a look that might have bored a hole in an inch board, and drew her skirts very close about her ankles. It is my belief that she started the noise about the rats for mischief, as she does all things, but had seen the grey thing that looped from Mistress Allison's petticoat into the darkness of the door. Then the terrors that she had prepared for others came home to herself. At this moment through the dark passage at the back there came the noise of scuffling and squeaking such as rats make, and a terrible white beast, with long, scaly tail and red eyes, bounded across the floor past the two stout dames standing on the chair, and ran beneath the window-sill upon which the young woman was standing. A treble-tongued and desperate scream went up.

"No, no!" cried Mistress Allison. "I'll take back every word I said, laird – I will indeed. I spoke hastily – I confess."

"Good-day to you Mistress MacWhirter," I said, quietly, lifting my cap from the table.

There was more squeaking and scuffling, and, I'm afraid, the sound of muffled laughter in the passage. I was only afraid now that the rogues would overdo the matter, so I made haste to be going.

"Master Heron. Master Heron." cried Mistress MacWhirter, "My boy can stay here for ever if he wants. I'd never say a word to hinder him."

"Thank you, mother," cried that youth from the door;"you might send me half a dozen pairs of socks when you get home, just for a keepsake."

On the window-sill May Mischief was standing, the graven image of apprehension.

"Good evening to you, Mistress Maxwell," said I.

The pet white rat, which the rascals in the passage had let loose from its box, gave a squeak of terror underneath. They had pinched its tail before they let it loose. This was more than enough for the young Amazon on the window-sill.

"Oh, Pat Heron," she cried, "don't leave me! Oh, I see the horrid beast! Don't, Pat, and I'll never call you 'Adullam' again. I'll forget what happened at the kirkyard o' Kirk Oswald."

I made as if to prove hard-hearted, and stepped towards the door. Then, without a word or a look to forewarn me of her intention, she launched herself from the sill of the window and caught me about the neck.

" Keep that beast off me, Patrick!" she cried, clasping me tight.

How we found ourselves outside in the still, silent, sunshine after all this noisy riot I never could tell. But before I knew where I was May Maxwell broke away from me in anger – she that had taken me tightly about the neck only a moment before. There is no end to the mystery of woman. Inside the wives were screaming both together, and then, just for a change, turn about.

" Think shame on yourself, you great hulk; you think it clever to frighten a few silly womenfolk. When I get time I'll tell you what I think of you. Go in and stop them."

Mistress Allison was crying "Murder!"and "Thieves!" turn about without pausing a moment.

May Maxwell looked so imperative and threatening that I went in again at once. I had meant to remind her that the matter was her own idea, and that she had mentioned rats first. But her anger and her imagination were working so handsomely that I did not dare. Besides, it is no use casting up anything to a woman. She can always put ten in return to anything you say. My father often said so.

So I went in.

No sooner was I within the dark kitchen than Mistress Allison, perhaps led by example, did as the Maxwell lass had done, and dropped upon my neck. I was under no illusions whatever as to why I found myself on the ground. Mistress Allison is no featherweight. But ultimately at long last I got them out, and on the green bank outside I gave them refreshment. Then I went into the house and brought the evil young men out to make their peace.

"I have caught the rat," cried little Jerry, "but it was at the peril of my life. See here!" He showed red teeth-marks on his arm.

His mother screamed in mixed fear and admiration.

"Oh, my laddie, how could you? A rat's bite is poisonous!"

"Do you think I care about that, mother, when I can do something to help you?"

He passed the limb round for inspection impartially, as though it belonged to someone else. There were certainly tooth-marks upon it, but they were broad and regular. I, who had seen many a rat bite, knew what the young scoundrel had done. Round the corner he had set his own teeth in his arm. Then he had rubbed the place hard for a moment to drive away the blood from under the skin. So the tooth marks now stood out with alarming distinctness. It would not have impressed a man for a moment, but it did well enough with women.

Thus peace was arranged.

But not one of them would venture back into the terrible house of Rathan; which was most strange, for later I saw one of these same fearful women loading muskets for the fighters under fire with great coolness, yet at the mention of a white rat with red eyes any of them to the end of her days would have got out upon the housetop and screamed.

The Almighty made all things very good without doubt, but He left some mighty queer kinks in woman. But then the whole affair of her creation was an afterthought.

When they finally rowed away with the morose keeper of the boat that evening all was kindliness and amity. May Mischief undid the great white parcel I had helped her to carry up from the boat. It was an immense pie with a most toothsome, flaky crust. To look at it made our mouths water.

"That's not a rat-pie!" she said, as a way of saying good-bye.

And the strange thing is, that from that day, though I took time to admit it to myself and though I continued to abuse her in front of others, I was becoming fond of her.

CHAPTER VI.

THE STILL HUNTER

BUT I promised Silver Sand a chapter to himself. Silver Sand was a conundrum like those they give to the students at Edinburgh University, which the longer you look at, grows more difficult. To begin with, there seemed nothing out of the ordinary about Silver Sand any more than about my clogs with their soles of birch. But after you knew him a while, one strange and unaccountable characteristic after another emerged and puzzled you.

Silver Sand was a slender man, of middle height, stooped in the shoulders, and with exceedingly long arms, which he carried swinging at his sides as if they belonged to somebody else who had hung them there to dry. These arms were somehow malformed, but as no one had seen Silver Sand without his coat, no one had found out exactly what was wrong. And no-one took the risk to find out. It was curious, however, to see him grasp everything from a spoon to a plough-handle or a long scythe, with the palm downwards.

Silver Sand made no secret of his calling and livelihood. He had a donkey and a dog, both wonderful beasts of their kind – the donkey, the largest and choicest of its breed – the dog, the greatest and fiercest of his – a wolf-hound of the type only kept by the hill gypsies, not many removes in blood from their hereditary enemy. This fierce brute padded softly by his master's side as he in his turn walked by the side of the donkey, not one of the three raising a head or apparently looking either to the right or to the left.

I had known Silver Sand ever since I was a lad. I had been over to the mainland by the shell-causeway to gather blackberries, which were not plentiful on Rogues' Island. In the tangle of the copse it happened that I heard a great outcry from a group of boys.

Out of instinct, since young boys are always attracted to a quarrel, I made straight for them. Here I found half a dozen lads of my own age, or a little older, who were torturing a donkey. There is no doubt that the animal could have turned the tables on its tormentors but for the fact that it was shackled with a chain and block about its forelegs, so that every time it turned to spread its hoofs at its enemies, it collapsed on its side. When I got near to it the poor beast had given up trying to defend itself, and stood most pitifully still, sleeking back its ears and shutting the lids down on its meek eyes to ward off the rain of blows.

Now, however wicked I could be, I could never stand mistreatment of animals. So I went into the fray like a young tiger. I had no fighting skill with my hands, but with nails and teeth, with clog-shod feet and the temper of a wild-cat, I made pretty fair handling of the first half-dozen, till a great lout came from behind, and with the knob of a branch laid me on the grass. It could have got more difficult for the donkey and even worse for me – for I was far from popular with the village lads – but for the arrival of Silver Sand and his dog, Quharrie. Hence there were sore bottoms and torn trousers among the Orraland boys that night. Their mothers also dealt with them soundly for coming home with their clothes in such a state. The donkey, Silver Sand, and I embraced each other. Afterwards Silver Sand introduced me to Quharrie – a fearsome dog – making him offer me a great paw in a solemn manner, which made me kin and blood-brother to him forever. And I have received many a gift which I have found less useful, as you shall hear.

In these troubled times to be a third partner with Silver Sand and Quharrie was better than to be the Pope's nephew. So in this curious way my friendship with Silver Sand began.

From then Silver Sand came to Rogues' Island and Rathan Tower every month. He made journeys of three weeks' length to all the farm-towns and herds' cot-houses in the hills, with red ochre in winter and scythe-sand in summer – and perhaps something stronger without King George's seal on it. But I never asked him about that.

As any rate he had the freedom of the hill fastness of the gypsies up by the Cooran and the Dungeon of Buchan, and he would make my blood run cold with tales of their cruelty and wrong-doing, and of the terror which they spread through all Carrick and the hill country of Galloway.

It was a cheering sight to see the encampment of Silver Sand by the side of the little burn, that came down from the high spring on Rathan Isle. It was like a breath of fresh air to me. For one thing the place was really green all the year round, and seemed to keep hidden about it the secrets of the spring.

So Silver Sand and Quharrie, his great wolf-dog, appeared there in a kind of regular irregularity, so that we began to expect them. Eventually, looking out from the high old house of Rathan, there would be a whiff of blue wood smoke rising down upon the side of the Rathan Linn, which made me dress in a hurry and forget my prayers, which I think are not so necessary in the morning.

When I came in sight of the encampment I usually ran, and I would see Silver Sand pottering about in front of his small tent, with a frying-pan or a little black drinking can hung above his fire from three crooked poles in the fashion he had learned from the gypsies.

Whenever I think of Paradise, to this day my mind sees the gypsy poles, with a clear stream flowing down among trees of birch and ash that huddle in the hollow of the glen from the south-west wind, and of Silver Sand frying Loch Grannoch trout upon a sizzling pan. Ah, it was always the best time of the year when Silver Sand camped on Rathan.

" Sure, the top of the morning to you, Patrick!" cried Silver Sand, as soon as he saw me.

He had a queer, deadpan humour of his own, and often used to pretend that I was Irish because my father had named me Patrick.

"Sure, and the same to you, and many of them, Brian Boru!" it was my invariable custom to reply, which much pleased him. Then I would get a red speckled trout fresh out of the pan, which the night before had found its way to Silver Sand through the clear granite-filtered water of Loch Skerrow. It was certainly not food for sinners. And always Silver Sand told me strange tales whilst he stirred the cold potatoes in the pan where the trouts had been frying, till they were burned crisp and delicious. On such mornings I did not eat breakfast at the house. Indeed as long as Silver Sand remained on Isle Rathan I only looked in occasionally at the tower to see that all was well, but if the weather was good I did not even go inside.

As for Silver Sand he was never was comfortable inside a room for more than half an hour. The open sky was his house, and sun or shine, rain or fair, made little difference to him.

The tales he told about the wild country by the springs of Dee made me keen to go there, and I often asked him to take me with him.

"Ah, Patrick, my lad, I should not take you there. It's a wild country with few decent folk. Why, I don't even take Neddy into the thick of it. 'No farther than the House of the Hill for me,' says Neddy, 'and thank you kindly.' But Quharrie and me are another matter. Where Quharrie and his master cannot go, Satan himself wouldn't dare. For Silver Sand can fill his bags of the fine, white granite sand from Loch Enoch's shore, watched by a dozen of the bloody Macatericks and the wild Marshalls, with not one of them any the wiser."

And this was no idle boast, as you shall hear before the story ends.

At this I sighed – these tales made my quiet life here on the island seem no livelier than that of the green mould which grew on the gravestones in the kirkyard.

I longed to hear the jingle-jangle of the Freetraders' harness or smell the outlaws' camp-fires among the great granite boulders.

"Not one of them any the wiser," said Silver Sand, striking a light with his flint and steel, and, transferring the flame to the bowl of his tiny elf's pipe, so small that it just let in the top of his little finger as he settled the tobacco in it as it began to burn.

So the days went on and the rest of the lads buzzed about and came and went to the house for their meals. Only little Jerry came down to us by the waterside, for Silver Sand could be "doing with him" – boys in general, and even those under my protection, he held in utter abhorrence. Once Jerry brought tidings.

"There's a sharp-nosed brig with high sails setting in for Brighouse Bay or Maxwell's landing. She's been beating off and on all day with her topsails reefed," said Jerry, in a clever way which suggested that he was of the opinion that his news was important, but which yet left him a way out if it did not turn out to be.

In a moment Silver Sand sprang up the side of the bank to a favourite lookout station of his own.

He came down shaking his head. The news appeared important enough to Silver Sand to please even Jerry, who loved excitement of every sort.

"There's devilry afoot!" he said." That's Yawkins and his crew, and Silver Sand knows what they're after, the ill-contriving demons – but we'll diddle them yet."

Then, looking down at the great dog, he cried, with a kind of daft glee -

"Up an' waur them a', Quharrie,
Up an' waur them a', man;
There's no a Dutchman i' the pack
That's ony good ava, man – *Hooch*!"

And Silver Sand, usually so dignified, executed a fandango on the beach, his long arms hanging wide of his sides and his light and nimble legs twinkling. Quharrie also lifted up his forepaws, moving them solemnly, as though he wished to join his master in his reel.

Evening came and the stars came out, but Silver Sand seemed far from easy. He ran repeatedly up to the lookout place, which he called Glim Point, but returned unsatisfied.

"It's not dark enough yet to see well!" he said, for his eyes seemed to be more effective at night than most.

"We'll have visitors tonight, down by the Rogue's Hole, I think." said Silver Sand.

It was about half past nine when Silver Sand's nervousness became very apparent and unsettling to me. He ran about his camp and up to the hilltop – in and out all the while, like a dog at a fair. Quharrie also bristled up his hair and shot his short, sharp ears forward, and under his black lip there was a gleam of white teeth, like the foam line on the shore on a dark, blowy night.

Quite suddenly a light flickered out of the gloom across the water from the direction of the farmhouse of Craigdarroch, and then Silver Sand's agitation became pitiful to see. He ordered me about like a dog – sometimes worse, but never said an uncivil word to his own dog, Quharrie. The beast seemed to understand him without a word, watching his look with fierce eyes that shone like untwinkling stars.

" Go to the House of Rathan, and tell the lads to bar every door and to stay awake tonight. Tell them to load all your father's guns, but not to shoot unless the ill-doers try to break down the door. It's unlikely that they'll meddle with the big house of Rathan, since you've no horses or stores. But who knows? – who knows? - the buzzards are gathering from the north and the south. Foreign Dutchmen and French monzies – broken men from all the ports of Scotland, and the riff-raff of the Dungeon o' Buchan."

I ran to the house and shared my news with the lads. And here again was a strange thing. The boys that had hidden from their mothers so recently perked up, and if any of them were concerned about the situation, they did not let the others see it. We had expected that we might have some trouble with the bad crew of smugglers, whom my father's reputation as a marksman and past-master in the Freetrade craft, had hitherto kept at a distance. But I was arrogant enough to believe that I could soon make myself as respected among any Yawkins and his crew as my father had been. In which, as it happened, I was grievously mistaken, for without Silver Sand, I was no better than a herring hung by the gills in the hands of these unscrupulous men. I named Andrew Allison captain of the stronghold of Rathan till my return, since we did everything in military fashion and gave him the key of the cupboard containing the guns, which we often spent our wet days in oiling with immense care and forethought. It made me pleased to see them shining like silver on the rack.

For myself I took a pair of pistols, and thought about bringing the same out for Silver Sand, when I remembered that without doubt he had his own.

CHAPTER VII.

THE RED COCK CROWS AT CRAIGDARROCH

WHEN I got back to the shore Silver Sand was already in the boat, Quharrie crouching in the bow. I offered one of my pistols.

"Leave these nasty things at home,' he said, with unusual shortness. "They'll go blasting off when there's more need to be as quiet as an ash-leaf twirling to the ground in a windless frost. Take a dirk, man, instead! "

He handed me a long, deadly-looking weapon in a leather case. Although I did not like the look of it, for the sake of peace, I stuck it in my black belt with the brass buckle, alongside the pistols in their cases.

Silver Sand took the oars. He did not stick his weapon – a dirk like mine – into his belt, but held it gripped between his knees as he rowed. His oars made no noise, neither on the rowlocks nor when he shipped them after I had got the little rag of a sail far forward to fill and draw. Then Silver Sand steered with an oar. He made direct for the Maxwells' landing-place. The light from Craigdarroch grew larger and larger then flames shot up far into the sky, so that the sea was lit up for miles.

Only under the shadow of the woods of Orraland, where the trees almost dipped their branches in the salt water at high tide, was there the safety of darkness.

So we kept far to the right, and skirted the shore almost under the trees. As we came close in, we lost the light wind which, a hundred yards from the cliff; seemed to slant upwards and leave the shore line breathlessly still, while from the burning farmstead of Craigdarroch the flames and smoke were tossed westward in the strong breeze.

Situated as I was in the bow, I could not ask any questions, and Silver Sand had not volunteered any information; but I remembered that there was bad blood between the lads of Craigdarroch and the evil crew of Captain Yawkins' gang. It might well be that they were now taking their revenge on the house and, little as I cared for May Maxwell, it made my blood run cold to think of her at the mercy of these sea scoundrels and hill gypsies, who thought no more of carrying away a lass from the Lowlands than of killing one of their neighbours' sheep.

When at last we got into the shadow of the trees, and ran the boat safely ashore in the slushy sand of the little cove under the beeches by Orraland Gate, Silver Sand whispered in my ear that we must "keep wide," which is a herd's term for keeping some distance from the flock in order not to alarm them.

"It's likely," said he, "that you may have some work to do with your guns. Keep them handy, and when you hear me calling like an owl, run to me, but don't fire if you can help it. The seven Maxwell lads are all over at the Isle of Man, and these vagabonds are doubtless taking advantage. It's the lassie that I'm worried about; the rest might go up in smoke as far as I care"- which surprised me to hear him say.

Quharrie and Silver Sand sprang clear of the boat, and I followed, stubbing my toe on a stone as I did so. I uttered a sharp exclamation.

"My man, it's as well to tell you sooner than later. In ten minutes if you make as much noise as that you'll get six inches of a smugglers' knife in your belly. They're not cautious, those boys, when anybody comes across them. There's Dago thieves among them, speakers of foreign tongues, but as handy with the knife as a shoemaker with his awl."

When we got up on the hillside clear of the woods we could look down on the farm steading of Craigdarroch. The ricks of corn which had been left unthreshed from last year's harvest were in a blaze. Black figures of men ran hither and thither about the house and round the fires. We could see them disappearing into the office-houses with blazing peats and torches. The thatch of the barn was just beginning to show red. Narrow tongues of fire and great sweeps of smoke drove to leeward against the clear west. It was strange that there seemed to be no help coming from the other neighbouring farm-towns. We heard afterwards that the Black Smugglers had sent a man with a loaded gun to stand at the gate of each farm entrance to keep everyone inside under the threat of death.

"It's the old man's brass chest they're after, I expect," said Silver Sand, "and maybe the young lass as well."

I had not the faintest idea what he meant by the brass chest but it grieved me to see the corn that had grown so golden on the slopes behind the isle go so quickly up in fire, and when he mentioned the lass my heart sank only to shoot up again like fire the moment after.

"Yawkins threatened that he would make the Red Cock crow on old man Maxwell's roof ridge before the year was out, and faith, he's done it. But the seven fiery brothers, believe me, but they'll be wild men when they come home."

We were now on a heathery hillock, dry above and wet beneath.

"Here's a hidie-hole for you, young Rathan," said Silver Sand, using my laird's title, which he did not often do."Lie down and wait till Quharrie and I come for you!"

With that he pointed with his finger to his great wolfhound, and away in opposite directions the two set off at top speed, the man bending nearly as low as the dog. The east wind whipped the rough grass, and I could hear the crackling of the burning rafters and blazing stacks. I wondered at the time why there was no men shouting. That was, I found out afterwards, due to Captain Yawkins of Sluys, a very notable man, who forbade it. When he was hung for piracy at Leith, some time afterwards, there were seventeen warrants out against him for all manner of crimes, from kidnapping a lass on the Isle of Gometra, near Mull, to bloody piracy on the high seas. When I was last in Edinburgh I saw him swing in chains on Leith sands, very well tarred, with the flesh dried flat to the bones by the east wind from the Baltic lands. And he is more comfortable there than if he'd been in old Richard Maxwell's hands that night.

This was his doing, and even then the cup of his sins was brimming perilously near the lip. Captain Yawkins would not see the port of Sluys much more often.

I was obliged, however, to lie low among the heather, and watch warily the tarry scullions that were making such a wreck of the wealthy and comfortable homestead. Only about two hundred yards from where I lay in the hollow of the moss-hagg, I could see, plain as black on white, a sailor with a musket which he carried over his shoulder as if he was one of His Majesty's soldiers – as indeed he was, but he was a deserter who was avoiding the noose or the ounce of lead which, fittingly, he received in due course.

Where I lay was on the edge of the wild country which reaches close to the shore, as it does all round Galloway, apart from the river estuaries. From there the moors run back, in broken moss-hagg and scattered boulder-stone, to the Screel o' Criffel, which is the highest hill in that locality and as they say, stands over the Solway, watching the tides and turning the weather.

I was to do nothing except lie prone on my front, with my nose just above the heather, and keep a watch till Silver Sand came back. It grieved me to be so inactive. I would have preferred to be in action, if it were only to avoid any jibes that lass might utter later. But my heart grew sore for the thought of her among all these uncaring men.

On this waste place, there were a number of low, dwarfish thorns, bent away from the sea by the wind, the moor being generally very flat and bare. I used to come to this place to raid kites' nests. So it came to my mind that there was both a higher and a safer place for me to keep watch quite near, as there was a little man-made mound that had been made for a gallows from the time that local barons were permitted to dispense justice. There was also a stone dyke round a well, which always flowed cool and clear from under a great rock in the middle stunted birches and ground-creeping thorns.

I did not think that Silver Sand would be disappointed or angry, because the place where I decided to go was only a few hundred yards further west, and at the head of a glen which led up from the shore. This would also, as I well knew, be our best way back to the boat we had left on the shingle. So, as silently as I could, I retreated through the long trough of the cold, black moss-haggs. I had not gone far, moving backwards like a crab, when a great rush of escaping cattle tore over the moor, and one great ox trod upon me and trampled me deeper into the black peat broth. For a long while I lay still as death, but as there seemed to be no pursuer I resumed my way more stealthily than ever.

Soon I was climbing, a fearsome spectacle of dirt, up the side of the thorn covered hillock. Suddenly I was seized from behind in a grasp that threatened to dislocate my neck, and a voice in my ear said, very low and deadly-

"One word, you crawling runt, and I'll let the life out of you!"

Now this was not at all a useful observation. It was a perfect impossibility for me to utter a word if my life depended on it, for his thumbs were choking me, and the pressure on my windpipe threatened to shut out the breath of life from me in a few moments. There were flashes of fire in my eyes, and stars that fell and burst; a sound of a great spate of waters roared in my ears; then came darkness.

To all intents and purposes I died then, for to lose consciousness by violence is to die. What more is there left to experience – in this life, at least?

CHAPTER VIII

NIGHT ON THE MOOR

WHEN I came to, I thought I could hear the buzzing of a hundred million bees, each as large as my hand. I wondered how such great bees came to be in this cold country and what flowers they were that they fed on, and who hived them, and what would happen if one of them stung me. I saw many other things which would take me too long to write down, even if there were a winter's evening to do it in. But after the bees there followed a thought of pie, and what a pity it was that I had not eaten that lass Maxwell's pie before I died. It was a good pie. It was warm, too, when she brought it, and I was so cold. Then I wondered where I was. I said to myself, "I do not know where this place is, but it is certainly not heaven." Yet I remember I was not very alarmed, nor disappointed but I had a sense of somehow being looked after.

When I came alive again there was a light on my face from somewhere, and somebody's arm was round my head, and there was a stronger suggestion of pie in my mind than ever.

"Has he come round?" said some one in a man's gruff voice, but quietly.

"Not yet, father. I think he has; but he was badly crushed, poor lad."

"It was a large bullock, May," said I, hoarsely, the words whistling in my throat like the night wind in the keyhole of the outer door. Being awake now I could remember thinking about pie, which is a very odd thing to think upon when you are dead.

"Aye, it was my father," she said, quietly, and quite in earnest, transferring my head from her shoulder to some kind of pillow made of young bracken and a shawl. "He thought you were one of the robbers."

"And it's as well for you, young Rathan, that my daughter knew you; for if you'd been one of Yawkins' crew, you would have supped in hell tonight," said the old man of Craigdarroch, solemnly and without emotion, since he was simply stating a true fact. It was surprising to hear him, for although he had been a wild man most of his days, in his later years he had become a great professor and a regular attendant on the Cameronian meeting at the Nine Mile Bar.

There was a cut on Richard Maxwell's forehead, made, as his daughter later told me, with a seaman's cutlass when he broke away from them.

They had been awakened by the herd-boy shouting that the outlaws were coming down from the hills to drive the cattle. Maxwell wakened easily, being a light sleeper, and his daughter was soon with him.

Her father asked her to come and help him carry away a chest of papers and valuables which the robbers were coming to search for in his house at Craigdarroch; Captain Yawkins had often threatened to do this, swearing that he would harry Maxwell the Psalm-singer (as they called him) with fire and sword, with the driving of cattle, and the hamstringing of horse. So before the mounted smugglers arrived, May and her father got clear of the farm and came out here to the moss-haggs where for the moment they were safe. But her father, not content with what he had saved already, ran back to get his Bible. Then some of the outrunners of the robber band took him unawares, and surrounded him; but he broke through them, leaving one on his back at the steading gate. And so he returned with his coat mostly torn from his back, a great ragged cut on his brow, yet holding his Bible in one hand and a naked sword in the other.

This was the substance of what I learned lying there on the moor on May Maxwell's shawl, while old Richard Maxwell in a low voice cursed the destroyers of his home, filling his own words with great curses out of the Book of Psalms. I admired how fluent he was in the words of the Bible.

Shortly, Silver Sand and Quharrie arrived, breathless and panting.

Silver Sand looked annoyed when I told him how I came to be there, away from the place and duty which he left me; but he said nothing, neither then, nor afterwards. May Maxwell and her father did not take his arrival as odd; and I now think the reason is that all Silver Sand's movements were so stealthy and secret that no one would have been astonished if he appeared at their door or suddenly vanished from their sight at any hour day or night. Yet to me he was always good and kind; and, indeed, remains to this day – though now he is, as he says, so stricken in years that the rheumatism in his joints keeps him nearer home, which means near the old house of Rathan.

"We must leave here quickly," said Silver Sand, "for they are firing the heather and grass, and it will spread like February moorburn in this dry, easterly wind."

"What do they want?" I asked Silver Sand, for I could now sit up, and was feeling infinitely better.

In truth it was the shock of the incident that hurt me more than the old man's thumbs, or even the hoofs of that great rampaging ox which trampled me into the moss-hole when the drove went over me.

"What do they want?" said Silver Sand, testily."The outlaws, whatever they can find – but Yawkins, he wants that chest," (pointing to the brass-bound box on which old Craigdarroch was sitting), " and another lad that I know wants the girl, I think."

At this May Maxwell, kneeling by her father, seemed to draw closer to me in the darkness; but whether it was from curiosity to hear, or only for company and the sense of safety, I was not sure.

The old man kept going, interposing prayers among his curses in a manner which, had our situation not been so serious, might have made us laugh. But none of us had a sense of humour that night.

"Curse them," he said, hissing his words---" curse them root and branch! But I must try to be patient. It's doubtless the Lord's will that my seven fine sons should be away at the Isle of Man when this has happened to me in my old age. I must try to bear this. *It's after all the Lord's will* – but wait till they get home and see the blackened walls of Craigdarroch, and the grey ash where the hayricks they built with their own hands stood, and all the bonny sheaves gone blazing up into the sky – there'll be a vengeance one day that will be spoken of for many a day. However, it's a mercy it's no worse, and we must try to be patient. It is the Lord's will! "

CHAPTER IX

IN RAMSAY BAY

I did not learn until long after how all this came about, nor what the Black Smugglers had taken from the Maxwells, though I was about to get deeply involved in their quarrels. In fact, I did not care; but it is a good story, and it is necessary to hear it from the beginning to properly understand the whole matter. It was told to me by Ebenezer Hook, who on that day steered Captain Yawkins' brig, the *Van Hoorn* into action, and also by Kennedy Maxwell, the youngest of the seven brothers who had gone for their spring cargo to the Isle of Man.

I shall try my best to untangle the two accounts. The motive of the Maxwells was plain. Will, the eldest, had news of a tidy cargo of French brandy, German perfumes, and Vallenceens lace stored on the northern shore of Ramsay Bay. So his brothers and he set sail in the *Spindrift*, a little fourteen ton lugger, which had run many cargoes and had brought much joy and sorrow to the adventurous house of the Maxwells of Craigdarroch.

At that time Captain Yawkins (the leader of the "Black " side of the traffic, just as the Maxwells claimed to be the "White") had been becalmed in Ramsay Bay but had sentinels on Maungold Head in case a ship of war surprised him within the harbour his boats were ready to tow him out of the bay.

It was the great Yawkins' custom to ask for what he wanted, and if it was refused, he would take it with violence. He had received word that the Galloway Maxwells were just about to lift a cargo of the finest ever rum from the island. No doubt some enemy took this news to Yawkins, for the Maxwells were a little over-fond of the strong hand themselves.

When Yawkins heard this, a longboat was despatched to seize the cargo. They arrived in the grey of the morning and took the linen-wrapped webs of the fine Vallenceens, the casks of French brandy, and the cases of the sweet-smelling water of Cologne from their snug hiding-place in the lee of the Red Fisherman's cottage.

The Red Fisherman ran to the shore as the men from Yawkins' longboat were landing, and with his fingers to his mouth gave the "kite's whistle" - the piercing signal agreed upon between himself and his employers, the Maxwells.

Up tumbled these seven dark-haired men from the tiny forepeak and from under the spread sail. In the stillness of the morning they could hear the rattle of their own beloved casks as they were swung into the boat of their adversary. However, the Maxwells were not going to let their goods go without an effort.

With his sheath-knife ready at his hip, Will Maxwell cut the rope of their small anchor as it ran over the stern.

"Away with the foresail!" he cried.

In a trice the great brown sail, darkened with tan-pit liquid as was common in Galloway, was mounted steadily aloft and took the wind. Will Maxwell ordered his crew to haul the sheet aft, and in a moment the dainty little lugger was dancing over the ripples, running straight for the robber longboat, which was now reaching out for Captain Yawkins' ship that lay at the mouth of the bay, just under Maungold Head.

Will Maxwell handled his little craft well. She ran with the breeze in her great square of sail faster than anything else would have done in that light wind, the ripples talking briskly under her forefoot, lapping and making a pleasant noise. So Kennedy Maxwell said, but he wonders how he had time to think about such things. He also admired a cormorant chase a pirate gull, and force it to drop a fish it had just taken from one of the white-breasted sea-birds which were wheeling and plunging about. Kennedy Maxwell says that he felt he was himself upon a similar quest.

They closed on the longboat so quickly that the man in the stern had only time to cry, "Hold off, you lubbers, or you'll run us down! " before the prow of the *Spindrift* crashed right along the larboard side of the ship's longboat, carrying away the oar-blades before there was time to ship them. Six of the Maxwells tumbled into the longboat in a moment and were hard at it with fists and short swords, while Will stayed aboard and made fast to the stern with his boathook.

The brothers had a great advantage in leaping from a height, and it may be that the Black Smugglers did not fight at all up to their reputation. Indeed, except for that peppery Welshman, Ap Evans, in the stern, none of them had much heart to fight. Moreover, a rowing boat did not give them enough room to use their skills. They required the sweep of a ship's deck, and there, as we shall see, they were no cowards.

Ap Evans gave David Maxwell a long, slashing cut down the outer arm, which bothered him for a long time after. But he was soon held by Kennedy, who had never been wounded before, and was therefore the most impetuous, while Will kept the others quiet with a pistol. It took no time for the other brothers to get their cargo on board their own boat again and sail away, feeling themselves proudly triumphant.

As they cast loose Will Maxwell cried, 'My compliments to Captain Yawkins, and thank him kindly for his assistance in getting our stuff aboard. It was done amicably and I won't forget it."

"The devil fly away with you, you ugly Galloway ox!" cried Ap Evans, the Welshman, his twinkling grey eyes contracted until their pupils had shrunk to the merest pin-points.

Kennedy says that he noticed this in particular, as it reminded him of their grim cat Toby when he was watching a caged bird.

So the seven bold brothers bore away with no more damage than a cutlass slash, which did not trouble David much as yet, the wound not having had time to stiffen.

However, all this time Captain Yawkins had not been idle. He had been awakened from his morning sleep by the news that his attempt on the Maxwells' cargo was likely to go wrong. So being, like all his kind, both swift and energetic, he at once ordered his boats out, made haste to get his anchor up, cast loose his Long Toms, and prepared to intercept the daring lads of Galloway as soon as they came between him and the shore.

He might have succeeded, but just when Will Maxwell was bandying compliments with old Ap Evans, the smugglers' watcher on Maungold Head signalled that there was danger approaching. Thrice the signal came, in a way that could not be misunderstood. Indeed it had been made before, but so intent were the men aboard of the *Van Hoorn* on watching the affray of the boats that no-one had seen the first signals.

Round the Head, beating up from the south in the light wind, came a vessel with tall spars sweeping the sky.

"A thousand devils," cried Captain Yawkins, "we have watched these landlubbers too long. We shall lose our ship. Here she comes. By the weathercock of Krabbendyk, it is the *Seahorse*, a sloop of war of eighteen guns. See the jack at her mizzen. Mark their sky scrapers. She means to have us, boys, but then *I* mean that she shall not. Captain Yawkins is not a man to be fooled twice in a morning."

The men bustled about the decks – Spanish rats and broad-beamed Dutchmen, hill country gypsies taken to smuggling – and the whole crew of outlaw men gave a rousing cheer, for they were angry and wanted to have it out with someone. Before the guns were cast loose and their muzzle sheetings removed, Ap Evans came on board, and his strident voice was to be heard setting the men to their quarters, as Captain Yawkins ran his brig like a Naval ship.

Indeed, many a Naval ship was less well armed. Two Long Tom stern chasers looked over the taffrail, six twelve-pounder carronades grinned through the ports; and besides these there was Yawkins' pet, a fine new twenty-four pounder on the forecastle, just shipped and never yet fired.

The Galloway lugger sped out between the heads of Ramsay Bay. In ordinary times she would have got a shot across her bows to heave her to, but Lieutenant Mountenay of the *Seahorse* had a bigger target than a possible score of brandy casks hidden under the sheepskins and bullock-hides on the *Spindrift.* So the Maxwells tossed their bonnets in relief and joy, and bore away north for White Horse Bay. It happened, however, that at the Point of Ayre they saw the spars of yet another king's ship, waiting in the seaway with her topsails backed, keeping in the clear morning a bright lookout upon four coastlines. It was not in the Maxwells' minds to take any more risks when they had come so far. So Will Maxwell turned the *Spindrift* southward in the direction of Derby Haven, where for safety they landed the goods again; and by the time that the second king's ship, which proved to be the preventive schooner *Ariel*, sent a boat aboard, the Maxwells were once more peaceful, coast-wise traders, with a cargo of salt, alum, barytes for the men of the Mona estate, and hides and sheepskins to take back in exchange to the tanneries of Dumfries.

So the young officer who came on board was obliged to report everything was in order. But MacCallum, the boatswain of the *Ariel*, said to Kennedy Maxwell – "My lad, this may happen once, or twice, and three times if you're lucky; but in the end you'll be cooling your heels in Kirkcudbright prison. And that's not a nice place, I can assure you."

"Away, Rab," said Kennedy, "it's not so long since you were running the bonny folds of lace with the best of us. Its not for you to say."

"Yes, Kennedy, to my shame that's more than true, but I have seen the error of my ways in time!"

"Perhaps," returned Kennedy, dryly, "and the promise of a pound a week with a pension at the end."

"Well, Kennedy, say what you like, my word was kindly meant, lad," said the boatswain.

"And kindly taken," said Kennedy, nursing his arm with his other hand,"but if I was you I would keep your distance from us. My father's a passionate man, in spite of having seen the error of his ways."

"Why should I keep away from your house or any other house?" cried Rab MacCallum. "You know Deputy Dallas, the exciseman, is there every other night."

"I know that." said Kennedy, "You see the way of it is this, MacCallum – my father can be doing with preventative men, and at a pinch he can put up with maybe a smuggler or two. But the man he can't do with is the man that has been one thing and now is another, yet who tries to keep a foot in each camp! "

"Nobody ever said that I provided information," said MacCallum.

"No," said Kennedy," but you come from Rerrick and the steel of the gallows there that hanged good men is in your eyes."

The boatswain flew into a passion.

"I'll catch you yet, you Maxwells; you and your proud sister. You all have a goading tongue and the look of contempt that disrespects honest folk. But I'll have you laid low some day yet."

"That proves," cried Kennedy, "that you have tried to do it before. A fig for your threats. You're like daft Tammy Norie's bladder that he carries dangling on a stick – full of wind, and maybe a pea or two rattling in your belly! Nothing else!"

CHAPTER X.

SMUGGLER AND KING'S MEN

MEANWHILE there was braver action happening between the Heads of Ramsay. For the account of this I am obliged to Ebie Hook, who all that day was at the tiller of the *Van Hoorn*, sometimes stretched across it, with a strong Dutchman to help him to twirl it round, and sometimes steering her with his finger and thumb to sail her precisely to the orders of Captain Yawkins.

Now there have been many things said against that impressive Dutchman, and no doubt he had many a sin on his soul, including murder in all its different degrees; but there are two things that no one could ever claim – that Yawkins was either a coward or a bad sailor.

Often in the ward-room when retelling the story of how the Dutchman ran across his bows off Ramsay Heads, Lieutenant Mountenay would admit-

"Tarred, wizened, sun-dried, and smoke-dried, if you were to take down old Yawkins from the shore end of Leith pier, you would find a better sailor than I or any man on King George's navy roster."

No-one dared to disagree, for it was usually after his sixth glass that he was in the habit of saying this, and he was strong and outspoken by then.

So on the quarter-deck of the *Van Hoorn*, which was kept as white and clean as a man-of-war, Ebie Hook stood taking his orders from the captain himself, and crying, "Aye, Aye, Sir," like clockwork.

He said that it was a pleasure to see the ship fall into her marks like a racing cutter, and stretch away on another tack as steady as one's married wife.

"She was the sweetest boat that ever sailed, was the *Van Hoorn*, and Yawkins was the very son-of-a-gun of a fine seaman – not an ounce of fat on him anywhere."

"Man, Rathan," Ebie would say," the way he sailed that ship in the freshening breeze that blew between the Heads was a miracle. When we set sail I imagined the gallows plain before me, for it wasn't just smuggling, it was black piracy they had against us, had we been taken with the plunder of a sunken Greenock barquentine in our hold. Man, I tell you I was afraid. I thought I would never again get merry at Stoneykirk Sacrament, or drunk at Keltonhill Fair.'It's all up with you now, Ebie,' says

I; 'I have told you many a time it would come to this. The tough tow-rope and the weary gallows have got you in the end.'"

"But oh, man, it wasn't to be at that time, whatever; and it was by clean-run seamanship that we won clear."

Now, being a landsman, I have not the skill of sea-terms to tell the story as Ebie told it, but the gist of it was as follows:-

"The way out of the fray, was this," Ebie Hook would begin (I see him yet, though he passed on years ago. He always sat by the chimney corner and puffed away on his short clay pipe, using tobacco of prodigious blackness and strength, that he had learned to smoke in foreign countries when he was a traveller – so vile that it was nauseous to stand the reek of his pipe after it had passed out of his mouth). "The bo'sun of our ship was Abraham Anderson, from the Crae Brig. As the king's ship came nearer he piped the men to quarters; and it was a pretty sight to see, though being at the wheel I had little time to see it. Between watching the binnacle and jumping to old Yawkins' word I had enough to do. There was no time for games when steering for that crossbones of a Dutchman, whether in a chase or a battle. He would have stuck a knife in you as quick as he could get married on shore – and they say he was married as many as sixty-seven times, the old Mohammedan!

"And it was bonny to see the boarding nets secured and the pikes ready, the pistols all primed and the matches burning, each one fixed to a linstock on the deck.

"The gunners were piling round shot on the boards, and the grape and shot canisters were coming up from below. Outside the harbour, near the entrance of the bay, lay the king's ship, waiting to catch us as we came out, with all their guns trimmed to rake us as we went past them.

"It was doubtless a good plan, but the king's officer was naive to think of old Captain Yawkins stepping meekly to his destruction like that.

"So in the lee of the land under Maungold Head we lay with our topsails aback, waiting for the enemy to come in and lay us alongside.

"Now, though the Captain was cursing the Maxwells and their impudence, and blaming them for sending the revenue men on us, it so happened that it was really due to them that we escaped the gallows, for that time at least.

"Now there is no doubt whatever that had the *Seahorse* known that the preventive boat *Ariel* was as close to Ramsay as the other side of the Point of Ayre, she would simply have lain still where she was and waited for assistance, which would have compelled us to come out and enter battle with her in her terms. But luckily for us the *Ariel* was at that moment rushing southward on a wild goose chase after the Maxwell lads. So we were left to fight it out on something like equal terms.

"It was awesome to hear the captain. He never stopped blaspheming. And the curious thing about the matter was that it wasn't the king's men that he was wild at, but the Maxwells, and more especially old Dick Maxwell, his partner who sailed the seas with him in the days before he got the brig *Van Hoorn* for himself.

" He cursed him as a thief, and there was something about a brass box and a treasure, and something, too, about a lass; but the message of his rant was, 'Be the day dark or clear, the night starlit or pitch black, and the if the Red Cock crows not on the roofs of Richard Maxwell by the cliffs of Craigdarroch, may I turn for ever and ever from side to side between the red coal and the brimstone flaming blue beyond the gates of hell.' A dreadful oath to speak once, but he said it often.

"It was indeed most fearsome to hear him. He swore like that all the time, even when we could see the king's ship coming through the narrows at the head of the bay and setting in for us with every piece of canvas set.

"Man, she was handsome as she came at us, the foam creamy white under her forefoot. She was like a tower dressed in snow-white clothes blowing light and airy from masthead to bowsprit and jib-boomend. Then as soon as she came round the point she began to fire the single guns, and the shot whistled through our rigging. At this time the job of the man at the wheel is not to be recommended as a livelihood, because the sharp-shooters fire at him, and if the ship gets raked fore and aft, he's the one that knows about it first, and all that's left of him can be swept overboard with a broom.

"But there was no disobeying orders in Yawkins' ship. You *might* be killed by the enemy if you obeyed; but you would certainly be killed if you didn't.

"'Put her about,' he cried, suddenly, and with that ran right across the bows of the *Seahorse* as she came swiftly at us, swaying with the undercurrent of the sea in the harbour mouth. She brought the wind with her, for as she closed on us we seemed to get it as well; and the sudden shift in our course, instead of leaving us becalmed, steadied us so we could send a broadside down her decks but also draw clear before she could alter her course.

"We were looking as though we might beach the *Van Hoorn* on the sand of the southernmost bay; but in a moment, just when it seemed that we had caught ourselves, 'All hands wear ship,' cried our captain, and the mates gave the orders while the Dutchman and I burst ourselves to bring the helm sharply round. Down dropped the peak, round went the spars, the yards were braced, and away we swung through the rising lift of the harbour bar till the wind caught us as she passed the heads of the bay, and, like a porpoise, buried her nose in the heaving swell where the wind and the tide met.

"As we left the king's ship astern, old Father Yawkins jumped onto our stern handrail, and waved his hand - 'Out-sailed, out-fought, out-witted – such a set of kiss-my-hands, you king's men. That's what I think of you! Ha!'

"And with that he leaped down, and snatching off his wig and broad, flapping hat, he crammed them into the right-hand Long Tom, and with his own hand shot them aboard the king's man.

"Now this insult angered Lieutenant Mountenay, commander of the *Seahorse,* more than losing the chase. It was partly this that caused a great eagerness among all the king's navy men to capture Captain Yawkins – an adventure which later succeeded despite many failures.

"So this was why the *Van Hoorn* ran directly north to land her cargo at Brighouse, and then burn the fine farmyard of Craigdarroch."

Ebie now took breath and blew upon his reeking pipe.

"But what stopped the *Seahorse* from chasing you?" I asked him. "She could not have been far enough behind to lose you in a run of less than thirty miles, to the Brighouse?"

"Well, that's a strange thing too." said Ebie, "It is just like a play. They tell me that the very last shot that was fired – the one that Captain Yawkins fired himself – carried away the whole of their steering gear, and left them without no option but to anchor. So they tell me. I don't know. But if that was the reason, it would seem that some of the old man's brains had stuck to the old man's wig.

"Eh, sir, but there's many wonderful things in the world.

"And my tobacco's finished. Have you a fill about you, do you think?"

CHAPTER XI

THE GREAT CAVE OF ISLE RATHAN

IN TRUTH, but it was good when we got under the brow of the land and underneath the shaggy shadows of the trees, to hear the sound of the water below the keel of the boat. We had Richard Maxwell and his brass chest, and May with her bundle of shirts tied in a spotted napkin. That boat was the most comfortable place that I had found since I saw the red star of a godless night rise over Craigdarroch.

Silver Sand rowed us back as silently as we had come. As we went I saw that he was not taking us to the house, but down towards the point of Rathan Island where the rocks were at their wildest and the surge constantly tossed and boiled about the perpendicular cliffs.

"Why are we not going to the House Bay?" I asked Silver Sand.

"Because I don't want my throat cut," he said. "Do you think Yawkins and his sea-thieves will not discover first thing in the morning that something heavy has been carried to the shore by two men, and that three men, a lassie, and a dog have got into a boat under the trees by the White Horse Bay? It's so plain to be seen that even a gamekeeper could make it out! "

"So what now, then?" I asked, the objective not yet being clear to me.

"What else?" said he. "I wish I didn't have to put up with such a pack of brainless fools with no initiative. Where else would they look for a boat to come from but the Rathan? Where would they be safe to search without hindrance but on the Rathan? Have you a regiment of horse and foot on the Rathan? Do the officers of King George pay you a visit every day? In the old days, it was on Rathan where your father brought many a fine cargo ashore, and it's there that they'll look for us."

"Then why are we going there; could we not make for Killantringan, or even Dumfries?" I asked, still unclear.

"Stop, Laird Heron," said Silver Sand, "you haven't the head of your father at all, or you wouldn't need to ask so many questions. If we went to Killantringan, we wouldn't be any safer than we are here. The hill outlawry could catch us before we'd gone two miles if we had to carry this box. And as for Dumfries, it would be just as feasible to aim for the moon. There's only two ways that I know to get to Dumfries – one along the shore, and we have no horses except my donkey and wee Donald, and the other road by the sea to the Nith Water, and it would be a job for us to race with the *Van Hoorn*, or even with her pinnace, that won a race at Rotterdam against the crews of the whole Dutch navy."

"Then there's nothing for it but the cave," I said.

Silver Sand pretended to admire my talent and perspicuity.

"Preserve us all, Patrick, but you mustn't put such a strain on yourself. That must have been so difficult to work out. Aye, as you say, it's the cave, and nothing else but the cave."

"But what's to come of the house of Rathan?" I asked, for though I was willing enough to take part in this quarrel of the Maxwells, I did not want all my earthly possessions burned within half a mile of me without doing my best to save them.

"You'll have to trust the house to me and Quharrie," said Silver Sand, still jesting. "You'll find that we are good at watching."

The night was already turning to bright yellow low on the east, and the red glow of the dying fire at Craigdarroch could be seen as a faint reflection on the water, as we began to draw near to the sea caves at the foot of Rathan Island. There were many tales about these caves. They were miles long, according to the ignorant. They were inhabited by the most terrible of sea beasts, by mermen and fearsome sea lions of exceptional ferocity.

But in fact they were rather pleasant places as caves go. I was especially fond of one of them, for not only had it a wide and high sea entrance, which made it safe to enter by boat, but as you climbed a long way through passages and halls, you came to a space of clear yellow sand, from which there was an opening to the sea like a window in a house high up above the doorway.

The cave entrance beneath was, as it were, the door of the house, and within it the tides surged and swirled, while the window at the top looked out to sea half way down the cliff, where not even a samphire gatherer could reach and not even a sea eagle could nest.

This was called the Great Rathan Cave, and it was the one Silver Sand had selected for us.

The wild calls of the gulls and gannets on the rocks was a great contrast to the night quiet of the moors. May Maxwell had been very silent, as well one might who has lost everything and found herself in the midst of blood and threats. But the pleasant daybreak and the cheerful nature of our surroundings seemed to lift her spirits.

The lower end of Rathan Isle toward the sea is almost separate from the rest, and is called the South Stack.

Further south was an isle, or rather a high single rock, where the sea-birds nested. We passed this on our right as we entered the Great Cave of Rathan. And as we went in, a cloud of gulls rose with an astonishing clamour, their many wings making a thunder of flappings like the beating of innumerable sails when a ship stands shivering in the eye of a breeze.

The air was clear and brisk, but the night dew had left a sticky, oily film on our faces and hands. A black diver flew hither and thither and seemingly tried to do away with his life by staying under water long enough to drown himself. It is a wonder that I took noticed that, although I have always heeded father's rule – "Remember all that you see, but forget all that folk say about you!" There are not many wiser observations than that to be got for nothing.

High up among the rocks a couple of ravens looked sneeringly and overbearingly down from the edge of their nest, and barked hoarsely at us as we went by. They had been watching the burning of some decent folks' house all night with some pleasure, but that is the nature of that bird.

"Glock! Glock! Glock!" they cried at us, as they do in the Norse sagas when the heroes are lying on the field of blood.

Now, these caves of the Solway are in a different rock to that which comprises the greater part of the seaboard. Here and there the rock is softer, like freestone, and it is readily eroded by the sea.

I wish that I could take you to see these wonderful spurs and arches that have been carved from the rock by the genius of the water. There are many sorts of caves there, and I used to play in them, often for the whole day. There was the Great Cave, that could house a thousand men in its depths, yet which could be defended by as few as ten men against any number who did not know its ways and outlets. In it there was the outlook to the sea, and the Hall which I called the Hall of Ossian.

The most part of these caves are sea caverns similar to those on the coast of Antrim in Ireland, which is the only other place where I have seen such resounding halls, with green water booming solemnly into them, and the noise of their roaring heard far along the coast. Some of these are deep, dark dens, accursed and gloomy, in which the tide sways blindly at all times, horrible to look upon from the sea, showing cruel teeth like an old wolf-dog that has drawn up its lip so that one may see the broken fangs and the cavernous dark behind. The dank, clammy air is compressed by the tide. A horrible ooze clings to every part of the rock, as though slimy worms from the sea-bottom had crawled over all of it.

On Rathan there were many sorts of caves. But most of all I loved the tiny cavelets in the White Sand coves, where the waves of a sheltered sea beat all day, lisping and lapping with a pleasant sound. There, on warm days, it was my habit to lie even naked, half in and half out of the water, the whole isle being so lonely.

We now drew quickly from under the frowning face of the South Stack.

As Silver Sand brought the boat near to the Great Cave, the entrance rose high above us, and the swaying of the waves in the mouth of it was so spectacular, that I felt as proud of possessing the Island as if I had made it myself.

Silver Sand, indeed, never glanced either above or below, but then he had no need, seemingly having a circle of eyes all around his head. Richard Maxwell seemed to be still muttering curses on his foes; and, by the jerking of his eyebrows and the twitching movement of his lips, I judged that he was imagining them captured and tortured somewhere so grim that they would have welcomed the cold salt water that sobbed and heaved into the cavern.

But May Maxwell, out of whom the mischief had died, glanced more than once up to the entrance, which opened for us like that water gate into the Tower of London, where the traitors enter but never leave. But she said nothing.

The upper arch of the cave is at least forty feet above the surface of the water, and the sea entrance beneath it is only three times the breadth of a boat. The cliffs rise so high above that seen from beneath, they seem as if they are holding up the sky. As we steered our way carefully into the mouth of the cave, we passed through floating balls of sea-spume so large that the prow of the boat was whitened with them. I have often taken them in my hands, chasing them, as puppies do, along the shore when the wind comes in off the sea.

The rock is worn everywhere into a myriad of holes and crevices, in which grow sea-pinks with dry, flaky flower heads. I also saw yellow tansy far above. On the sheltered crannies, where a little earth collects and the birds leave droppings, there was some parched sea-grass, and I think that I caught the pale-blue glint of the sea-holly. I remember that I thought it was early for it to bloom, and I imagined climbing to get a piece for May Mischief. This when I had infinitely more serious things to think about.

Quharrie sat beside May Maxwell in the boat with his paws on the seat, heaving his head aloft and sniffing in an uncertain fashion, as if his experience, though a wide one, did not include sea caves.

May Maxwell settled her shawl closer about her as we drew away from the wholesome light of day, and the greenish glimmer grew about us. It made my heart waver to and fro within me like a sunbeam in a basin of water, tingling and quivering, when she laid a little hand on my arm. She trembled as a maid can, and it was a cold hand, and it shook. But it made the last remnant of my dislike of her fly away.

Nor do I think now, looking back, that I ever disliked her greatly. In my heart of hearts I always liked her – even when she pursed her mouth and cried, "BAA!"

It was sweetest, perhaps, when out of the depths of the great cave burst a clamorous cloud of rock pigeons. As we entered we could hear their voices peep-peeping and chuntering to their young, some of the old cock-birds meanwhile *roo-hooing* on the higher ledges with a sound wonderfully varied and pleasant. Also at the entrance there were a few solitary maids and bachelors sitting in the clefts sunning themselves with drooping wings, like barn door hens in the dust. Some were preening their feathers, the sheen on their necks shining red because at that moment the sun was rising.

When the boat got well within the cave, where the narrows of the passage open into the wide Hall of Ossian, the boat ground harshly on the sand and shingle. At this the doves took instant alarm, and with a startling whirr and clatter they swooped down on us in a perfect cloud, their shining breasts extraordinarily near to us, so that the wind fanned our faces as the living stream poured out of the narrow and fetid darkness of the cave into the splendid sunshine of the young morning.

It was then that May Maxwell cried aloud, as a lass well might. The clamour of the doves startled me, even though I was used to it, far less a young lass that had seen her home burnt over her head that night. There was no shame or wonder in it. Nor is there any need that I should write about it, except that I could not quite hear what name it was that she cried out. But I had hopes that I knew.

CHAPTER XII.

MORNING IN THE CAVE

THE entrance was the grandest part of our cave. It was not very wonderful inside – as caves often are. There was the dark hall of sand and pebbles, in which the water broke either at the end of the long sea passage or half-way up the incline of the floor, according to the state of the tide. But except for purposes of landing or defence we never stayed long in this dank and cold place, but climbed directly up to the little chamber, which could have been the cave of a hermit, as it was comfortable in all weathers, except when a heavy wind blew in straight from the south, when the large window faced the gale. But mercifully during the time we spent there the air was fairly still, and we only heard the swell sobbing and swishing along the edges of the rocks far beneath us.

So we climbed through the dank and dripping passages, which did not take long, I carrying May Maxwell's parcels and guiding her. But it was pleasant to emerge opposite the window into the early morning sunlight, coming from the direction of Southerness and turning the cold, white crests of the chilly indigo waves to a rosy colour. I took pleasure in leading her to the window, which was shaped almost oblong, with sea-rockets and stonecrop growing around it. I shall always consider it as a special omen that, when I looked past the end of the ledge, I saw a little sod of heather growing in the cleft, and in the middle of it, early for the season, a few waxen lobes of perfectly white bell-heath. I still held her hand, in case coming into the light suddenly might cause a giddiness, and pulled some white, waxen bells, which I presented to her with all the courtesy of which I was capable. This she took gracefully, and she looked at me with eyes that were full of tears, and said, speaking unlike her former way-

"Thank you, Patrick; what makes you so mindful of me? I don't deserve it."

I had intended here to have said something exceedingly fine and appropriate, but all that I could get out was just, "Yes, of course you do!"

And even then I stammered. However, I am not sure that I could have improved it even after a week's practice.

So in the early morning we sat and looked over the sea. The air was still fresh, but the sun had already taken the chill off. The sea was like a painted cloth hung up before us, since we were so high above the water –

a cloth on which the ships and boats were drawn prettily one above the other.

The natural window at which we sat was not as high as it was broad – and there was a stone shelf in front of it; it looked almost man made.

"It is very quiet and peaceful here," May said; but Richard, her father, said nothing. I think he hardly noticed where he had been taken. He had lived at Craigdarroch all his life apart when he was on the seas, and indeed had been born there. It went hard with him to lose it all in a single night.

"As peaceful," May continued, "as though there were no wicked men in the world."

This moment now seems to me so strange and peaceful – the calm before the storm breaks and the lightning flashes.

At this she shuddered slightly, and I later found out that at Craigdarroch Hector Faa himself had taken hold of her, but that she had broken free from him, fleeing hot-foot into the wood. It was Hector Faa, who as with his tribe was an outcast from sweet Yethom, who had sent a message to Richard Maxwell that he was coming to the low country for a wife, according to the custom of his tribe. And he and his mother boasted that a Faa bride had never been led home without her hands tied behind her back. This was Faa custom, considered as sacred by these wild gypsy clans.

So Black Hector, who was the brother of John Faa himself, was simply doing the bidding of his mother, as well as following his own inclination, when he sent this message to Craigdarroch. His mother had adopted the ways of the clan and had become more Faa than the Faas themselves, as they say all of these abducted gypsy wives become.

The curse that Richard Maxwell sent back in response is still remembered in the hill country, and his descendants mention it with a kind of pride. It was considered as fine a thing as the old man ever did since he dropped profane swearing and took to quoting condemnations from the Psalms – which served just as well.

The answer that came back was short and sweet."Tell the old man at Craigdarroch," Black Hector sent his message, "that I'll have the lass in spite of him and the seven illustrious brothers."

And it is likely that he would have succeeded, had it not been for one man, but not one of May Maxwell's brothers.

Once we were safe within the cave, Silver Sand went away with Quharrie, taking the boat with him, and leaving us shut in with no chance of escape, if the smugglers had followed us to the Stacks outside the cave.

But I had my pistols, and set about priming them, and carefully checking the condition of the locks, for I was proud of my marksmanship. As a boy I had set a stone on the dyke and knocked it over with another at thirty yards' distance, four times out of five. In later days, since my friends came to reside on the isle with me, I often used a pebble to win an argument.

Indeed there were few places about the Isle Rathan from which I could not reach an erring youth with pebble cunningly thrown from the hip. Later, I had practised a great deal with pistols until I considered that a smuggler, great or small, would have little chance with me at twenty yards. I was also skilled with the claymore and small sword, taught by my father during the wet days of winter, keeping me at it till my limbs ached and my back felt broken.

It was not long before Silver Sand brought back a boatload of provisions from the house. He brought with him only one reinforcement, Jerry MacWhirter, with the news that in the morning the father of the Allison lads had appeared with two stout apprentices and a very large whip, and had driven the three boys – Andrew, John, and Rab Nicoll – into his boat. Meanwhile, Jerry had stood on the cliff above, and, according to him, had exhorted their father to beat them soundly. Which I have little doubt that he did.

It was a loss, but one I was not sorry for. If the smugglers came, there was less responsibility for me, and Jerry was of an age to decide for himself. Besides, he had never been under control in his life. He would give us no anxiety, and would often amuse us. I think we were all more cheerful and hopeful as soon as he joined us.

But Silver Sand brought also another passenger, a bare-footed, barearmed lass, freckled and well built, with arms and legs like those of a man.

"This is a lass," he said, as soon as he came in," that I found knocking at the front door, which is not safe to do. So I brought her with me. She can speak for herself. She doesn't appear to be troubled with shyness."

As soon as May Maxwell saw her she got up off the stone shelf by the window and ran to her cheerfully, as does a child amongst grown folk when another child comes in.

"Father," she cried, "do you not see this is Bell MacTurk?"

"Aye," said the old man, "I see that!"

But apparently the sight did not do him much good, for he sank again into a morose silence.

"Bell," said Mary, "shake hands with Master Patrick Heron this minute, for you're on his Isle of Rathan – or, rather, in it – and very far in too!"

Bell came forward and shook hands.

"Laird or not," said she,"you might have had the sense to give a bonny lass an embrace in salutation."

Mary Maxwell laughed.

"Oh, Bell, Bell," she said, "is this a day for your jesting?"

"Oh, away with you, Mistress May, it's not every day Bell MacTurk gets the chance of a little kiss from a laird! And why should you be sad? There's some things and stores burned, and the thatch is off the byre, and the stockyard's empty; but there are people coming home who will build it all up again, and put a bigger harvest than ever under thatch and rope. For there was no end to the wickedness of that crew of Black Smugglers and robbers. But now the whole country will rise against them, and then they will be finished."

While she was speaking Richard Maxwell looked at her from under his bushy eyebrows. There was a grey pallor about his face that did not look right in the full light of the morning, because the sun had now come round so that it shone upon the face of the cliff.

"Aye, lass," he exclaimed, rising to his feet, "these are words wise beyond your years. They shall be rooted out, for the destruction of the farmhouse that was my home and where I raised my children. This I swear and declare before the Almighty."

"Now, sit down, father," said May, anxiously "don't walk about, you are not steady on your feet and you might fall down the cliff. Besides you are putting those who are helping you into danger with the loud sound of your voice."

The old man sat down without another word, and wrapped himself again in his gloomy reflections. But all the rest of us were visibly cheered by the arrival of Jerry and Bell, as well as by the food which they had brought from the house. The only worry I had was the thought of Rathan House, which was all I had, lying vacant and open to the crew that had burned Richard Maxwell's farmstead and all of his goods.

But Silver Sand relieved some part of my anxiety by declaring that he meant to remain outside, and be both scout and watchman.

"The house is perfectly safe in my hands. I'll set Quharrie to watch it," he said, "and no smuggler will come near it when Quharrie is looking after it."

So it was arranged that if the waterway should be barred Silver Sand was to lower any message or package for us over the cliff in such a way that it would swing opposite the window – a plan which was afterwards carried out with complete success.

But despite that I thought it strange that Silver Sand would take no part in the real warfare against the outlaws, whilst giving us help in every other way.

CHAPTER XIII

THE DEFENCE OF THE CAVE

BUT our good humour did not last long, for we were to hear from the enemy in a very sudden and surprising manner. How Yawkins found us to this day remains a mystery. Not even Ebie Hook, to whom I owe the answer to many questions, can unravel this, since he was not present at the attack, being one of the watch who remained on the *Van Hoorn* by order of Captain Yawkins.

It is likely that one of the lookouts upon the mainland saw us go into the cave, or noted Silver Sand's return from the house with his load.

However, it is certain that just before nine in the morning, before the *Van Hoorn*, having embarked those of her crew who had joined with the gypsies in destroying the homestead of Craigdarroch, bore up to the south of Isle Rathan under easy sail. When she came abreast of the entrance of the cave a puff of white smoke rose from her side, and a great round shot came plumping into the mouth of the cavern, breaking away a fragment from the cliff, which plunged like thunder into the deep water of the entrance. Myriads of chips flew every way, but not so much as a speck of dust reached the great central hall, where only the echoes reverberated, though the swells raised by the round shot and the fall of the great fragment came rolling up to our feet in an arching wall of green water crested with white.

From our secret watch-tower window on the face of the cliff we could see the brig hanging in the wind to give her stern chasers another chance. I sent May Maxwell and Bell into the little passage at the back, where they might be tolerably safe in the event of a ball striking through the window of our retreat.

As soon as the noise raised by the second round shot died away – it struck the cliff without doing any harm – we saw two boatloads of men from the brig setting off with the evident intention of attacking us. The *Van Hoorn*, as it must have been obvious from her deck, had been firing uselessly at a vast hole in the sea cliff. Even so the men at quarters on board of her watched it; and some of them muttered to one another that it had been better to have turned the ship about and made off with what plunder they had before the king's ships found them. But the captain, it is said, had private information about the chest which Richard Maxwell had carried away, and cared for no other part of the spoil.

At any rate he decided to try the entrance of the cave, having little doubt that so large a force would be able immediately to subdue our weak defence, which must have appeared feeble to him even though he did not know the strength of our position.

There was nothing very wonderful about the cavern in which we were concealed. It consisted simply of a sea entrance practicable for boats, and a cliff entrance accessible only by gulls and pigeons.

The passage between the two chambers was narrow, but with many twists and turns, having small chambers and one or two side passages which returned back upon the main one. At the bottom of this natural winding stair there was the large hall which we called Ossian's Hall, where the sea passage ended and where the swell broke upon a beach of shingle and sand. Indeed the whole cavern, as far as we knew, did not extend more than two hundred yards in all its turns and windings, entrances and passages.

There were no footholds on any of the cliffs that lined the sea edge, which were steep, black, and slippery. You may find this, the second on the right hand in sailing along Rathan, between the South Stack of Rathan, and the east point that looks to Killantringan and Southerness. Indeed, the entrance is so wide that you cannot miss it. The arched cliff that is called the Needle's Eye is within fifty feet of it, and the reverse suction of the sea pouring out of the Great Cave of Rathan sets through the Needle's Eye in a boiling swell at every turn of the tide. It is thus easily found.

So much, then, for our situation. Now a word concerning our preparations for defence: we had plenty of arms and ammunition, and, speaking for myself, I was optimistic about the coming fray, that I am sure I would not have been in open country where a hundred might fire at you from all sides. I thought it best that Richard Maxwell, Jerry, and myself should go down to the Hall of Ossian, and by getting as far out into the passage as possible, kneeling upon ledges and jutting rocks, be ready to beat back our assailants as they entered.

There was, indeed, about thirty feet from the Hall of Ossian a kind of platform on which two of us could stand. This commanded the entrance, and from it we could see the wide span of the outer arch and the rock-doves flitting to and fro in the sunshine. May Maxwell came with us to help in loading the guns – in which she was exceedingly expert, having been trained in this by her brothers when they went shooting at birds or when practising.

Bell remained in the chamber over the gate, both to give us intelligence on the approach of the enemy and also to receive any message from Silver Sand on the cliff above, which he might swing downwards in the way that had been arranged. We had just gone to our positions before one such message did reach us. It was wrapped about a stone and tied with willow shoots. This ball swung clear of the cliff; so that Bell had to take the hooks used for hanging the porridge pot upon the cave fireplace, in order to draw it in, which might have been dangerous had the smugglers seen her.

But in a trice she had detached the stone and brought Silver Sand's message to me, which said in correct enough English but in a curious ancient hand and without punctuations –

"IT IS THE CHEST THEY WANT AND THE LASS THE HOUSE IS SAFE ENOUGH FIRE AT THE GYPSIES THEY ARE THE DEVILS THE SAILORS HAVE NO HEART IN THE MATTER YOUR OBLIGED SERV^T SILVER SAND."

We had to be content with this information. The one thing I was now sure of, was that Silver Sand would be of greater service free and above ground than down with us in the sea cave. But we were all in good spirits, especially when Bell came down with the letter and served us with courage of the Dutch sort out of a square, wide-mouthed bottle, scandalously overserving Jerry because he was a favourite of her – which she thought that I did not notice.

So we went to our posts to be ready, since the boats were approaching. From the window in the cliff we could note their numbers and bearing. There were about twenty of them in two boats. Most of them were not sailors, but wild fellows from the hills, bonnetless and unkempt.

Yawkins himself was in one boat and Hector Faa in the stern of the other, monstrously fine in a buff coat and a shirt with lace upon it, both of which he had taken from the house of Richard Maxwell at the burning of Craigdarroch.

When I mentioned this to May Maxwell she ran up to take a peep at the window, and came down furious, saying, " That is the shirt that I got ready for my father to go to Stoneykirk Communion in, and to think that that ignorant fool should be wearing it!"

"Let him sup with the Devil," cried Bell,"and I turned it and bleached it on the courtyard and sprinkled spring water from the well upon it."

"Load the muskets, May," said I. "It's not much use quibbling about a man running away with your father's shirt, when he wants to run away with you yourself."

But she did not somehow seem to think that this last point was nearly so heinous a crime as the dirty rogue wearing her father's shirt.

"It took me two hours to do the ruffles," she said. However, this foolish care for a trifling insult almost made me angry.

"Maybe you wouldn't have been so annoyed if he had run off with you!" I said, with as ill-natured an expression as I could manage, for such superfine care for her father's ruffles was beyond my comprehension at such a time.

"It might not concern me," says she, "since it's good that at least some folk in the world think something of me."

"Even a broken land squatting gallows cheat like Hector Faa! "

"Aye," says she, "better him than nobody!" At this moment came the roar of the third shot from the brig. She was firing again into the cave, and the shot, being aimed low, came skipping in, rebounding from side to side of the cavern and filling the long sea passage with dust and the clamour of echoes. But it did no harm, for the first time it touched the roof it rebounded and fell heavily to the bottom where, without doubt, it lies to this day.

Upon this Jerry cried, "I am going up to see what they are doing. I have a biscuit up there I would like to toss them for their breakfast."

"Come back to your post, you wildcat," I shouted after him. "If you play any tricks at such a time as this, I'll break your back!"

Now I understood how he must have angered his mother and relations, and for the first time I had some sympathy with them and their free use of the birch rod.

"I'll be back soon!" he cried, far up the passage.

I could only bare my teeth at him and go over in my own mind what I would give him when I got him quietly by himself for all this. Then the first musket-shot went off outside.

There was a crash and a loud yell.

"That will be Jerry's biscuit!" said May Maxwell, who knew something of his intentions, having heard Bell and him talk together. Now there was a disturbance at the outer gate of the cave; though being in the dark far back and standing to our posts with our muskets ready, we could see nothing. Yet we could hear shouting, cursings, blasphemings, and multitudinous splashings in the water sounding like a thousand wounded wild ducks.

"They've sunk the boat, blood them!" cried someone, hoarsely.

"Let us get on, Yawkins!" cried another. "We've too many on board already; shift for yourselves!" was the answer. Then came a burst of swearing and more splashing.

"Back her! Back her!" cried the strong voice of Yawkins. "Keep the rascals off with your boathook; here comes another stone."

There was another resounding splash, and a loud, universal "AH!"

Then a cry of "Into the cave mouth, lads, and you'll be out of reach of the stones!"

I could have bitten my thumbs that I had not thought of this plan before. I was indeed, as Mistress

MacWhirter had said, "a poor general."

I was also angry with Jerry for being quicker witted than me. It turned out, however, that the plan was May Mischief's, told firstly to Bell and then carried out successfully by Jerry and Bell together.

All this was indeed mighty fortunate for us, for the first great stone, after a drop of fifty feet, drove a hole in the leading boat – that of Hector Faa – and in a moment he and all his ragged regiment were struggling in the water. They scrambled onto the rocks, however, swimming with one hand and holding their matchlocks above their heads with the other, since that is how it is done when swimming across the narrows of Loch Enoch and Loch Neldricken in their home country.

But the swell and tossing of the sea water was difficult for them to cope with, and many of them got their tinder wet as well as their powder; so that their pieces were no use to them, fortunately for us in the cave.

In a trice we could see them climbing and crawling like wild cats of the hills, as indeed they were, on the knobs and ragged edges of the sea entrance.

We could also hear the grating of the oars of the boat against the sides of the cave as they scraped along, and the voice of Yawkins ordering his men to take their oars out of the rowlocks and push the boat along by hand. Then came a splatter of musketry up the passage, and May Maxwell cried out in a way that caused my heart to leap.

In an instant both her father and I set our Queen Anne muskets to our shoulders and fired. This halted the boat and one of the smugglers dropped forward. He fell amongst the feet of the others and seriously impeded them with his moaning and grasping at them as they trod upon him.

Some of them cried "Back!" and some "Have at them!" So they were greatly confused. I did not fire again, hoping that there might not be any need for more bloodshed. But Richard Maxwell did not agree, and he nimbly climbed down with the discharged pieces and ran up again with the loaded ones which his daughter had prepared for him. He took no notice when she cried out, for as soon as he had fired his first shot he broke out into a great rapture of singing. This was his song:

"There arrows of the bow He brake,
The shield, the sword, the war;
More glorious Thou than hills of prey,
More excellent art far.

"Those that were stout of heart are spoil'd,
They slept their sleep outright,
And none of those their hands did find,
That were the men of might."

The vigour with which the old man sang this psalm was something to marvel at, since not for a moment did he stop his musketry practice, and at the end of every verse dropped a deadly shot among his enemies.

The boat's crew soon had their bellyful of fighting in the dark, and were now only anxious to get away with their skins intact. Some of them lay down in the bottom of the boat, while others stood up and fired into the darkness of the cave; but apart from a pigeon or two which fell flapping and struggling into the water, no one was a penny-piece the worse, for May Maxwell's cry was only a sudden exclamation at the crack of the musket, though to me it had sounded disturbingly plaintive.

The boat backed out, narrowly escaping another of Jerry's dangerous biscuits, and in a little while we heard the noise of shooting above us, which made me fear that the gypsies had found a way of scrambling down the cliff. But it was nothing more than Jerry trying his hand at the gun, for in a little while Bell came flying down for more ammunition in a high state of excitement, crying, " We soaked them all. Hector Faa got his bonny French coat drenched." And this seemed to her to be the highlight.

Our cave, which was shaped much like a tadpole with a very wide head and a very long body, was full of gunpowder smoke, so that we could not see those we were firing at. But Richard Maxwell continued to discharge his gun as often as he could get it loaded, angrily sending each shot with double powder and a text of Scripture.

Presently another great gun went off from the *Van Hoorn* but there was no lead or iron in it this time. It was the signal of recall, and in a few minutes the single remaining boat's crew was taken on board, and the brig steered away to the south. This was not a moment too soon; for the outsailed *Seahorse* and the deceived *Ariel* had gathered off the Isle of

Man and were speeding north to hem the Black Smuggler into the blind alley of the estuary of the Solway.

Now, though Yawkins was no doubt eager for revenge, and even more eager to capture the brass-bound box which Richard Maxwell kept so carefully, he had too great a regard for his neck to risk the gallows on the slim chance of achieving either. He ran, therefore, towards the entrance of Wigtown Bay to turn before the slower king's ships could trap him, then he steered south to escape, at least this time. His day had not come yet. But the shadow ship was following hard after, and the Fate that travels by land and sea, but most surely and completely by sea, waited to lay the final arrest upon him, and on Leith Sands she hove him to. Where he remains to this day.

CHAPTER XIV.

THE HILL GYPSIES

THEN it was peaceful for some hours.

As Silver Sand had predicted, there was little heart for the fight among the sailors. They fought best at sea. But the gypsies of the hills, accustomed to the crags and caves, the screes and precipices of the Dungeon, were quite different adversaries.

Since these days the countryside has settled back to normal and it is easy to forget that it was only a few years ago when the Marshalls and Macatericks levied blackmail and drove cattle from half the land of Galloway. Many of them were gypsies of pure blood, like Faa himself; and Marshall. Indeed, the Faas, though expelled from the Border country, regarded themselves above the Stuarts or Douglasses, or any other ancient, dignified names. In some ways, I am inclined to agree; but whether the blood is improved in quality by the long descent through cattle-thieves and wizards is a moot point. But, Hector Faa was little more than a chicken-coop thief, and confined himself to maids from the Lowlands and droves of cattle from anywhere; and as for the lost John Faa himself; did he not still hold King James' patent of nobility, and describe himself with justice and full heraldic right as "Lord and Earl of Little Egypt"?

The greater part of these tribes that herded together in the upper hill country – the No Man's Land, on the borders of the three counties of Kirkcudbright, Wigtown, and Ayr, were broken men from the Border clans and septs – wild Eliots, upstart Beatties from the disputed lands, or outlaw Scotts fleeing from the wrath of their own chief, the Warden of the Marches. With them there were the Macatericks, a sept of sturdy rascals from the wilder parts of North Carrick.

All these outlaw folk used to plunder the men of the lower lands and valleys until the Leshmahago Whigs rose to power in the high days of Presbyterianism before the return of Charles Stewart, the second of the name, King Charles II. Then these, decent, God-fearing men, of a dour and high spirit, and all united by the tie of a common religion and by the Covenants (National and Solemn League), rose and made defeated the Macatericks, driving them out of their country with fire and sword.

Those that escaped took themselves to the wilds of the moorlands, where no law was obeyed, and no warrant was good unless countersigned with a musket.

In the dark days of the Killing Times, this country (which seems destined to be the great sanctuary of the persecuted), was also where god fearing Presbyterians worshipped in secret. But it was unsafe for them there because there were always informers there who for hire would bring the troopers on the poor, hunted wretches, cowering with their ragged clothes and tender consciences in the moss-haggs and among the great rocks of granite.

Then in the times which followed, as some still alive are old enough to remember, all the land was swiftly pacified apart from in the wild country – the wild men being an assembly of the outlaw clans that had gathered there. It is curious that, as long as their crimes were not excessive, their marauding was tolerated, so that they took as many cattle and as many sheep as they had need of. As to their country itself, no man had the lairdship of it. For centuries all of it belonged to the Kennedies, though the Lord Stewarts of Garlies have long claimed some rights over it. As for lifting a drove of cattle from the Lowlands, it had been done by every Macaterick for generations, though generally from Carrick or the Machars, where the people are less inclined to fight, than those from Galloway.

It was therefore not just bravado, but more a declaration of his rights, that Hector Faa should send word to the Maxwells, the strongest of all the patriarchal smuggling families of the Solway seaboard, that their only sister was intended to be the bride of a gypsy chief.

Hector Faa had seen May Maxwell at the great fair of Keltonhill, where she had gone every year since she was a girl, under the guardianship of her bodyguard of brothers. Only a year ago Kennedy had struck Hector on the mouth and drew blood, and Hector had drawn his knife on the Maxwells, but, at Keltonhill, they were in their own country and in overwhelming force.

"Till another day!" cried Hector Faa, as they dragged him away.

The other day had now come.

I have no doubt that the gypsies knew well that the Maxwell brothers were some distance away or they would have been far less bold and infinitely more wary.

All this takes a long time to tell, yet the sailing away of the smugglers, and the second attack of the gypsies followed within a few minutes of each other.

We were still standing in the Hall of Ossian waving our hands before our faces to clear the cave of the sulphurous smoke of the powder.

"Run," said Richard Maxwell to his daughter, "bring me my canister. I left it at the cave-head."

I was about to do it instead, when he called sharply to me, "Don't leave your stance. I hear them coming again – ah, if I could only see them!"

A moment afterwards, out of the smoke, appeared half a dozen heads, black and fierce, with long hair drifting in the tide as their owners swam towards us.

Richard Maxwell, Jerry, and I fired, but what with the darkness of the place, the thickness of the smoke, and the horror of shooting at men's heads so close, I think that no one except old Richard hit his man.

In a moment they were on us with daggers drawn, all except one of them who still swimming and seemed to be grievously hurt.

It was a scrappy fight in that crowded little cave, and I was not expert at fighting with daggers. I stood in the corner in front of the niche where May had been loading the muskets, and swung my sword in that St. Andrew's cross movement which even skilled swordsman find hard to overcome. I felt it strike flesh at least twice, but in the darkness of the cave could see only flashes of blade and pistol. The oaths of the gypsy, the shouts of old Richard whose pistols cracked again and again, the crying of the womenfolk, all thundered in my ears, and in the midst of all the sulphur of the powder set me sneezing.

It is not an experience I would recommend but I had had no choice ever since I saw Craigdarroch in flames. In a little the light grew clearer in the cave, and I could see dimly. Richard Maxwell was in death grips with a tall gypsy, and little Jerry was engaging another. One lay on his face at the edge of the water, and one at my feet. The fifth was nowhere to be seen. I rushed to Richard Maxwell's assistance, but the man at my feet gripped me as I ran and I fell over him.

Outside there was a noise of guns and the sound of a boat coming up the passage.

"This is the end," I said to myself as I felt the best we could do was to repel the first assault. We could not hope to beat back another boatload. The man who had brought me to the ground could only grip and hold and he apparently had no weapon. I could not see if he was wounded or not, but the horror of his face so near my own, revolted me. He drew me nearer and nearer to him as if he intended to bite me. I had heard terrible rumours of the ferocity and cannibalism of the folk of the hills. I could not resist with my full strength, and I truly believe that by strength of arm the fierce wounded gypsy could have drawn me into his embrace and sunk his teeth into my face, had not the boat we had heard coming along the cave at that moment discharged her cargo of men, who, springing out, soon put an end to the combat.

I must have passed out before I knew my fate – but more from the unusual excitement than from any hurt, and also because I had not yet attained the full strength I now have as an adult.

When I awoke Kennedy Maxwell was bending over me. He shook me roughly.

"Where is my sister?" he said.

What I said in answer I did not know, my head spun, and the darkness of the cave, together with the turmoil of the struggle and the lashing of the sea on the pebbles, made me confused.

Kennedy, seeing that I had nothing sensible to say, instantly ran from me, leaving me lying. I tried to rise; and in a little, holding the rock and leaning my shoulder against it, I stood up. Two of the Maxwells, Will the eldest and his brother Peter, next oldest, were bending over their father where he had fallen at the other side of the wide room where we had fought. Silver Sand knelt on the opposite side, and the old man appeared to speak to him earnestly but with great difficulty. The other five of the Maxwells – Kennedy, and young Richard, David, Archibald, and Steenie – were nowhere to be seen.

"Is he badly hurt?" I asked, seeing their grave faces.

Silver Sand looked up quickly and motioned me to be silent moving the fingers of his right hand quickly up and down. The old man was close to death, perhaps even in the act of passing.

Richard Maxwell looked around, as if seeking what in the dusk of the cave he could not see.

"Where are the rest?" he said, speaking with difficulty

"They are looking for May!" said Peter cautiously.

His brother Will turned on him with a fiercely threatening frown.

"They may look but they won't find her," cried the old man "Alas, I am like Job, both my house and my children stricken at once! Fetch the lads."

Silver Sand went and called them in. They were scattered through all the passages, but no trace of May Maxwell could be found. Jerry also had vanished, and there was no way they could have left the cave. Bell came reluctantly out of the nook where in the thick of the fight she had hidden but she had nothing to tell.

The seven Maxwells stood about their father, who sat half supported in the arms of Silver Sand. Only Kennedy hid his face, and he was the youngest. The rest stood stern and calm, accepting the fact without showing emotion.

"In one day, they have taken from me my home, my daughter and my life. The Lord knows that I have never done harm to those that sought my blood. Listen, my sons; forgiveness belongs to the

Lord, and I forgive these sons of Zeruiah. I, that am about to die, and shall never carry spear or pistol again, forgive them. But you should not do the same, at least till you be as near the presence of the Judge as I am. Follow after them with a great vengeance. Vindicate the right. Smite with the sword of the Lord and of Gideon. Let the Lord smite and He will, or hold His sword and He will; but see you that you be as Gideon and do not spare your swords. Show no pity until that evil tribe is rooted out – robbers of houses and murderers of men."

He paused, his hand on his side.

"I see," continued the old man, "a time coming, horses and men upon the green. I see the waving of their banners. The companies are marching to the beat of the drum. They are clattering up the Wolf's Slock. I see them go."

"It is the second sight," whispered Silver Sand.

"Listen to him. No horses can go up the Wolf's Slock."

"I see them go," he cried, turning sightless eyes upon the roof of the cavern, in so vivid a manner that we all turned our eyes also that way; but we saw nothing there save the tremulous gathering and scattering of the light which came out of the deep water at the cave's mouth.

"I hear the horses' shoes ringing on the granite. They slide and scrape the lichen from the stones. O Lord, let me see the height of the battle and who is the victor before I go, and then I'll go quietly, like a lamb. Do not strike unless it be for justice, Lord, and if it is, do not sheath Thy sword. Ah, I see them, I see them. Help, Lord, for Thy servant is failing. The bloody and deceitful men shall not live half their days. Their winding-sheet is drawn, and is smoothed white and fair. The Lord has let down His corpse cloth upon them."

There was a long silence, very still, in which I could hear the breathing of the strong men inside, and the pulsing of the sea outside. Then the old man's high-pitched voice, that was like the crying of an unearthly wind about the rooftops, again took up the vision."They have been struck to death. Thou hast done it! Death and destruction are written on our Lord's banners. The battle is over. The rain has gone. The snowstorm will never return! Loch-in-loch! I see thee, little loch. Thou art clear this morning. Thou art red in the evening, and there is a pile of mangled heads by thee. Praise to the God of battles. I see the end. It is a glimpse of a mountain. I see the victors come riding home. There is a maid leading on a white horse."

He sat up using his own strength, Silver Sand keeping behind him to catch him in case he should fall.

Waving his hand, he cried, "It is my own lass. Praise the Lord, Himself has cast the hem of His cloak about the child. Pure within and without, I see her come home, for the intent of the wicked is ended. The Lord that is a strong Lord deals tenderly with the young plants and waters them often."

He fell back, but his voice went on, though the tide was plainly on the ebb.

"But there is much to do – and little time to do it in. Up and away back by the east door, the dry door, that we hadn't the sense to see. Follow them that way. Leave me! Leave me! Can you not let an old man die on his own? It's between him and his Maker now. Let the dead bury their dead, you follow the living! Off you go! Off you go! Lord, into Thy hands I commit my spirit."

For a moment, he rallied, opening his eyes on the dusky cave, and seeing the light at the far end of it which came in from the wide sunlit sea.

"*Ebb tide and a dark, misty morning!*" he said very quietly and made his way towards the light.

So the spirit passed, battling and warring to the very end, just as he had lived, to where there is peace beyond the shadows.

Richard Maxwell had gone out with the ebb tide as the spirit of man ever does.

CHAPTER XV.

THE DRY CAVE

THE dead father lay in the cave. The living sister had gone from it. The Maxwells all stood about their father as Silver Sand, in whose arms he died, laid him down softly and closed his eyes.

"And now concerning May," said Will Maxwell, like one who passes calmly to the next subject."Who saw her last?"

"She was in the corner where the guns were loaded when the rush of men came," I said; "she passed me a gun just after we saw the black heads on the water."

"And she was not in the cave when we entered, neither did she pass out by the way we came," said Will.

"There is a hope for her," I said, "Jerry is also missing. He may be with her." For I knew the tricks of that youth.

"You heard my father's words," continued Will Maxwell. "It is for us to follow them. We are all fit and able. The track is plain. Why are we standing here?"

"Where shall we follow?" said David Maxwell. "Sea or land – Yawkins or Marshall?"

"She's never gone with Yawkins. He was downwind before she was out of the cave. We must look for her amongst the outlaws," said Kennedy.

The Maxwells did not reveal their intentions, but immediately decided among themselves how they were to follow. Four were to ride the Raiders' track, while three were to gather wide and raise the country. And they were all to meet at the Bridge of the Black Water of Dee.

"And you?" said Will Maxwell, looking to Silver Sand and myself. Silver Sand answered for both of us.

"We are with you immediately. As soon as we have searched the cave for Jerry we will follow after you."

"Why will you not stay with us?" said Will.

"Because," said Silver Sand, "if the outlaws have taken May with them, they will separate, and some will leave the cattle-trail to take the fastest road to the Dungeon of Buchan. We will seek the track of the riders. You follow the cattle as you wish."

Will Maxwell still appeared not to understand. He had little thought of any options for the pursuit. He desired only to come swiftly to blows with the outcasts and have the matter over. He assumed that he would then find his sister, if indeed she had been carried off.

Silver Sand, being versed in the ways of the hillmen, read deeper, and was determined to follow his own council.

But concerning the purpose of our search we all made a vow, standing about the dead body of Richard Maxwell, to seek until we found and to strike until we had finished the matter – all except Silver Sand, who had gone aloft to search the higher chamber, from where Jerry, earlier in the combat, had thrown his biscuits.

We laid Richard Maxwell to rest on the sandy hill behind the cave at the farthest end of Rathan. As we came out the seagulls clanged about, and a rock dove flew down and perched on the prow of the boat above the dead body, which was unusual, and mightily admired, for none of us had ever seen such a thing before. But the Maxwells took it as a sign from out of this world, so they all took off their bonnets and put them in the bottom of the boat; for which I thought none the worse of them, although I kept mine on (for, in fact, it was just a young pigeon which was tired of flying, and it soon left), and so we drew to the shore. We buried him quickly, but with due reverence, and Silver Sand said a prayer that moved me, since I did not know that he was a religious man. Then I thought about many things I had said to him that did me no credit, and I regretted them. Yet I remembered that he had never rebuked me as a strict teacher would have done.

So before we left we made a grave for Richard Maxwell, with spades I had brought from the House of Rathan. When I was in the house I took a hasty look round to see that all was well. Nothing had been touched. There was not so much as the print of a dirty foot. But in the kitchen I found Jerry lying in a wet pool on the floor, I thought he was dead, but as I pulled him to the window he recovered somewhat, and said, lifting up his hand to the light and letting the moisture drip from it, "It is only sea water. It was a fine morning, so I took a dip for my health."

This amused me, but I could not wait to ask him more, having come for the spades.

"You saw nothing of May Maxwell?" I said.

"I left her in the cave," he said, glancing quickly up; "she'll still be there."

Knowing this not to be true, I left him hastily, commending him to a square bottle of Hollands to help him recover.

So we laid old Craigdarroch in a fine sandy grave. We had no grave clothes, apart from a sheet which I brought from the house, but his face and wounds were washed clean, and he had the look of one who died well pleased. We left him without a coffin, to the kindly chemistry of the earth. For me, I would not have silver plate or polished oak delay by one day the solemn "dust to dust" which is the requiem of us all.

But we could not start on our search till we had gone back to the cave and tried to understand the words of the vision concerning the unknown entrance of which the old man spoke. So Silver Sand and I took the boat back to the cave where the blood could still be seen and the fetid stench of gunpowder had yet to clear. We made a complete search, beginning at the uppermost chamber. We went into every cranny that we could enter as did Quharrie, who went forward with his head down, and growling as though he was tracking a wild beast.

But we did not find an outlet big enough even for a rat until we came down to the great cave, the scene of the deadly strife.

"'The dry door – the east door!'" he said, "muttered Silver Sand, musing. Suddenly he clapped his hand on his knee like a man that solves a riddle.

"What idiots!" he cried, and with that he got into the boat as if to leave the cave. But he did not put the oar into the water but used it to feel along the dark rock above his head on his right, whilst pulling the boat along by his left hand using any projection of the rock that could be found. The oar scraped and slid along the ledges, bringing down the straws and dirt of the doves' nests into the boat. He went two or three yards in this way, pulling the boat with him. Then he came to a sudden dark bend of the rock which looked almost like a corner cupboard to the cave. All at once his oar, which had been scraping and rasping along the dead wall, fell forward till the leather that lay in the rowlock rested on a ledge of rock.

"I thought as much." cried Silver Sand, "This is the way we lost our maid. The old man saw clearly, as the dying ever see."

He put his hands on the ledge as if it was a parapet and leapt up, pushing the boat back as he did so till the stern hit the opposite wall.

"Throw me a rope," he cried from above, "and come here and see!"

I did so. He caught the rope deftly, and in a few moments I was up beside him. I was taken by surprise by what I saw. I had passed that way a thousand times, and even taken my skiff round, sitting in it and feeling with my hand to see if there was anything unexpected; for in those days I expected to find a wondrous mermaid in every sea hole. Now I discovered that the rock barrier, which seemed continuous to the roof to one sitting in a boat, was when one was standing erect was little more than breast high. I called myself a fool for not having seen it before.

"Not compared to me,"said Silver Sand,"I have been here before, and not always in good company. Even worse, I have seen something very similar in Antrim, in Ireland, at a place they call Port Coon, where much good stuff used to be run."

This, then, was the "dry door – the east door" that the dying visionary had spoken of. Silver Sand went back to the cave again for a candle, but I was happy to remain by the boat, for I had no stomach any more for the Hall of Ossian. I would not have gone even for all the contents of the brass chest that lay hidden in the sand there.

When Silver Sand came back, he lit the candle. Standing still in the boat and shielding it with his hand, he looked narrowly at the rock, with his eyes within an inch or two of the wall.

"I thought as much," he said."Hector, my man, this is the way you went."And he pointed out to me a series of irregular steps, not much larger than notches, that went up from the water to the edge of the rock parapet. They were not one above another, like steps in a ladder, but more like the step over a stone dyke. Some of them might be natural, but most were man-made. No wonder Hector Faa knew of these, was this not the Isle of Rogues?

"Up, my man!" cried Silver Sand to me."If you want your lass, you have no time to waste. The Faas don't wait for a priest or a minister when they decide to marry!"

"*My* lass," he had said. Though May Maxwell was no lass of mine, and at another time I would have said so. But she and I had been friendly during these last few days, and I had done my best for her, which would have been noticed. But "*My* lass," he said."My faith, that was an over-quick word," I said to myself.

But this was no time to argue about words if we were to save this bright and cheery young maid, albeit a knowingly mischievous one, from the grip of the wild and ungodly gypsies of the hills. With the candle lit we looked at this new cave, which was bone dry on the other side of the barrier. The bottom was a smooth bed of freestone rock, as if the water had worn it, but there were no pebbles on it.

"Hector Faa was running barefoot, and carrying the lass," said Silver Sand.

"How do you know that?" I said, since I could not conceive how he knew.

"Because there's neither nail nor shoe marks, but some limpets have been moved here and there, so somebody has come by this way fairly quickly, and not long ago."

We tracked the dry cave some way till we could hear the wash of the waves again. Then we came to a narrow opening very low down, through which the tide was rippling brightly and softly. The roof of the cave came to within three feet of the water, like the blue hood of a pack man's waggon. Silver Sand stepped down and out. I followed him, and we found ourselves standing in the broad sunlight in a little bay that looks to the south-east. Silver Sand was gazing all about him, looking so extraordinarily foolish with the lighted candle in his hand in the broad sun that I laughed aloud.

He looked at me crossly. "What are you so pleased about?" he asked.

I said nothing, but pointed to the candle in his hand. He blew it out, and looked at me with his eyes closed to pin-points, like a cat's in the sun.

"If she were my lass, I would not be laughing."

He said this sharply, in a way that I did not expect, for it was surprising to me that a man like Silver Sand, who could be so uncanny and mysterious, would take as much offence at being laughed at, like a little girl.

Meanwhile his eyes, roving quickly hither and thither, fixed on something that seemed to greatly interest him. He pointed with his finger to the bottom of the water in which we stood up to our knees. Looking, I saw a little shoe sitting on its sole on the sand, as though it had been set afloat to sail as a game and had softly filled and sunk. I lifted it and held it in my hand, and from that moment all day I lost all good humour. Silver Sand had indeed struck the laugh out of my face. It was May Mischief's shoe, and it looked so pretty and simple with its little wet silver buckle glinting in the sun that I could only grieve. It felt even worse for me because it was the shoe which she wore the day I called her "Impudent Besom." I could see her as she sat on the window seat, dangling her feet in the air, sitting on the fingers of both hands turned with the palms down on the sill, her hair like a boy's, and she with a very pretty mouth whistling away like a blackbird. I felt so badly about this that it was a comfort to sob and make myself small in front of Silver Sand, who stood looking at me, not woefully, but as one might look at a child who has broken his toy and thinks he will never be happy any more.

But despite that I was now glad that he had said, "Your lass!"

So we waded our way to the shore, and before we came out Silver Sand threw the old tin candle stock into the tide, which I went and carefully picked out again. There was no point in being wasteful that day or any other day, as it was the candle which used to sit on the stone shelf of the milkhouse at Rathan in my father's time. And it stands there to this day.

When we got to the house we found Jerry MacWhirter much recovered, but not yet able to move far.

"I'll take care of the house for you till you come back," he said. "It'll be all I'm good for. I'll be obliged to you for the loan of the cellar key, and if you'll hand me down that side of bacon ham, the frying-pan, and some butter, I'll manage fine," said that cheerful youth.

"Have any of the Maxwells been here?" I asked him as I gave him what he asked for.

"Aye," said Jerry, "and they have taken muskets and ammunition, and went off on the chase. I wish I could go after them, but falling flat on my belly on the water like a frog is not good for one's insides."

This was all that Jerry had to say, and we could not get another word out of him. He did not seem at all concerned that May Maxwell had been carried off. He treated it as an excellent prank.

"Well, it's doubtless poor taste to run off with a gypsy, but I've heard it happen before," he said.

"I'll break your neck for that, Jerry MacWhirter, when I come back!" I cried as I went out of the door.

"Make sure that you come back on your legs," he cried. "If you're going to chase after hussies that run to Gretna with gypsies, you are more likely to come back with your feet facing forward, or I'll be mistaken."

The last I heard of Jerry was some words that he called after me as I went along the stone passage: "You could leave me a written letter, Laird, that would make me heir to Rathan – just in case"

And I heard no more. I had, however, heard enough to make me swear to twist his neck on my return – which, indeed, I may say now, that I lived to perform as a man of his word.

CHAPTER XVI.

THE CAMP OF SILVER SAND

HOWEVER fast as I went, with my pistols newly primed with an extra powder flask at my hip, Silver Sand went faster. We were to take the boat over to the Orraland Cove, where there were white shell sands. Quharrie was in the front of the boat, looking fearsome, because he had somehow been in the fight and had been struck on the mouth, which his master stitched in a neat and surgeon-like manner, doing it like one bred to the business.

As we went, I at the tiller, Silver Sand at the oars, as was usual (for Silver Sand liked exercise, while I was in not especially partial to it), I said to him, "We are to follow the Maxwells, I suppose?"

"Suppose here, suppose there," said Silver Sand, who seemed a little disturbed for some reason that I could not fathom. "If you want to play follow to the Maxwell lads, you can do it. That's the way to find the cattle, if that's what you're wanting. But if you want the lass, before Hector Faa's mother ties him and her up over the tongs, you'll have to try another way to do it." Being wise I said nothing, but waited for explanations, knowing better than to interfere with Silver Sand when he was in such a mood.

Suddenly a thought made me check my pockets. We had no money, and though steel blades and steel pistol barrels were imperative, some might be useful. I mentioned my concern to Silver Sand and he smiled.

"Don't worry about money," said he," there's a good strong purse inside this sleeved waistcoat that is at your service – every Dutch and Scottish coin!"

I must have looked very strangely at him, for he answered -

"You needn't turn up your eyes at me like tea-dishes. I am neither thief nor robber – though I am with a laird with an island that I can nearly cover with my trousers when I sit down on it. Do you think I have no silver because I am only a packman and a seller of scythe sand and red ochre?"said he."Certainly don't forget the red ochre!"

"Sometimes I think, Silver Sand," said I, quietly, without any show of temper,"that you are very different from what you appear to be."

A very futile and foolish remark, as I now understand.

"My, do you know," said he, pleased," but I'm sometimes of that opinion myself."

He had quite recovered his good humour.

I think it was that the matter of the candle that still stuck in his throat, and how badly he took to being laughed at.

"But have you really money enough for us both?" I asked, just to make sure.

Silver Sand put his hand into his pocket and poured out of a purse a double handful of golden guineas, more than I had never seen before.

"Red ochre is remarkably profitable," he said.

"Indeed,"I replied wistfully."I'd swap Rathan for your donkey if that was the case. And by the ribs of the Curate o' Carsphairn, there's that very donkey!"

But I knew well he was only joking about the profit on red ochre.

As we landed and pulled up the boat, Silver Sand's donkey, a beautiful beast of a dun mouse colour, and far larger than common donkeys, came trotting down to meet us.

"It's as well," said I, "that the gypsies didn't get their hands on that donkey or you would have had to buy another."

"Aye," he said drily, "but I'm thinking that even the hardest fighting man that lives between here and John o' Groats will think twice before he meddles with Silver Sand and his donkey."

Then we made our way up to the tent in the wood which Silver Sand had pitched the morning before opposite to the Isle Rathan. It was standing intact, without disorder inside or out. There were, however, many footmarks around it, as if hoofed feet of cattle, broad pads of unshod horses, sharp horseshoes, and the slipping prints of bare human feet had passed by.

To me, this was now even more mysterious than ever. The wild gypsies had indeed been in this quiet nook of Orraland Glen. It was here that they had gathered their drove to make for the hills. How was it that all the property, left here so openly with only a donkey for a guard, was as secure as if it had been locked in Kirkcudbright jail? The solution was beyond me. I saw, however, that the answer was linked to the way in which Silver Sand undertook to keep Rathan House safe against the hill gypsies and black smugglers. The two things hung together. But as I was the one to benefit, I had nothing to say in the matter. As we came near to the tent (which was bell shaped, with a pole of un-trimmed birch stuck through the roof), I saw a plain willow wand, peeled white, leaning against the door flap. It was stuck deep into the ground, and was easy to be seen by all that came near. Then on the flap itself there were curious signs, like those they say can be seen in Egypt, the country out of which the children of Israel escaped. In the centre of these was the sign which is known among Eastern peoples as the Shield of David. This was painted in black, but there were two bars of red across it, a thick and a thin, the thick being topmost. Strange letter-signs as of lions and gryphons, and many eagle-faced things were also painted on the canvas in outline.

"What might these be," I asked of Silver Sand, somewhat incautiously. I might have known that if there was anything worth knowing, it was unlikely that he would tell me his mysteries just then.

"Well," said he, " they might have been drawn to amuse the donkey, or they might be made by the bird droppings, or perhaps it might be myself trying the quality of my tar and ochre; but they're none of these, but thank you for asking."

I might have expected such an answer, but the truth is I asked the question without thinking.

He paused a moment as if he was asking himself if it was worthwhile to give me any information. "They're just my lock and key," he said, drily, and that was all I got out of him.

He went into his tent, putting aside the peeled rod, but he did not invite me to enter; yet, when he came out, he brought a bottle of foreign wine with him and some sweet cakes, which he offered me.

I mentioned that I did not care for wine, and never used it.

"You'll be the better for it to help you to your journey's end," he said; "those that go walking quickly through the moss-haggs and the moors with Silver Sand and Quharrie need some strong provisions, in any case."

So I took a little, and what with me being unaccustomed to it, and the rarity of the vintage, it ran through my veins like soft liquid fire, extraordinarily hearty and vivid.

"That's surely unusual and rare," said I.

"Aye," he said, "there's nothing like this in the whole of Scotland. That comes from where the swallows go in the winter."

"And where's that?" I asked, interested to hear him mention that, as it was something that I had often wondered about but could get no satisfactory answer.

But he did nothing but laugh and say, "Maybe at the bottom of Carlinwark Loch!"

And though that was the currently accepted opinion, I knew well that he was joking. On the other hand, he did not like my quip about the candle. It is odd that people who make fun of others are the most thin-skinned themselves.

But it is something I have noticed particularly, and many times at that.

CHAPTER XVII.

COUNCIL OF WAR

So we set out, travelling forward with all speed, but, as our custom was, talking as we went. We spoke of the daring of the outlaws. No raid for fifty years had reached so far south as the shores of the Solway, though the smugglers and the gypsies had a regular route by which they conveyed their smuggled stuff to Edinburgh on the east, and Glasgow or Paisley on the west. Their organisation was both so audacious and so far reaching that it is safe to say that there was not a farmer's pitcher between the Lothians and the Solway filled with spirit that had excise paid to King George, and not a burgher's wife that had duty-paid lace on her Sabbath headwear. The excisemen were few and harmless, and mostly contented themselves with lingering round public-houses in towns, and carrying a measure cup and gauging-stick about the markets – occupations for which they were entirely suited.

I suggested to Silver Sand that such actions as kidnapping and fire-raising ought to be punished with hanging.

"That has been said before, Laird Rathan," he said in an ironical manner," but as for me, though I'm trying to get your lass back for you, it's because I like you both – not because I find any fault with Hector Faa or any of his Clan."

"But it's cruel abduction and murder," said I, " and disappoints me to hear you defending such actions."

"You're young, you're young, Rathan," said he, "and in time you'll learn sense. Man, where did all the gipsy wives come from that have kept the Faas alive for so many generations? They were all taken, every one. There's Meggat Faa, who is the mother of Hector and John Faa himself. Do you think Meggat is a Faa by birth? Not her, I tell you – she came from a decent Border family – the Kerrs of Blackshiels over by Yethom. But she's more Faa today than any of her sons. Now, how did that come about? I can tell you that in this age of immoral acts and behaviour (just like the tales that we hear about the wee German, King George, and his Dutch women – and perhaps others closer to home), there's not a Faa that wouldn't make a good man, loyal and kind at all times. Indeed, let me tell you there's many a lass that might be proud to be in the place of Mistress May Maxwell tonight."

"Then if that's what you believe, I've had enough of you," cried I, hotly flaming up at the way he spoke about the man who had abducted by force the daughter of Richard Maxwell, who lay without a coffin in his shroud under the sands of Rathan. But as I grew hot Silver Sand grew cool.

"No, no, laddie, I'm up to the neck with you, dirk and dagger and I have thrown away the scabbard; but I'll never say that the Faas are bad to their wives, or, in fact, that they are evil at all."

"Then who does the murders that they are blamed for? " said I.

"Of course, there's plenty bloodshed, and no doubt the Faas are involved and they shall be hanged for it, and I'll have no pity for them. But, I don't like to hear of folk that are pleasant and comfortable, living together like they were in a beehive, caught up with the scoundrels of the hills. Man, I've been there myself, and I know what it means never to get justice nor even the chance of justice – to be tried by sheriffs and judges that have you judged and condemned before you even get to the court."

"But surely you wouldn't condone murder and robbery, would you? For if you do, much as I admire you, you and me must part," said I.

"My lad," said Silver Sand, "you and me will agree. I'm as much on the side of the law as it's possible to be in these uncertain times, when who knows when they go to their beds whether they'll wake up under the King or the Pretender, or indeed who is the correct King and who is the Pretender."

"As for me," I said, with a self-righteousness that must have made Silver Sand flinch – "as for me, I am on the side of the law at *all* times."

"My word, just imagine that!" said Silver Sand. "They'll make you an exciseman! You have some job ahead of you with these brothers-in-law of yours, the Maxwell rogues. As far as I can see, they're not so fond of the law."

I declare that I could have pistolled him there and then for saying such a thing about the kin of the poor young lass that had lost her father, and was at that moment in the hands of a ruffian.

I said as much to him, whereupon he laughed, having regained much of his former good humour, and treated me with a glance of affection, which, from one so strange in appearance and mysterious in antecedents as he, made me wonder why I liked it so well.

"Come now, Patrick," he said," you and me have known each other a good while. You know that I am with you to the last breath – aye, and beyond it, if they'll let the like of me through Peter's Gates. I'll fight with you against Faas and Macatericks and Marshalls, and especially against Marshalls, so I think you and me had best stick together. You are a fine lad and a tough fighter, but you lack judgment. Man, the great art is to keep clear of fighting till you cannot avoid it. And then – why, then – do it once. Don't make two jobs of it."

He clapped me on the shoulder. "Sit down. A council of war is needed," he said.

Having said all this so rapidly that he left me breathless, he plumped down on an anthill, and motioned me to do the same. But I sat on a stone and said nothing. I watched for the ants to come out, but the hill was empty and none came, which disappointed me.

The night was drawing in quickly, and we were in a deserted place under the fine rocky hill that is called Screel, which rises from the Solway side, and is visible against the sky all over the south of Galloway. We had made our way among rocks that crumbled under our feet, and rang with a kind of iron clang as we trod across them. I was most hungry, and nothing edible grew here, and there was no farm within our sight. It seemed, however, that the clouds were very close.

"Let us look at our options," said Silver Sand.

"The first thing is to make up our minds what the enemy is likely to do, and then we can plan our own course. First, then, there's the smugglers with their casks of brandy and wine. We must let them go. They are far on the road to Edinburgh with the Preventive men keeping well out of their way. Then, secondly, there are the cattle rustlers. They have had a long start – more than fifteen hours, because they never came near the Cave at Rathan. They would start when Craigdarroch was in flames. Then there's our friend that you are more interested in, Hector Faa and his bridal company who have, you can be sure, the best horses and the best of advice and assistance on the road. They'll be the hardest to catch up! "

"Silver Sand, I ask you not to speak of the young lass like that."

"Well, well, Rathan, then I won't; but don't fret. I'm kind of related to the gypsies myself, and I can tell you that until the marriage ceremony is completed at the end of the three days of feasting, May Maxwell will be attended to and treated like a lady – and also will be after that, more than ever, because she'll then be a Faa herself."

"God forbid!" said I, fervently.

"Amen to that" said Silver Sand. "We could even make her a Heron, though the Herons are only long-nosed frog peckers to the Faas."

Despite this, I was relieved to know that the young maid was safe from harm, and also that we had at least three days after Hector and his prisoner reached the outlaws' hold on the side of Loch Enoch. It was not much to be thankful for, but it was so much better than I'd feared, that I was almost relieved.

As Silver Sand sat on the ground, he laid his long arms, from the elbow to the wrist on the heather before him, as though they were actual weapons; and sitting there, I saw that the joints seemed to be the other way, either naturally or through some extra-ordinary torture. Seeing this, I felt a great pity for him, and my eyes welled up as I remembered all his past kindnesses. I put my arm round his neck and said to him earnestly,

"Forgive me for every wrong thing I have said to you, for man, I like you – I do admire you!"

For a moment Silver Sand glared at me as if he was angry, then suddenly placed his face between his hands and sobbed from the bottom of his throat. It was terrible. I did not know what to do in that lonely place, but I laid my head on his shoulder to see if that would comfort him.

"O, Patrick!" he cried at last, "you have given me back my manhood. I have been treated like a beast. I have been a beast. I have lived with beasts, but you are the first that has come close to me for thirty years. Patrick, for as long as Silver Sand can trail his old twisted bones after you, you will not be in need of a friend for you and yours. Man, I would go for you into Hell itself, despite the brimstone smoke, the red flames dodging through the bars, and the poor, poor creatures wailing behind"

He turned away for a moment, and when he looked up again all trace of his emotion had gone.

"But this is not what we are here for," he said, with one of his quick changes, "we didn't come here for our health, like Jerry Macwhirter jumping out of the cave-hole." He went on calmly. "The question is, what road should we take? I'll tell you what I think, and then you can tell me what you think. The cattle are easily tracked. You can't drive cattle without leaving plenty marks. There's only one road for them, and that's the straightest. If they pass the fords of the Black Water, and get past Cairn Edward and the Black Craig, the Maxwells might as well say, "Fare you well, Kilaivie,' to every one of them. Now, secondly, you can assume that Hector, the lass, and one or two others not driving cattle, will be thrashing horses hard on the road towards the Dungeon of Buchan and the ridges of Loch Enoch. Which way they would go, I don't know, but I have my own opinion. It'll not be the direct road, in any case, for Hector will know well that the country will be raised to pursue him, and that the Glenkens wouldn't be safe for horses. At the moment, a horse is a necessity to him. The lass wouldn't walk, and they couldn't carry her tied up for twenty miles. I'll guarantee that they're at the Gatehouse of Fleet by now, and heading for the Ferrytoon o' Cree as fast as the horses can gallop. Then they'll stay for an hour or two up at the Herd's House, or likely Cassencary, which is a favourite haunt of smugglers and gypsies."

"Mistress Ogilvy will look after the lass, and pat her on the back when she cries, and tell her tales of the fine wives he has gotten, and how many grand lasses would be eager for Hector."

"The conniving hag," said I, exceedingly angry, "I'll have her called out as a witch."

"No, no," said Silver Sand,"you won't do that, for Mistress Ogilvy's a friend of mine and a decent woman besides."

But I was of a very different opinion. Silver Sand paused a while, considering and pondering till I was weary. At last he appeared to reach a decision, for he took a piece of oatcake out of his pocket, halving it fairly as he did so.

"I think that you and me must separate before we have gone much further. I am sad to think so,

Patrick, but it is the best that I can come up with. I must go there across the heather and run as fast as I can to get there using the Cree road before a horse with six hours start. Now that might be possible for Quharrie and me, but not for you. What you must do is to get ahead of the cattle that's making for the old Brig of Dee four mile to the north of Clachanpluck, between that and New Galloway."

"How do you manage to make that out?" I asked. "Is it not more likely that they would take straight to the hills?"

Silver Sand turned on me with a look of scorn.

"It's obvious that you are a shore-dweller, and not a flower of the heather, or you wouldn't consider driving cattle fast through the moors. Man, to go fast they can only use a drove road. This means they must stay on the west side of the Ken, and the east side of the Grenoch Loch near Clachanpluck. They daren't use the Parton Road, since that is too public, and besides, Ken Bridge is easy blocked and is sure to be guarded. They can't take the Lochenbreck hills, as I mean to do, straight from here, for the cattle wouldn't drive over the wild moor."

"Now, you must get to the Dungeon of Buchan before the cattle; they won't be expecting rescuers before that, and I must get quickly to Eschonquhan by the Loch Trool. Whichever one of us finds the lass must stay put until the other comes, unless a completely safe chance opens up."

"But how shall we find one another?" I said, for in that wild, unknown country it seemed madness, especially for me who had never been there in my life before. I already saw myself as a poor lost bewildered lad, out on the hungry hill, with May Maxwell the bride of the Faa.

Indeed, the thought of parting with Silver Sand, and even from the companionship of Quharrie, discouraged me so much that I could have wept; but I remembered the grey hair of Richard Maxwell, dabbled with his blood and his roof blazing, and I resolved that whoever should have mercy on the wild gypsies, it would not be me.

The bushel barrel of their iniquity was nearly full measure, heaped and running over, and it would soon be sharpened with the Lord's own level and plumb line.

CHAPTER XVIII.

TO INTRODUCE MISTRESS CRUMMIE

So, as night fell on this most eventful day in my life, Silver Sand and Patrick Heron, set forward over the dreary stretch of Ingleston Moor that lies on the hip of Screel. Though it was May and the green leaves were shooting out from the branches, the air came from the north and I longed for my father's great sea-cloak; since I had only a small, checked plaid which was made for my father to see the sheep in after he had left the sea and settled on Rathan. Though Silver Sand had no cloak or plaid whatsoever he did not appear at all inconvenienced. As I write, I am advised by someone looking over my shoulder without permission, that those who read tales love to have a description of the clothing of the heroes. But I am no hero, God knows; and as for Silver Sand, he was not dressed in a manner fitting to be described in print.

Nevertheless, because the old fashion has passed away along with the old lawless time, it may be worth mentioning the ancient style of dress. Silver Sand was clad in a rough cap of badger skin with the fur outside, and the ears cocked up on either side above his own, which gave him an appearance of being extraordinarily alert. He wore homespun grey knee-breeches and a roundcoat of the same material but without tails. His arms stood through his tight body-coat a great way, and when he travelled he usually took off his loose overall and travel only in his sleeved waistcoat, carrying his coat over his arm, as is the summer fashion in Galloway even to this day.

On the day before, I had put on my best suit, thinking I might see May Maxwell – not because I wished to find favour from her in the way of romance, but because she had teased and scorned me when she came to my own house with Mistress Allison and Mistress MacWhirter, and I was resolved that she should never do that again.

I wore my own hair without powder, which also my father never used, but I had it tied behind in a ribbon. My body-coat was of fine blue cloth, more light blue than dark, long in the waist, with large pierced silver buttons, and creamy lace at the sleeves. Underneath I wore a waistcoat which I thought fitted me very well. It was cut with long flaps on the thighs, in which were pockets, with broad mother-of-pearl buttons. Then as for my legs, I wore grey tweed breeches, but of a finer quality than usual, which they weave somewhere near the Border. I wore pearl buckles at the knees. I also had long knitted ribbed stockings and sharp pointed shoes that I bent upwards with care and effort – and which had silver buckles. Thus was I dressed in an attire more befitting the Kirk of Dullarg on a Sabbath than nights and days on the wild hills of the Dungeon of Buchan.

During the fight in the cave, and in the adventures of the previous night, the lace had been so torn off that I judged it better to remove it all, and safely kept it in my pocket, intending to have it stitched and put on again in due course.

When first setting out on this quest I was careful of my clothing, but by the end I thought as little of it as I would a corn sack with leg and arm-holes pierced at the four corners, which some landsmen in the remoter parts of Galloway still use. So under the cloud of night, and with some comfort from the little food Silver Sand had brought, we set out over the heather-bushes of Airieland Moor. We went down a little glen where there were trees, birches, and oaks, I think – as far as I could tell from the sound that their leaves made in the dry, cold north night wind.

We passed a row of cot-houses by a mill-dam, and came down to the farm-town of Airieland, where there is a large steading. The cows tossing their heads and jingling their chains in the byre sounded both homely and welcoming, considering what we had been through. So an extraordinary desire for a drink of warm milk came over me, just like I got from May Maxwell when I rowed across to Craigdarroch in the morning, as well as, of course, the many disdainful words.

So I said to Silver Sand, "Can we not wake the people here and ask for a drink of good fresh milk?"

"You may," says he," but, mind you, Hector Faa does not wait for fresh milk – his is beyond the hill, and he's running for it!"

"But," said I, "unless I get something I don't think I can go any further."

"If that is so, we'll soon fix that!" says he, and with no more words he turned into the byre, drew a milking stool down from between the thatch and the wall, and looked around for a vessel to milk in.

He could see none in the dim light of the byre; but after looking at his own hat he said, "Give me a loan of your bonnet!" which, when I had given it to him, he carefully knocked in the crown, then out of the high-peaked cock that stood upwards he made a tolerable drinking vessel. He set this on his knees, and began to milk a cow into it, which, I thought was most impressive, having had little experience of cows. But Silver Sand was calm, and in a few moments he handed me a hatful of most excellent warm milk, which, when I had drunk, followed by a second, completely refreshed me.

Then I urged upon Silver Sand to take some himself, using my hat, which had been used twice already.

"No," he said, slily, "it's better to keep the stock separate. It saves marking them with red ochre, which, as you know, is extraordinarily expensive."

Then, having refused my hat, he showed me a trick that I had never seen before, though I have no idea how he managed it in the darkness of the byre.

I heard the *sough, sough* of the milk streaming into some receptacle.

"Have you found a vessel to hold the milk?" I asked, thinking that it would have been better if he had, before he spoiled my hat.

"Aye," said he, "I have found a vessel, but the problem is that there's a hole in the bottom of it, and it all runs out as fast as I can milk it in."

I asked, in my simplicity, "Why do you do it, then?"

He laughed, but didn't answer. Then, as my eyes became accustomed to the dusk of the byre, I saw that the madcap had made an extraordinarily wide mouth, and was milking sideways into it, which made me wonder why the cow did not kick him. Because the only time that I had tried milking was at Craigdarroch, having been persuaded by the smooth words of May Maxwell; but the cow, that was a noted kicker, spilled me and the milking-pail head over heels. This caused a great laughter at which I had to join in, but privately thought it a poor joke to spoil my suit of second-best clothes in the gutter of a shed. But this trick of Silver Sand was new to me, and I stood and gaped until, seeing with that my mouth was open, he suddenly directed a stream of milk towards it, to my great shock. Considering the gravity of our situation, this seemed to me to be inappropriate. Besides, I was afraid that some drops had fallen on my coat. So I said to him, sharply -

"Now, when you have quite done playing the fool, perhaps you will tell me how you mean to pay the man of the house for his hospitality."

"Hold on," he said, "who pays for a drink of milk?"

"I do," said I," and I shall wake up the man of the house and give him a penny."

"Do," said Silver Sand," and I'll tell you what you'll get, and that's two ounces of lead drops underneath your coat-tails for disturbing the house at this time of night. That's what old Airie gives to young fellows like you that come in grand coats to play 'chase and kiss' with his lasses. See, that's his window," he went on, "but just be so kind as to let me get behind the midden first, for I'm not fond of lead drops."

He skipped off behind the shelter of a mountain of some dark material that was piled in the yard.

"Now go off with your penny," he cried, "I like fair play. Nothing like honesty."

His high spirits made me exceedingly angry.

"Come away," I cried, " let us have no more tomfoolery. I believe you just want to hold me back till your fine friend, Hector Faa, the murderer, gets the lass."

"Hold you back?" he said. "Far from that, Laird Rathan, it's your fine sense of breeding that holds you back – so much so that you can't even take a drink of good fresh milk till you have wakened the gentleman of the house from his bed to introduce you to the cow! Goodness me, I could do that myself."

And with that the madcap went to the door of the byre, and, lifting his hat with the air of His Majesty's Lion-King-at-Arms, he said,"Mistress Crummie Cooshairn, let me make you acquainted with the Laird o' Rathan, that did you the honour of drinking a drop of your own making. Your good health, and many of them, Crummie!"

I turned on my heel and walked away, for I had no words to express my indignation.

He called after me, "Patrick, don't sulk, man. It's not becoming you. Take a lesson from this jolly wife Crummie. *She* bears no malice. Here, Crummie, my lass, there's a handful of grass to make more milk, and there, master of Airieland, is a halfpenny to pay for the grass. And so all is correct, and we're honest, honest – and honour is restored!"

Somewhere about the steading I heard a window go up, followed by bad tempered bellowing, the purpose of which was to ask what night-hawks of not doubtful parentage we were that came crawling and stealing about his premises, that he would have the blunderbuss on us in a moment, together with other resourceful amenities.

"Good evening to you, Airie," said Silver Sand, calling back from the little narrow stile that led into a field among trees -"Good evening to you, and all your fair daughters. My compliments to them, and tell them I cannot stay the night, but I'll call again soon."

The roaring of oaths from the window became a very thunderstorm.

As we went down the banks of a small burn that flows through a smooth meadow beneath the house, we heard behind us still the wrathful roaring of the great voice, as yet unappeased. Silver Sand chuckled to himself as if he had done something very clever.

"Why didn't you stop and explain," he said. "you might possibly have dodged the blunderbuss and had time to put in a word to satisfy your honour before he got time to load again."

But I avoided saying anything to him on the subject. So we went on our journey.

Now, although these episodes take a long time to tell, and perhaps occupy too much space, but they happened very quickly. I do not believe that we were at the farm of Airieland for more than a quarter of an hour.

Now, when I recall it much later, I cannot sufficiently admire the wonderful foresight and patient kindness of Silver Sand in insisting we rest periodically. I would have carried on regardless, and so in a short time, due to weariness and the need for sleep, I would have worn myself out long before we reached the hill country.

So we carried on our way, going over fairly level, boggy country, where there was some cultivation, and some cattle in the field. Coming past the farm of Auchlane I jumped a high dyke to show my agility, since the double draught of Crummie's milk had invigorated me. Also the night was not yet quite set in, though people had gone to bed, it being the custom in Galloway to go to bed very early. So, as I say, I leapt a stone dyke, but found one side much higher than on the other. I alighted on my feet, but fell forward against something that bellowed and rose instantly beneath me, throwing me off and which then ran across the field. This shocked me, and I may have shouted out loud.

"Were you screaming because you thought that little cow was the Devil himself? " cried Silver Sand, who had climbed the dyke quietly with Quharrie.

I answered that it was not me but the cow that made the noise.

"It sounded very like you, Laird!" he said.

These were the sort of things that used to keep me wondering whether Silver Sand was the best of company or the most insolent and forward of tinkers. Yet five minutes after he had said such things I would laugh at them inside, though I continued to hold down my head like the sulky dog I was. At the poor little hamlet of Bridge of Dee we crossed the river, which looked cold and grey, the night wind ruffling it beneath us. Beyond this we got into very bleak, unkind country, and continued through this for more than an hour. It was all wet, marshy peat, with black ditches; and, even worse, green, deceptive "quakkin-qua's," covered with a scum that looked like tender young grass, but in which, at the first step, one might sink to the neck. Here and there we came upon some sheep grazing as best they could on the wet, sour grass. Nevertheless it was pleasant and cheery to hear them cropping the grass with short, quick bites, then moving on to another clump. As we passed by, one of them gave a cough, sounding just like a human, just like a man in church does behind his hand so that he does not disturb the worshippers.

In a little while we were among the lochs of Bargatton and Glentoo, dreary stretches of reedy water in the middle of marshy ground, so that in the night it made one shiver to look at them. But we went onward to the lilt of Silver Sand's song or the rise and fall of Silver Sand's voice, as he told stories of the old Killing days, and the pallid men who had lain in the wilderness to which we were going before it was utterly given up to the rustlers and outlaws.

Quharrie stalked in front, never once coursing about after rabbits and hares like other dogs, even when they popped out just under his nose, but followed his master's eye and hand. With his head very high, his sharp ears set forward, cocked like the feather in a Highlandman's bonnet, his legs wide apart as though to guard against sudden surprise, he would run ahead and then stand a moment till we came up. In this manner he scouted in front of his master, so that there was nothing, not even a grouse cock, that was not indicated before we came to it. As we reached the little farm of Drumbreck, where the moss ends in a great flow of black peat, in which there are deep and dangerous holes half full of water from former fuel cuttings, Quharrie stopped and growled.

Motioning me to stand where I was, Silver Sand passed the dog and went carefully to the dyke to look over. Then he waved to me to come on. It was only a tinker and his family camped under three great beeches that grow in the courtyard of the little farm, for Drumbreck has always been a well known place for the travelling people.

"It's just Tyke Lowrie and his family," said Silver Sand; "no harm in them, though the mistress of Drumbreck is well advised not to let them in among the sacks in the barn."

The little village of Clachanpluck lay ahead, which was inviting to my weary limbs, with its whitewashed houses, and trees growing about the little fringes of garden, and dogs barking as I went down the long street. At the end, where the roads separated, it was time for Silver Sand and me to part.

"The Lord keep us both!" said I, and parted without shaking hands, yet not so fast but that I heard Silver Sand say, " Amen!"

I am sure he was a Christian man, but there are many queer Christians in this land of Galloway.

Indeed I fear that I am one myself.

CHAPTER XIX.

ON THE TRACK OF THE RAIDERS

IT had darkened slowly, and now the night was at its prime when I passed down the street of the little clachan. The north wind met me in the face like a wall as I made my way alone through this hamlet of sleeping folk, silent under the peace of their cottage eaves of thatch – too poor to be worth robbing, but numerous enough to render good account of themselves in case of an attack.

Now while the wildest members of the smugglers and the gypsies attacked the cave for the purposes I have described, there was a much larger number who carried out the easier work of driving off the cattle of the Maxwells and others, and packing the cargo of the brig upon horses, in order to clear the country before the alarm arose.

This was a safer task since in those days news did not spread with the extraordinary rapidity with which it does now. The country was sparsely populated and there were fewer dwellings. A man might ride a long day among the hills of heather and see not one smoking chimney or any place where kindly folk dwelt. There was a district of thirty miles square in Carrick, in Galloway, and the moors of the Shire, over whose border exciseman never ventured, except with a force of red soldiers behind him, and this might happen only once in twenty years. Moreover, the farmers and small proprietors of the day were content to pay the hill raiders for protection rather than be in constant fear of them.

Therefore, as long as their own cattle were left alone, the bonnet lairds and farmers of Balmaghie and the Glenkens were unlikely to come to blows with the gypsies or the smugglers in defence of other people's flocks and herds. But murder and house burning were a different matter, as the outlaws were about to learn. So the chief desire of those who were driving the cattle was that they might get to the Craigencallie and Loch Dee drove-road before the country rose behind them.

This is the account of how they set out from the Craigdarroch beach.

From the coves by the shore a great number of men came running with the cargo – kegs of spirit, Hollands boxes wrapped about with wheat-straw – strange cases from the Indies, where the Hollanders have many plantations – and, most precious of all, iron-lined boxes of lace. The horses were loaded with as many of these as they could carry and the rest were taken to pits dug out under the clifftops, or in the sides of the glens, and covered with green turf. So the long train set off, a band of wild rogues keeping the pack-horses moving with slender pointed sticks, cut from the nearest coppice. The horsemen of the smuggling party clattered ahead with great barrels slung at each side of their horses, secured under the belly with broad leather straps, and tightened by strength of arm and the leverage of foot against the side of the poor beast – although the jolting of the load soon eased the straps and fastenings, when they were on the way.

The smugglers were the more relaxed of the two parties, since the gypsies were deeper in crime than the Freetraders, having been responsible for the house-burning and the cattle-stealing, and so rode with their necks in danger. But the land smugglers, most of whom had no interest in the affair beyond ensuring their goods were safely stored, were more than merry, for it was their custom that a cask was kept free and open for use on the way. And as they went they sang -

"Where'er we see a bonny lass, we'll caa' as we gae by;
Where'er we meet wi' liquor good, we'll drink an we be dry.
There's brandy at the Abbeyburn, then there's rum at Heston Bay,
And we will go a-smuggling afore the break o' day."

Now we have no further concern with the smugglers. They ride out of the story as soon as they cleared the cattle and the raiders who were driving them. As they went the jingling of their horse-harness told the country folk that the Black Riders were abroad, and in the night many a wife reached over to check if her husband was there; for though none of them objected to the cask of spirit which they would find at the back of the high road dyke the next morning, nor did they fail to leave money for it in a cup in the same position, it was not business that the housewives wanted their husbands involved in.

But for the cattle drovers the situation was different. They could only pick the best and speediest of the stock, and drive it with the horses in front, and a regiment of half-naked rogues from the hills keeping the poor beasts on the trot from behind. If a Galloway cow lagged and threatened to hold back the column, she received a sharp lash across the nose and was driven off into the darkness. Sometimes, however, after a drink at a wayside burn, the terrors of loneliness so pressed upon her that she would come racing after the company, bellowing as loud as she could, and so rejoin the herd.

As soon, then, as I had passed the little forge at the lower end of Clachanpluck, where there is a tree plantation, I became aware that I must be close upon the track of the stolen cattle. The road was deeply trampled, and in the softer places there were many signs of a large herd having passed only an hour or two before.

It was now that I missed Silver Sand, for he could have declared the number, condition, and intentions of the herd and their drivers, and even how fast they were going from the marks on the road. I had no such skill. But on the other hand I have always had a good opinion of my own luck and resource in emergency. So that on the whole it was with a beating heart, but with a certain sense of elation, that I went forward along the road.

The track ran between two rows of trees – beech for the most part, as I knew by the dry clash and rattle of their leaves when the winds brushed them against each other. I could see over the low hedges into the meadows, and a bloom of the fair blonde flower that is called Queen of the Meadow looked over and nodded at me, which I thought to be very early for the season, being but the end of May.

As I went on, a remarkable thought came over me, that I had been here before with May Maxwell, though I knew very well that it was not true. Yet the fantasy took hold of me, and as I walked I looked from side to side, saying to myself, "Here she and I plucked the honeysuckle and the bindweed in the hedge. Here we sat and wove them into crowns on this low bridge of turf. Up this bramble-interlaced slope we wandered, our arms entwined." Yet all the time I knew full well that I had never seen these places before. Though there was no reason why the thought should please me so much, I do not deny that it did comfort me; so that I continued to walk with enthusiasm along the highway – such as it was – till it came to the side of the long narrow loch called Grenoch, not to be confused with the larger Loch Grannoch that lies among the granite hills at the head end of Girthon parish.

There I began to meet lagging cattle so often that it was not safe for me to continue using the road. I climbed, therefore, to the moorland above the loch, where, from the ridge I would be able to see in all directions.

Now I was speeding along, like a beast that has had both food and drink, and spurred on by the thought of coming back this way again with May Maxwell at my side. Which, indeed, I never did – at least, not till many years afterwards, after everything had changed. But the feeling did me good at the time.

I checked that my pistols were primed more than once, as much as the dim light would allow. There was a beast roaring at the foot of the Duchrae Craigs, where the road kept away to the right straight for the old Bridge of the Black Water.

The cattle were now on the road immediately in front of me. I could hear them quite plainly. A low and continuous moaning came to me on the north wind, mixed with sharper noises of the shouting of men and the occasional barking of dogs. I did not think that these were the gypsies' dogs, which are trained to hunt silently, but dogs that had been gathered up of their own accord from the farms on the way. These did not bark long, however, either falling behind or getting a knife in their ribs from a gypsy driver that silenced their yelping for ever. At this point the drove-road went over the Folds Hill, and I needed to get upon the river side of the herd, to avoid being driven up to the moors and away from the bridge, which made it necessary for me to cross the road. I did this at the little hut which I now know to be the farm of the Clownie – now only a ruin of walls – I now so far behind I thought I was safe but slowly crossed the dusky white road with dark patches upon it, looking both ways, unsure of the correct direction to take.

CHAPTER XX.

THE GREAT FIGHT AT THE BRIDGE – HEAD

BUT I had not stood there for long when a voice from the foot of the dyke, by the well of excellent water that lies by the path over to the Duchrae, called on me to stand or take the consequences. Though these were not elaborated, I elected to take them, and so ran as fast as I could towards the loch, which I could see as a dull red colour beneath me.

Apparently the consequences spoken of were up a gun-barrel at the time, and consisted of two ounces of lead, for "Crack!" went a musket, and something whistled like a dor beetle past me. Reaching down, my finger encountered a hole in the flap of my blue coat. It was warm at the edges, and appeared to be clean cut. In a moment I was in the heart of a willow bush, where I sat giving thanks to God for my escape. I would have been more pleased with the help of Providence if the bullet had gone through my trousers, since I had more pairs of them, and besides, they were only of grey homespun when all was said and done. But I had only this one coat, and that was made of fine blue cloth.

The bush by the waterside was safe, but from its depths I could see nothing, and I knew that every moment the dumb, hard-driven herd of beasts was drawing away in the direction of the bridge, and I would not be able to cross before them. I might have done it easily, but I was deceived by the great turn which the road makes at Parkhill towards the Folds of Tornorrach Wood. It is always the same when I try to take short cuts or cut corners. When will I learn to be content to stay on the main path? Possibly in the next world, when I shall not be able – for there, as we are told by authority, all things shall be new.

As I went, the light wind carried a strange, low, continuous moaning sound. From the willow-bush I went slowly along the waterside until I lost the track of the cattle. Then, when the loch had narrowed into a lane of running water, I struck up through the tangled brush of the thick wood called the Duchrae Bank, where many hazels grow, to the top of the hill that looks toward the Bennan and the valley of the Ken. Day was just beginning to show, which in early May does about two hours before the sun rises. The cold grey of the sky became the colour of a Water of Dee pearl – silken grey shot with quivering rays of white.

As I ascended, the moaning grew into a hoarse, tumultuous roaring. There they are at last! It is so dark that I can only guess at their position, but I can see that the head of the column is making for the bridge. The riders ride before, their heads low between their shoulders, glancing forward. The whippers-in run tirelessly on the flanks, keeping the column tight. The moaning of the herd comes to me on the wind like the crying of a single mighty beast in pain. It is pitiful and heart-rending.

The Black Water looms dark – the bridge a grey purple arch spanning blackness.

But a row of sparks flashes out at the bridge-head. *"Crack! crack! crack!"* go the guns. There is a sudden turmoil in the densely packed herd. The horsemen at the head of the column form up, and also from them red sparks, with the clang a little behind them, spit angrily out.

"Hurrah!" I cannot help crying out loud, for my friends are there, and at the bridge-head.

They are fighting to turn the robbers. Perhaps Hector and May are among them. I was foolish not to hasten and get to the bridge-head before them!

Ah, there they are at it! Listen to the rattle of the guns, the splutter of the pistols – how they go! I find myself running forward at full speed, keeping close to the water, and alongside the Holland Isle. I wonder as I run, if I shall ever return when the nuts are ripe, for that place is well known for them. In a little while I am abreast of the packed and frightened cattle. The outlaws are playing a bold game. Their mounted fighting men are pushing along the front. The silent, eager dogs and the limber gypsy laddies are dressing the sides of the column, which, indeed, is being naturally held by the lie of the land – the rocky glen of the Black Water being in front, and the deep dark lane of Grenoch on the other side. The unmounted men who are not armed keep circulating along the rear. Between them and the bridge there is a lowing, roaring, horn tossing sea of wild cattle, the best and the strongest in Galloway.

I get down by the water's edge, and I am pushing on all the time. I hear my feet crash on the shingles. I fall on my face among the hard stones before I know it. That is fortunate for me, for with the instinct of a sea-bred boy I feel for the water. It is within ten feet of me, roaring deep. With my leather belt I fasten my napkin, filled with my powder-flask and pistols, upon the top of my head. The strap is caught in my teeth, and without a moment's delay I push off. Though I can wade nearly all the way, in the end I am swept off my feet. Ten strokes, however, take me over, and I stand shivering on the north side of the Black Water.

But my powder and my pistols are dry, though I myself am streaming wet. Crying my name, to let the Maxwells know not to shoot, in a moment

I am at the bridge-end and among them. As I had imagined, the defenders are my friends, with another ten men whom they had gathered as they came along, mostly kinsmen of their own, Maxwell's and Sproats, from the coastlands. Kennedy Maxwell, who is the one I am closest to, has only time to say, "Don't throw a shot away, Patrick. We're turning them. This is the third time they have come at us."

As he spoke the mounted men came on again, but a storm of balls tore through their ranks, and set the horses plunging and the cattle wild with terror. So again they were driven back. The men hung half over the parapet of the bridge and kneeled with their muskets upon it, yelling with challenge in their voices.

"We have them," cried Will Maxwell, "we'll not let one of the cowardly crew escape!"

The word was ill-chosen, and the rejoicing premature. Again the mounted outlaws drew off to the rear, and for a time only the dogs kept the column within its lines.

Gradually their front widened, as though to flank the bridge and make for the water. We spread out to meet them. The others were soon blazing away, but the gypsies were far off, and I saw little point in maddening the poor dumb beasts with pistol balls.

Yet it was an amazing sight – Dee Bridge with its high-arched span – men standing two deep in the centre of it; men astride its parapet; gunshots cracking, pistols spitting. Then in front of us the white, pitiful eyes of a myriad (so it seemed) of wild cattle – maimed and tortured without knowing why, sending up a great roaring of dumb prayer to the God of all ill-used, over-driven beasts that never did any harm. Beyond these, the dark forms of the mounted outlaws contriving new plots in the rear.

I wanted the Maxwells to charge and break the column of cattle, but Will Maxwell overruled, saying, "No; we will hold the bridge." So the bridge was held.

Then suddenly a great fierce light arose in the rear. The outlaws had kindled a fire, and the red light burned up, filtering through the ranks of the cattle, and projecting great horned shadows against the clouds. For a few minutes this picture stood like a painted show, with the Dee Water running dark and cool beneath – a kind of Satan's Inferno where the beasts are tortured for ever.

Two half-naked fiends ran alongside the column of cattle; carrying what was apparently a pot of blazing fire, which they threw in great ladlefuls on the backs of the packed beasts that stood frantically heaving their heads up to the sky. Then in a moment deafening yells arose from all sides. Fire lighted and ran along the hides of the rough red Highland and black Galloway cattle. Desperate men sprang on their backs, yelling. Dogs drove them forward. With one wild, irresistible, universal rush the maddened column of beasts drove at the bridge, and swept us aside like chaff.

I have never seen anything so extraordinary and awesome as this tide of wild animals, frantic with pain and terror, which surged in waves irresistibly to the bridge-head. It was a dance of demons. Between me and the burning backs of the cattle there rose a gigantic Highland steer with fiery eyes and matted front. On his back was a black devil that waved a torch with his hands, scattering contagious fire over the furious herd. The rush of the maddened beasts swept us off the bridge as chaff is driven before the wind. There was no question of standing firm. I shot off my pistol into the mass. I might as well have shot them into the Black Water. I declare some of the yelling devils were laughing as they rode, like fiends snarling and crying incessantly when Hell wins a soul. It is hard to make any who did not see it, believe what we saw that night. Indeed, as I write in this warm and comfortable winter room, with the storm outside, and my wife in bed calling on me to put my writing aside and let her get to sleep, it is well-nigh impossible for me to believe it. Yet it was as I describe. I who write it down was there. These eyes saw the tossing, fiery waves of maddened creatures that ran forward seeking death to escape from torture, while the smoke of their burning backs went up to heaven.

I looked again. Beneath at the ford I saw a thousand wild cattle with their thick hair blazing with fire, their tails in the air, tossing wide-arched horns. I saw the steam of their nostrils going up like smoke as they surged through the water, a hundred mad Faas and Marshalls on their backs yelling like fiends of the pit. In a score of pulse beats there was not a beast that had not forced the bridge or crossed the ford. We defenders were broken and scattered; some of us swept down by the water, powder damp, guns trampled shapeless – we that had been so sure of victory were dispirited and annihilated.

(But before I tell of other things let me add how the outlaws scattered Greek fire over their cattle, unwittingly using a stratagem of the ancient world. In a field by the waterside, within a hundred yards of where the column halted, were the Duchrae Sheepfolds, where there was a store of pitch and oil for sheep dipping and cattle marking, of which, in some devilish fashion of their own, the outlaws, skilled in such horrid chemistry, made their cruel fiery brew.)

CHAPTER XXI.

SAMMLE TAMSON FETCHES THE WATER

WHEN I came to myself (for I was just as frenzied as the beasts themselves while the turmoil lasted), I found myself lying on the heather having been tossed from the bull's back. My hands were burned and black where I had slapped the poor beast's hide to put out the flames. But despite that, it did not favour me above any of its persecutors. I think the impulse to stampede did not come so much from the pain as from the sudden blind fury, which at any moment can seize a large crowd of half-wild cattle in the presence of some unknown threat.

I do not know how I came to be on the beast's back, but it may have been to avoid being trampled; but once on this shaggy charger I reached safety, somewhere between Mossdale and the Stroan Loch. I now found myself pitched out onto the heather, almost falling on a cock grouse that had heard only the thudding of a bullock's heels, and no doubt wondered where the blundering beast was going. His cockship got something of a surprise, I think, when the enemy of his kind was shot out upon the top of him with pistols shining in his belt. At any rate, he rose with a strong protest of "*Geck-kek-kek-a-kek!*" that such a trick should be played upon him – as quiet a self-respecting bird as he was.

In a few minutes I was knocking at the door of Mossdale house, that sits on its own on a pleasant slope facing the rising sun and I thought the long, low, whitewashed cottage made an exceedingly quaint picture. There was a man just coming to the door with a wooden platter of hens' meat in his hands. His eyes were red with sleep, and as he approached, his jaws opened like a rat-trap, for he was yawning as if he had not had nearly enough of his bed.

"Good morning, sir," said I.

"And you have brought the top of the morning with you, friend," he said, but not at all suspiciously, passing me with the hens' meat. I stood at the door, not venturing in. The man, who was built long and thin with a stoop in the shoulders, opened a little door in a wooden construction. A hen or two with many chickens emerged tumultuously, making that screeching noise which hens make when they are hungry, as much as to say, "I'm as empty as a whistle! Are you going to be long with that meat?"

The man put down the little trencher and stood over them with a long wand, holding back the greedy and making room for the poor, puny, backward ones, that were not able to elbow forward with their short callow chicken wings. The scene was one of exceptional peace, and affected me strangely, still having the noise of that wild riot at the bridge-head in my ears, and the sound of that mighty bellowing, like the roaring of all the bulls in Bastian.

"It's been a fine night!" said he. "Where have you come from this morning, friend, so early. Did you stay the night at the Duchrae? "

"Indeed." said I, frankly – at least with more frankness than I had intended when I knocked at the door, "I did not sleep much, as there was a considerable number of wild men on the road yesterday, and it was better for peaceful folk to keep out of the way."

"I'm with you there," he said, scraping up some of the hen meat, that had fallen on the ground, giving it to a peeping, peevish little chicken that came complaining and pecking about his feet.

"Neither deal nor trade with the likes of them. For me I keep out of their way."

"Did you hear anything at all, yesterday?" I asked watching him pretty carefully, for my own back was to the sun.

"I was thinking," he said, "that the Dee Water had come down hard in the night, and that I heard the falls roaring. I thought I would try fishing this morning. I might catch a fine fish."

"You might catch a four-legged salmon, with horns," said I.

"You don't say?" said the man. "Then Sammle Tamson will be staying close by his own doorstep."

For the first time there came a shade of suspicion over his face as he glanced at me from head to toe.

"You're well armed, friend, to be out so early."

He looked at my pistols and silver-mounted sword.

"I'm an honest man," said I, reassuringly.

"I expect so," said he that had called himself Samuel Tamson, "there's a lot of honest men travelling on the road. I never met with one that said he wasn't."

But nevertheless he viewed me again with a somewhat reassured look.

"You'll not be a Faa?" he asked, in a sly, shrewd manner.

"No," said I, "I'm no Faa, thank Heaven!"

"As I expected," he answered. Then he added reflectively, "The Faas are a good-looking race when all is said and done."

He looked at me still longer.

"You kind of resemble the Macatericks – long and lanky, but your mouth's too big to be a Macaterick, and none of the Marshalls have turned-up noses!"

Which (I may remark) neither had I. Sammle Tamson seemed reassured. But he was still cautious.

"You'll have a name of your own," he said he; "let me hear it."

"My name is Patrick Heron!" said I, a little nettled at the man's obvious suspicion, though indeed I would never have so much as looked at any one coming to my own door in the same way.

"You'll not be related to John Heron of Isle Rathan?"

"I am his son," I replied, briefly.

"Is that so, Oh man---"said Sammle, yet he did not seemed inclined to take any action beyond the exclamation. He still stood with the empty trough meat in his hand. A voice from the house cried behind us, sharply. "What's all that chattering about? Am I to wait a day for you to light my fire, Sammle Tamson? Is this why I married you, when I had many better offers? I wish to goodness I had never left Parton!"

The voice was sharp, but by no means unkindly. On the contrary, it amused me.

"There's a young man here, goodwife," said Sammle Tamson at the door, leaning from the outside to put his head within as one might point the bending top of a fishing-rod into an upper window.

"Fetch him in, and let us see what he is like," said the voice.

Sammle silently motioned to me to put down my pistols and sword on the window sill outside, which I would not have done even if he had asked; but the voice from inside made it feel as if it was necessary.

Then he went inside before me, and I followed. Hardly had I got inside when I wanted to be out again, for I saw, for the first time in my life, a goodwife in some disarray sitting on the edge of the bed settee engaged in completing her attire. I would have fled in an instant, but the voice said, encouragingly:"Come away; sit down, young man-"

"But, wife—"began Sammle Tamson in a tone that implied he disagreed.

"Hold your tongue, husband. I'm not so unattractive yet, but I am old enough to be the laddie's mother, you would think I was a wench in a short skirt to hear you. Don't be so decent with Eppie Tamson."

"He says he's a son of the old laird of Rathan's." This came sulkily and somewhat grudgingly from Sammle.

"Come here and let me look at you, laddie," commanded the dame, from the bedside.

I had been standing modestly with my face to the window, looking over the wide moss, now bright with the red of the sun rising. I turned at the word with some diffidence. But the dame was already in her woollen gown, which she was busy buckling at the waist. She was a plump matron of forty-five, with pleasant apple-red cheeks, and very bright blue eyes. Even while I turned she took her feet, one at a time, into her hand, and shod them with a neater shoe than I had ever seen on the foot of a Galloway wife – whose normal footwear was a shapeless slipper, often worn with a loose double stocking. Altogether Eppie Tamson was a respectable and attractive lady – a desirable friend, as I could tell from her voice.

Sammle Tamson was blowing up the fire – on his knees, with his back extraordinarily high in the air, and his head so close to the bars that it seemed as though he was trying to crawl between them. And he did seem slender enough to succeed.

So I went obediently enough to Mistress Tamson. who, rising from the oak bed settee on which she had been sitting, took me by the shoulders, led me across the room to the window, and looked at me for a moment in a way which made me blush. I blushed still more when she took me fairly round the neck and gave me a sound kiss saying,"Aye, laddie, what would I not have given for a boy like you! Get up, there, off your knees, Sammle Tamson; you can't even light that fire. You are but a feckless weakling. Let me at it!"

Sammle rose in a discouraged way, as one that was not appreciated in life, and proceeded to put some water in the porridge pot.

"Go to the well for fresh water," threw his wife at him over her shoulder as she puffed and blew.

"But I brought in fresh water late yesterday," he said, complainingly.

His wife rose off her knees rapidly. Like a flash Sammie ran to the back of the door, and seized a couple of bright water cans. He was making out of the door with them when his wife came at him with the broom handle. Sammle protected himself instinctively with the cans, and the stick rattled harmlessly on the tin. But he did not smile as he hurried down the path, nor did his wife send a single word after him. It seemed to be entirely routine to them.

"Did you ever see such a man?" queried the dame, as she returned to the fire."He can't do anything without needing to argue about it. And he's that thoughtless and unmindful that he can hardly be relied on to do anything but feed the hens,"-here she paused; then, as if something had been called to her mind, she added-"*if that!*"

"Just go to the door," she continued, after another pause, and see if he has gone to the well. He goes to the dung-heap for worms for his fishing when he's sent for water," she explained.

I looked and saw Sammle Tamson standing by the well, emptying the water out of the cans. I came in and reported accordingly.

"Aye," said his wife," what a man – Lord, what a man! It's just like him. He would never think of emptying yesterday's water at the door here. He must carry it to the well and empty it there. It's a mercy he did even that. The morning before last, do you know what he did? He took the water-cans to the well with the water that had been standing all night, and he brought them back as they went, with the selfsame water in them!"

The mistress paused.

"But he caught it for that!" she said, righteously.

"But he can't make any mistake this time," I said.

"I don't know – I don't know," she said, shaking her head."It's barely possible; but if it is possible at all to make a mistake, Sammle Tamson's the man to make it."

The fire was blazing up the chimney now, and the house of Mossdale, on its sunny hillside, was very cheerful. I saw a prospect of porridge.

I opened my heart. I began to tell, willingly, all of my story to the good dame. She heard me with constant expressions of sympathy and pity, standing with the porridge spurtle in her hand in the middle of the floor, while the water in the pot steamed away unheeded.

I told more of my story.

"Well I never! Dear me – just think on that! And the wild cats burned the house -"

I told still more.

"And you fought them in the cave for the sake of the girl. My word, but she'll be a proud lass. Upon my word! But she'll have given you a different kind of a kiss than would an old wife like me."

I said, "Not so," but went on with my tale.

"The Almighty preserve us," cried Eppie. "And the ill bred heather-cat ran off with the young lass, and now you're looking for her. Did you ever hear the like of that! My man shall go and help you. Oh, that he was any good! If I had a pair of breeches, I declare that I would go with you myself! And you have no mother, you tell me. Poor laddie! Poor laddie!"

The white apron went up to the eyes that were no longer merry, and she took me in her arms and kissed me again.

Then she ran to the door, and cried out loud," Sammle Tamson, you big slowcoach, come home with the water this minute, or you shall get words from the devil from your beloved!"

Through the window I could see Samuel Tamson standing gazing moonstruck at the well.

"You great dozy oaf, do you think that this is miracle morning, and that the good well-water is going to turn into wine?"

Samuel recovered his cans in haste and started for home.

His wife saw his legs beginning to move like compasses, and then, thinking that at last all was well, she came back in to the fire. She said no word, either good or bad, as Samuel came through the door and put down his cans behind it, with a look of self-righteousness which did one good to see.

Eppie took the great tankard from the shelf and went to get it filled with the fresh, cool water from the well. She thrust her dish into the nearest can. It struck the bottom with a hollow sound. In great surprise she looked inside.

The can was empty and dry.

It was too much. A sin such as this deserved punishment more than broom handles. She gave her husband a look that would have weaned a foal. Then with great politeness, she turned to me and asked if I would be so kind as to fetch some water from the well.

When I left on my errand, I was anxious for the poor man inside. I expected that I should have to collect the fragments on my return.

I do not know what really happened, for when I came back Sammle was sitting on the wooden bench in the corner of the fireplace with an extraordinarily subdued face, and his wife was standing, silent also, by the inglenook.

It was Sammle who looked up first.

"It's fine cold water," he said,"and a nice cheerful walk in the morning to give you an appetite for your porridge – it's a pleasant task to fetch the water."

But his wife said no word; she only stirred the oatmeal into the pot.

In a few minutes there was a great steaming dish of porridge on the table – a wonderful sight for a famished man.

Then as soon as I had finished Eppie came to me and said,"Now, off with your clothes, into my warm bed, and get you some sleep for at least four hours."

"But," I urged, "I dare not lose a moment. I must cross the hills to Loch Enoch straight away."

"You'll do no such thing. I know the look of a troubled and sickening lad. You'll do as Eppie Tamson says in her own house of Mossdale. Better to lose four hours than lose the lass. You have had no sleep for two nights, and you'll never see Loch Enoch or your May if you carry on as you are doing."

All the while she was unbuttoning my coat and waistcoat as if she had been my own mother, which I thought strange – but it seemed somehow natural to me

"You see I have no children of my own!"she said in explanation, which somehow, perhaps because I was asleep on my feet, seemed perfectly logical.

I think I was asleep before I was out of her hands. At least I have no memory of my head ever touching the pillow. I was rising up, up – on warm, white, fleecy clouds – up, up, till I put out my hands to keep from being squeezed flat against the arch of the blue sky. I saw angels. I remember what they are like. There are two kinds of them. One pattern has merry eyes and white teeth, with sunny curls cropped short like a boy's. The others are about forty-five, very buxom and are all named Eppie. I did not hear the name of the first sort.

CHAPTER XXII.

I GET THE RIGHT SIDE OF EPPIE TAMSON

IT is strange that when you are very tired folk will never let you sleep for more than five minutes. You'll have noticed that. So have I. As soon as you drop asleep, in a quarter of an hour or less they are at you, saying that it is some frankly impossible time, and that you must get up.

As I lay asleep I heard some one say, about a million miles away (or maybe more), that it was eleven o'clock. I turned over, for this was no concern of mine.

Somebody said, a little nearer this time – maybe a thousand miles away, "Poor laddie! Another half-hour won't hurt him."

So I turned over again and went to sleep for what felt like a year.

But the contrariness of things is such that in less than three moments (and short ones at that) some one with a pair of strong arms – although comfortable ones – was raising me gently up.

"My lad, I'm sorry to wake you, but it's nearly twelve and dinner's ready, and the man of the house is also ready to take you to the Wolf's Stock, which is the best way to Loch Enoch. He knows that if he doesn't keep you safe, he need never again show his face at Mossdale or call Eppie Tamson his wife!"

I sat up. Wakening from a deep sleep in a strange house is the eeriest of things. The house seemed to be spinning round but in a strange kind of whirling silence. I do not think that Lazarus felt any different when he awoke after his four days in the tomb with that big flat gravestone covering him.

Eppie helped me on with my things just as she had helped me take them off; as if in a former existence she had been my mother. It was a comfort to me to have some one to pull up my socks and undo the ties of my boots, since I had never known a mother.

While she was bent over me in this way, whilst tying my shoe, I saw Samuel Tamson lift his head and give her a look, which was both wistful and pitying, though I could not for the life of me understand why – it was him who needed pity, in my opinion.

So now dressed, and dinner was on the table; and before I sat down I noticed that my coat was neatly mended where the bullet had cut through the previous night, at the side of the Clownie dyke when I ran headlong into the willow bush by the waterside. This pleased me as much as anything. I also noticed that my clothes were clean brushed and exceedingly neat and in good order.

I was about to thank her, but she cut me short.

"Get your dinner, laddie, and see and not dirty your clothes. I have spent a lot of time on them."

"I am sorry to put you to so much inconvenience," said I, politely.

"Nonsense! 'Inconvenience,' he says, the boy lacks judgement. I'm proud and glad to do what little I can for your mother's son."

"Did you know my mother?" I asked, for my father had rarely spoken about her, and I would like to have heard more.

"No, it's just a way of speaking," said Eppie Tamson; "but I know her son, and if ever there was a lad needing somebody to look after him, it's him. And you sorely need that lass about the old Isle of Rathan. If she is worthy of you, God keep you and help you to get her. If you win her out of the claws of the buzzards, she won't go home without a ring on her finger, or my name's not Eppie."

After dinner she had a great number of directions to give to her husband, who said not a word, but only looked at her and me time about in the same extraordinary wistful and mournful way. Then she gave me my pistols. They were cleaned and oiled, loaded and primed.

I was about to thank her again for having put them to rights, when she said,"No, not me – I wouldn't touch the nasty things. It was him that did them, and I hope to your satisfaction? "

I quickly assured her that they were.

"It's just as well," said Mistress Tamson.

Then she pressed on me a fine engraved silver flask, which she said she had been given by the Laird of Parton when she married; because she had been a servant in the big house there.

"It's full of the best. *You* carry it!" she said, pointedly.

Also she had scones and oatcake done up with fine ham between the slices in an appetising way I had never seen before, which no doubt she had learned in the kitchens of the great.

As I went out she asked if I had any money. I showed her Silver Sand's handful, and she was more or less satisfied.

"Oh well!" she said, sounding disappointed, that made it obvious that she had also meant to supply me with that, if I had needed it, but which made me grateful all the same.

Then when she bade me good-bye, after giving me a fine hazel staff with an iron tip to it, she burst out crying like a child and went indoors without speaking, shutting to the door.

But we had barely left the grounds of the cottage on our way to the great hill of Cairn Edward, before Eppie came after us again with something bright in her hand.

"I brought this," she said; "it might be useful to you." It was a brass pocket telescope, very short, but as thick as my wrist. It had many stages, all closing up into one, and closed with brass caps at both ends.

I did not want to take so many things from her, and began to say so. But I saw her husband motioning me to be silent from behind her back.

Following the direction of my eyes (for unlike some people, I do not have the art of looking without seeming to), she caught him in the act.

"Make him take it," she said.

"You had better," said Sammle, feebly.

So I put the telescope in my tail-pocket, where, to tell the truth, it was extraordinarily heavy, and at the time, I did not expect it to be useful.

Then, standing in front of me on the heather which was not yet in bloom, this woman, whom I had not met until that morning, made me promise that I would to return to her as soon as I had completed my mission.

"Mind you," she said,"if you're not here by Wednesday, I'll come among the gypsies to look for you myself – breeches or no breeches!" As she said this, she went back into the little cottage at Mossdale that you may see above the Flow to this day. Only you need not call, for Eppie Tamson is not there now.

So at noon on this fine day in May, Sammle Tamson and I took to the hill. At first I doubted him, and I thought I was a better mountaineer than him. But I was soon to learn different. Samuel Tamson walked with a strange forward stoop which approached a right angle. He leaned heavily on his shepherd's staff as he went – his thin, pallid face with its lack-lustre eyes going before him. He had the air of a man who carries his own head like a hand lantern. He carried a tall stick, and often the hand that grasped it was higher than his head. Yet he could beat me on the hill without turning a hair. His legs moved over the heather and stones as though they could not help themselves, and never stopped. He carried his left hand pressed into the small of his back.

And as we went the man that had been so silent began to talk without ceasing, walking all the time and speaking as though talking on the slope of a Galloway hill, up to the knees in heather and shin-twisting holes, was as easy as breathing. The subject of his dialogue also astonished me. It was all about Eppie.

"She's most extraordinary woman, the wife. There isn't anyone like her in the six parishes. Very thorough, well-prepared and tidy, clever with hand and tongue, and with a heart as kind as – well, you've seen it for yourself. It's a neverending wonder to me why she ever took to the likes of me, or how she puts up with me now she has."

"She was exceedingly kind to me," I said.

"Yes, but," said Sammle, speeding up Cairn Edward at a pace that made me pant like a wind-blown nag, "man, I saw that you had the right side of her from the start."

Then he stopped for a moment, and I thought he was weary after the short, hot burst uphill. But this was not the case. He only wanted to assure himself he had my attention.

"You may think she's unpleasant to me," he said, earnestly."I'm always pleased when she takes enough notice to look after me by keeping me at my work. I know I would try a saint. I have no memory at all, and the mind that I do have is not worth as much as a whelk. Sometimes I think I must have hidden my mental ability during my sleep, and forgotten where I put it, for I can't see hide nor hair of it. And everyone is born with that, the minister says. He has speaking about that very subject in Kells Kirk not long ago. What do you think of that question yourself, Laird Heron?"

This was said with the earnestness and desire of a Scot for a theological discussion. But I had little knowledge of theology, and an even smaller to engage in any debate at that moment. So I tried to keep him to his story.

"Indeed, aye, I'm a great trial and vexation to her, I know, and she was used to better things. You see the way of it is this: I had been a widower for three years when I began to visit Parton House to see her in the evenings. I had one daughter, who was five years old. Well, I asked Eppie, again and again, but she always said no. In fact, she made fun of me to my face; till I plucked up enough courage to say that I wouldn't come again just to be slighted in front of people. No, and then I didn't look to her for nearly for a fortnight. Then I met her on the Boat O'Rhone road, at the edge of the Big Wood of Turnorrach.

"'Good evening to you," says she, ' have you forgotten the way to Parton?'

'I said, "No, I haven't, but I was made well aware that I wasn't wanted at Parton."

"She answered that she wasn't so sure of that.

"Now, I'm not a bright man nor a forward man, but I'm not exactly a fool, so I embraced her round the neck, and you'll find that a more successful argument with a girl than any talking – provided, that is, that she likes you at all. That's my advice to you, Laird Rathan."

We were now on the brow of the high, rocky hill that is called Cairn Edward, or Cairn Ethart, which rises bleak and grey above the rushing of the Black Water of Dee.

"We'll keep high," said Sammle. "It'll be better for seeing and less easy to be seen."

So as we went, he again took up the burden of his tale.

"So, of course, after Tornorrach Wood, there was no more ado but to get married. And we were married as soon the banns had been called, and a fine wedding was held the big house. The lady of the house was very taken with her, and among other things that she was given was the flask you have in your pocket, and the telescope. Perhaps you wouldn't be the ready for a drop now? No ---- well, well!

"But then there was my daughter, Marion, that was mine and my first wife's – a pretty little lass. Now some silly, scheming people had been telling her stories about step-mothers, and when we came up to the door, or as near it as the laird's pony could take us, there is little Marion sitting on the doorstep (and you could see that she was heartbroken, although she had finished crying and she looked at us with a puckered and pitiful face). It pains me to remind myself of it!

"Then when we dismounted, little Marion comes to meet us, with her lower lip quivering and her large blue eyes watering – O man, man, to think about it! And, she says, as clever as if she had been saying it over and over to herself to learn it by heart before we came -

"'This house is yours now, I know,' she says to Eppie (she was five year only last September). 'But, maybe, you'll allow little Marion to stay in the hen-house beside the calf. I wont disturb him at all,' she says.

'Marion will be really quiet, and see, I have taken Black Andy there already!'

"Black Andy was her little dolly that I had made out of a small stick and painted red and black.

"'See,' she said,'Black Andy's there now, waiting amongst the hay, and he and I will never make a sound - will you let us stay in the hen-house? '

"O man, O man," burst out Sammle Tamson, sobbing to himself in a passion as he leaned on his staff. "it was like death to me to hear the child.

"And the wife, Eppie, oh, but she took it to heart. She sat down on the doorstep and sobbed till she started laughing. And then she couldn't stop.

Never in my life had I seen anybody taken like that. It was a most pitiful homecoming.

"Then, when she recovered, she took the little girl in her arms and kissed her; but Marion had been talked to by silly folk, and had set her mind on going to the hen-house, so she would not go to Eppie willingly.

"But I sent Marion to bed in the parlour, and saw her happily snuggled up to Black Andy, who was only a stick painted with tar and cart-red, and covered in an old cloth - yet she took him in her arms and sobbed quietly on the pillow, for she loved him.

"So I left them.

"But in the morning it so happened that I had to rise early – and it served us right for marring during the lambing time; so it was just before dawn that I closed the door behind me, and unwillingly went my way to the hill.

"Eppie was lying wide awake in the dark of the morning, thinking, no doubt, and perhaps not the pleasantest of thoughts, about what she would do with Marion.

"When, as she has told me fifty times, and fifty times more, the parlour door opened slightly as if the cat was coming in. Then a little white face looked round the corner of the door, and small bare feet padded across the floor till they stopped by Eppie's bed.

"It was Marion. She looked for a while before she spoke, but Eppie didn't say a word.

"'They say that you are my mother now,' said wee Marion, holding up one bare foot off the cold stone.

"'And what if I was your mother?' said Eppie, as kind as she could.

"'WELL THEN,' says Marion, emphatically, 'if you are to be my mother, I thought that I would like to creep in beside you for a while in your warm bed, for it's very, very cold in the parlour.'

"Eppie was out of bed in a moment, and had the child in her arms, crying over her and rejoicing all at once.

"'Can I come in, then?" said Marion.

"'Yes, bless you, you can so' said Eppie, heartily.

"'And stay? ' continued the wee lass in white.

"'Yes, come on' ' said Eppie.

"'And put my cold feet on you?'"

"'Of course, child, anything you like.'

"'Then I'll go and get Black Andy!'

"When I came back from the hill there was no room for me, for Eppie and Marion and Black Andy' were all lying sleeping with their arms about each other!

"And that was how it began!"said Sammle Tamson of Mossdale.

"And where is the lassie now? I would like to see her. Is she up and married, or out to service? "I said, without thinking.

Sammle shook his head. He did not sob again, but there was a look of anguish on his face that was heart rending.

"She's gone!" he said.

"Gone!" said I, startled. "Did she die?"

"No, not that; she was lost on the hills – it's a long story, but we're nearly over by the Black Craig o' Dee now and we'll have to be cautious."

But he went on.

"So, sir, for a year that lass was the very apple of Eppie's eye. We never had any children of our own, and Eppie was just devoted to Marion. I often spoke to her about it, but as you'd understand, I might as well have saved my breath."

I understood, and signified it with a nod.

Sammle Tamson went on, feet and tongue working together, till we drew towards the verge of the Black Craig of Dee, and saw beneath us the whole of the land behind, with its lochs and lochans, clints and mosses, away to the little white house of Mossdale itself, where I have no doubt there was one watching us as we journeyed.

CHAPTER XXIII.

THE FORWANDERED BAIRN

AND this was the rest of his tale.

"After the wife had been at the Bennan for nineteen months, she allowed Marion come out over the hills with my dinner in a napkin. I seldom went so far away that she could not see me from the doorstep; for the most part herding is done within sight of the house, since the land all slopes to the Water of Dee, where the wee house of Mossdale sits, as you are well aware.

"But it so happened one day that I had a job up at the Englishman's Dub which is at the back the Bennan hill, up by the springs o' the Lowran Burn.

"I remember it as if it was yesterday. I had an eye on the sheep, of course; but I was cutting some birch, that was twisted, to carry it home to make a fancy low stool for wee Marion.

"And, faith, here she comes herself, singing with my broth in a tin can that she was carrying by the handle, being careful not to spill it, and my small sandwich in a bag that she called her school bag, though there was no school near for her to go to. I can see her, hopping and skipping over the moor – despite the stones and the deep heather that sometimes were higher than her head – cavorting along and singing like a skylark. Oh, but she was a cheery wee lass."

I will admit that I found all this extraordinarily interesting, perhaps more than readers will; but to hear it from the strange, laughable-tragic man on the great hills of heather maybe made all the difference.

Sammle Tamson went on. "While I was at my dinner, she sat and talked bits of child's talk, and ate scraps that I gave to her, or that she pulled off for herself, for she always took great pleasure in sitting and eating the crumbs when Eppie was baking.

"I remember she asked about the wee crooked birches – and if God made them crooked. Or if it was their own badness that made them crooked, or was there another reason? And she wouldn't be put off with no answer at all, but pressed me so much that she had me clean out my depth, and I had to say:"'Well, Marion, you'll have to ask the minister when he comes to talk to you. You'll have to ask him *his* questions for him as well!'

"'Indeed I will!' says she.

"So when I had taken my fill, I buckled on the bag and gave her the can, and the young lady took the road home as cheerful as a lark."

By the time Sammle Tamson had got this far in his tale we reached the great Corry that lies to the west of the Black Craig of Dee, between the Hill o' the Hope and the Rig o' Craig Gilbert. We could see the smoking chimneys of the steading of Laggan of Dee, that was said to have decent folk in it, even though it was close to the outlaw country.

Sammie stopped deliberately, and faced me in order to say emphatically, "So I saw wee Marion leave me, her little white legs twinkling among the heather beneath her short skirts. She went over the hilltop, standing on the top just long enough to wave her can, and cry a word that she had learned from Eppie:"'Noo, Sammle, see and be home before the night.'"

"'You wee rascal!' I cried, and she ducked down."

Sammle looked me in the face. I had not thought he could look so solemn.

"From that moment to this," he said, "I have never set eyes on my child."

We were silent for a while, Sammle Tamson looking directly at me as if he had forgotten to look away, while I was trying to hold back my emotions.

"But did you not look for her?" I asked very foolishly, and without thinking.

"Look for her – yes, we searched near and far. There were search parties out on the hills for ten days. I didn't get to bed for nearly three weeks. It was then that the pain in my back began. The wife went out of her mind altogether. She was wild, and dead set against me, though I could not help it. The child had come home from further than that over fifty times.

"But I'm going too quickly," said Sammle; "I'll tell you the whole story.

"The day after Marion was lost on the moors, Eppie went missing as well. She had risen and taken to the hills before dawn. My sister from Clachanpluck, a married woman, was with her; but Tibby was always a sound sleeper and when she awoke Eppie was up and away.

"So there was another hunt.

"I tracked Eppie all along the side of Dee Water, here by a footprint and there a strip of her gown tangled on a blackthorn, till the next day at noon I found her away up on the links of the Cooran Lane far beyond Loch Dee, completely out of her mind. As far as I could make out the outlaw folk had found her, but she had frightened them. All of these sorts are afraid of people that are out of their minds, and don't think it's safe to meddle with them – otherwise, I don't like to think what might have happened.

"When I found Eppie she was lying on a the riverbank in the sun with nothing on her head. As soon as she saw me coming close, she let out a scream and ran as fast as she could.

"Now, it's odd when a wife of nineteen months runs away like a fox from her husband. That hurt me but I saw there was nothing for it but to run her down. But it was a long chase.

"She had the strength of six. I don't think I could have caught her, had she not dropped something she was carrying.

"So in a hollow of the heather I took Eppie in my arms, and called her 'my darling,' and spoke to her as I used to do in the hay at Parton on the nights when I first went to see her.

"Bit by bit she came to, till she saw the thing that she had found. It was the same can that Marion had taken my dinner broth in, the last time she was sent to me. Every time that her eyes fell on that can, she would go off again in a trance, and speak wild, wild words when she came out of it.

"But at long last I got her home. That was no joke. That was the hardest job that ever I had. The can was half full of blackberries that the child had been gathering (so we thought), because Eppie had said that of all the sugar conserves that are made, she was fondest of blackberry jelly. So the child almost certainly had thought to please Eppie but in doing so, had gone to her death.

"And the strange thing is that even when Eppie came back to normal, she said time and again that she had seen the lass running ahead of her over the *quakkin' quas* and the green morasses of the Silver Flow o' Buchan. Oh, I know that's not possible, but this is what Eppie declares to this day: She was on a hill that they call Craigeazle, and down below her she saw our little girl running, and, in relief, she called after her. She ran down the hillside among the rocks and clattering slate-stones, but the wee lass kept running. It was terrible ground, wet and mossy at every step, but the child ran on light footed; when suddenly something like an arm shot up out of the quagmire and pulled the child down, and Eppie saw only the oily bubbles rising out the black glossy mud of the moss-hole).

"O man, Laird Heron, I know the story is not believable. It's only a distracted woman's dream; but if she mentions it to you, you must not contradict her, for she believes it like her Bible. Sir, it was a pleasure to me to see her take such an interest in you today. It takes her mind off what is not good for it. I'm often glad when my stupidity angers her, and it's a kind of pleasure to me when she comes at me with the broomstick. Sometimes I even make myself look stupider than I am, just to humour her."

Sammle Tamson finished here. What a dolt and ass I had been to look on this man as no more than a mockery and a laughing-stock! Underneath that strange outward appearance and behind his comical relations with his wife lay, unsuspected, a whole world of tragedy. The Lord keep me in the future from hasty judgments. We see our neighbour's face, but not what is behind it.

It had been more than two hours since we left the house at Mossdale, and before we knew it, had reached the ridge. As soon as Sammle looked over it, he dropped like a shot.

"Down," he said under his breath;"for the love God, lie down!"

I was beside him in an instant. Together we peered cautiously over the worn and water-pitted edge of the blue whinstone rock, our bodies buried up to the chin in the heather.

Sammle pointed with his nose, as if he was a curlew.

"There," he whispered, although we a thousand feet in the air above the drove-road,"Do you see that?"

What I saw was the bends of the Black Water of Dee shining amid the dull yellows and greys of the grim mosses through which it slowly made its way. I saw the untenanted cottage of Clattering Shaws and the drove-road to the Cree Bridge winding across the heather. But what was most noticeable was a long, straggling line of black dots crawling irregularly over the moor by the waterside.

"There's the drove, and there's your Macatericks and Marshalls, and I expect a Faa or two among them." said Sammle.

I got out the prospect glass in a flash, and Sammle, knowing how to use it, set it for me. But he let me look first, which was thoughtful.

I soon found them, and though they were only blurs when I first saw them, by dint of a little screwing of the slides and learning how to shut one eye, I was soon able to see quite clearly.

There were ten or twelve mounted men in the party, riding loosely behind, but two of the horses carried wounded men. They seemed unable to sit by themselves, and were held up by a man at either side. Then there were a great many cattle, some limping wearily, and others trying to snatch a bite of fodder by the way. I was astonished to discover that I could see all quite plainly at this distance. I had never seen telescope as good as this one. Then ahead and behind the herd there were boys with rags as clothes holding the beasts in check and playing pranks among themselves. But what I was looking for, although I hoped I would not see, was not there – Hector Faa and May Maxwell were not part of the procession.

Silver Sand had been correct in his predictions: it would remain to be seen if he was also correct about the outcome.

"Thank the Lord," I said aloud.

The Edinburgh road takes a turn at Clattering Shaws, and there is also a wide plain where the country folks say that King Robert the Bruce fought a battle. But it was a difficult place for us to cross to the other side of the glen; but we had to cross it, and quickly, because it was evident that the outlaws now considered themselves perfectly safe in their own country and would not hurry the cattle.

I told Sammle as much of Silver Sand's plans as I thought prudent – which, to be honest, was nearly as much as I knew myself. He approved of them generally, and was able to shed a great deal of light upon the intentions of the gypsies, the lie of the country, and on what my own movements ought to be.

The cattle reivers would certainly, he said, take the easiest road, and slowly use the track by Loch Dee to Loch Trool, then past Glenhead, and up the narrow defile of the Gairland Burn, into that tangle of lochs and mountains under the brow of Merrick, which formed their robbers' stronghold. There would be better grazing by the loch shores than anywhere else, though indeed the Faas never wanted for fodder as long as there were hay crops on the Cree water or corn in the Glenkens. It was easy work taking down a bevy of horses and bringing up a supply – easier than cutting and winning the meadow hay upon their own sparse watersides.

It was therefore necessary for me to cross and take to the hills on the eastern side of the Dungeon, then make for the Wolf's Slock as fast as could, and trust to Providence after that. At least, so said Sammle Tamson, evidently thinking that Providence would be no improvement upon himself as a guide among the hills of the Dungeon.

CHAPTER XXIV.

A MEETING WITH BILLY MARSHALL

AS WE WENT I began to see my guide hanging back and halting on one foot, instead of bravely striding forward as he had done before.

"What is the matter, Sammle?" I said.

"We'll have to cross in the open," said Sammle Tamson, "and I don't like it."

Yet there was no one in sight to the east or south. We stood alone in a wide vacant area, more usually crawling in the heather, with only our noses peeping out.

"You see that large V the road takes there," said he, "that's a king's highway, although few of the king's men ever sets foot on it now. Do you wonder why it doesn't go in a straight line, like an ordinary road? It's because that bog down there is not safe. They say that King Robert, who came from Carrick, managed to trap a whole English army in that bog. Now, my man, if you're to get to the Wolf's Slock, there's only two options as far as I can see. To cross straight ahead is dangerous, but also a great deal faster. On the other hand, it's safer to go back to the Black Craig o' Dee and cross where the road winds like a snake, and you won't be seen."

Sammle looked at me to choose.

"On!" I said briefly.

"It's as I would have expected, but be aware that in half an hour both of us may be lying on the heather gasping like a couple of shot partridges."

Sammle began to crawl cautiously among the boulders, keeping to leeward of every stone. The dots of cattle and men were now so far away that caution seemed needless; I did not ask why he was taking such extraordinary care, for I had great trust in the moorman. It might be that the outlaws had watchers on all the tops, who could discern every movement of both beast and body on that great empty waste.

In ten minutes we were crossing the little Dee water, which there flows sluggish and brown from the peat mosses. It was deeper than I thought, and I had to hold my powder and pistols high up in order that they might stay dry. While we were crossing, we saw two decent-like men come out of the little farmstead of Craignell and wave to us with friendly gestures. They were so near that we could see them distinctly, and could make out the colour of their hair and the pearl buttons on their coats, and I was prepared to turn back to see what they wanted.

Sammle Tamson, however, became a different man as soon as he saw them.

"Run for it," he cried, and instantly turned towards the hill and went upward like a fox, turning and twisting so quickly that I could hardly follow him.

Over my shoulder I could see the men running through the heather, and waving at us to stop. It seemed a wrong to be running from men who I thought were decent moor folk, though at least one of them had matted unkempt hair like the outlaws.

But since Sammle ran, I ran too; and it was just as well, for in a moment, *Wang! Crack!* came a bullet and the sound of guns hard on the back of each other. Sammle was going at top speed, digging his staff into the earth as he went up the side of the hill, as if he was running with an extra leg.

Presently we reached what was one of the roughest parts of the country for heather and stones that I have ever seen. It is called, I hear, the Rig of Drumquhat, and whoever is its laird has a barren heritage and plenty heather. If it had not been for the latter, indeed, I think we would have been as good as dead. As soon as we had weaved ourselves into the thickest of it, Sammle dropped on his knees and put his hands on the ground and panted with his head down and his tongue out.

"Look out," he said between his gasps, "and see if you can see those blasted villains."

I said that I did, but they were far away, and going very slowly, as men that were not keen on their job.

"No!" he said." Young Billy Marshall is over fond of the brandy bottle and loose women to be a good hill runner."

"Billy Marshall!" said I, looking, I am sure, very puzzled about the mention of the name of the great smuggler. "Billy Marshall's in Holland, and doesn't dare show his face in Scotland any more than Johnny Faa himself."

" Well, Laird, believe me, that chap with the Roman nose was none other than Billy, or else I'm Billy myself. Just keep track of them, will you?"

And he lay down flat on the grass, with his arms wide and his hands limp and open.

Out of my heather bush I watched the glen. They had turned back to go into the house of Craignell again.

"There's something more attractive inside there, you can be sure," said Sammle. "You'll not be bothered with Billy joining the rascals you have to fight up by the Dungeon."

Then we set off again over two very desolate hills that are called, as Sammle told me, Craignell and Darnaw. We were high up on them and kept the crown of the causeway, the brown moors and grey rocks running from horizon to horizon beneath us.

So we believed we were safe for the moment. The sun was now beginning to sink, and a great bank of cloud was gathering over in the west, and we could hear the wind as it came to us on the mountain-tops.

"You'll have a dark night in the Wolf's Slock. It'll be as dark up there as the inside of the devil himself. But that'll make it easier for you."

I had a question to ask.

"I heard you say that Billy Marshall could easily come across the Channel from Holland. Now, is it your opinion that John Faa himself, who has a price on his head, might come as well?"

"There's no knowing," said Sammle "Faa might never have been out of the country since he broke with his clan. You know the Faas are considered gentry over by on the Border. And they say that Johnny Faa keeps away from his mother and brother since they took to cattle stealing and murder, but still gets his share of any money that is earned honestly. He takes no share of the cattle; but every penny that rattles in a beggar's wooden cup, or a copper that is given to him at an alehouse, Johnny Faa himself gets his tenth of it. He's treated as a kind of pope amongst them, though the ragged clan wouldn't remain civilised, and instead of doing nothing, would have fought for the Pretender, as Johnny would have preferred. Faith, they even say that Billy Marshall is afraid of the Faa himself. Johnny Faa is not supernatural but he comes and goes like a ghost, or like the wind – no-one knows where he goes or from where he comes."

Soon we were on the height above Cairndarroch Ford. Sammle did not cower now, but strode boldly down, staff in hand, kicking up the dust of the heather with his feet. When I asked him why his mood had changed, he said,"I'm less worried now. They believe the rear of the cattle herd is guarded by Billy Marshall at Craignell, where he is safe inside by now, drinking wine – a sweetheart sitting by each arm. If anyone saw us, they would think Billy was keeping a good watch, sending people to cross the country quickly to keep everything safe."

And it was as he said. When we got to the ford of the Dee Water, Sammle went splashing through, his feet casting up the water about him in a kind of glee, like a horse trampling into the Solway tide for a bath. Far up on the hillside somebody waved something white.

"Have you a napkin?" said Sammle."I have lost mine, and I'm loath to pull off my other shirt tail. Eppie made such a fuss about the last one. I'll tell you the story some other day, when we have less entertaining things about us."

I handed him my handkerchief that was not so white, but served his purpose, which was indeed no more than to wave back to the rascal who saluted us from the hilltop as we went through the ford. Sammle waved the napkin twice to his right hand and once to his left, touching the heather on each occasion.

"That means 'All well,' "he said; "three times round your head is 'Danger – Run!' and holding the napkin out at arm's length from your left hand is 'Wait till I come'; but that last one will be not much use to you."

We were now among the burnt heather, whistling as we went, and kicking up the ashy dust of the March moorburn with our feet. This dust got in Sammle's throat and kept him coughing.

"I think I have to leave you now, Rathan," he said. "I may have been a help to you so far, but any further and I'll be just a burden and a danger. I can do many things, but neither in the church or market can I keep from coughing when I get that dry itching in my throat. I expect I'm to be hanged, for its always in my Adam's apple that I have a prickling feeling as if I had eaten pepper-pods."

We were now high above the misty basin of Loch Dee, which we saw shining blue away in the hazy south, with the burn running out of it into the Cooran Lane. We could see with the prospect glass the drovers letting the cattle stray wide, watched only by boys, on the green meadows of the two Laggans by the loch side. A great number of the poor beasts were standing in the water of the loch cooling their travel-weary feet and drinking deep draughts.

We were now on the smooth side of the furthest spur of Millyea, the last mountain of the Kells Range, which stretched northwards, in a series of broad, rounded summits, like a school of porpoises in the Firth. I was astonished at their height and greenness, never having seen a green hill before, and I had supposed that all mountains were as rugged and purple with heather or as grey with boulder as my own Screel and Ben Gairn by the Balcary shore. But I now saw these as being specially granted by a kind Providence to provide secret caves and hiding places for our Solway smugglers.

On the other hand, it was thought to be a Divine judgment on the people of the Glenkens that their hills are so smooth that the comings and goings of men and horses upon them can be seen from afar, and the smoke of a still could be tracked for a whole summer day's journey. But then, again, had the Glenkens folk been able to supply themselves with whisky, the Solway farmers, like my friends the Maxwells, would have had to go farther afield in order to seek a market for their wares.

But things are wisely ordered, and amongst other things it was ordained that I should now be on the side of Millyea looking towards the great breastwork of the Dungeon of Buchan, behind which lay the outlaw country shrouded in dark and threatening mist.

CHAPTER XXV.

THE DUNGEON O' BUCHAN

NOW, because nothing can be more uncertain and uncanny than the changes of the weather in the Dungeon of Buchan, Samuel Tamson, that very honest man, and I were obliged to part. The thought of the poor lass, May Maxwell, was heavy on my heart, and I craved to see her, even if I could not rescue her – which in the disturbed state of the country, and the mountain men having won so great a victory at the Black Water of Dee, did not seem likely.

It was time to part, so we looked at one another and found nothing to say. Sammle Tamson turned on his heel. When he had gone maybe ten steps, he stopped, looked back and said to me,"The God of Jacob be your reward."

But even then I found nothing to say, and so parted with remorse. The great clouds were topping the black and terrible ramparts opposite to me. Along the long cliff line, scarred and broken by the thunderbolt, the clouds lay piled, making the Merrick, the Star, the Dungeon, and the other hills of that centre massif of the hill country look twice their proper height. The darkness drew swiftly down like a curtain. The valley was filled with a steely blue smother. From the white clouds along the top of the Dungeon of Buchan fleecy streamers were blown upwards, and swift gusts were forced down. Behind, the thunder growled like a continuous roll of drums, and little vivid flames played like devils' smiles about the grim features of Breesha and the Snibe.

The frowning rocks of the Dungeon lay beyond, and further north was that great hollow-throated pass through which still a peep of sunshine mistily shot down, and bore the grim name of the Wolf's Slock. It was that I had to climb. Although there was no light in it, it was by that route I would be best able to see the hell-brew of human activity that was going on up there. I lay down on the opposite slope on the grass and heather, looked upwards and reflected on my position. All the while, the wind came in curious extremes – now in mild, warm puffs and gusts, and then in sharp, cold blasts that froze the blood in one's veins.

It was then and for the first and last time, a kind of shuddering horror came over me, which I am now ashamed to think about. What right had I to be there? – when I might have sat safe and smiling on my Isle Rathan? Had anyone interfered with me there, that made me go and take up a stranger's quarrel? What a fool to bring myself so close to the point of a dagger – and that for someone who had no thought or tenderness for me, but only scoffs and jeers! I did not even know if she had not been playing with me. For all I knew she might have gone willingly enough on the pillion behind handsome Hector Faa, himself a brother to John Faa; a gentleman in upon the Borders; and who might even, when the turmoil died down, become respected. What was I, who might have been sailing in the tall ships to see strange lands (and I had enough money to do so) – eating breadfruit and drinking of the coco brew that is like wine and milk all at once – doing here on this perilous hill on such a desperate quest among desperate men?

But, truth to tell, I did not believe this unshakable logic. I did not believe in being cautious, and in my heart I only longed to meet Silver Sand and to come to grips with a dozen Faas on their own ground – at least until I could get first sight of the self-same smile that was on May Mischief's face when I called her "Impudent besom!" aloud that day, when my tongue slipped and I let the words slip from me unawares.

Thus I let Satan tempt me, but I resisted. However, he was not so easily deceived, for he flew away out of my heart, crying, "Fool, thou hast the desire to go, only so a slight girl may lead thee to the death – one that cares naught for thee." But I said to him, "Thou liest, Foul Thief, and if thou didst speak truth I do not care. I will go!" Whereat I felt mighty manly, and so rose and went.

But to decide is always easier than to do. Between me and the frowning ridges – now the colour of darkest indigo, with the mists clammily creeping up and down and making the rocks unwholesomely white, as if great slimy slugs had crawled over them – were the lanes of the Cooran, winding slow, leaden, and dangerous. And beyond them was the Silver Flowe of Buchan, where the little Marion had been drawn to her death either by the clinging sand or the dread arm of the water horse demon.

As I went the ground became wetter and boggier. My foot often sank to the ankle, and I had to shift my weight suddenly with an effort, drawing my imprisoned foot out of the oozy, clinging sand with a great "cloop," as if I had begun to decant some mighty bottle. Green, unwholesome scum on the edges of black pools frothed about my brogues, which were soon wet through. Then came a link of silver flat where to the eye, the sand was firm. This was a pleasant sight, but when I set foot on it a shivering flash like lightning flamed suddenly over it, and it gripped my feet like a vice. Had I not been shore bred, more particularly on the Solway, I could have perished. But I knew the trick of it, and threw myself flat towards the nearest bank of grass, kicking my feet free horizontally, and so crawled an inch at a time back to the firm peat again. Then I found a great shepherd's stick lying on a link of the Cooran - a wide, black, unkindly water, when seen under that gloomy sky, however it may appear in other circumstances.

It had been placed there by some shepherd who had business on the other side, or perhaps had been cast up by that dangerous water after it had drowned the man who used it.

But at any rate it was a fortunate for me, for this great staff, was more than two yards long and prodigiously stout, with a pike at one end, and on the other a crooked handle, close enough at its end to catch a sheep by the leg. I took it with gratitude, and I hope the man who left it there has never missed it. It was of great service to me, and, moreover, the chances were a hundred to one that the fellow was a Marshall, a Miller, or a Macaterick, for on the handle was a great M very roughly cut. Yet it was a good staff, and served me well, so why care about who made it? Thus in time, by the grace of God, and by taking great care, I crossed both the Silver Flowe of Buchan and the Links of the Cooran. It is always the custom in Galloway to share the credit of any victory with Providence, but to blame it entirely for any disaster. "Wasn't that well done," we say when we succeed. "We might as well give up," we say when we fail – a comfortable theology, shared by the majority of those Galloway men who took to the hills out of obstinacy, not fanaticism when Lag came riding with his mandates and letters judiciary.

CHAPTER XXVI.

THE WOLF'S SLOCK

BUT I had no such thoughts as I went up the side of the Dungeon towards the Throat of the Wolf. It was indeed obstinacy and not courage which took me there. I had done no harm that meant I should be afraid of any Faa. But all the same there was a small cold contraction about the pit of my stomach, where ordinarily my courage lies. Other folks may say that they feel bold as lions – at the heart – or have a mortal fear – at the heart. They are different to me, for it is low down, even in my stomach, that my courage lies.

The truth is I was most mortally afraid. To begin with, I was wet through – not that I minded that much in itself, for I was usually wet all day at the shore; but there the salt in the air, and the kindliness of the sea breeze, make it a comfortable wetness. Here, on the other hand, the wind off the hills had a cold nip about it, and seemed to freeze the very clothes on one's back. I also felt a sting of sleet on my face.

I clambered upwards through the great boulders and loose stones.

It was serious now. I could see only a hundred yards or so above me, but overhead the thunder was moaning and rattling, coming ever closer. There was a faint blue light, more unpleasant than darkness, high in the sky. Then little tongues of crawling cloud shot down, seemingly to snatch at me, but curling upward like the eyelids of an old man's eye as they came near me. I hated them.

As often as they approached there was a soft hissing, and the rocks grew dim and misty blue.

My hands stung at the thin fine skin in the webs of my the fingers. I had a strange prickling tightness about my brow, and my bonnet lifted. So for all my brave stubbornness, it was harrowing, and I do not know how I came through it. If I had to do it again, I believe that I would instantly turn tail and make for Rathan's Isle and its most defensible turret. Indeed I do not know how I continued, but certainly it was not out of courage.

What I least liked were the little spouts of stones that discharged themselves downward with a crash and a rattle. I don't why they did, since the clouds had not broken and there was no rainfall. They came with a dry noise, like bones rattling into a vault, as I'd heard once when they were clearing the Dullarg kirkyard to make room for new parishioners – a most unholy sound. I have wished many a time since that I had stayed at home and not gone to hear it – as in fact my father had asked me. So I got what I deserved.

Most of these spouts of stones fell onto great tails of stones that spread down the mountain's steep slopes, like rubble from a quarry dump. I had to cross some of these, which was both difficult and hazardous. Little sharp slate stones came down with a whizz, spinning like wheels, and passed quite close to my ear with a vicious *clip;* as when the teeth of a dog snaps when he bites and misses, but means to succeed the next time – a most vile feeling. One went past like a bullet of lead and clipped a piece of skin from my ear, which came nearly made me swear – which I never do, since it benefits no-one. But I ought rather to have said a prayer and given thanks, but that I did not do that either.

Then I came to one very wide spout, and I plunged my feet into it quickly and eagerly, because I wanted to get across as quickly as I could. But when I was half way across, everything began to move slowly beneath my feet, and immediately I felt dizzy and sick at the same time, because nothing is so unsettling as losing trust in the solid earth underfoot. I stood a moment till I felt the whole side of the hill, as it were, moving downward. Then I remembered the quicksand, and when I felt the motion of the stones speeding up, all slithering along as one, with an ominous rattling at the edges, I decided on a leap of faith. I flung myself out as flat on my stomach as I could and dug my fingers and toes, yes and my face too, into the moving stone slide.

We went slowly and slowly, and for some years (so it seemed, and I took careful note of the time), I could not tell whether we were going faster to fall or slower to stop. But I prayed more intensely than I had done for months. I resolved that if I could only get out of this I would be quite a different man. I made as many as sixteen promises that I would give up various sins, most of which I had been meaning to do for a long time, since they meant little to me. Then when I felt that the slide was speeding up, I added sixteen more sins, but those were ones that I really cared about. After that I called on Providence to do whatever it wished to me if I did not give all these sins up, if only this once I could survive this ordeal. (However, I had no intention of ever coming that way again). Then suddenly in the midst of my promises and petitions I remembered the great precipice which was below me, which I had admired as I lay safely on the opposite hillside. I had watched the spouts of white stones shoot over it and clatter against the rocks far below. I had seen ravens, too, flitting heavily about the face of that cliff; and eagles balancing themselves above. In my current predicament, I regretted that I remembered everything so clearly.

Would we never stop?

We must be near the top of the sheer fall by now – we were still moving, slowly, little by little, but still moving. Would this never come to an end?

I began to long for the fall and wonder if it would hurt much. One thing came into my mind and stayed there. I was glad I had called May Maxwell "Impudent Besom," but I regretted that I had not kissed her there and then. I even thought that she might have liked it. And I would have, certainly. But now it was too late.

We had stopped! No, we were moving on again. Stopped again! It was dark now for what seemed like several years, and I lay as dead with my hands dug into the sharp-edged silty gravel, my arms stiff-set in it to the armpits, my toes also covered, and all my soul and body strained, as one that is ready to be broken on the wheel and sets his teeth to bear the first wrench, praying only that it may be soon over.

I do not know how long I lay like that, daring not to breathe or move. Then, with infinite softness and caution, I began to move off, drawing out my arms inch by inch, and quivering with fear if a single slate stone the size of a crown coin clicked away downwards, or when the gravel moved an inch to fill up my empty arm hold. I did not mind so much about dying, but the picture of that great raven calling lustily to his mate, and plumping on the ground within two yards of me, chilled me to the bone. Again I cursed my imagination – which, indeed, has been unwelcome to me, since it made me endure not one but many deaths by anticipation.

For example, as I lay there I could see the black fiend alighting close to me with an interrogative croak, cocking his rough head to the side. I could see him keeping his wings a little off his sides ready for flight, and the purple gloss on his black satin cloak, with his beak sharp as a chisel. He waddled a foot nearer, gave a 'Craw' to alarm me, then hopped to my head, took a look round, and.....There was, I declare, a horrid pain in my eye as I lay on the loose slate heaps. For a moment, I thought that the raven had struck it out. And that is just one example of the way my vivid imagination worked for me.

As I crawled and wriggled across that wide spout of rock, I felt as if all my interior and vital parts were missing. Now I would crawl a yard; then I would lie all so cold and still, so that even the stones felt warm and soft athough they were cutting my hands, and ice was forming on them where they had been wet.

Eventually I was clear and sitting on a solid knuckle of rock that shot up from the ribs of the mountain, which was more comfortable to me at that moment than the great armchair at Rathan, in which indeed I now sit and write.

I was trembling like a leaf. One moment I chattered with heat, and the next shivered with cold. I was drenched with perspiration, and then when I had time to look I saw that my hump of rock was right on the edge of a deep overhang. Blue-white mist was surging up from beneath on some reverse current and boiling over the lip of the cauldron. The reason I had not heard the stones falling over the edge of the slide, was that they fell so far that they returned no noise up here. There, too, was the raven, black against the darkness, sitting like the devil I had dreamed of, cocking his eye at me from a neighbouring rock.

Such is the nature of man, that this lifted my spirits. I taunted the raven with names. I threw stones at him. I pulled out my silver flask and toasted him, calling him "old Mahoun" – which seemed to annoy him, because he rose abruptly, which he had not even done during all the stone-throwing. He sailed away, crying as he went something that sounded like, "Till another day!"

My courage had returned to me, and I pressed upward into the belt of cloud. I was well within the Wolf's Stock now, and found it as dark as I had been told. The iron pike of my staff shone with scintillating light as it touched the rocks, and I again had the prickling feeling all over my body. But somehow the tingling air dried me, and thus probably kept me from taking my death of cold.

And so ever upward I went. I did not rest, because I had a kind of strength and a desire to see the thing through, which greatly supported me when it lasted.

It was comparatively quiet where I was, but the wind shrieked and howled among the teeth of the shattered rocks above. It yelled overhead as I got nearer to the top. Yet hardly a breath reached me, except some hissing down-draughts of chill wind that came and went in a minute. I thought that I would be lucky in the darkness to find the shelter of a rock, or the space between two that might act as shelter from the rain. But suddenly everything changed.

I came to the summit suddenly like getting to the edge of a wall when a comrade gives a hoist up. The wind met me like a knife, and cut me in two – the lower part of me being warm behind the wall of rock and the top half nearly devoid of feeling; also the rain drops were driven level like bullets. I had on a coat that buttoned, a waistcoat with flaps, and other things beneath; but the rain drops were able to reach my naked skin, as though I had no more on me than a ladies' handkerchief that she uses to hold scent to her nose in church. As for my face, I had to bend my neck and put the crown of my hat to the blast.

Yet I could not stay there all night like a fly on a wall, and though the discomfort was infinite, the fear I was in of another stone spout was far greater. So without stopping to think, I set my elbows and then hands upon the brink and pulled myself up. Thereafter, for some minutes I could do nothing but lie prone among the rocks, gasping for breath like a trout on the bank.

However, there was no advantage to that, in fact very much the reverse, for it was as chill up there as it is an hour before a March snowstorm. I stood up and went stumbling forward, all the time feeling with my pike for the stones and hollows. Sometimes I fell over a lump of heather. Sometimes my foot skated on a slippery granite slab and fell flat on my face; yet strangely I felt no pain, either then or afterwards, perhaps owing to the quivering excitement I was in.

In this way, I advanced for some way, blindly and doggedly – beaten so deaf and dumb, dazed and stupid by the tempest, that I did not know whether I was living or dead – nor cared.

CHAPTER XXVII

IN WHICH BY THE BLESSING OF PROVIDENCE I LIE BRAVELY

SUDDENLY my pike struck something that was neither stone nor peat bog. It seemed strange to me, having recently experienced a prolonged strain of unfamiliar experiences things, to encounter something familiar. I struck again and again. It was like an outhouse or a wooden door. What good fortune, I thought! Some shepherd's shelter with a sheep pen, used during the nights of the recent lambing time which in the hills had barely finished.

But I heard a commotion inside above the noise of the storm. I struck again, louder. Like a flash a door opened and a great light blazed in my eyes, which blinded me. A number of men sprang on me all at once, and dragged me in. The door was shut, and there was a knife at my throat.

Then I thought I would rather be back in the stone spout of the Wolf's Slock. I was certainly out of the throat, but now I found myself in the wolf's teeth. I had clipped the wings of the raven but I was in the eagle's claws – although I did not think so poetically at the time.

But even though I did not see anything clearly then, being dazzled – all of what I saw as they dragged me in is printed on my memory indelibly – vivid, white and clear as the angry sea with a struggling ship upon it nearing the breakers, which I once saw off Rathan Head by a flash of lightning. So, though blurred at the time, the outlines of all that passed is now clear in my mind.

As the dark men dragged me forward I saw another two of the same breed, curly-haired, olive-skinned men, hastily crushing something heavy into a chest in a little back room, on the floor of which there stood a candle. A smooth-faced old woman with white hair was sprinkling sand all over the floor of the kitchen, and a great butcher's knife lay plain to see on a pine table. A fire blazed in a wide ingle, and the roof was hung with hams – a cheerful place on such a night, yet somehow it felt sinister.

But all the while I saw this the knife was at my throat. The point drove inward and pricked.

The old woman seemed to finish her task, and looked up.

"Let be, Gil," she said, standing with a handful of white sand in one hand and a foul red cloth in the other. "Let be; first ask him his name,"

The word "first" stuck in my throat, further in than the knife.

"Your name?" said one of the men kneeling on my breast.

I would have answered gladly, but instead I only cried hoarsely like a rough-legged fowl.

"Your name?" cried he of the long locks again, setting his knee in my ribs till I thought he would send my immortal soul flying out of my mouth as a chewed cloth bullet is shot from a boy's popgun.

"Speak!" he yelled, more fiercely than ever.

It was a most unreasonable request in the circumstances, yet as my eyes goggled I tried to speak, but instead I only crowed like a cock. The others pulled the man off and propped me up against the side of the fireplace.

"No hurry,"they said, giving him a look that went to deeper to my marrow than the knife. I began to prefer Gil's approach. I always took medicine quickly, and there are worse ways of dying than by the knife – which indeed is nothing after the first cut, in the way a pin does not hurt when you put it into the thick of your leg up to its head, after the first prick of the skin. A ploy which you can try or take my word for, just as you please.

"Hand him a drink," said the old woman, with a face was as smooth as an eggshell but a look as false as a pine door painted mahogany.

They gave me something that tasted like liquid fire and it burned as it ran down. I began to find my power of speech.

"Now, honey, your name? " said the old woman softly, putting back her white locks. Her hair was yellow white of a strange dry texture, but there was a dirty rusty mark across it as if she had wiped something upon it – her hand or a knife, perhaps. For me, they were altogether too ready with both in this house.

"Patrick Burgess,"said I, telling as little of a lie as I could. Burgess was my mother's name, and as I was her sole heir and successor, surely that name was mine too – if it was anybody's.

"Aye, Patrick Burgess," said she. "It is a fine name, and whaur micht ye come frae, Patrick?"

Her use of dialect reassured me a great deal. No one could speak good Galloway Scots and be a complete blackguard. But I was soon to find out.

"I come from New Abbey," I said.

"You are far from home, lad," said Mother Eggface, speaking softly, but with a dangerous glint in her eyes that made me uneasy. "What brought you so far on such a night?"

She might well ask that.

So I prayed to the Almighty that I might be enabled to lie convincingly. Certainly, I intended to do my best.

"I am a pedlar by trade," said I. "I am on my way to Dalmellington, and I have lost my way."

I was satisfied with this last statement comforted me mightily, for by accident it was true. I had indeed lost my way.

"Good Master Pedlar, Patrick Burgess, bound from the New Abbey, and where might your pack be? Have you also lost that?"

She had fallen back into English, which, apart from its use in the Bible, I did not care for. There was also a dry and deadly mockery in her tone, which made me dislike this old woman most of all of them.

"Let him settle first, and hear his story after," said one of the men genially. "He'll carry it about him somewhere."

Eggface looked at him with a glance like the light on a new knife when the blue sky is reflected on the untarnished blade, and he sat down and took a drink, saying no more for a while.

But I lied on and on for my very existence, and I never stopped praying, and I think I was helped, although whether this came from above or below I cannot say.

"I am on my way to Dalmellington to take delivery of a new pack of goods brought by the carrier from Glasgow," I ventured.

"What is the name of that carrier?" put in a man from the back.

"Richard Brown, and a decent man," said I, like a flash.

Now either Providence or you-know-who was at my elbow, and I answered promptly, as I would at a church service. There was never such lying since the Garden of Eden and I did not know I could master it so well.

The man at the back grunted and began whittling a stick.

Knives again – plenty of knives.

I was relieved, not so much that Silver Sand had told me in one of his many stories of this Dalmellington carrier's name, as that I had remembered it – for I find names hard to remember, particularly in my later years.

"What did you say your name was?" said the old dame again, looking at me with her gimlet eyes. Why would a woman have eyes with three-cornered pupils that look at you like bayonets?

"Patrick Burgess," said I.

I had almost said "Heron" before I remembered, and might have done were it not for the thought of the knife. Iron sharpens iron, and also my wits.

She turned round. "Ivie," she said, abruptly.

A great hulk lying in the corner grunted.

"Kick him awake somebody," she ordered, without looking at the lout, still keeping her eyes fixed on me.

The long-haired tyke called Gil took my piked staff and thrust it into his ribs, which made the giant grunt, exactly like a great swine that lies in the filth of the sty when you poke it.

"Rise and speak to granny," said he of the locks.

"A sweet granny," thought I but all the same I tried to appear happy, thawing myself in front of the fire, and thinking up more lies. However, for me, lies like mine should not be planned. They must come spontaneously or not at all.

The hog arose.

The hog rubbed his midrib and grunted a question. He wanted to know why he had been woken up.

Granny turned her eye on him and said, "Do you know anyone of the name of Burgess in New

Abbey?"

The hog scratched his bristles, grumbling.

"Show him the staff!"she said;"he'll fall asleep again."

Gil took up the staff and dug it in once more, this time strong and fierce.

Whereupon Hog turned like a wildcat, snarling with a flash of white teeth, and red murder leaping up in his eyes like flame at the touch-hole of a musket.

"Can't you leave a man alone; I'll knife the next brute,"he said, recognising his comrade's position in the group.

Then he rubbed his head, and said slowly, "Man of the name of Burgess in New Abbey? Yes, there's Isaac Burgess, the pig dealer – a fine man, and a friend of mine."

For my sins – this was my uncle, the brother of my mother and as rank a rogue as ever smelled Holland's gin.

"Here is a nephew of his, or says he is. Sit up and see if you know him." It was a trying moment.

"Aye," said the hog, slowly,"you look like him – you'll be the son of John who left and became a packman!"

"Well said, hog!" I thought, but yet if it is true that I resemble my uncle, it is no wonder that I have had little success with women. For, indeed, he was as ugly as sin.

But for the time being, I was safe. As far as they were concerned, I was a pedlar, and I had told the truth. At this there was a general easing of the tension. The men began to polish up their guns and pistols.

This reminded Gil – that long-haired thief – of some unfinished business. He walked over to me and said, "Your pistols are in your way. I'll look after them for you."

The other men turned to see how would I take this.

I gave the weapons to him, pulling them out of my belt, as well as my clasp knife with the horn handle, which I also gave him. Then I lay back and stretched as if I was glad to be rid of them.

I began to relax slightly, but I now felt my throat, where Gil's knife had been, grow sorer than ever. I was roasting in front of the fire, gradually drying off. The old woman came to stir the pot now and again. She kept eyeing me as I toasted first one foot and then the other, taking off my wet brogues to do it, and commented on the cleanliness of the house. I told them what a night it was outside, and how glad I was to have a roof over my head.

"Indeed," said Granny Eggface,"it's not a night to let a dog outside, let alone a lad like you. But you are well away from the road to Dalmellington, lad. What took you up the Wolf's Slock? I didn't think Dalmellington lay on top of a hill I heard!"

"I was striking a short cut for Loch Doon," said I, for lying now came as easy as breathing. I toasted my feet at the fire, setting them on the hot hearthstone to dry. The pot boiled and let out little puffs of steam, and gave a warm and comfortable smell, full of promise. I began to feel more at home.

Eggface went to the foot of a ladder that reached up to a room above – it seemed to me to be a mere garret, under the roof. "Come down, child," she said in a more human tone than I had yet heard her use.

"This might help. When a child comes in, the devil flies out at the window!"I said to myself, as I heard a light foot on the stairs. But I forgot that he would return.

A little girl of six came downstairs, looking terribly thin and pinched; despite being a well-grown girl, and one that would soon fill out with proper nourishment.

The old woman set her to washing the tables and laying wooden basins round the board. I counted them. There was none set for me. This was not so good, for I was starving, and had no food of my own.

But I kept watching the child. She was, as I said, pinched and haggard but her eyes were full and clear. Yet she shrunk at the least sound, and only answered "Yes" and "No" when she was directly spoken to. One of the men kicked her as she passed, because in looking to her plates she had stumbled over his foot. The kick only a slight one, which would not have hurt even if it had reached her. But the girl winced and moaned, with a look of fear that disturbed me.

Granny Eggface turned sharply with a questioning look, holding a heavy potato masher in her hand. Her eye flushed into sudden anger as she noted the cause. With a strength that I could not have believed from that skinny body, she struck the fellow with the heavy end of the masher on the side of his thick head making a dull sound, and stretched him senseless along the wall.

"I'll teach you to meddle with the bairn," she said. "The next time we'll find out what you have inside you, you halfwit!"

The other men laughed a little at this, saying, "Served him right, Granny, the big bully!"

And even the Hog laughed aloud, till the stricken man, stirring, looked evilly at him. Gil, who, under Granny Eggface, seemed to be somewhat of a leader, set a poker to his backside and told him to get up. This he did sulkily, and with an unpleasant expression in his face.

When the supper was served it was a fragrant stew of all sorts of meat, boiled with vegetable to a kind of pottage, and very nutritious.

The men spoke among themselves in a language of which I could not understand, and the old woman joined them with the occasional word.

The little girl and I sat apart. She dipped a tin skillet in the pot and gave it to me with a whole partridge in it, and much of the fragrant stew. I thought it was a good opportunity to thank Eggface for her hospitality, and to say that it was a blessing that there was such a house in so wild a place.

"Aye," she said, dryly, "it's fortunate in more ways than one. We often have a visitor for a night, but they seldom stay much longer. The air up by Loch Enoch and the Dungeon, is very hard on the health, you see!"

"What kind of travellers come mostly?" I asked, as carelessly as I could.

"Oh, nearly every sort," said Eggface. "We had a stranger last night, who has only just left us, and, indeed, we have hardly cleaned up after him yet."

Gil frowned and shook his head at her. But the old witch-wife only chuckled and laughed to herself.

"Away," she said to Gil, "it'll be just the same in a hundred years – or perhaps even less."

Which was thought among them to be an extraordinary fine joke, and the whole table laughed at it wholeheartedly. For my part I could not see not the point of the joke – and I still don't – and why the telling of it created such laughter. But it's easy for the headmaster to get a laugh in school, especially if he is standing with the belt in his hand.

"What kind of goods do you travel in?"asked the old lady when they were at supper, looking over her shoulder at me.

I told her dress pieces remnants, laces, Welsh flannel, and other things for the farmer's wives and maids of Galloway and Ayrshire.

"How do you pay for them in Dalmellington?"

"With the money I got for the last pack,"I said, thinking myself particularly clever. "I have it with me now!"

CHAPTER XXVIII.

THE BLACK SEA-CHEST

I THOUGHT this was my best shot. It was, in fact, my worst, and undid any good that might have accrued to me from the lies that I had told before. It was ever thus. It's like renting one of the devil's farms. It is of little use. His leases are too short, and there are no compensations for disturbance.

I had barely spoken when I saw the whole party look at one another, and the little lass steal away with a quivering lip. She slipped quietly upstairs.

"What's that you're taking up the stairs?"cried the old woman, sharply.

"Just a basin of stew," said the little girl.

"Come here, and let me see it," commanded the old lady.

"Now, you'll be tired," said Grannie a little while later, "and you had better go to your bed, my man, for we must be up early in the morning. I have no lazy bones in my house."

I said I was in agreement with this.

At that she lit a candle of the thinnest kind, and showed me into the little back room, the door of which had stood open all the evening. It was furnished with a low stool, a bed, and a great black sea-chest.

"And a good evening to you," said the old woman, as she shut the door.

So there I stood, with my brogues in one hand and my candle in the other, and surveyed my narrow chamber. I turned down the bedclothes.

They were clean sheets that had only been slept in once or twice. But I turned down the sheet also, for I am particular in these matters. Something black and glutinous was clogged and hardened on the bed. So I turned over the bed. The dark, red stuff had soaked through and dripped onto the earthen floor. It was not yet dry, though some sand had been thrown upon it. I did not need to examine the substance more closely to determine its nature. I felt sick, and felt my time was up. But it was necessary that I should make the best of things, even if I were to die.

So I then lifted the lid of the great sea-chest.

Merciful Heaven! In there was the back of a dead man, broad and naked. There were two open gashes on the right side, livid and ghastly. The rest of the man seemed to be cut up and piled within, the way a winter bullock is pressed into a salt barrel ready for the brine.

Now the God who had preserved me from so many perils, and has forgiven me for the lies I told, once again came to my assistance.

At any rate, down to His supreme and undeserved mercy that I did not pass out in shock then, or let the lid of the great chest fall with a clang. However, I put it down very softly, took off my coat, and knelt down to pray. And as I knelt, I was aware that someone came to the door and spied upon me through the latch-hole, then went and reported what he saw, whereupon there was much laughter.

While I knelt in the silence after the great guffaw of laughter, I heard the noise of a woman sobbing somewhere above; not the child, but the slower, sharper sob of a woman.

Also somewhere else in the house someone was sharpening a knife.

As I rose to my feet a folded piece of paper fluttered down from a crack in the black boards of the ceiling. I took it in my hand as I went shuffling towards the bed. There was writing upon it.

"For God's sake try the window. You are near your end by cruel men. The Murder Hole gapes wide. A friend writes this."

Then written below in smaller characters –

"If by any chance you that read are Patrick Heron, I that write am May Maxwell. But whoever you are, God pity you!"

Again the Lord of Hosts was my help, since I could have died then, overcome by the wonders that surrounded me and overladen with the horrors I had experienced.

The Murder Hole – its name was foul and notorious. There had long been a legend of such a place in the stories that went around the countryside, and made our flesh creep as we told tales by the fire in the winter evening. I had never accepted its existence, believing it to be foolish chatter; but now it seemed likely that I would discover some proof concerning it.

Yet I went to the bed and threw myself down, firstly taking a look at the window to see what kind of fastenings were used. They were of thick wood, but looked old and worm-eaten.

As I lay on my bed a whirling universe of thoughts buzzed through my mind and huge, dark clouds tracked each other across my brain. Yet, despite that, I was in danger of falling asleep. Indeed I must have, for I awoke with a start of horror. A cold sweat burst over me as I realised my position. I sprang to the window and tried it. It was tightly fastened. I had to kneel on the sea-chest for a while, and cold thrills ran up my spine, like darning needles of ice.

I groped round for something to use as a lever. By good fortune my hand touched my own staff which Gil had thrown there when he had finished exploring the Hog's ribs with its iron prod. I took it, and inserted the point under the frame between the stone wall and the wood. Being glazed only with sheepskin the window, there was no need to worry about the jangling of glass when it gave outward. I threw myself at the little square of open space. There was a swirl just then, and only a slight cold draught sucked in. Had the opening been on the stormy side, the gust would have roused the men who slept or lay on the floor in the next room.

I was outside in a moment and had replaced the window, so I might have more time without discovery. I found myself in a narrow passage between the rock of the hillside and the wall of the cottage, which was all but built against the precipice.

Climbing up the rock I crept slowly along the thatch, feeling for an opening into the room from where the letter had fallen. With a throb of fear that was almost overpowering, my hand suddenly encountered a hand stretched out in the darkness – a human hand which closed upon mine. It was as startling as though if had come up from the grave; but it was warm and small, and was in no doubt whatsoever that it was the hand of May Maxwell, whom in my heart I called May Mischief.

I pulled the little hand but the little hand pulled me down. In a moment my ear was close to her lips. There was only a little unglazed skylight, like the window below, but far too small to let any one through.

"Run for your life, Patrick! Oh, they are cruel! They show no mercy!"she said.

"I shall never go without you," said I. "What! Leave you – the one that I came to save?"

"You must," she said. "They will not kill me. And….and….I have a knife!"

"Give me the knife!"I said.

She leapt down like a feather and handed up to me a great knife, which was almost like a sword set in a haft.

I quickly cut away the thatch till I felt the skylight was about to fall on the floor. "Catch it, May," I said softly and the next moment the iron frame gave way and fell into her lap, for in the darkness she was holding out her dress, as I had asked her.

She laid this down so that there was no noise.

"But the little maid," she said, "she is in the next room asleep?"

"They will not harm her. We must get help," I said hastily, to get May away for, to my shame, I thought only of her.

She tripped down again, swung a bag about her by a strap, and was beside me in a twinkling.

We slid off the roof and found ourselves on the ground in a moment. Then hand in hand we stole out of the lee of Craignairny into the wild war of the elements. The wilder the better for us. I had thought to try for the Wolf's Stock again, but two things were against that; first, the murderers knew that that was the way I had come and, second, there was that terrible spout of broken stone which needed to be crossed.

We stood towards the west along the margin of a loch that was lashing its waves on a rocky shore – a wild, tormented chaos of greyness. This I now know to have been Loch Enoch. Since then I have more than once followed our route that night with men of the hills who knew the ground, so that I am now able to give the names of the localities, which I had not been able to do then when the places were as new to me as the city of Solomon.

CHAPTER XXIX.

THE MURDER HOLE

IT seemed as though we had only gone a hundred yards when behind us we heard a fearsome crying "The pedlar has escaped – the pedlar has escaped! Loose the bloodhounds!"

At this threatening cry May and I instantly set off running at the top speed, and by the guiding of Providence we managed to run a long way, keeping our feet somehow among those slippery screes that lie between Craignairny and Craig Neldricken.

It was indeed an eerie night. The wind shrieked overhead, passing above us in a constant screaming yell, that sometimes sharpened into a whistle and later dulled into a roar. There was no moon but the storm-clouds had thinned, and soon the mist lifted. The wind scattered the thick, white clouds and threw a strange semi-darkness over the wild moorland.

Behind us we now heard that most terrible of sounds – the baying of bloodhounds on the trail of blood. May Maxwell ran steadily, with her hand in mine.

"I have another knife; you carry that now!" she said.

"But you may need it," I urged.

"Indeed I may," she said; "but I want to carry my skirt."

I thought I understood women. So do you. We are both in the wrong, my good man – we know nothing about the matter.

Behind us on the uneven wind, high above its top note, rose the crying of the hounds.

"How many?" I said, succinctly.

"Two," she said as briefly.

We came to the bed of a little burn that trickled down the steep sides of the Clints of Neldricken. I went first, feeling with my staff striking from side to side like a blind man because of the darkness.

Sometimes as we scrambled down I would catch her by the waist and carry her many yards before I set her down, then ran on just as fast as though I had been carrying a feather. So we ran our wild race, and I think gained on our pursuers.

Lanterns began to dance on the slopes above us – that grim land, the outlaw's fortress, which we were leaving. Only the booming of the dogs came nearer. We ran on down and down so lightly it almost felt as if we were flying. We passed a little tarn among the rocks which is called Loch Arron, and then on again among the heather.

Suddenly in trying to lift May Maxwell I stumbled all my length on a heap of stones, dashing myself on the sharp corners till I felt the rough granite scrape my flesh.

I fell and hit my head on a stone, and knew no more.

When I came to, May Maxwell had me in her arms, and was trying to stagger away from the place where I had fallen; but it was too much and we dropped down together on the heather.

I passed out again. I seemed to lie for a long time devoid of speech and hearing, the blood draining from my head and my brain reeling.

But I had a dream which was more vivid than the yelling of the bloodhounds.

It was a dream, but one of those which had great clarity. I thought that May Maxwell took me in her arms, saying, "I will kiss him once before I die. Only once – for I love him and he is mine. He came on his own to find me, when my own family had forsaken me. And he did find me, and we shall die together."

Then in my dream May Maxwell gave me not one but many kisses, and laid me down. I knew it must have been a dream. It could not be otherwise.

It was bright when I awoke as the sky was now clear of clouds. I saw May Maxwell with a knife in either hand, looking so different that I hardly knew her. She crouched like a lithe, wild cat ready to spring, and there was a glint of fire in her eyes. The sound of baying, and the soft gallop of feet on the heather came from not far away. Then like a bolt came a great dog out of the darkness, with white fangs dripping froth. Making no sound, it sprang at May, but with the knife in her hand this girl, the one that had held up her skirt as she ran, thrust the steel with more force than many a man into the open mouth of the beast, which fell roaring and snapping upon the iron. Yet she recovered the weapon and struck again and again. Then another brute sprang past her towards me as I lay helpless, for it was my trail the dogs were following. But my bravest girl drove sideways with her knife as the dog came on; yet so heavy and fierce was the beast that it brushed the knife aside, and would have fallen full upon me had she not thrown herself across me.

The beast seized her left arm and bit savagely before, with her right hand free, she struck home with the knife that had killed the first hound. The brute rolled over, and with a long whine like a whipped puppy, it died.

Then came the dancing rows of lanterns, and I knew that we must be doomed. But there was the spirit of an army of men in this girl, for she knelt over me with my bleeding head on her knee, leaned her back to the rock, and waited.

It would not be good for the first man who would come upon us.

We we were on a platform on the north side of Loch Neldricken, but close to the waterside. There was a strange thing below us. It was at the western end of the loch, where it looked as level as a bowling green, and in daylight the same colour, but in the middle there was a black round eye of water, oily and murky, as though it was bottomless and the water seemed to arch up in the middle. It was fearsome to look upon.

As she knelt over me May Maxwell pointed it out to me, with the knife which was in her hand.

"That is their Murder Hole," she said," but if we are to lie there we shall not lie there alone."

The lights of the pursuers were dancing now among the heather, and their cries came from here and there, scattered and broken.

In a little, waiting together, we could see Gil clear against the sky. He also could see us, for he cried out to the outlaws behind him.

But in that moment of great terror, suddenly something vast and terrible sprang past us – a shaggy beast infinitely greater than the dead bloodhounds, followed by another beast, less in size but even swifter in action. They were the same we had seen together that first night in the kirkyard of Kirk Oswald. They flashed out of sight and disappeared in the direction of our pursuers.

It was the Ghost Hunters that hunted only at the Dark of the Moon.

Gil turned in his tracks and began to flee.

"The Loathly Beasts!"we heard them cry. "The Witch Dogs are out!"

Then there was a shriek of pure animal terror, the lights were darkened, and the cries came from everywhere – but not now of hunters encouraging each other, rather of men fleeing singly in the deadliest terror and crying out as they ran.

"Oh, the Beasts – they are not of this earth," cried May, holding my hand tightly."Oh, Patrick, do not pass out again and leave me all on my own."

On this, I sat up and looked about. The two dead beasts were lying there. May took a napkin out of her bag and very tenderly wiped my face. Then she put it back and dropped, unconscious herself, into my arms.

So we were lying side by side when suddenly Silver Sand came and found us. We had been so close to the dead bloodhounds that they had blown their bloody froth upon us in their last gasps. Silver Sand brought water from Loch Neldricken to throw on May's face.

"Not from the Murder Hole," I cried in terror, "from the burn."

So he went again and brought it and she awoke.

"What was that terrible beast?" she said, clutching me.

"It was no greater beast than myself," said Silver Sand,"my twisted arms are turned the wrong way about for some good purpose. It was only a matter of a furry coat, a little phosphorus, and Quharrie."

"But we must leave.Can you move?"he asked anxiously.

"I think so," I answered cautiously.

He tried my limbs and got me to my feet.

"Where does it hurt?"he asked.

"In my head," I said.

"That's fine,"said he, "that's thick enough. Now try to walk."

I soon found that, though dizzy, I could still walk a little. So we set off with May Maxwell and Silver Sand supporting me.

The night wind blew on my wounded head, cooling it, and May Maxwell's arm was about me. I could have walked to Jericho.

"There's horses at the Gairland Burn," said Silver Sand, encouragingly. "It was touch and go that time, though, but we'll beat them yet."

CHAPTER XXX.

A WOOING NOT LONG A-DOING

IT was no doubt partly due to my wound, but also exhilaration, which made me spring forward as if I was flying. The blow to my head, the bitter conflict I had seen, yet been unable to take part in and the sweet dream I had dreamed, all acted on my senses like wine on an empty stomach.

There was no one like May Maxwell, and I had seen her fight for me. This is what I kept thinking.

And who could blame me?

We were making down the glen of the Midburn as swiftly as we could. We could hear it rushing, as if it was as eager to escape from the Accursed Country as we ourselves. Silver Sand kept his ears set backwards; and Quharrie, instead of marching before us as usual, patrolled behind us, going from side to side, and occasionally taking a run up over the rugged boulders on the side of Meaul which rose above us.

"I think they have had a bellyful," said Silver Sand.

"The Faas?" I questioned.

"No – not the Faas," he said, with a sudden and strange temper, "why are you talking about the Faas. Those vagabonds were not Faas. They were Macatericks – of bad black blood."

"Does that matter?" I said. They could be Faas or the devil as far as I was concerned, I only wanted them to leave us alone.

We passed a large sheep pen on our left. Silver Sand pointed it out.

"Had the worst come to the worst," he said, "we might have had to fight in that place against a dozen Macatericks."

We saw it only dimly through the starlight, so we could not pick out the great stones of which it was built, set firm and solid upon a foundation of the most ancient rocks of the world. But I had finished with fighting. There was a smell of blood in my nostrils, and I kept thinking of that poor fellow's body in the sea-chest. I could not rid myself of it.

Then we went off again, Silver Sand, though he was both twisted and slender, was almost carrying me in his arms, and May Maxwell, in silence, helping even more than he. We were soon at the Loch Valley, and heard the crunching of the granite sand along its margin underfoot. It was on the feet after the miles of heather. We left the loch behind us, with its crisp white sandy shore. It seemed to run a great distance eastward, with its little waves lapping against the ledges of its rocky basin.

A watcher from somewhere cried out a word at us, and in the same tone and tongue he was answered by Silver Sand – the sudden voices sounding startling on the chill night air. But whether he was one of the outlaws, or an ally of Silver Sand I did not know then. There was something glimmering in front of us. This roaring white torrent was just the Gairland Burn seen through the darkness, and I began to wonder how far away were the horses. Surely they were not far away now?

"Courage," said Silver Sand,"they are under that star!"

Which was a comfort – but then again, so was Rome.

"If they are more than a mile I'll be exhausted," I said,"I can go on further."

"They are within half a mile," he said gently, as if he was speaking to a complaining child.

So we went on. May Maxwell was so attentive and kind, that tears rolled down my cheeks when I thought of her and of her goodness. Even in the starlight she seemed to have some kind of second sight, since whenever blood from my wound was in danger of running into my eyes, she wiped it with some linen, soft as napkin, which she carried with her. The touch of her hand upon me was gentle as gossamer and cool as the night.

"The horses are at the Gairland!"said Silver Sand again."Courage – Laird."

A poor laird, poor as his lairdship. But the pressure of May Mischief's hand was more helpful than the words of Silver Sand.

We heard a curlew crying periodically in the darkness down by the side of the burn.

Silver Sand paused, put his hand to his mouth like a trumpet, and beat softly upon it with the other.

Instantly the tremulous whirr like a snipe when it drops sideways began in the air above us, so marvellously imitated, that we could hardly believe that it was possible. However, it was something I could also do well myself, as you shall hear. For some time now we had been descending rapidly, and the exertion of going downward seemed to send the blood to my head. I reeled and quivered and I began to fall.

May Maxwell slipped from my arm and went in front of me."Put your hands on my shoulders,"she said, "and lean on me as you go."

"But I might hurt you," I said.

"You will hurt me far more if you don't." she replied quickly.

I still hesitated, but Silver Sand, who walked beside me with his arm about me, said, "Do as the lassie tells you. She has good sense – better than you."

I thought that was rather hard on me, having done so much that night, before Quharrie and his master arrived. But from the front, from where she could not see me, May Maxwell said, "But Patrick had good sense too, or I would not have been here by now."

"Good!" said Silver Sand, and that was all he said.

As we went it was a delight to lean my hands on May Maxwell's little shoulders, one after the other, but unfortunately the ground was too uneven to permit me to place them both there at once.

But a strange warm magic – white magic – passed up my arm and settled happily about my heart.

Suddenly we came to more level ground. The terrible pressure upon my wounded head, which came from going downhill, ceased; and some large moving shapes emerged out of the dim starlight.

Silver Sand ran forward and said some words. A man stole off, up the waterside, jumping across it in running skips like a dipper bird. We were on the verge of the little island called Gale Island, and the man ran westward along Loch Trool. Three ponies stood patiently tethered together, Silver Sand helped me onto one.

"Can you sit?" he said.

I could sit, indeed, but I was not so sure about riding.

Then we began moving steadily along the edge of Loch Trool. The path was no more than a peat waggon track, and rough beyond the understanding of southern folk. Silver Sand went first, I came next, and May Maxwell came last but she seemed to be lagging.

I turned as best as I could.

"Ride across the pony, May," I said; "this is a terrible road, and you have no saddle".

But she did not answer. She had always ridden that way in the old days when she tormented me during my visits to Craigdarroch to collect the milk. But although in the past she had a quick tongue, now she was silent. Although dawn was about to break, it was still very but I think she did as I asked, at least until we were past the difficult narrows of Glen Trool.

I could still hear the curlew we had heard when we came down the Glen of the Gairland, and its cry from the blackness of the birchwood was very comforting.

The day was breaking as we reached a great height above the lake and paused for a moment to breathe our sturdy ponies.

"May!" I said, softly.

Her pony was behind me, but she did not move forward.

"May!" I said again.

She still didn't come, yet she must have heard me.

"Oh, my head!"I said, and she was at my side in a flash.

"Does it hurt?" she said; and by the tremble of her voice I am sure she was close to weeping out of sympathy. I felt guilty as my head was no worse than it had been.

She came up close so that she could touch my brow by leaning over. Her touch healed my head, and after that she rode alongside all the way.

"When all is said and done," she said, "it does not matter. It is only Patrick."

What happened next was extraordinary. All this happened at a the great height above Loch Trool when the morning sun was turning golden-white in a violet sky. May Maxwell and I never said a word of love – such as asking one another whether we loved each other, as lovers do in books.

But as she leaned to wipe my brow, she came very close. So I put my arm around her to steady her, and being so near, when she looked up I kissed her. It can be done on horseback if the ponies are good and move smoothly.

"I dreamed that in a dream," I said before I let her go, "and now it has come true."

I expected her to be angry, or even pretend to be. But for a girl so lively and quick witted she took it tenderly, which I liked very much. Indeed, she kissed me back willingly, without embarrassment, a good true-hearted kiss, which I will never forget. All the while, Silver Sand had been busy with his pony's girths. Whilst I am not someone who talks about their romantic experiences, but that kiss I am proud of, and I don't care who knows. But I will say no more since my tale is of grimmer business.

Now I promise and declare this was the extent of our love-making at that time. When we made love after that we did it intentionally, and neither of us pretended not to enjoy it, which is not at all what I would have expected from May Mischief. But one never knows!

The morning broke as we rode through the shallow water of the Trool at Fordmouth, and we came out in the open. Then Silver Sand flung up his cap with the shaggy ears into the air and we all cheered, "Hurrah!" For we were at last clear of the wild country, and May Maxwell now again sat soberly and properly on her pony by side-saddle like a great lady.

CHAPTER XXXI.

MAY MISCHIEF PROVES HER METTLE

WE all dismounted by the waterside, and May came and washed my face like she would a child's, and bound up my head with strips of the finest linen. It was warm and soft. I do not know where she carried it. I had one deep cut, ragged and sore, on the right side of my head, and a smaller cut by the temple, which was the one that had bled the most and weakened me.

May bathed them, and Silver Sand helped her to bind them up. We drank what remained of Mistress Eppie's tonic. Then we remounted and rode off.

It was a good, wide road now, especially after we turned south at the House of the Hill and rode towards Cree Bridge. There were pleasant farmhouses all around, where the cocks near and far were crowing, and the smoke rose up slowly into the sunshine. Men came out and looked around at the sky, and they seemed well pleased. And so were we. I often looked at May Maxwell, and strangely enough she always seemed to look at me at the same time, though I was not a pretty sight with my bandaged head and my bonnet cocked on the top of the white rags. I had never seen her look at me that way before.

We rode alongside one another, Silver Sand cantering easily in front, with Quharrie trotting ahead of him. I was on May's left, and as our horses clattered along, making a pleasing rhythm on the hard road, I took her hand, saying, "This is the hand that saved me."

"No, I'd rather say that this is the hand that pulled me out of the House of Murders." she returned.

But she shuddered and lifted up her hand to her face. I saw something that made my blood run cold. Three great fang marks on her forearm, from which the sleeve had fallen back as she lifted up her hand.

I was off my beast in a moment, crying out to Silver Sand, who turned.

"What a fool I was not to check!" I said, "the dogs have bitten you, May."

Silver Sand looked grave.

"This must be burned," he said, briefly.

"Let me ride on to Cree Bridge," she said; but he would not hear of it.

There was a farmhouse near by, called Borgan. Kind folk live there, and it is not far from a bridge where the waters come down tumbling white, almost as a waterfall.

We went there, and told them as much of our story as we chose to, then they took us into the kitchen and sent out a boy to attend to our horses.

May asked for a knitting-needle, which she heated white hot among the peats, and, turning, looked at me. But it was too much for me to burn her. Which made me ashamed, because I knew that she would have done it to me without blinking, since this is the way of women when they need to help those they love. But I was always a coward in such matters. So May took the needle herself, turned back her sleeve, and placed the white point on her arm, which hissed and made some faint blue smoke. Still being weak in my head, this made me need to sit down. But she thoroughly burned the fang-marks; and then, sitting down beside me, asked quietly for a drink of water, which she then gave to me.

The kind people of the Borgan were keen for us to stay, but May was anxious to get eastward to see her brothers and her father – but I had not yet had the heart or indeed the time to tell her that the old man was dead. This may be thought to be both wicked and selfish of me, particularly as I allowed her to ride happily with me, at times touching my hand, and at other times singing. But I could not bring myself to tell her yet and could not think of the best way to do it.

I convinced myself by saying that it would not have been wise to tell her when we were still in danger; but as soon as we sat together in the inn at the Cree Bridge I told her plainly and tenderly, judging that it was better to have it over with. Even then she said very little – only that she had suspected all along that something terrible must have happened since there was no pursuit of her after her capture and abduction.

Then after a while her tears flowed suddenly, as though it had taken time to sink in.

"Oh, why did they do it?" she cried. "He was such an old man."

Then she put her hand in mine, and looking up at me in a way that was heartbreaking, said

"Patrick, you must not think about me any more. We are not safe to live with, we Maxwells; and this, I see, will be only the beginning of trouble and bloodshed. My brothers will never rest till my father's murderers are destroyed."

"My lass," I said, "I did not think of marrying your brothers."

"Aye – but," she said sadly, "we are all the same."

"God forbid!" said I – to myself.

But on the whole she took the news very well but she stopped looking at me, nor did she give me her hand any more. But when we left the inn, some strange people looked at us curiously, so she walked very close to me, and nestled her shoulder against mine; which comforted me much, and I think, her as well.

She did not like to cry in front of people, but when we were on the road again, her tears ran silently down her cheeks; and I think that she either forgot about the burns on her arm, or she may even have wished that there were more of them. But all she said was this, over and over again – "He was such an old man."

Although Silver Sand rode further ahead there was no more courting. I regretted this, and I wished that I had kissed her more often – but a young man in love can be very unthinking and selfish.

It occurred to me, while May rode so silently, to speak to Silver Sand concerning the report that we should give to the Sheriff at Kirkcudbright.

To my surprise he was very much opposed to this suggestion.

"Report me no reports," he said."What good would that do for you?"

"But I want it known that there is murder happening the hills, and nobody is any the wiser," said I.

"Do you think the Sheriff doesn't know that by now?" said Silver Sand.

"It's easy for you, my man," I said to him."You didn't see the poor lad's bloody back in that great sea-chest, nor did you hear the knives being honed on the sharpening stones being made ready to cut your own throat."

"Not tonight, maybe," said Silver Sand," but look here."

He opened his coat a little, and showed me the blue-white scar of a great wound. "That was a Macaterick knife," he said, "but I reported no reports. Only," he said, grimly, "I paid my debt."

"And what, then, shall we do?" I said, for I was in a genuine difficulty. I was a laird and I did not support of private war, although I had become involved in one during the last day or two.

"This is certain," he said. "I know the Maxwell lads, and I know the hill rogues – the Marshalls and the Macatericks. Neither will rest till there's more of this."

"And the Faas?" I asked, for I blamed Hector Faa for all that had happened to me, and it was mainly with him that I wanted to get even.

Silver Sand turned in one of his sudden excesses of temper.

"I tell you," he said, firmly, "that the Faas have had no part in the murders."

I longed to ask him which side he was on, but for the sake of what he had done for us that night, I thought better of it.

"But what, then, was the lass that Hector Faa ran away with doing in a house of the Macatericks?"

"That I don't know," he said, "but I am certain that Hector Faa will have had his reasons. But he is no murderer."

"What, then, was that honest man doing pickled in that devil's chest? Friends of murderers are no better as far as I'm concerned."

Silver Sand answered very quietly."It's not right to talk in that way between friends. Surely you know Silver Sand well enough by now, and that you can trust him."

Now, I had not been thinking that way about Silver Sand at all, but only of Hector Faa, and it was no wonder that I was angry with him. I told him this, and his anger, the reason for which I could not then understand, cooled in a moment.

"You're in love, laddie, and that excuses everything."

And from then on he carried on in his ordinary placid demeanour. We passed Kirkcudbright by the sea (which looked very like a low-lying English town), always keeping ourselves on the crown of the causeway, and were soon within sight of Rathan Isle. I could see the old house shining white across the blue of the sea, and my spirits rose. Here we met Kennedy Maxwell, and sent him onwards to announce our return.

As she went along May Maxwell kept her eyes to the ground, being, I think, afraid of seeing the roofless walls of Craigdarroch with its gables pointing so hopelessly upward, all blackened on the inside.

Half an hour later, a man came across the fields toward us. He was a well-set-up man in faded clothing, with moleskin trousers underneath, as are worn by labourers. He went up to May Maxwell and with an elaborate bow said to her, "My Lady Grizel Maxwell's compliments, and she would be pleased to see you at Earlstoun. She thinks that her house is the best place for young Maxwell lady, who is a second cousin."

May looked astonished. It was not often that a message had come to her from the old lady of Earlstoun. Silver Sand turned round sharply.

"I'll ride with you to Earlstoun gate," he said to May. Then turning to the messenger, "And whose dog gave birth to you?" he queried.

Now this was a distinctly uncivil question, and Silver Sand was normally so polite. He told me afterwards that he could not abide anything pompous from flunkies, and that Quharrie and he always took such matters into their own hands – sometimes, also, in Quharrie's own teeth.

Moleskins, however, was tolerant.

"Just the bitch that was your own mother's sister,"said he, pleasantly.

"Served me right,"said Silver Sand; "that's no flunkie's answer. What made you wear that coat? "

"Just the same that makes you ride on another man's animal," said the sturdy serving-man, unruffled -"not enough money to buy one of my own."

Silver Sand looked him straight in the face, and the serving-man looked straight back again, standing with his hands on his hips.

"And how do you know that this horse is not my own?"

"Because that horse is Johnny Faa's and it came from the Borders. I know the breed by the bonny white flash on his face."

Silver Sand took this patiently, and said only,"Does your mistress wish to keep young Mistress Maxwell with her? "

"I believe that to be her wish and intention."

"You were in the wars, weren't you?" said Silver Sand, quickly.

"Yes," said the man, "I rode with the wild Bonshaw. Who did you ride with? "

"You are a man of sense," said Silver Sand,"and men of sense know when to hold their tongues."

"When it's worth their while," said the serving-man, who had ridden with Bonshaw to the Whig shooting.

"It'll be well worth your while," said Silver Sand.

"I don't mean money," said the other, quickly.

"I never met a soldier that didn't. Don't be shy," retorted Silver Sand.

"Well, if you insist," said the other.

Something passed from hand to hand. I suspected that it was a guinea or two out of the same bag which had supplied me with mine.

CHAPTER XXXII.

I SALUTE THE LADY GRIZEL

So we rode on to the great house of Earlstoun. Its occupant was the Lady Grizel Maxwell, the daughter of old Earl Maxwell, and a woman well known and respected through all the Stewartry and beyond. She had her peculiarities, but she was known to be so exceedingly hospitable that often her own table went short in order that dainties might be sent to those of her poorer neighbours.

She met us at the garden gate. She was a large woman of masculine features, with a prominent nose and a clear and fearless grey eye that looked unblinking at each of us.

It was Silver Sand she looked at first.

"Preserve us, man!" she said. "Surely hemp's not so expensive that they can't afford to make a rope for you. What brings you to this country?"

Silver Sand was manifestly put out.

"I think your ladyship is mistaken," he said.

"Mistake here! - mistake there! - Grizel Maxwell knows a —"

"Shush, shush, my lady! There's names that shouldn't be spoken of at a lodge-gate."

"Indeed, yes,"said her ladyship, taking off the broad, blue, man's bonnet that she wore, and showing a beautiful head of lint-white hair rippling away from her brow, "it's myself that should know that."

"Well, then!" said Silver Sand for all answer.

She greeted May next. Opening her arms to lift her down, which she did as a grenadier might dismount a drummer-boy, she said —

"My daughter, you and me have both lost fathers; it runs in the family. The Maxwell men are never likely to die in their beds. No, they ride gaily, and you can hear the clattering of their spurs down the dark valley as they go away, never to return. You are grieving for your father. Come with me and we'll stay a while together, till you get over it. It can't be helped, my lassie. You see that coat, May, lass. There was a head taken off close to the collar – you see the velvet looks as if it's rusty. That was my father's head. That's been the way of the Maxwells ever since they came to Galloway, where, indeed, they had no business to be."

Then she turned to me, looking at me fiercely to see how I would meet her eye.

"And who might you be, young man, that rides so freely by my cousin's side?"

Before I had time to speak, May Maxwell began to tell how that, when all others had hung back, I had ventured out and saved her from the most terrible perils, but saying nothing about her own role.

"Patrick Heron of Rathan! An old name, though nowadays with little to show for it. It's none the worse for that. Indeed, the Maxwell's took all but that small barren isle, and I know they would have taken that if it that been worth their while. Yes, man, I didn't know your father, but your grandfather was a gallant young man, and many a time he met me after the planting season – just for fun and because we were young, you understand; nothing else. He had the most attractive ankle and calf. Yes, lad, you resemble him in the leg, but not in your features. Come down and pay me your respects."

So I came and very respectfully gave her a salutation.

"Indeed, sir, your mouth is not at all like his; but I doubt that's how you kiss a pretty girl. No, an old gossiping wife can't expect anything else at her time of life. Well, well!"

We stood before her as meek as a flock of chickens, and she held up her apron by the corners as if she had corn in it to feed us with.

"But it's a fine thing for you to stand here on the steps of my house. I'm an Earl's daughter, you know. Didn't you know? If you didn't, there's Gib Gowdie that calls himself a butler, he'll soon tell you – silly old man, Gib! Will you come in, man?" she said to Silver Sand, who stood with his hat in his hand as the gentry do in front of a lady."It's a long time I saw you ride off with— you-know-who—"

But Silver Sand said, "I thank your ladyship exceedingly, but I have much business to transact."

She took both of us through the door, and closed it herself, closing the bars as in a prison. We found ourselves in an immense bare hall with only old buff coats and black armour hanging about, in the faint light which filtered down the great staircase.

The Lady Grizel went to the top of the kitchen stair, which opened downwards like a great deep well.

"Jen!" she cried.

"Yes ma'am; don't get in a fidget, ma'am! Can't you wait for a while? I'll be there in a moment."

Her ladyship stamped her foot.

"Come here this instant, you impudent woman!"

"Then your ladyship will have to come and pluck the chicken, and you know you never were good at it," said a voice from below.

"Jen!" cried Lady Grizel from the stairhead, "this is the last straw. You and I must part."

"And why would that be?" inquired a goodnatured woman of dark complexion and mature good looks, with very red cheeks and dark eyebrows, who looked up at us as we stood at the top and she at the bottom of the kitchen stairs. She had a sheet about her and a great pullet in her hand."Why, your ladyship, were you thinking of leaving Earlstoun?"

"No, Jen, but if you won't come when I ask, I'll have to part with you."

"No, no, your ladyship, you know well you couldn't do that. You couldn't put up that nice head of hair yourself. Besides, if you don't know a good servant when you have one, I know a good mistress."

"Jen, get to your work in the kitchen this minute,"cried her ladyship, turning on her heel. "Don't answer me back! I'll have to show you to your room myself, May, and you, Laird Rathan, can go to the reception room, where you'll have some company till I come down."

I went towards the room indicated. I could hear a great noise within of barking, screaming, and coughing. The entrance was exceedingly high and the doors opened like a gate, outwards. Here in a large room were a collie dog, a longhaired cat of some foreign breed, a parrot on a stick, and a monkey, an ugly beast dressed in a red coat, capering about everywhere and keeping the whole room in a turmoil.

As soon as I came in there was silence, and the monkey ran to the top of the red velvet curtains, and there tilted his head most comically in order to see if anyone were following me into the room. The action was like that of a bad lad at school looking out for the teacher with his strap or birch rod. At this moment I could not forbear laughing.

"Have some manners, you fool!" shouted a loud voice which startled me, and instinctively I begged its pardon. But it was only the parrot, a strange bird which I had often heard about but never before seen. So I remained in this room with these curious companions till her ladyship came down to me.

"This lass of mine tells me that you saved her from the claws of the buzzards at the risk of your own life. You'll be thinking that was a brave thing. But, it's nothing at all.

"Your grandfather would have done as much for a kiss and a cuddle from a bonny lass; but I guess, indeed I know, that you have spoken about the farm and want to rent it for life. I don't doubt that you are a decent lad, though you haven't much money. We'll see, we'll see, Patrick. A

Maxwell's not to be picked up every day as a hen picks corn. You may get her, and you may not. What's that you say, that you have got her already? No, my fine man; if there had not been slips between the cup and the lip, I would not be here today, with the same name given to me by the Priest when I was christened – we won't say how many years ago!"

CHAPTER XXXIII.

JEN GEDDES' SAMPLER BAG

JEN GEDDES appeared at the door. She had dressed herself in a black gown of very thick silk, and her grey hair was over her ears in most elaborate ringlets.

"I have never seen such a silly old woman," said Lady Grizel, "at your time of life, Jen, to dress up for a young man; I'm embarrassed."

Jen said, without turning a hair, " Whatever my age, it's well known your ladyship was a grown woman when I was christened."

"Never, Jen, I was just a little girl. I don't remember it at all," said her ladyship, firmly.

"No, No, Lady Girzie, you know well that the name of Janet Geddes is written in your own handwriting in the big hall Bible." This said with an air of triumph.

But I went forward, and seeing that Jen was a privileged person, I waited for Lady Grizel to introduce me.

"You'll know Laird Heron of the Rathan, Jen – a gallant young man. He takes after his grandfather about the leg, don't you think, Jen? "

"That's something your ladyship would know. I have heard my father say he often came to visit you. As for me, I'm a far too young to remember."

"Nonsense, Jen, you know well that it was you that used to let him in when he came knocking at the door, and you that rushed him out of the back door that night when his lordship, my father, took us by surprise."

Jen chuckled at the recollection, and so was caught.

"Yes, my lady, and was it not something to see him make the sparks fly from striking the iron of the door guards so quickly. Yes, he was a free spirit, and knew a bonny lass when he saw one."

"You and he were too intimate for me, Jen," said her ladyship, craftily. "I don't care for a man that goes after both mistress and maid."

"Nonsense," said Jen, "there's no harm done, for a gallant lad to take a little kiss from the maid on his way in to the mistress; and why not? Do you think the maid is not as good a judge of men as the lady; besides sometimes being a deal prettier? She can't help being a greater temptation sometimes."

And Jen tossed her stately ringlets before her well-preserved apple cheeks.

"Indeed, Jen, now that you have given away that you and me are about the same age, I'll won't deny that in your youth you were an attractive lass."

Jen held her head high.

"Perhaps I'm not so bad looking even now," she said.

"An opinion in which I heartily agree," said I, taking her hand in mine, while I held my hat in the other. "Let me claim the privilege of my grandfather, who, I realise, had excellent taste!"

Whereupon I bowed to mistress and then to maid, who both dropped me a curtsy – that of Lady Grizel graceful and sweeping, that of Jen Geddes ample and hearty, like a boat that rises and falls in a mill-pond.

"Well bowed! You are graceful," said the Lady Grizel, very much pleased, "and a lad with courage will win the heart of old wives more than looks."

"But he's good looking for all that," said Jen. "I think he's even as bonny as his grandfather ever was."

"That was always your way, Jen; and there's nothing wrong with it. The apple you *had* was always the best apple, the nicest, rosiest one. That's what it is to be happy."

She sighed.

"As for me," she went on, "the lad I liked best was always the one that I couldn't get, and that's maybe the reason that I lie my own at night, with only another old mischievous woman like myself between me and the bedside."

"You might have had the Laird of Rathan," said Jen to her mistress," had your family never driven him out of Orraland and Rascarrel. But you were an earl's daughter, and wouldn't deign to think of living in just the old tower of Rathan, no better than a commoner."

"Indeed, Jen," said Lady Grizel, tossing her head on a way which reminded me exceedingly of May Maxwell when she is mischievous, " it wasn't me that was unwilling. I would have given away all my best clothes to live there; but it wasn't to be."

She reflected for a moment; then she spoke, waving her hand sideways as though to drive all these things away.

"But this is nothing but old women's idle talk. It's Patrick Heron that's come to my door with a pretty girl on his arm, riding lively and cheerfully – him with a three-cornered wound on his forehead, and her with a bandage on her arm that they have got, by fighting each other to win the other. Jen! we'll even have a wedding. I must get down Father John, and Jen, you can air the sheets."

"My goodness," said Jen, "you always have been one to eat your porridge before it has been cooked. They're Whigs and not of the Roman religion, and more than that, the young lass's father is not long under the sod."

"Fine, fine, Jen," said her ladyship," it's maybe as well, but I know I have made this young man's heart go boom boody boom tonight. Let me listen!"

And the abominable old woman put her hand on my heart, which was certainly thumping with surprising quickness at the thought.

"A good honest heart," she said," that hasn't been wasted on other lasses. You won't have long to wait, my lad, and I'll butter your bread for you that day, my man."

I was grateful for that promise of a gift. Lady Grizel was not such a bad old lady.

"Do you remember,"said Jen, "how you used to come gathering blackberries, and then the mistress would call you into the house for a bite to eat?"

I remembered clearly, and said so enthusiastically, that Jen was moved to relate of other recollections, while her mistress left us to ourselves.

"She's a wonderful woman, the mistress; there is no-one like her in the three counties. She might have had the choice of men – as I did; but whenever one of them tried too hard to impress her, she became unmanageable with him, and she wouldn't be controlled; and even your grandfather only pleased her by pretending not to care a pin for her."

"She has been very kind to me already," I said.

"Yes, and she'll be even kinder, for I can see she likes you. My name will not be Jen Geddes of Parton if she's not good to you, far beyond what you might expect. But be standoffish and contrary, fiery as mustard, and fly out with your hat in your hand and your head in the air at a word. That's the way to please the mistress; yes, and a great number of women. They don't like men that just make feeble sounds and mutter – except for my sister Eppie," she added.

"Your sister Eppie?" I said, a strange thought coming into my head.

"Yes, and that reminds me, where did you get that bag with the bloody knives in it that's lying on the table? I hope haven't been involved in some terrible business, you and the Maxwell lass."

I told her as best I could our great and wonderful story when her exclamations would permit me. Before I had finished telling of the broad back of the man in the sea-chest, she had to sit down; describing the two gashes in it nearly finished her, as the sight of them had almost done for me; but she still wanted to hear more.

"But the bag; where did you get the bag? "she cried.

I knew nothing about the bag. It was one that May Maxwell had brought from the House of Death beside Loch Enoch.

"That's my sister's bag, I can swear to it," she said. "She's married to soft Sammle Tamson of Mossdale. It was me that made it and gave it to her before she left Parton House. Look here!" she cried suddenly.

She ripped away a part of the lining. "JANET GEDDES; HER SAMPLER WORK," was cross stitched on the inside of the lining.

Then I remembered the story of Marion, and the little lass that we had left with Mistress Eggface and the evil men in that terrible house on the hill of Craignairny.

"The poor little girl," I said again and again, "and we left her in that house amongst murdering devils."

My heart sunk, as maybe it had no need to do, for it was certain we would have a horrible death had we tried to take her with us then. I tried to reassure myself, but it did not do any good.

The Lady Grizel now came in.

"I remember," she said," when you came to Earlstoun as a small boy, that you liked a little bread with butter and sweet conserves. Now, you'll have to be on your way soon, for the sake of Jen's honour and mine. It will not do for a handsome young man to be on his own in the house with three bonny lasses. You were in the Wolf's Slock at the dead of night with the prettiest of them, according to you; my faith, but you are not embarrassed to say that to my face. You're not to come into my house if you don't learn to be civil. However, it was a piece of cake with conserves that you liked. See now, boy, there's some set out for you in that room there. Go inside and get it."

So saying, she took me by the shoulders and roughly pushed me out. I went through the door, and there in front of me, standing alone by the window, was my May. I shut the door behind me and looked about for Lady Grizel's sweet cake and conserves.

CHAPTER XXXIV.

SWEET CAKE AND CONSERVES

"MAY!" I said softly.

She turned and came near to me and stood very close against me in a sweet way, but I knew that she did not wish me to touch her then, but only to stand there. We remained like that for a considerable time, and I ached to hold and comfort her. Which at last I did with satisfaction to both of us, and the time flew away.

I told her that I had to go to the old Tower of Rathan, and see what it was like there in the hands of Jerry. I told her, too, about little Marion, who she was; and she cheered me by telling me that the wild and murderous folk were not all unkind to the little child, but that she was treated like the daughter of the old woman – as I had seen when I was in the kitchen. Also she was not old enough to know the full extent of their enormities. All of which, being the words of my beloved, reassured me, because I did not wish to have to undertake a second journey just at that time.

We looked around for a place to sit down, for we needed to talk together as if it was for the last time (or at least a night and a day). There was only one great chair in that large room, though there was much tapestry and some high tables and corner cupboards. So we sat down on it happily, and in truth I did not know how I could leave her – so soon does one depend on the sight and touch of a dear young lass.

But I knew well that she would be true to me, and she promised to think about me every hour; and asked the same from me. This made me laugh, for I knew that I should think of nothing else at any time, far less every hour. So I asked her when she would come to the Rathan and stay.

"It is a poor place," I said," but there is no reason why, with hard work and good farming, it should not be the most comfortable and happiest of homes for us. We Herons have lived frugally for two generations, and we can afford to remove a little money out of the Dumfries lawyer's hands when a bonny bride comes home to Rathan."

I strongly urged her, and at last she admitted she would come when I was ready, for she said, "I have no heart to go back to Craigdarroch, for I know my brothers, and they are not men to let bygones be bygones. There'll be more and worse spilling of blood before it is all over!"

"Are you sure you would come to the Rathan?" I asked, to try her; for indeed I knew she had agreed, but I wanted to hear her say it again.

"Indeed I do, Patrick, body and soul and everything – just for you own, when you're ready to call for them."

"Then," said I," I'll just take them now,"

At which she cried out, but she was not displeased.

"Have you licked all the conserves off the cake yet?" cried a voice from the door, which opened just a little.

We were surprised and answered nothing, and the door closed again as softly as it had opened.

May laughed May Mischief's laugh for, I think, the first time since the beginning of the troubles.

"Have you?" said she, looking at me.

Now we sat on a single chair, and though I do not consider myself particularly bright, and I had no experience, but that was good enough for me.

There is nothing to report of the next half hour.

"It's my turn, May," said Lady Grizel, who had been coughing at the door for five minutes. " I do sometimes have a cough, but I like a quiet hour in the evening with a merry lad as much as anyone."

"His grandfather, wasn't it?" asked my witch wickedly.

"Indeed but you're nothing but a couple of scamps that need turning upside down and smacked – and in a trice I would send you both out of the door. Do you hear me?"said the old lady, secretly pleased.

Then she turned to me.

"Now away with you, Patrick, and tell those Maxwell lads that they are welcome to the farm buildings at Earlstoun to stow their goods and cattle in when they get any. And say that they can sleep well in the granary and the stable loft. But there's to be no fighting near the house," she added, having in mind, no doubt, the manners and customs of the Maxwell brothers.

"And another thing – they must find their own caves and hidy-holes for the Hollands gin and the lace. I'm not going to have the kings men rampaging through my house, rummaging and thrashing about, at my time of life. A keg over the back of the Dyke is one thing but a cellar full of brandy is another."

So I said goodbye to them, kissing them both, and also Jen Geddes, who boxed me on the ear for an "impudent rascal, who isn't able to leave a decent woman's bonnet straight on her head."

And this was all the magic I ever used to win three women's hearts.

The Maxwells had already heard the whole story of their sister's rescue from Silver Sand, and I was given much credit. So they came upon me like bees when I arrived, leaving their work of putting new roofs on their barns and outhouses. They wanted me to stay and celebrate the occasion with them, but I was eager to get to the Rathan; so I took their boat and rowed across, with the familiar tidal flows swirling in the smooth places, bubbling like oil and rippling along the side of the boat, a pleasant sound which is always nice to hear.

I beached the Maxwells' boat at the Shell Cove behind of the house, and went up the path, looking like a man that has come back from foreign parts and is trying to spot the changes made to his home. Rathan House looked better than ever I saw it. There was a platform hanging out of one of the windows, for no apparent reason, with a dark vessel sitting upon it. It was a very silent place, but I heard the hens cackling and pecking at newly scattered meat, so I knew that someone was there.

I went quietly around the house till I came to the main door, which was deep set in the wall. It was wide open, and there sat Jerry Macwhirter, peeling potatoes and piping as he worked, "Awa, Whigs awa'," and other ungodly tunes.

"The Whig is not so far away, my lad! - And how do you like that?" said I.

Whereupon I took him by the back of the neck to shake him, but he twisted himself round, and would have knifed me had not he recognised me and dropped it with a hearty cry of joy.

But I still shook him, and he responded by kicking my shins. This restored our friendship, since I had now paid him his dues for his insolence when we parted. Then I had to tell him the whole story, which astonished him greatly. There had been, it seemed, a great quietness about Rathan and the whole countryside. It was said, however, that the sheriff was organising a party to go against the outlaws, but no one believed it.

On the other hand, it was thought that the Maxwells were preparing themselves for a great raid on the hill country. Many had given in their names to Will and Kennedy Maxwell, and it was said that a large body of men exercised every night under moonlight on the farm of Craigdarroch. What was true, was that a party of preventive men from Kirkcudbright had come across a body of fifty horse by the Darroch islets, and had fled without firing a shot. But these might only be the regular Freetraders, since the Maxwells had sworn never to run another cargo till the evil beasts were destroyed, root and branch, from off the face of Galloway.

I wondered what the evil beasts had to say to this.

Inside everything was in such beautiful order that I could hardly recognise it. Jerry (to pass the time he said) had cleaned and decorated so much that it was fit for a bride and I wished May was with me.

When I told him about May he looked sulkier than I had ever seen him. The further I got on with my story the gloomier he got. At last he broke out – "Then I suppose nothing will suit you better than to get this lass to come to the Rathan, set up house like a grocer, and read the Bible night and morning?"

I said that these things were far away

"But I can see they are coming, and not so far away either – nearer than I like."

"It won't make any difference to you, Jerry." I said with the innocence of inexperience.

"Whistle on my thumb!" he said irreverently; "I'm finished with it; I know my jug's been to the well too often. I'll even take to a tent, like Silver Sand. Him and me will go travelling the country. That's what we'll do. I can at least paint a door. I'll tell you this. Jerry will not prepare your drinks or nurse your screaming children. I cannot stand them."

Whereupon he took me round the house, and in a mournful, valedictory manner (which amused me much) he showed me all his improvements. He really had brightened up the old house wonderfully. But of course his improvements, such as they were, only showed me how much needed to be done before a young bride could be brought home. I resolved, therefore, to go to Dumfries the very next day to see the lawyer that looked after my assets; but all this time I was burning hot and cold in flashes and my head was buzzing strangely.

"Well, you're not to do that," he said, "I have a small job to do myself, and since I kept house for you, you should wait for me."

I nodded, asking only when he would be back again.

I told him about the matter of the bag and little Marion.

"I'll call at Mossdale on my way to New Galloway, and tell them. It's something they should know, and it'll probably be best for your health to keep clear of the Macaterick's country for a while. I'm only an unwanted lame duck, and I don't matter much. But Jerry MacWhirter is as slippery as an eel."

So he sped on his way to Earlstoun, with a message that everything was fine, and to ask May to let him have the bag in which the knives had been.

To ease my head I strolled down to where Silver Sand had made his camp by the side of the little Rathan burn. His donkey was there, having been brought to the isle from the other side. Silver Sand looked a little oddly at me as I approached, and I wondered whether he was thinking if I had asked Lady Grizel more of his history, which I would not do if he didn't want to tell me himself. The camp was very fresh and pleasant, and made me very happy, were it not for the queer humming machinery which was working in my head. In the excitement of being with May and returning to my home, I had completely forgotten my battered head, but the pain had returned. Silver Sand, as soon as he saw me, forcefully ordered me to go to bed, calling himself ill-names for not having thought to do so sooner.

So he sent me to bed and helped me off with my clothes, then took them away. Then he laid cool, wet cloths on my head, and gave me something to drink. Whereupon I slept for many hours, and when I awoke I could not tell what day or hour of the day it might be. But I was unhappy since I had not sent a message to Earlstoun, so he went there himself, leaving me on my own. Outside, the salt water sounded cool and pleasant and it felt as if the spray from the sea was breaking on my hot head. So I lay, with many earnest thoughts of the goodness of God, between sleeping and waking. Indeed I reproached myself with remorse that I had so seldom thought upon the Maker and the Giver of all good. My nature is not to be ungrateful, but recently things had happened so quickly that I had neglected to do so.

Perhaps this was the reason I was now lying upon my back.

CHAPTER XXXV.

SILVER SAND'S WHITE MAGIC

IT was in the light of day when I came to, as Silver Sand, using his white magic, had put something in the drink which had caused me to sleep. But I was remarkably refreshed and my head was cool.

"Give me my shirt!" I cried, for I could hear him at the wood block where we cut branches and prepared logs for the great fireplace.

"Eppie will bring it from the store-room," said the voice, not of Silver Sand as I had expected, but of Jerry, who sat at the foot of the bed smirking at my surprise.

"What Eppie?" said I.

"Listen to him," said Jerry, scratching his bare foot,"how many Eppies do you know? Are there Eppies tumbling over one another in this house? "

But I let him ramble on, because there in the doorway stood my kind friend Eppie Tamson of Mossdale, with her buxom person and apple cheeks, and she was drying her hands.

"Well, laddie." she said. "This is a happy sight – you clothed and in your right mind. You have had a tough battle, but you have come through it."

"I want a dish of porridge," I said, for I was hungry.

She went to the door and cried, "]en, he's woken; fetch the porridge!"

And then who should put her head in at the door but my dear May Mischief, who came quietly and sat at the head of my bed and put her head down beside mine on the pillow. Though just a small gesture, it made my heart soar, and I thought about it long after she was gone. She told me how that I had been unconscious for nearly ten days and had raved on about many things, some of which she said, " I would not have wanted anyone but me to hear." But she smiled as she said it.

"And I heard more about your wrongdoings than I am likely to hear about for the rest of my life," she said.

Seeing me look a little anxious, she said, "There was nothing to cause me any anxiety, Patrick; for though I heard everything, you only ever mentioned one lass."

She smiled and waited for me to speak. So, to please her, I asked who that might be.

"It was just that daft May Maxwell," she said, looking down at her lap, and then up at me very simply and sweetly.

"Well," said I, "was that it? I thought it would have been either Jen Geddes or Eppie Tamson."

"You're obviously getting better," says she, "and we'd better keep it at one, my lad!"

And in my state this seemed to me to be a fine piece of wit that I laughed until May, now frowning and looking anxious, asked me to stop. Then I said that I would get up; but she put her hand on mine and said, "Look, Patrick, it'll be a few days before you're ready for that."

And indeed she was right, for I could see my arms were wasted to the bone.

"My boy," she said, and I loved to hear her so speak, "you are not fit enough to climb the Wolf's Slock tonight."

Then I asked her about Lady Grizel and how she was, and she told me that she sent over to ask how the lad was every day, and to know when they were coming back, because the time was dragging at Earlstoun without both Jen and May, and with only a common monkey and an impudent parrot to keep her company. I thought the Lady Grizel was acting like an impolite old woman.

Also she told me that Mossdale, being on the verge of the outlaw country, was no longer safe; for it was known to the Macatericks that Sammle Tamson had been with me at the Cooran that day, and the gypsies had vowed vengeance against him. So by borrowing two carts from Clachanpluck, Sammle and Eppie had brought all their belongings to Earlstoun. Sammle was now with the Maxwells, busy making plans for vengeance on the marauders of the hills.

"And Eppie came here to nurse you," she said, "but I have done most of it myself, since they let me come," she said, with some pride.

All this was news to me, and it took me some time to understand that so much should happen in such a short time.

The next day May and Jen went back to Earlstoun, with the promise that Sammle Tamson would bring her (meaning May) over to see me one day a week until I was able to go to Earlstoun myself.

Then Sammle himself came to transport the belongings of May and Jen, and with him was Kennedy Maxwell looking much less serious than the others.

Then I agreed with Sammle Tamson something that I had been thinking about. I asked if if he would come to the Rathan with all of his goods, using the lodge by the stable whenever he wanted; and in the meantime (at least, until the bride arrived) Eppie and he were to live in the house of Rathan itself and look after both me and it. And it was good for me to have a man of my own.

"To think that you and our May have made it up!" said Kennedy; "that beats everything."

I told him tartly that it beat him at any rate, with his night-time roaming and dealings with a dozen floozies – whereat, more pleased than rebuked, he laughed.

And so it was settled. I was to give Sammle all that he required of bread, meat and ale, four rows of potatoes, half an acre of barley and an acre of oats, and also twelve pounds sterling a year for the services of himself and of his wife. All which I think very generous, considering that most farm servants are happy with two pounds and his meat. But I wanted to make sure that in the home which May and I looked forward to with so much pleasure, that others who live there would also be contented. Besides, with my father's savings I could well afford it.

Kennedy Maxwell told me that the hill folk were all eager to avenge the retaking of May and the discovery of their villainy. He also told me that nearly a hundred stout and brave lads had sworn to go later in the year, to root them out of their stronghold with force and destruction. These men came from all the parishes, from Minnigaff to Rerrick, and from Carsphairn to the edge of Kells. Sammle Tamson had been up raising the men of the head end of the Stewartry, and there were many, even from the Doon Water and the Shalloch-on-Minnoch, sturdy men of Carrick, who would gladly join, having been badly tormented by the outlaws in the past.

So the days and weeks went by and then it was time for harvest, and the reaping of the scanty fields that I had taken so little interest in. But the Maxwells and their friends came and did it for me; and I shared it fairly with them, because I did not need a great of corn, while they, who were restocking their farm, desperately needed it. I had no livestock to speak of apart from some sheep; and all the corn I had, had been consumed by horses that had been hired from local farmers, which was easier for me, though less profitable. But I did not care a great deal, apart from growing what was needed for the house of Rathan, since I could get any money I needed from the funds and property held by Mr Erskine, that well-known and most honest lawyer in Dumfries.

But all the same I intended to keep horses in the future, to drain and plough the land, which would improve Rathan and its productivity. I also believed that if the sea could be shut out from a particular narrow gulf, I would gain a great extent of fertile land for my estate. All of which I have now done, and I mention this to show that the days of enforced idleness were very fruitful in regard to the future.

Also as I said, I had concerns about the state of my soul, about which I sensed that I had neglected. I intended to go and open my mind to Mr. Macmillan of Balmaghie, who was a leading man among the Societies and a man of great holiness and fearlessness. In due course I did this, and became a member of good standing, but not until after this dangerous quarrel had ended and peace had returned.

Then, when I could sit up, Silver Sand came and told me tales, teaching me all the lore of the woods and the strange old sayings of the gypsies. I wondered where he had learned them but he did seemed to be well learned in everything. He had set up his tent again, he had gone back to his trade of selling scythe sand, all made out of the hardest white grit of the granite which had been ground down and sifted by the rain and the worn by the rocks on the edges of the lochs in the granite districts.

He brought me three kinds of sand to see, but not being a scythe-man I could not tell the difference.

Then, very enthusiastically, Silver Sand described them to me.

"This," he said, running his hand through the fine, white, sand that he had in one bag, "is the sand which I gather from the edge of the little Loch of Skerrow near Mossdale which Sammle Tamson knows so well. This is the commonest kind, yet good for coarse work, such as mowing ordinary grass, or the weeds and grass at the edge of field. It is the cheapest: but this," he said, showing me another very fine sand, "is the sand from Loch Valley, which, when we were last there, I did not have time to show you."

"It is fine, and sticks smoothly on the sharpening board, and is used for corn on the hillsides, and for short hay that is easy mown.

"But this," he said, taking up a smaller bag as if it had was fine gold, "is the sand from Loch Enoch itself. It is the best, the keenest, and lies closest to the blade of the scythe. It is used for the mowing of meadow hay, which is hard to cut, because it has to be cut about the beginning of August, before the floods come.

Then it is hard work to mow for a long summer's day, and a great swing of the scythe is indeed needed. At that time of year you can hear the ' strake, strake ' of the mower in the shade as he puts an edge on his tool, and nothing else is used throughout all of Galloway, Carrick, and the Upper Ward of Lanarkshire than Loch Enoch sand – that is, when they can get it."

He passed it over to me in a canvas bag. It was certainly very beautiful, and I let it trickle through my fingers.

"But how did you get this, Silver Sand?" I said. "Have you been back again since —— ."

"No," he said, "but I have people who can go for me."

The sand ran through my fingers, clean and dry, until I felt something like a coin. It looked very like a token that the ministers give to those who are judged fit to come to the Communion table. But there was no text on it; only some markings which I could not make anything out of. Yet Silver Sand snatched it from me in an instant, and I think I saw him change colour as he did so.

"God forgive me! How could I have missed it?" he said. Then, having looked at it, he muttered, "So soon!" and was silent.

Now although Silver Sand had proved himself, and I knew him to be trustworthy to the core, I had certainly suspected him of double dealing. But to me he was utterly beyond reproach and above suspicion. It was simply not possible that he could be manoeuvring with a foot in either camp. However, I knew he was certainly a man with more secrets of his own, and dangerous ones to boot, than I would care to carry about without a suit of armour.

Soon after this he headed off to Earlstoun, taking the boat with him to the White Horse Bay, the closest landing point to the house in which May was living.

When I was well enough to sit at the high window of my room again, the prospect glass was of great use to me. I could see the camp of Silver Sand, with Quharrie on guard by the stream, and the white streak of the sprig of peeled willow against the black opening of the tent. That was part of Silver Sand's magic. In fact I often told him that he would be likely be burned for being a wizard, and that (as they did to Major Weir) they would throw in Quharrie and the peeled sprig to keep him company.

"If that happens, some will suffer, I'm sure!" was all his answer.

Yet it is true that when he wanted water for the cattle that we kept later on, it was by using this same peeled wand that Silver Sand was able to find a spring anywhere on Rathan. Whether this was by foreknowledge or some science that was hidden from the rest of us, I could not say, and indeed I still do not know.

Then beyond, over the tide which I watched come and go twice a day, I could see the farmstead of Craigdarroch, where the Maxwells were busy at their thatching or working in the fields with their guns standing cocked close by, which was an unusual thing to see in Scotland at that time of day.

But what I looked for most often, until my eye ached and I had to take it from the eyepiece, was the topmost turret of Earlstoun, and the little bit of the terrace of the Italian garden at the corner beneath where there was a smooth piece of turf on which May Maxwell often walked and (as arranged) waved a white handkerchief to me to lift my spirits.

CHAPTER XXXVI

THE BARRING OF THE DOOR

But it was not long before I grew as strong as ever, and could make my own way over to Earlstoun to see my girl. Eppie and Samuel remained in the house and Samuel occupied much of his time in going over to Craigdarroch to hear the latest plans for the great raid that the Maxwells were to make as soon as the winter frosts came and froze the upland waters; for there was no point in going there in force when the bogs and lochs were unfrozen. Boats could not be dragged up to the summits of these wild mountains, and even if the Lowlanders came in force and defeated the outlaws they would all escape among the peat bogs, because of their knowledge of the ground.

This had been a wild year in Galloway. His Majesty King George had recently come to the throne, and many of those inclined to crime seized the occasion to plunder their neighbours. Agnew of Lochnaw took out letters from the Privy Council, and, as the warrant ran, "bought commission of judiciary to pursue and slay the red-handed clans of gypsies and broken men living in the fastnesses of Carrick and Galloway, who do continually plunder, slay, and put in fear His subjects." These clans were the Millers, Baillies. Macatericks, and Marshalls – though, noticeably, the Faas were not nominated in the warrant.

But nothing came of this. Agnew stayed in Lochnaw, along with his warrant of justiciary, and the plundering of the Lowland parishes and the terrorism of the upper districts carried on as before.

As William Maxwell of Craigdarroch, when he heard of it, put it, "Lochnaw may scratch his feet, his act is but a puff of wind. Those that are too far away to bear the brunt, are too far away to bring the redress."

By that he meant that Agnew, the King's Sheriff; was too distant to be attacked, and therefore did not feel the need for action. But the Maxwells were not the men to let their burnt thatching, their stolen cattle and the blood splashes on the white hairs of their father stay unavenged. Moreover, their scouts, sprinkled here and there on the edges of the wild lands, brought news of the extraordinary activity and boldness of the outlaws – these "wolves and thieving rogues" as they were described in the Acts of Council.

In these secret meetings of the Maxwells, Samuel Tamson was, of course, deeply involved, having a greater stake in the business than most

– a child's life. But it was through Silver Sand, who took no part in these preparations for battle, that Eppie heard that, so far, all was well with Marion. In fact, Silver Sand's silence in the midst of the noise of these war preparations was remarkable. Generally, he lived very quietly on the lands of Rathan whilst making only short journeys to sell his sand in the other parishes that lay on the south of the disturbed country. Nevertheless, it was through him that we heard of the acts of raiding and fighting with which the "wolves of the hills" were charged.

But soon after my recovery a remarkable day arrived. I remember it like yesterday, and it is unlikely that I shall ever forget it.

It was towards six o'clock on a wet, rainy September evening, when Silver Sand rode up to the House of Rathan. He came in and shook the raindrops from his coat, stood and warmed himself silently with his back to the fire in the hall, for the evening was cold and a fire was welcome. The time of the summer fruits was past, and the days of storms were approaching. For me it had been a year of years in spite of all the pain and the difficulty, for it had brought me great and continual joy; and, more than all, the hope of May coming to the House of Rathan before the new year, was like sunshine in the gathering night.

Silver Sand stood and looked at me for a while without speaking.

At last he said, " You had better get yourself over to the House of Earlstoun. It's likely you'll be needed there before the morning."

Then I asked him why. But he gave me no answer, saying that he and Eppie were quite sufficient to keep the House of Rathan against all comers.

"But," he added, "there will be no comers here, so take your musket and pistols and make your way. Them that bearded the lion can fight with Grimalkin."

I could not understand what he meant. So in some fear I took my arms and the boat, and went over towards Craigdarroch. There were no cattle around, nor any sign of habitation; but some one whistled to me as I went by in such a way that I knew David Maxwell was on watch there. So I kept on, hearing nothing but this single whistle coming out of the scattered buildings of the farmstead, the new thatch of which shone yellow in the gloaming.

The House of Earlstoun had previously been a baron's castle with a high wall around it and a centre keep; but within the outer wall there were now many buildings of stone and lime, roofed with red tiles. These had been built in more settled times, so that now there was only one great open space in the courtyard, in front of the gate. In ancient days, that gate was shut nightly, but this had not been the case for many years; and now it stood open, a mass of useless iron, which the Lady Grizel had often threatened to sell as scrap metal if the smith would only give her sixpence for it to make plough blades out of.

Lady Grizel had a reputation for being very rich, although she lived very plainly, and went about the house like one of her own servants. She listened to all the gossip of the country from Jen and the coachman-butler, but she was never considered to be a miser. On the contrary, she was credited as being "just as free and homely as any normal person." But her father's gold plate (which he had got from Charles the Second for his services to the cause of ridding the country of Whigs) was a favourite topic of conversation all over Galloway, and the House of Earlstoun, having never been broken, was always thought to be one of the richest in the country-side.

But to me it was only rich because my lass was there. As I went towards the dark and silent house I looked up at the windows for her but saw no one. There was not a gleam of light about the whole great hulk of the tower. This made me more anxious, thinking I had come too late. So, with some inward anxiety, I knocked at the door, and someone inside asked me who I was and what I did. When I answered there was a noise of voices consulting, and I got my pistols ready in my hands, while my gun swung at my back. For, indeed, I did not know what, if anything, might have happened.

But I heard the voice of my beloved asking them to open the door, since it was indeed myself, and she could not be mistaken.

So presently, with much creaking and noise of very rusty chains and bolts, the door swung open a little and my sweet love's hand came emerged to pull me in quickly. Then the door was slammed with a clang, and the bolts were made fast and a great barricade set up again at the back of it.

I was a little bewildered coming out of the windless silence of the night into the bustle of so many men, for I soon saw that the House of Earlstoun was held by no fewer than thirty stout fellows, with William Maxwell in command. But I did not yet understand the cause nor the need for such warlike preparations.

May took me through many passages until we arrived at the keep; then up a narrow winding stair which was so dark that it made it difficult for us to ascend (but as lovers together in a confined space, we did not rush), up into a well-lit room in which there was a fire, but all the windows were barred and bolted and the curtains were closely drawn.

There was the Lady Grizel, sitting with her feet in a great pair of slippers, and toasting them before the fire. Jen Geddes was also there, and May went and sat down by the side of the fireplace with a stocking she was knitting.

"You are welcome, Patrick. This is a strange situation. Have you ever heard the like of it? " said Lady Grizel, after I had saluted her.

I answered that I had heard nothing of the purpose of our coming together, except that Silver Sand had sent me, telling me that I would be of use.

"Silver Sand?" said she."What's Johnny-ah-hum-ah-hum—"

Then she suddenly stopped, and remained deep in thought for a long time.

"I suppose its the attitude of nobility that's about the creature that makes him do it, but it's a strange thing to stand against one's own flesh and blood."

Concerning which Delphic utterance I knew better than to attempt any question.

"Who are here?" I said."And what can I do, Lady Grizel?"

"There's all the Maxwell clan here, as well as the Taits of the Torr, Maclellans of Colin, Lennoxes of Millhouse, Cairnses from Hardhills, lads from Balmaghie, Sproats, and Charterses – such a crew to feed – but all men of mettle, with some skill in aiming a Queen Anne musket half full of slugs."

"And what is all the gathering for?" I asked.

"Jen!" said Lady Grizel.

"Yes, ma'am," says Jen, who was making a garment for herself and had a pin in her mouth.

"Why are you speaking so primly? Tell Patrick about your lad that came to see you this afternoon."

"Wait a moment," says Jen.

Then she carefully stuck pins all over her seam looking critically at it as she did so, and all of us waited on her to finish.

"You see," she said at last, "I had finished my work and had swept my kitchen. Then I was even making myself tidy —"

"Making yourself spruce for the lads, Jen," said her ladyship, swaying in her chair and laughing till the floor shook. She often laughed at the littlest things.

"And why not?" said Jen.

"He may come yet, Jen," said her mistress. "You haven't waited too long yet – only forty years to my knowledge!"

"Of course, I haven't lost hope yet, any more than your ladyship has," said Jen, very much unabashed.

"Well, as I was saying, I had just put on my bonnet and was tying the strings when up came a lad to the kitchen door. He had a look of tar about him that made me know he was a sailor.

"'Good-day to you, mistress! Do you want any sea coal?' says he.

"Now 'sea coal' means only one thing in Galloway, and it's the coal that warms you from the inside. So I went upstairs to see the mistress, for I wasn't sure whether she might want a drop put behind the wall when the Freetraders next passed by in the early hours.

"When I came down again, I took the other stair that enters by the larder.

"My slippers made no noise. I just looked in and what was my fine lad doing but trying the bars of the windows and looking around the parlours? He had a footrule in his hand as well, but what he was measuring is more than I can tell.

"So I went back out of sight, and made a little cough and then went in.

"My man was sitting on a chair by the kitchen table as innocent as a pussycat when she has half a pound of fresh butter in her belly.

"'You have a fine view,' he says, looking out of the window, as though he hadn't moved.

"'Pff. It's a fine night for oatcakes," says I. 'Your back as you walk down the lane would be a far finer view. Walk, my lad, I want no spies and snoopers in my house!"

"So he went on his way. But before he went, he gave me a black look and a black word.

"'I'll be seeing you again,'says he.

" 'Almost certainly,' says I.'I go to all the hangings. You're a fine lad, but you'll dance the dance which has no steps some morning soon – and you'll make a bonny tassel at the end of a rope!'

"Then he told me where witches meet their end.

"'No,' says I,'I'll not be going there, even if it was only to keep out of your way'

"Then in came Silver Sand with a tale of raid, murder, and robbery, and in a little while the Maxwells came here with all their band, and I had my lady's orders to let them in. That's all I know, except that we are just three poor women that's to be murdered."

There was silence after Jen's tale, and May gave me something to eat and drink, the which I swiftly despatched, and went out – for it was not meet that on such a night I should detain the women, even though one of them was my own dear May. She came to the door with me, and told me, as all women do when their men go out to war or danger, to be sure to take good care of myself for her sake.

"I would come with you," she said, "and help, as I did on the Gairy of Neldricken, but my lady says I'm to stay with her in the keep."

So with a little pain but a great eagerness, I bade her farewell for the night.

Then I looked for Kennedy Maxwell, who was my closest friend among all of May's brothers. He was on watch at a window opposite to the great iron gate that stood open. I said I would prefer to be near him during what was coming. So he told me to go and speak to his brother Will, who was the captain and organiser of the band. Accordingly I did so, and in a little while was at my window within a couple of yards of Kennedy, where I could see down into the courtyard, and also over the main wall of the castle to the fields. I could even see the gravelled walk sweeping away through the trees of the avenue.

It was almost pitch black, for the stars were dim and lost in the thin cloud overhead. As we stood to our posts, steadily and clearly in a gallery behind, a clock struck the hours.

Once I thought that I heard horses, as though an iron shoe had slipped on a stone; but again it might only have been from the stables of Earlstoun, the noise of a horse rising to its feet.

"What do you think they might want?" said I to Kennedy. "It cannot be Hector Faa looking for May again?"

"Hector Faa – my foot!" he said, in a contemptuous whisper. "This is a bigger job than the kidnapping of your sweetheart," he said. "They're after the old wife's rents and lease payments, and maybe they think that my father's brass chest is here as well."

I was both relieved and disappointed to hear that Hector Faa had nothing to do with the raid.

"Mind you there are those in this business," continued Maxwell,"that have some pride. This is no Macaterick's ploy – though of course there'll be both Macatericks and Marshalls there. But the finest of the Solway Freetraders will be riding through that door before the morning, and afterwards you and me will either be eating our porridge in Earlstoun kitchen or getting our kale broth somewhere else, depending on circumstances and upbringing."

" What set them against her? " said I, for the Lady of Earlstoun had always been well thought of as one of the old stock, and favoured natural justice before the law.

"Goodness knows," said Kennedy. "Mostly greed and bad blood. Besides they have a quarrel with us, and they know she has given shelter to May. So they think, no doubt, that she is in cahoots with us."

"I knew well what would happen," continued Kennedy, in a discontented tone. "Our Will is always so fond of keeping within the law he wanted permits from Sir Andrew Agnew to pursue and make an end of the outlaws of the hill country. So of course he got it for the asking, and thank you very much – for the Government of King George has enough to do in the north for them not to be pleased to get any jobs like this off its hand. But the warrant was posted in Edinburgh and as soon as word of it came to Carrick and Galloway I knew they would be all down on us, buzzing like a bees' nest.

CHAPTER XXXVII.

THE SILVER WHISTLE BLOWS

"GREAT HEAVENS! Do you hear that? "said Kennedy.

A clear jingling came from over the moor.

"That's a horse shaking its bridle reins,"said I.

I began to feel unsettled. It was eery to sit by the unglazed narrow window straining one's ears, and with every bird that cried on the moors making the heart jump. A corncrake among the long grass cried, " Crake – crake!" but there was something in the tone of it which told me that that bird wore a buff jacket and steel cap, if I was not mistaken. An owl flew by with a soft waft of its wing. I had thought, but was not sure, that I had heard a hoot from the centre tower where Neil Cochrane stood on guard. He was an Ayrshireman, and I heard him say, " Shoo, you beast!" under his breath.

My nerves were tugging at my arms, and had a cat crossed the courtyard I declare that I should have loosed off my musket at it. I could not see much from my window, apart from the blackness of the courtyard, and the glimmering grey space of the great open doorway which was where, if anywhere, danger would come.

Suddenly something black, like a four-footed beast appeared in that grey space. I had my gun at my shoulder to fire, but the shape was familiar, so I dropped it. I recognised the spread of his hind legs. It was Quharrie, and I am sure it was his master moving furtively like a shadow across the grass plot behind him.

Where could he be going? Was he warning the enemy or acting as our advance guard? The questions which had tormented me ever since Silver Sand became involved in our matters returned with a new and overwhelming intensity.

Was it possible that Silver Sand was still playing on both sides? Could it be that he was, through all his twisting and secrecies, working for the interests of our cruel and revengeful enemies?

I had good cause to think so, but then again simply could not believe it. Yet again Silver Sand had all of us in his power. Had he wished to destroy us on this occasion, all that he needed to do was simply to lie in his camp and wait for our destruction. Yet he may have come to save us. Why did he always hang about on the edge of the fray?

How was it that whenever it came to a fight and the swords had been sharpened for war, Silver Sand disappeared and was never to be seen, reappearing only to cover the retreat of the foe? I found no answer, and, in fact, it would not have been possible for me to find one at that time. The matter was far beyond me at that moment, and depended on something which I never suspected. So I need not have troubled myself that night by trying to solve the problem.

But I knew that the enemy could not be far off, for Silver Sand was often like a stormy petrel where danger was concerned. But the night closed in again, and I grew deadly weary out of inaction. I heard Kennedy softly cursing the entire universe, but particularly his brother Will, because he was numb with cold and had been forbidden to smoke or so much as to spit – a dire prohibition to an untamed Galloway man who spits in his sleep, and still more especially in church, regurgitating all through the sermon like Solway tide in the narrows of Rathan.

Outside, the corncrake cried as if it was beneath the wall. There was more of the steel cap in the sound than before. The fellow was near by, perhaps under the wall. Then farther off a snipe, whose note is the clan call of the wolves of Buchan, called out with a whinnying noise. To my imagination, it was as if the bird had once been given a soul, but had now lost it forever, although it was destined to search for it all over the moorland.

Whilst on Rathan, I had learned to imitate all the moorland sounds, and those of the sea fowl, and there was no bird call that I could not easily reproduce, apart from the snipe. So, as a lad does, I practised the call night and day, till one day the bird itself came nearer and landed clumsily beside me like a cherub with a broken wing. I was so proud that I never made soup out of him, but sent him off, a very astonished bird, to bleat again after his lost soul upon the moor. In this matter I thought that I could beat even Silver Sand.

I grew so utterly weary of the tension that I put my head out of the window to look about me, despite inviting a shot had any enemy been near enough. For some moments I drank in the night air, and it invigorated me. Again the bird whinnied in the air. I looked closely for him, since it was early for the snipe to be on the move, even in the nesting time of the year.

Before I knew it my pride overcame me. With my tongue vibrating upon my palate, and my hand directing my voice upward, I let the weird sound float out three times on the night air. I thought I performed it so accurately that I felt sorry for the lonely bird seeking its soul. It sounded like the whisper of the air as the bird took off, then the quiver of the stoop, and the sharpening *crescendo* as the bird caught itself up again and began to ascend. Never had I done it better. Indeed I did it too well, and had Will Maxwell known then what he will know now, if someone reads this account to him, he might well have taken my life. But even Kennedy at my elbow was deceived, and cursed heartily at the noisy bird, which pleased me, despite my having disobeyed the orders we had been given.

But what happened next was more astonishing. The crake I had heard before immediately cried three times beneath the wall and this time, it was certainly from a human. That fellow deserved a bullet in him for doing it so poorly. The snipe which I had answered went on crying. Again I sent my voice up into the dark night, and this time was answered from below with a crake. I called out once more, and then all soft and mellow from out on the waste, as clear as a flute, a silver whistle blew.

Then knew I that at last the fat was in the fire and I looked carefully at the lock of my weapon.

I heard Will Maxwell speak behind me.

"Fire when the gate darkens!" he said, and moved on, like a keen soldier with the eye of the Duke of Ramillies himself.

Then suddenly the Great House of Earlstoun and all of its entrances and approaches was surrounded by a ring of noise. Hoofs clattered up the pebbled avenue, feet clambered upon the wall, and from the other side where the office-houses were, came the sound of a sledgehammer thundering on a gate somewhere.

A deep voice cried, "Open!" but no answer was given from the other side. The hammer again thundered upon the wood with a hideous clamour. Then with a crash, the gate gave, and there came a rush of trampling feet.

Horse iron clanged on the hard pavement beneath the gate. A man on a gigantic horse filled up the doorway.

"Hector Faa, as I'm a living soul," said I to myself, and then fired. The echo from the little opening through which I had set my gun deafened me. I did not hear the noise of any other shots, but I am told that as soon as my piece had given the signal, a dropping and irregular fire came from all around the house, first from our side at the ports and wickets, and then a return from the enemy from outside.

I saw that the man in the doorway had fallen, and lay across the entrance. Then those outside the gate drew the horse away, and in the darkness I could see the man trying to crawl clear attempting to lie down in the shelter of the wall.

But now, riding two abreast, a crowd of men drove right into the quadrangle of the court from the entrance. They had been astonished by their reception, never dreaming that the tower was garrisoned. Yet they were not men who would be discouraged. So they rode in. Why they came on horseback, when it would have been a more effective tactic to come on foot, I know not; but they did. Perhaps the outlaw men never cared to trust themselves far from their horses while they raided in the low country, and certainly every smuggler on the shore kept a swift beast as the main tool of his craft.

In any event they trampled in upon their garrons till the courtyard was nearly full, and on the strong main door that I had used to enter the house, the sledgehammers began to thunder.

"Fire!" cried Will Maxwell at last, and almost as one the guns went off, and men tumbled right and left among the horses' feet.

"Load with lead shot!" cried the voice of Will Maxwell, high up on the tower.

"Let me do it for you, just like I did in the cave!" said a voice in my ear, softly. It was May Maxwell, standing with shawl over her head in the stone passage.

Without a word I handed her my piece, and the flask and lead lay on the stone sill. Was she not a soldier's daughter – a Maxwell – and about to become the Lady of Rathan?

What right had I to forbid her? Her kind had stood behind fathers and husband for many a day, with the powder-flask in recent years and before that with the dirk. May was good with either, as I had found out.

The next volley came irregularly, according to how quickly the Maxwells and their men could reload.

The shots scattered widely among the animals, and the whole courtyard became a leaping and plunging hell of maddened horses. They blocked the gate. They fought with each other, biting and kicking. The breaching blows upon the great door ceased. The strikers with the sledge hammer had been swept away, most likely by the feet of the horses, for I heard confused cries and groans as the turmoil swept beneath me.

It was pitiful, but I thought once more about the body in the sea-chest, since the image of that broad, cold, white expanse with the two red gashes in it had stayed in my memory ever since. So I hardened my heart again and fired into the brown mass, and all the while May handed me my piece as deftly and calmly as a man-at-arms.

The tide of men and horses now pushed through the gate, and though the men had seemed to take a long time to get inside, the rush of the maddened horses carried them out swiftly, and the courtyard emptied itself like the White Horse Sands when the ebb surges back through the gut of Solway.

But there were three men and a horse that lay still on the red flags. One of the men was groaning, but I thanked God that the horse was dead, since I never could bear a dumb brute in pain.

"If that wasn't the Miller of Barnboard that I put a shot into, my name's not Kennedy Maxwell," said a voice."The foul thief – he owes us for four steers!"

CHAPTER XXXVIII

THE SECOND CROWING OF THE RED COCK

MAY had silently stolen away from my side during the outlaws' retreat, no doubt to carry the news to the Lady Grizel. Again there was a period of waiting, and it was wearing, as such pauses during action always are. But the next attack was from the side which I could not see. First there came a bank of thick smoke drifting and eddying round the tower, followed by the uncertain flicker of flames, casting red reflections on the already crimson-splashed courtyard. The repulsive men were lying there with black masks across their faces; but one, in the corner beneath us, had in his agony torn his off, and revealed the features of Gil Macaterick, whom I had seen last by the "Murder Hole " on the side of Craig Neldricken.

We were still waiting until Will Maxwell cried from the top of the battlements for ten men to come from the north side to the high tower wall. I sprang up to get in front of Kennedy, for I knew that one of us would surely be sent back. Then it seemed that Kennedy was certain to get there ahead of me, being able to reach the stair first, so I said, "Kennedy, have you your ramrod? " which made him search for it, whereupon I leapt in front of him, putting my hand on his chest and pushing him out of the way. I left him using, as was his custom, the language for which our soldiers were noted in Flanders. For this may I be forgiven?

From the tower top there was an astonishing sight. Men were hurrying about the outhouses with brushwood bundles, and half a dozen of our picked marksmen were shooting at them as if they were running deer — impressive to see, as one and another dropped his man.

So here, on the top of the keep, I stood still in wonder, until Will Maxwell came and gave me a great clap on the back, ordering me to crouch behind the wall, and do some good shooting for my board and lodging. He kept marching up and down, and must have made a conspicuous target to those below, for just as I dropped behind the stepped battlements a bullet came"spat" against the wall by which I had been standing, driving most viciously, and fell flattened and frayed at my feet. It was quite warm. Will Maxwell was rolling up one arm with a napkin, using the other hand and his teeth, but always looking mighty coolly at the men running round the office-houses with firebrands. The ball had just nicked him as it passed.

The burning sticks crackled and a great cloud of dense smoke arose, especially from the back of the stables, where we could hear the poor horses plunging. But the enemy now kept carefully under cover, and though we continued shooting at them I could see it was having no effect.

"This is the second time I have heard the Red Cock crow," said Will Maxwell. "The third time I'll be doing the crowing myself."

He stood on the tower top looking around as calmly as though he had been setting out a day's work at building walls, and then said --

"This will not do, boys; we'll have to go out to get at them!" So with that he took twenty of us (of whom alas! I was not one), and made ten to go out of each of the two opposite doors, with orders to run round the back of the byre and stables to slay all who opposed them, while he and three other men scattered and put out the fires already kindled.

So this they did, while two of the Maxwells kept the gates.

Although I was not included in those chosen to leave the walls, nevertheless I slipped out after them from the lesser door on the south side, the one which the outlaw men had attacked first. It was the great Nick Haining of Dalsleuth who was leading our advance, and the men made their way to the corner of the barn, dropping on their knees to take aim when they rounded it – no doubt raking the enemy sheltering there with a severe cross fire, for at that moment Will Maxwells party began to shoot from the corner by the carriage house. I did not get involved with either party, since I only had my pistols with me, but I ran to the stables, where I loosened the plunging horses and turned them out, for I could not bear to see the poor beasts burnt or hear their crying.

They had been driven wild with the noise, the flickering lights of the torches, and the smoke. Since I was not known to them, they would not let me near them, but they almost knocked out my brains against the wall with their flying heels. However, from the ancient corn-crib that stood in the corner and had a good high lid, I swung myself up among the rough joists; and with my great clasp knife I leaned down and cut their halters one by one, scrambling perilously along the rafters. Whereupon each turned and made for the door, I giving them a sound slap on the hip as they went past for the little trouble they had caused me. So in a trice the stable was emptied and I went on to see after the cows.

The smoke was thicker in the barn, but luckily all the cows were out and only one little late-dropped calf was in its stall, bleating most piteously. I also freed it and turned to the door.

But no sooner had I done so than I saw our men, with Will Maxwell in the lead, running across the yard and through an open gate, which clashed in the face of the crowd of men that pursued them. It was done so quickly that I could not see everything, and in the uncertain light of coming dawn and the flickering of the dying fires I could not clearly make out their numbers. But it seemed to me that there were only eight of them. Several, therefore, must be dead or taken.

As I considered my own position it seemed exceedingly likely to me that there might be more missing at roll-call, and that one of them would be myself.

The men who had rushed after Will Maxwell's small band returned quickly to where they came from because a gun or two cracked from the walls, and a man stumbled and came down on his hands and knees, crawling away painfully on all fours. As for me, I lay a long time stretched out on a beam in the barn, but since the beam was an untrimmed rough log, I was exceedingly uncomfortable. I was in constant pain and thought I was bound to fall even though half of me was on either side of the wretched thing. I forgot that barn joists are not meant for places of concealment.

Suddenly there was a noise from outside. A man came in and looked all around the barn, standing tall in the doorway. I could easily have shot him from where I lay, for I saw the whites of his eyes. He walked stealthily, and the dancing lights from outside glinted on the blade of the long knife he was carrying. He crept around with a stooped slouch that looked sinister. That was distasteful enough, but I hated even more the red gleam of the fired stack which shone in the man's eyes through a narrow wicket of the byre as he looked about. A man could be hanged for having such a face like that in broad daylight; but in the dark of a cowshed, and with the whites of his eyes flickering red, and his upper lip pulled high over his gleaming teeth, I thought it could have been the devil himself looking for me. I think that if even Hector Faa had come into the byre just then I would have craved protection from him.

Just then the tread of a light foot at the door could be heard, and my gentleman with the red eyes leapt swiftly under me with his knife point down, and sprang into the darkness of the haystack at the end of the byre. Then there was stillness. But what a stillness! My heart beat against the beam like a hammer. I listened till I could hear the spiders spinning their webs. I heard the mice creep, and the woodlice and little beasties running among the thatch. I almost heard my own flesh crawl on my bones – as perhaps I did, for I feared that it would get down by itself, leaving my skeleton hanging there on the joist.

I do not know how long this suspense could have continued, but the light noise at the door could still be heard. Something called from outside, but weakly; and I could hear my gentleman of the eyes and teeth stirring in the hay.

At last the grey oblong of the door was filled by the outline of a living shape.

"Patrick!" said a voice I knew well, in a whisper.

Gracious Providence above be merciful! *It was May Maxwell!*

With a quick snarl like a wild beast, the creeping rascal sprang from the haystack at the end of the barn. As he sped underneath me I could see his knife gleam when he turned the blade upwards to strike at May. But he never reached the door, for one of my pistols went off in my hand, more by instinct than of intention. He staggered a moment, and then fell forward, falling flat on his face in the gutter of the byre. His knife flew and fell at May Maxwell's feet. Down I leapt, and taking her right hand with my left as she stood amazed, and with my undischarged pistol in the other, we ran to the little side entrance swift as ghosts and hammered on it.

No doubt the guard was at his wicket, for it was some moments before we were noticed and could make them understand who we were. Inside I heard Jen raging like one possessed for some man to come and help her to turn the key. It had been jammed with a bar to keep any from turning it with nippers from the outside. The keyholes at the Great House of Earlstoun were large enough to put a fist into, and turning the key was a burden, even for a sturdy lad.

It was only for a moment or two that we stood there, but to us it seemed an eternity. For as we waited, nervously, for the door to open, some men ran to the cowshed to find out the reason for the shot, and when the first man crossed the threshold he shouted aloud and threw up his hands. Then another turned and saw us at the door, then he levelled his piece at us. I saw the gleaming gun barrel turn into a black dot, and with all my strength I thrust May behind me. A horrid burning pain in my leg and the jerk of every nerve and muscle threw me back, telling me that I had been hit somewhere. I never heard any gunshot at all, but I knew that May had caught me and dragged me inside just as the door opened.

Jen was there with a candle, and they quickly ripped away my stocking and saw the wound. It was nothing. A shot had gone clean through the fleshy part of my calf, happily without injuring either bone or muscle.

The wound was not serious, as even May saw.

So they washed it and bound it up, and I insisted on going back again to my post with my gun.

But the great raid was over. The Red Cock would crow no more. The day was dawning, and the outlaws and their friends stole away like the grey night-wolves that they were. But as May and I looked down we saw a something horrific. Each dead man seemed to rise by himself and crawl backward towards the gate. We remained stiff with terror, rooted to the spot with fear, and soon nothing remained in the courtyard but the red splashes and the broad, shallow pools of blood. I do not know how they managed it, but probably, under the cover of a cloud, they sent some of their smaller and more dextrous thieves to carry off the dead to prevent their discovery. These, getting beneath, may have slunk off with the body, which in the darkness was both a protective shield and a terror to the onlooker. However it was done, I know that not a shot was fired. For me, I would rather fire at a corpse at a funeral as at these dead men who had apparently come to life again and went crawling off, trailing their blood behind them on the slippery flags of the courtyard.

The silver whistle blew time and again, farther and farther away. Then the morning came and the sun rose. There was a great silence about the house till we heard the cocks crowing upon the midden at the end of the barn. It was ironic that they had slept safely through all the clamour of the Red Cock crowing. The cocks of Craigdarroch answered in the distance, and from the Rathan Isle I thought I heard my own noble rooster crowing faintly and airily, like a cock in fairyland when the bells are ringing for the little folk to come home.

Then we all went out to see what we could find.

In the courtyard there were only the stiffening pools of blood, scarlet splashes blackening rapidly to crimson and puce – unwholesome and horrible. The marks of the sledgehammers could be seen on the spiked and plated doors, mostly around the handles and keyholes. The windows in the inner dwellings had all been smashed by bullets, and the sashes were splintered. On the roof the flagstaff had been hit and hung at an angle in a very sad and melancholy manner. The dead horse in the corner, with its eyes wide open, lay on its side. It was well dressed, and the mounting of the harness was of silver, of good quality but plain and wholly without crest or motto.

"That's no hill-country horse!" said Will Maxwell.

"I think I have seen the like about Barnboard," said Kennedy, lifting up the head, "and I'm thinking that if we opened the beast's stomach we would find some of our own meal."

And true it is that the Miller of Barnboard was never seen again in the countryside – neither at church or market, holy fair or cock-fighting.

On the threshold of the barn door lay the knife of the man with the teeth, which I removed and I still have it on the wall above me as I write here at Rathan.

My wife once took it down from over the mantelpiece and put it in a parlour cupboard where she never goes; but I found it and brought it back again. That is perhaps the difference between her and me. I had almost said between men and women but that might not be wholly true. She does not like think about these old dangerous black days when all is now peaceful, and Galloway is once more a sober place to live in. On the contrary, I enjoy thinking about every old memory, except the white body in the great sea-chest. That disgusts me.

CHAPTER XXXIX.

THE EARL'S GREAT CHAIR

IT was six weeks before I was myself again, and I remained at the Great House of Earlstoun under the watch of Jen Geddes and the Lady Grizel. It was wild weather and the winter was setting in earlier than usual, as it often does when we have a summer season better than usual -"two summers in a year," as the folk say.

There was indeed nothing to take me over to the Rathan, for the Dumfries masons and joiners were in, making such improvements to it as the age of the house and its ancient construction would allow. Eppie was on their backs all day long (so Silver Sand told me), scolding and raging at them, calling them useless, ham-fisted scoundrels. I could hear her in my head, and thought myself well out of the dust and the noise, especially as May Maxwell bandaged and bathed my leg with her own hands each day. Most of her cheerful spirit had returned, and it was entirely pleasurable to have her look in upon me with a smile and a bright word as she went up and down the stairs with a duster or feather brush in her hand.

Sometimes I would call to her to come to me for a moment. If it was morning and she had her house business to do, it was her custom to tiptoe round and kiss the top of my head where the parting of the hair is. Although, since I mainly have a wiry wisp of bristles, this mode of kissing is not particularly satisfying. But there was no point in complaining. I sat there in a great black oak armchair, which was not made any more comfortable because of the fact (of which Lady Grizel and Gib Gowdie reminded me twice a day) that three Earls had died in it. It was a monstrously cumbersome article of furniture, and there was no way of getting round to the back of it to reach her with my leg resting on a stool. Usually before I could even move, May Mischief would already be kissing her hand at me from the door, and saying in a tantalising way,"Wasn't that nice?"

The wretch!

But it was not always like that, for I played fox several times, by pretending to be in pain, which with one harder hearted than May was a game which would soon have stopped working. But she never quite knew whether I was pretending or not, and so (perhaps wanting just a little to give in) she would approach at long last to within my reach. Whereupon she retired for a considerable time into the depths of the Earl's chair.

"People are different," she once said, merrily. "Jen says that three Earls have sat here; but I'm thinking if two of them sat together at once in it, they would hardly have fitted as well as us."

Which made us become closer and even more of a match. So I continued to live in the snug shelter of the great house, and in the evenings Kennedy Maxwell would slip over and tell me tales of how the great raid on the outlaws was progressing. He described the ambitious plans. There were preparations being made on the borders of the Kells. Bands of men from Minnigaff and the edge of the next county were to be led by one of the MacKies of Glencaird. They were all to move as soon as the bad weather set in, for the only time to hunt the broken men out of their fastnesses was in the days of hard frost and when the moon was bright.

It was not until November that I could get out at all, and I was still a little lame in the middle of the month. Yet by the first week in December I could run with any of them up the Rathan Hill. However, I still stayed on in the great house by the command of Lady Grizel, who now openly assured us of her intention of leaving her whole estate to May Maxwell and her heirs for ever.

"But it will depend on how you behave yourself, Patrick my man, whether you and yours get any benefit. Men are not to be trusted, so I'll get Rab MacMonnies the lawyer to arrange the documents so that if you are not a good boy, May can put you out of the door with a mere 'good-evening to you!' How does that sound, May, my lass?"

But May, being of Scots blood and far from reckless, said nothing, bad nor good.

Whereupon the old lady would say, " You're all alike, you women, before you get married; your own lad is always 'like the little white hen that never lays away'; but afterwards – my word, you never stop pecking at his comb."

But for all Lady Grizel's kindness I do not think that either May or I thought anything would come out of her good will and even her promises. I have never yearned for great possessions, and the old house at Rathan was enough for me, and to this day I maintain that there is no place in the world like it. Because I have a warm affection for the land which nurtured and supported me in my youth. And May thinks so too.

But during these weeks there was always a suggestion of worry on May's brow, and I knew what was causing it. She knew of the preparations for the great raid on the den of the Wolves; but she, being the daughter of Richard Maxwell after all, did not dare to say a word to dissuade me from taking part in it. Yet I felt that she was anxious for me.

I could tell by the way that she would hang on the words of Kennedy when he came in the evening and we all sat by the fire.

On the other hand Kennedy and the rest of the Maxwells looked forward to this raid as being the greatest pleasure and excitement of their lives. They had taken out a Privy Council warranty for the extermination of the outlaws just as one might take out a license to shoot game in these present peaceful times, and they cleaned their guns joyously and jested about the sport they expected. Particularly for William Maxwell and some of the elder hands there was a deep and even a kind of perverted religious earnestness in the ploy. They had scores of death and burning to settle against the outlaws. They had a deeper, keener, even a religious hatred also, because the Faas and the Marshalls had been recruited by the remnants of the wild Highland Host that had ravaged the Lowlands a generation before, carrying away all that it could carry and burning whatever it could not. It was believed that in the gypsies' country there were hoards of the rich plunder of halls and the poor heirlooms of farm cottages, stolen by force in the terrible years that culminated in the unforgotten and unforgiven "Killing Times."

There was once a minister in Balmaghie who used to add a rider to the prayer, "Forgive us our trespasses as we forgive them that trespass against us," by saying, "But for Thy glory take the Laird of Lag and all the rest of the Malignants in Thine own hand, in case they repent and are forgiven!"

At last, the great raid was ready to begin by the 17th of December. From all sides, the men of the Lowland parishes were to close in upon the outlaw country. Men were mustered and equipped along the Solway shore, but there was no doubt that the Marshalls, Millers, Macatericks, and all the hideous crew that gathered about them knew what was in store for them, for the most part of their women were sent into Ayrshire, and out along the Freetrade routes to Edinburgh and Glasgow. Many of these were arrested by the Sheriffs of Ayr and Lanark as beggars and prostitutes, and were safely in prison when the attack was launched on the men whose worthy mates they were. Only a few of the most hardened and cruel, like my friend Eggface, remained to face the brunt of the coming storm.

CHAPTER XL

THE BREAKING OF THE BARRIER

IT was a cold morning when I put my fighting harness on my back, secured my sword by my side, kissed my lass, and swung into the stirrup with a sinking heart within me and wet eyes behind me.

I promised myself that if I managed to return safely to the old tower of Rathan (whose smoking chimney I could see, looking homely and friendly yet so far away), I would never again wear a leather jerkin, nor carry a heavy broadsword.

A soldier never rode to battle more unwillingly than I did, at least for the first three miles. But when I met Samuel Tamson, equipped with sword and pistol like the best – who was on foot, but moved as fast as a horse could trot, I changed my mind. I saw a strange glint in his eye, and I thought of little Marion whom only I had seen, and only May Maxwell had spoken to, since she was lost on the Silver Flow of Buchan so long ago. I was mustered into Will Maxwell's company, and fell in behind him in the front rank with Kennedy. Three or four young lads, handsome fellows with good horses that were brisk jumpers at fences, went on ahead as sentries.

It was a cold, dim, raw day, with a thick yellow haze in the air, and a grim grip of black frost underfoot. The horses' feet fell on the road, which was as hard as a pavement, and sounds carried a great distance. There was a flurry of snow in the air. The wind came in little gusts and swirls, raising blood into our cheeks as though they had been brushed with the lashed end of a whip.

I had risen late after a long night's rest, since nobody knew when we might sleep again with so much wild work ahead of us. I had been given a soldier's blue military cloak that had been worn by one of the Earls and in it, I found many useful and pleasant things, which were ideal for a hungry man in a winter campaign.

It was very touching to think of one of the very last things May said to me through her tears --

"See and keep your feet dry. There's a pair of socks in your left pistol holster."

This was as precious to me as many other affectionate words.

We were now riding westward to meet the men of Lower Minnigaff at the bridge of Cree. As we went the air became extraordinarily bitter. The wind dropped as we passed Cassencary, where in the estuary the tide was full with a turbid yellowish brown colour. As we rode clanking across Cree Bridge, snow began to swirl around us. I thought we were in for a great fall, and momentarily we thought to turn back, or at least to shelter for the night. But the entire operation had all been thoroughly planned, and to pause would likely result in putting off the attack indefinitely. Moreover, Will rightly argued that it was doubtful whether we would ever be able to get so many men and horses to come together for the same purpose again.

So we continued, and after a while I realised it was for the best, since I could not bear the thought of having to go through the parting with May all over again, and I became as eager as any to go through with it at once.

It was arranged that we were to leave our horses at the Lodge of Eschonchan near Loch Trool, where Lord Galloway had a post. Men were stationed here at all times of the year – making payments, of course, to the Marshalls to escape retribution, and also in the name of protection. Here we would leave a guard and push northward to finish the job once and for all.

We counted upon having the young moon, but it now seemed that moonlight would not be available to light us on our way, though she should have been in the sky by seven o'clock.

The snow flew thicker but in a curious, uncertain way, as though little breezes were blowing it back up from the ground. A flake would fall softly down till it neared the earth, then suddenly reel and swirl, rising again with a tossing motion as when a child blows a feather into the air.

As we went along the pale purple branches of the trees grew fuzzy with rime, which thickened till every tree looked like a wintry image of itself carved in whitest marble.

In truth I disliked the conditions, and I liked them less the more we went on. For the yellow mist was dense and clammy about us as we advanced. It had a raw, unpleasant feel about it, and as we rose higher up the Water of Trool it hung in fleecy waves and drifts against the brows of the hills. But what I least liked was the awesome darkness of the sky. The mist was almost white against it wherever there was a break, but the sky itself was dark and foreboding. A dismal, unnatural light seemed to pursue us and it barely enabled us to see. I cannot say that any of us were in good humour.

The feelings of most of us were expressed by old Rab MacQuhirr who had long been the shepherd on the Merrick and was now our guide.

"God save us and bless us!" said Rab; "I do not like this day. This is a devil's day! No day of God's making was ever like this! "

Which indeed may seem a foolish if not irreverent thing to say, but then had you been there and under the shadow of that loathsome cloud, maybe a belief in Providence would not have served you quite so well either.

The Glen of the Trool was dark and narrow as we went down into it along the waterside, and the loch itself lay black as night at the bottom of its precipices. It was like the entrance to the pit of blackness itself. The faintly falling snow had not lain on its surface, which made me want to unbind my father's Dutch ice-runners from the saddle. He had brought them home with him from the Low Countries as curiosities for people to admire; and often I used to amuse myself on the White Loch of the Clonyard, or upon the Orraland milldam when I did not want to go so far.

I took them with me, knowing that when we had to storm the fortress of the isle in Loch Enoch, my life might depend on my speed. Moreover, ice running was an accomplishment seldom tried in Galloway at that time, and I had hopes of returning with my honour and reputation enhanced.

After a long and weary plod up hill and down dale, the Lodge of Eschonchan came into sight. This was a place which the Lords of Galloway had used as a hunting lodge ever since they came to be overlords of that part of the Forest of Buchan – an area only Cassillis and the Kennedies had ruled in the past.

It is not large, but it is a strongly built house – though with hardly any articles of furniture, and bowls and platters of the poorest quality, because it is not wise to trust anything of value to the gypsies, even under the protection of the payment of mail. So my Lord the Earl does not keep his legal documents and treasure chests at the Lodge of Eschonchan.

Here, though, we had some refreshment, and rested for an hour. Then, leaving a guard with the horses just sufficient to protect them in case of attack, we walked on with most of the younger men.

Our route was up the same Gairland Burn which May, Silver Sand, and I had descended in such pain on that morning long ago. But I was not eager to go up it under that gloomy winter sky, because now every step took me further away from all I loved. I tried to think that it was for the best, which was certainly true; but somehow that had no effect on the state of my courage which had (as usual) sunk down into the pit of my stomach. It was, in truth, cold comfort.

We marched in close array with skirmishers searching higher up the slope to engage any hidden enemies, while the rest took the narrow path by the waterside, where the burn roared and swirled about the great grey stones.

We were soon deep among the hills, and yet not a shot had been fired at us. Not a frond of dry red bracken had waved. The rime lay close and thick, and the brown heather kept our footsteps quiet. The only sound which could be heard was when a scabbard rang now and then when it glanced on a granite slab, or a nail in some brogue screamed noisily against a stone, harsh and slippery with frost. No curlew or peewit cried. Only on a rock high on the Clints of the Nether Hill of Buchan, a black raven croaked his dismal song of gloom.

I was apprehensive, but I felt some exhilaration at the thought that we were soon to come to grips with the enemy.

We were just at the corner of the burn where, under a great black face of rock it is confined in a deep defile, when our scouts on the hillside raised cries of alarm, the reason for which we did not understand at the time.

"Come up!"they cried."The water's broken loose!"

Our shepherd guide and I took to the hill immediately, and so did many who were acquainted with the wild lochs and precipices about us, and with the nature of the wild men we were dealing with.

Suddenly from above we heard a tremendous roaring noise, as though the bowels of creation were gushing out in a great convulsion. Echoes came back from the hills on every side. I found myself climbing the slope with considerable speed until I reached the higher rocks. I was so nimble that I ran straight into the path of a hairy savage with matted locks, whose weapon was in his hand – the long dirk of the Highlander. But he had not expected any one to come at him over a rock in such a spectacular manner. He took my approach as a dangerous assault, thinking that to be so bold, I must have men behind me, because he instantly threw down his knife and raised his hands in surrender.

"Himself is only a poor Gregor lad, and doing no harm!" was his statement.

Behind me came our guide, Rab MacQuhirr and Kennedy Maxwell, at the sight of whom my captive plunged upwards weaponless among the rocks, and as it was a rough place, with many hiding-places between the boulders, he was soon out of sight. I was not unhappy about this because, had Will Maxwell come upon him and his dirk, that would have been the end of "himself", the poor Gregor lad.

But I placed the MacGregor dirk in my belt as a trophy.

The great roaring noise still continued. Suddenly those of us that were up on the side of the Gairy saw an awesome sight. A great wall of water, glassy black, tinged at the top with brown and crowned with a surging crest of white with many dancing overlapping folds, sped down the glen. Apart from those who had climbed the hill following the first alarm, our party was sheltered in the narrow passage. As the wave came down upon them there was overwhelming confusion. Men threw away their guns and took blindly to the hillside, running upward like rabbits that have been disturbed whilst feeding. From where we stood the water seemed to travel at a steady rate, but nevertheless many of our men were caught in the wash of it and spun downwards like corks in the inrush of the Solway tide.

The black, white-crested wave eventually passed, and the great flood subsided and ran clear with a creamy froth on it, but we could hear the boulders grinding and plunging at the bottom of the burn.

Then upon us, scattered as we were in confusion over the hillside, a storm of bullets came from behind the rocks higher up the Gairy. It was the first sign of the enemy, and we felt insulted.

I felt a sense of the unfairness of the deed. We had come prepared to give battle and to deliver an assault; but we wanted to do it in our own way and on our own terms. We felt that it was most deceitful (as well as unfair and two-faced) to scatter us over a great area of ground, and then attack us when we were least prepared.

But Will Maxwell had the spirit of a general. Standing on a rock, he sounded his pipe, calling all down from the bare hillside, where each man was exposed to the guns of the outlaws, to the burnside, which was strewn with boulders which could be used for cover.

The flood was still running, but was evidently past its peak. The great roaring sped farther and farther down the valley. We scrambled off the hill, running like foxes around the stones, and taking advantage of any chance of cover as we went. Bullets spatted uncomfortably among the rocks, but the aim of the hill men was not good, and the light was poor, so that very few of our men were wounded.

As soon as he had us all collected in the valley, our captain began moving in loose skirmishing formation along the side of the burn towards the loch. The outlaws above us also kept parallel with our march, shots cracked, and on the hillside there were sounds of cheering. But we kept on our way, and so far no one was seriously hurt, which showed that the aim of the enemy had been bad. But we did not know if ours was any better.

CHAPTER XLI

A RACE FOR LIFE UPON THE ICE

WHEN we came to the southern side of Loch Valley, from where the Gairland Burn issues, we saw a strange and surprising sight. There was a deep trench, the upper part of which had been cut through recently by hand, since spoil lay all around where the spades had been at work. The ends of a weir across the outlet of the loch were still to be seen jutting into the rushing waters. This had evidently been constructed with considerable care and certainly with immense labour. But now it was cut clean through, and we could see where their labourers had first used their picks; the power of the flood had done the rest. So great had been the force of the water that the passage was clean cut down to the bedrock as if it had been cut with a knife. The deep ridge of sand and pebbles, which lies like a barrier across the mouth of the loch, had been severed as one cuts sweet-milk cheese, and the black waters were still pouring out from an abyss under an arch of ice that spanned the loch.

But as we looked over the black and glistering expanse of hollow ice which swept away to our left, bright cracks began to form like forked lightning across its whole surface. The water had been sucked from beneath it, and it was held up only by its own weight.

The sounds made as the cracks and splits ran in all directions built up into a great roar, echoing from the hills. Gradually, most of this flashing and thundering turmoil centred at a point right in the middle of the loch. An intensely black spot began to gape there, from which the white, roaring cracks rayed out like the spoke of a wheel from the hub. On the edge of the loch we stood as if we were on the rim of a whirlpool, for the ice sloped down from our feet towards the black centre. Had any one set foot upon the edge of it they would have been carried down to the yawning hole, for the entire ice of the loch was giving way as the roof of a great cavern slopes and sways before it falls in.

Then with a crash that shook the ground the ice cave fell in upon the water in a thousand pieces, sending white foam mixed with dark lumps of ice high into the air, while underneath the broken fragments tumbled and crunched against one another like icebergs in a heavy sea. Then little by little, groaning and wheezing, the turmoil settled down; and Loch Valley, with its shivering cover of broken ice, settled down ten feet beneath its level of the morning.

Hardly anywhere else in Scotland could such a thing have been possible; but the outlaws took advantage of a high barrier of sand and shingle which had dammed the waters of the deep rockbound lake since the ice age. It was a true stroke of generalship, and showed us that we had more than the ignorant redhanded Marshalls and bloody Macatericks to deal with. It was so well thought out and nothing like the rough-and-ready knife and-bullet method of the common hill rogues.

Moreover, nothing more calculated to shake our nerve could be thought possible. We were thankful to regroup our scattered force, but there is no doubt that by this time most wished themselves well out of it. For me, at least, that six-foot wave of black water and the shining whirlpool of breaking ice had taken away any desire for revenge.

Nevertheless, as the darkness grew deeper, we made our way to the old sheep pens by the Midburn, which are solidly built like a fortress of great granite stones , with footings on the bedrock of the hills. There was room for all of us. By nature the place was strongly protected – on the one side by the roaring and dangerous Midburn, and on the other by an extensive peat bog. We hoped to be safe here, if not particularly comfortable, through the long winter night. We all had our cloaks wrapped around us; and my friend Kennedy had carried the Earls great military coat, partly for the warmth it gave him but also for the good things from Lady Grizel which it contained We had agreed to share both the cloak and its contents.

But this outcome was not at all what I had foreseen. My chances of glory were few, and the raid seemed likely to end in disaster. To run uphill and take prisoner a shaggy highlander (who immediately escaped again), and to be penned like one of a score of sheep in a granite sheep pen, were not what I had expected. But how could I improve on it?

The outlaws on the hill had given us no further trouble, in fact their engagement with us had been limited to the moment when the rush of the gaping waters of Loch Valley made us retreat and scatter.

"The Carrick men should be coming by now,"said Will Maxwell. "Oh, if only we had some one to go up and see what they are doing!"

The old shepherd of the Merrick knew the country but he was old and stiff; and, besides, he had little interest in the matter. I felt the same way, except that I wanted to burn the Shieling of Craignairny and get that accursed sea-chest out of my dreams. But I think the devil must have been at work because, without thinking, I suddenly announced to everyone that I would put on my ice-runners and go. This caused great astonishment and admiration. I regretted this immediately and silently called myself a fool many times over; but my accursed pride would not let me take back what I had already said.

May Maxwell says today that that was the wickedest thing I ever did, because I forgot my promise to her and that I should have let one of the others go. All which I know is true, but then none of the others would have offered.

But all the lads of the raid encouraged me, and said that I was the bravest of the brave, and other things which young men like to hear. So I took my ice-runners in my hand – which I have said my father had brought from Holland. Kennedy Maxwell and four others, all proper young men with well grown beards on their faces, which often made me envious, came to see me safely off. I proposed to circle Loch Neldricken on the ice first, so that I could be sure there were no enemies lurking about it. I did this, not because I thought that the outlaw men would camp there, but so that these young men who had formerly scorned me, especially Colin Screel and Kennedy Maxwell, might observe me bravely going off into the night alone. Such a thick-skull was I, and so void of common understanding! But I enjoyed being admired and to be recognised for doing something that others would not attempt. And this same odd form of cowardice, for I had little real courage, has often carried me through with credit. I am like the old soldier who said, when complimented on his bravery in battle, "We are all black afraid, only – we do not all show it!"

I had enough sense to keep my fears to myself at the time. Now it does not matter, for I am a middle aged man, and such is the power of having a reputation that I cannot change it by myself. Even this plain confession of weakness will not be believed; which is perhaps, after all, the reason why I have mentioned it in this account. So apt is man at deceiving others – and himself.

But I went forth, binding my ice-runners of curved iron to my feet at the little inlet where the Midburn issues – too strong and fierce to ever freeze, except at the edges where the frost and spray hung in fringes, reaching down like cold fingers into the rapid waters.

Away to the left stretched Loch Neldricken, the midmost of the three lochs of that wild highland region – Valley, Neldricken and Enoch. I set foot gingerly on the smooth black ice, with hardly even a sprinkling of snow upon it, for the winds had swept away the little feathery fall, and the surface was smooth as glass beneath my feet. Each of the young men shook me silently by the hand. I suppose they thought me brave but foolish, for I had lost no cattle and had a bride-to-be safe at home. Yet there I was, setting off into the black night in the face of unknown danger

– dangers which made the close-packed well-fenced camp in the sheep pen seem as safe as one's own fireside.

I struck out from the edge with great strokes, moving my hands with each sway of my body as I had been taught by my father. In a moment the four lads were far behind me and I was alone on the black ice; yet I had that feeling of arrogance which all swift motion gives. The ice whirled behind. Following the southern edge, I was between the narrows in a minute. Here a jutting promontory of land – a mere tongue of sand and boulder – cut the loch almost in two. There was a fire kindled on the south shore, the one nearest our camp. On the opposite side as I sped by I thought I saw two men standing with muskets in their hands; but it was so dark I could not be sure if they saw me. However, with the fire on the shore opposite to them and the passage through which I went was not more than twenty yards wide, they could hardly fail to. They must have thought me the evil one himself, flitting by on the wings of the wind.

I sped away with the blades on my feet cutting crisply through the thin-sprinkled snow, the imposing mass of the Black Gairy casting a gloomy shadow overhead. An odd flake or two of snow hit my face as I bent low to look sideways up the hill. I went slowly, moving only my body and hardly making a sound, as the night parted before and closed behind me.

It took only a short time to make the circuit of the loch and return to the narrows; but as I passed I accelerated, for I knew that this time it would be dangerous. The watchers would now be on the alert and might have realised that the devil would not use iron runners, but instead use wings like the bat. So I bent low and scudded through the strait with the dying fire on one side and the land closing in to trip me upon the other. I was just in the middle and running my best, when a couple of shots went off, and the bullets tore past behind me screaming like plovers whistling down the wind.

I was so excited with my escape and proud of my daring that I shouted as I flew; but I should have held my tongue, for shortly after I saw that my speed was taking me out of the region of flat ice into a low forest of dense green reeds. I turned quickly, but my momentum was too great. I was carried straight into them, and there, not twenty yards in front, lay the bottomless depths of the Murder Hole, like a hideous black demon's eye looking up at me. For the second time I came close to being its victim. I remembered the tales told of it. It never froze and it was never white with snow. With its open mouth it lay waiting like an insatiable beast for its offering of human life; it never gave up a body committed to its depths, nor betrayed a murderer.

The thin ice swayed beneath me, but did not crack – which was a bad sign, since that meant it was brittle and weakened by the reeds. The edge of the horrid place seemed to rush towards me, and the reeds opened to show me the way. I had gone down on all fours as I entered the rushes; now I grabbed hold of them as I swept along, and so came to a standstill, but only a short distance from the edge. I hardly dared to move, until, inch by inch, by pulling myself forward and pushing backward, I once more found safe ice; then I made directly for the shore, for the Murder Hole was more terrifying to me than a tribe of Faas armed to the teeth.

In a few moments I had unshipped my runners, reached the heather, and was making the best of my way over the Ewe Rig towards the great barrier of Craig Neldricken, behind which Loch Enoch lay. As I went I heard the moor-birds cry – the wild whirl of the curlew and the croak of the raven. Now I knew well that most of these would be the signals of my foes answering one another, because the gypsies can imitate any bird that flies; besides which, the curlew is seldom seen on these moors in winter and the snipe never is. A thought struck me. I set my hands to my mouth in the way that I have already described, and made the whinny of the snipe palpitate across the moor.

Instantly, as on the night of the blowing of the silver whistle, I was answered from both sides; my summons had aroused a whole colony. But towards Loch Arron, lying straight in front of me, there was not a single sound. So I called again more persistently and, as it were, querulously; and immediately set off running headlong upward in the direction of Loch Arron, which I felt would be my best chance of safety.

More than once I had to crouch among the rocks to let a man run past me, so effective and imperative had my second call been. It was a blessing that almost everywhere over all that country there is a hiding-place within each half-dozen yards; or else had I would have been a dead man ten times over.

I skirted Loch Arron without putting on my ice-runners, because it is little more than a mountain tarn, and I knew that if there were any guards in the direction I was travelling they would be up at the Nicks of Neldricken, or at the Slock of the Dungeon – the passes which are the usual roads to the tableland of Enoch. Without a moment's hesitation, therefore, I set my feet upon the rugged Clints, hoary with rime and slippery with frost.

Born by the shore of the Solway, with cliffs at my door, and gulls' eggs for my playthings, I was at home wherever there was a need to hold myself up by my arms. Dark or light did not make any great difference to me, and as my fingers thrilled with cold as they caught the rocks, I cannot say that I was agitated by the perils of climbing the Clints of Neldricken.

CHAPTER XLII

THE FASTNESSES OF UTMOST ENOCH

AS I went, part of me thought that I would never see the sun shining on my own house at home on a pleasant day again. I was more angry about the pride that had carried me up here among the hills where I had no business than I was hopeful of success. I could well have stayed in my walled dwelling of Rathan, and, with some of the credit I had earned from my previous deeds, could have settled comfortably with my wife. But seemingly I needed to be climbing here on the edges of creation like a tom-cat on the tiles just for the pride of being spoken about. And for what? So that young men might wonder and admire, and the message would spread across the country that no-one was as brave as Patrick Heron! This, though, was untrue; for even now I was unhappy with the course of action I was taking, and I was fearful, having the bravery of a mouse, and even then a poor mean one.

Yet I had to go on, because the hunters were both behind me and ahead of me. I gripped the icy crags of the granite rock tightly, and looked up at the dense bank of stars above me, for the clouds had now blown clear. Or perhaps, since the cliff was so high, I may have risen above the frosty mist. At any rate it was a deadly cold place, and my fingers soon became numb. Later they seemed to swell and throb with heat to the point that I thought they were dropping off.

Eventually I reached the topmost ledge of all, and crawling a few paces, I looked down upon the desolate waste of Loch Enoch under the pale light of the stars. It is almost impossible to describe what I saw, yet I shall try.

I saw a weird wide world, new and strange, as if it was emerging from the chaos of creation – but was not yet approved by God. Such a scene might have been on the far side of the moon, which no man has seen nor can he see. I thought with some sadness and pity about the poor souls condemned, because of the crimes they had committed, to live there. I also thought that, if I been living so far from honest society and friendly people, I might have become no better than the outlaws. I blamed myself that I had been so slack and careless in my attendance to religious matters, promising (for the comfort of my soul as I lay there looking at the terrible scene) that when I was back in Rathan, May and I would ride each day to church upon a good horse, she behind me upon a pillion – and that thought gave me strength. At any rate I convinced myself that God could not destroy a youth like myself with such excellent intentions.

But this is what I saw, as clearly as the light permitted – a huge, conical hill in front, the Hill of the Star, glimmering snow-sprinkled as it rose above the desolations of Loch Enoch and the depths of the Dungeon of the Buchan. To the left the great steep slopes of the Merrick, bounding upward to heaven like the lowest steps of Jacob's ladder. Loch Enoch lay beneath, very black, set in a grey whiteness of sparse snow and sheered granite. Then I saw in the midst of the loch, the Island of Outlaws, and on it, I thought, a glimmering light.

So I began to crawl downward. I now moved as if I had left my fear behind me sticking to the frosty

Clints of Neldricken. The distance between me and the loch was hardly as far as a bowshot, and I soon found myself putting on my runners on the edge of the ice behind a huge rocking-stone, my heart racing. Then I was not at all afraid, thinking that on the ice, which was so black and polished, I could out-distance all pursuers, for nobody in Galloway could skate as well as myself.

The ice sloped away from the edge, and I had some concerns as I slid downwards, in case I was slipping into another chasm like the one I had seen open for me at the Murder Hole of Loch Neldricken.

But there was only a great expanse of flat ice ahead of me, and I struck out softly. It was beautiful ice, smoother than I had ever seen, since it had frozen early, and had a skin on it like fine bottle glass. But the air was now so clear and still that, whatever I did, I could not prevent my ice-runners ringing, and the whole loch now twanged like a fiddle-string when one hooks it with the forefinger and then lets go. Yet as I swept along, swinging my arms nearly as low as the ice, and taking sweeping strides like a Low Countryman, I was proud that nothing in Galloway could come near me for speed.

I was so sure, that with a sweep like an albatross (so I imagined) I circled about to the island where the dying fire was. It seemed as if the light came from a kind of turf-covered shelter – not a clay-built house with windows like that in which I had spent that night of terror on the slopes of Craignairny. There were men crouching around the fire, all looking out to the loch, from which came the strange ringing of my ice-runners, the like of which had never been heard there before. Suddenly these men seemed to take alarm, and like a brood of partridges dispersing when one steps among them, they sped every way into cover. I laughed to myself. But I didn't laugh for long, for as I went I had a sense that I was being hunted, which often comes suddenly and is quite unnerving. I did not hear or see my pursuer. I did not know whether the thing was man or beast, ghost or devil. But I was being followed, and swiftly, silently. There was something behind me – I did not know what, which made it even more fearful. In wild terror I clenched my hands and flew. My runners cut the smooth ice in long, crisp whistlings. The black shores sped backward. Behind me, I heard the relentless patter of feet galloping like a horse, yet noiselessly, as though shod in velvet. As I turned at the eastern end of the loch something grey and fierce and horribly bristling sprang past open-mouthed, straining to take me. It was going so fast that it overshot the mark, and the beast shot past with all four feet hissing taut on the glistening ice, yet it looked back showing its gleaming white fangs.

So we raced to and fro across the glassy ice of Enoch – the beast that hunted me always gaining on the straight, and I gaining at the turns. After a time or two I regained my composure to some degree. This was like a boy's game, and I had played it on the ice before, though not with such a fearsome playmate; nor with savage men scrambling and watching among the stones at the edge, knives in their hands and murder in their hearts.

But I clearly saw that I only had an advantage as long as I could keep up my speed. If I had slackened or tripped only once, the fangs would have been quickly at my throat.

Likewise, though the nights were long, morning must eventually arrive, and then I would be like a poor hare waiting for the shot of the huntsmen, driven by the hounds to die. I thought this was inevitable and regretted there would be no-one there to tell May Maxwell and the people of my country how I met my end.

But the chase ended very suddenly. As I darted between two isles that stand out of the middle of the loch, my runner scraped the edge of a long ridge of granite, and I pitched over on my face. In a moment I felt the horrible breath of the beast on my face, as it came rushing after me and drove headlong at me.

I had my knife out in an instant, and struck wildly again and again at nothing till my arm was seized as if in a vice.

Then I heard the sound of men's voices, but faint and far away, as though I was hearing in a dream. A lantern was shone at me, and a band of men came clattering over the ice towards me. But there was something that stood between me and the stars, something black and large and panting, which looked towards the men who were coming, but stood across me like a lion that guards its prey. Moreover, the beast done me no harm, as far as I could feel, except that my arm was a little stiff.

As the men came nearer the beast emitted many short, hoarse growls from deep within. Its body seemed to quiver with rage, and I could not be sure whether this was because it had been hindered in the disposal of its prey.

"Quharrie, good Quharrie, come here!" said a voice from the group which halted three yards away.

"*Quharrie at Loch Enoch!*" I thought, and it all came clear to me. If Quharrie was at Enoch, Silver Sand was also there, and I was betrayed! That was what I thought. Yet I was not any more afraid. On the contrary, I became angry, and I began to compose, even as I lay on the ice, the speech that I would make when I met my false friend face to face. It was a good speech and exceptionally cutting, and it made me feel that I would meet a noble death. I was ready to be a martyr, but I was resolved that every one should know how I had been brought to my death — especially Silver Sand, who had been my friend. I was determined not to be silent. For once, I would speak my mind.

The men about me kept calling to Quharrie — sometimes threateningly, and sometimes coaxing with promises. But the great wolf-dog only growled more fiercely, standing across my body with a wide-arched stride.

One of the men wished, I think, to do the dog a mischief, but the others held him back, and grappled with him to deprive him of his pistol. Then two came from opposite sides to snatch at me as I lay, still a little stunned with my fall; but this so excited the fierce beast that he wheeled this way and that, roaring and snapping, and made such dangerous swift charges that they were compelled to withdraw.

Then, from the island, two men came by themselves over the ice towards us. As they entered within the shining circle of the lantern light I saw it was Silver Sand and one other. The men made way for them. Silver Sand strode through them, and I thought he had never seemed so large and strong. I saw him coming long before he knew who I was, and I hugged myself at the thought of what I was about to say to him.

"Give me the lantern," he said.

As he came, Quharrie left me and fell in behind his master. His work was done. I looked around and regained my knife. But not to strike out. I was now sitting up and Silver Sand came up and shone the light of the lantern on my face.

I took the dagger by the point, and offered it to him, saying, "Silver Sand, true friend, here is a knife; strike quickly at my heart, and make it a swift end. Thou knowest where to strike, for thou hast lain against it many a time."

I thought this was mighty fine at the time, and original; but now I know that I had heard my father read something like it out of an old book of stage plays.

Silver Sand looked at me, coolly and cruelly as I thought then, nobly and gently as I now know.

"Patrick!" was all he said.

"Yes," said I, "the same – Patrick Heron of Rathan – where the tent of Silver Sand has stood many times in the last seventeen years – and now stands ready for him – after - " (I said, nodding my head) –"after-------"

"Can you walk?" he said, briefly.

I took off my ice-runners and stood.

So with not a word spoken we went back to the infamous island on which I set foot for the first time.

There on the grey-green grass were many turf huts and shelters. We did not go into these, but only into a wider sod-built shelter, open to the sky, where the fire I had seen was still smouldering.

As we went Silver Sand spoke neither good nor ill to me. I believed that his conscience was troubling him, and I rejoiced like a spoilt child who says he is going to die, and *then* his mother will be sorry.

The dusky followers crouched around, talking together in whispers, whilst casting deadly looks at me. I sat on a stone and warmed my fingers at the embers. I was so obsessed with getting the upper hand of my former friend Silver Sand, that I just acted a part at that fire among the outlaws as willingly as if in a stage play, though I knew that I was as good as dead.

Then one sprang up and made a speech, pointing often at me, as if he was denouncing me. I did not understand what he was saying, as much of the talk was gypsy gibberish. But I knew that the gist was that it was I who had been in the Hut of Craignairny – and I who had been their undoing.

One after another spoke their minds, but Silver Sand remained silent. The dark man who had come with him over the ice whispered to him.

Then the outlaw that had spoken first, the lout from the kitchen, took his knife and came over to me as if to bring matters to an end. Suddenly the expression on the face of Silver Sand changed. He sprang to his feet, and stood in front of them straighter and prouder than I had ever seen him.

"To me, Faas!" he cried."Back, or I will blast you with the black curse of Little Egypt, Roderick Macaterick!"

The man slunk back; but, as it seemed, dourly and unconvinced by the threatening finger.

Of the men that were there, some ten gathered themselves beside Silver Sand. The others grouped closer together, crouching in a bunch with their heads forward.

"Who are you," said their spokesmen," to come among us after all these years, when you have taken no part in the danger, and to think to lord it over us now? "

"Silence, hound!" said Silver Sand, with consuming vehemence."You know well who I am. I am John Faa, of the blood royal of Egypt. You remember well why I left you: because I am not one of those that do murder. You know well that I have kept free, not from the danger, but from the plunder. Now that the plunder is done with, and danger has arrived, I am here. Is it not so?"

There was no answer, but his own followers gathered closer about him.

"I am here," he cried again, "and here is this lad – Patrick Heron of the Rathan. It is true what he says, that I have eaten his bread for seventeen years and my tent stands now with its peeled rod in front of it by the side of the water on Rathan Isle."

"And you would break the clan to save this lad that comes to spy on us and destroy us!" cried another voice from the thick of the hostile crowd, with great bitterness, and, I am bound to admit, with some accuracy.

But Silver Sand had this of the royal blood in him – he assumed the proper demeanour of a man of action.

He commanded; he never explained.

"Down, dog!" he cried. "Who dares to thwart John Faa – by the king's belting, Lord and Earl of Little Egypt? Not you that are no Egyptians, but cowardly fools and unwashed ruffians from the four seas? I will hunt you with the Loathly Beasts. I will press on you with the Faa's curse. I will wither the flesh from your bones, for I am your king, John Faa, and the power is mine, alone and without bound among this people of Egypt."

The man who had hitherto faced up to him attempted to say something, but he did not find the strength. His words withered on his lips.

"Roderick Macaterick," said Silver Sand, solemnly, "on the grave of him that you slew by the Loch of Neldricken when he was lost in the moss, stands the white wraith that curses and the Grey Dog that waits. I deliver your soul to them!"

The man fell moaning on the ground.

Then Silver Sand took to speaking in the language which I could not understand, but chiefly, as it seemed, to his own people. He took me by the arm and drew me away. Then, as one, those men that stood with him moved off from the island and out upon the ice. Some of the others started to follow.

Silver Sand turned and faced them.

"Any that sets his feet on the ice to follow us shall be blasted quickly and surely. He shall never see good days again. You had best scatter and save yourselves, for a heavier hand than the Lowlanders' shall fall upon you before to-morrow, and you will pay for your murders and iniquities."

The men stood still, hesitating and afraid, and we went our way.

It was towards the Hill of the Star that we went, Silver Sand leading. When we came to the side of the loch Silver Sand turned to his followers.

"Faas," said he, "and you, Hector, leave this place. There shall be no assault delivered by your enemies, but one more sure and terrible will come from the Almighty. The judgment for murder and crime will come swiftly. Do not return to take part in it again, for I foresee that no one shall escape. Haste you up the Doon Water. Do not wait for pursuers nor turn aside to meet foes, but scatter over the country as soon as you have passed the boundaries! "

The men stood silent and irresolute.

"I know that you obey me only because I am your master, John Faa, and your chief. You obey without question, like Egyptians of the pure blood. You have done well. Go now and be honest, or as honest as you can, for never more shall you or I inhabit the dens of the Dungeon of Buchan. Fare you well! "

"And who is to be the chief?" said Hector Faa.

"I that speak am the chief. As long as I live I cannot be other than the chief, but I give to you my hand and my authority, Hector. "and he added, "It is a poor throne, that of Little Egypt, and no wise man would covet it, but such as it is you are next in line."

So on the side of the Star Hill they left us, diving into the black night, and we were left standing alone – Silver Sand, who was John Faa, King of the Gypsies, Patrick Heron of the Rathan, and Quharrie, that had hunted me like vermin an hour ago, but afterwards fought for me like a blood brother.

CHAPTER XLIII

THE AUGHTY ON THE STAR HILL

We shook hands in the darkness.

"Now we shall go to the Aughty!" he said.

I did not know where that might be, but I was content to go there, being dazed and unable to speak. As ever, Quharrie went ahead.

"And the Maxwells?" I said. "I must get back to them."

"They did not wait for you," he said, "they are all back at the house of Eschonchan by now."

"But they were meant to attack tonight," I said. "They were only waiting for my return."

"Well, Patrick. I tell you they are waiting at the house at Eschonchan, with tankards of ale in front of them. Don't be concerned about them. They will be glad to see you when you get back, but they thought it better to stay warm at the Lodge of Eschonchan than freeze in the snow in the sheep pen of the Midburn. In which they showed good judgment."

As he said this, he pushed back a matted covering of heather which hung down the face of a rock, and a light briefly flashed through the opening, and showed some bleached grey-yellow grass.

"And it's just as well!" said he, "for there's such a storm brewing that has never been seen in your days nor mine."

The air was chill and damp, but gusts of warmish wind blew at times, and in the south there was a luminous brightness. Just before I entered the cave I looked over the hip of the Merrick, and there, through a cleft of a cloud, I saw the stars and the flickering brightness of the northern lights. They shone with a strange green colour that I had never seen before.

"This," said Silver Sand, "is the Aughty of the Star. You have heard of it, but few have seen it since the Killing Time. It is the best hiding-place in all broad Scotland."

I looked around the famous cave which had sheltered nearly all the wanderers, from Cargill to Renwick – which had been a safe haven in many a storm and one which neither Clavers nor Lag ever found. My father had told me also how he and Patrick Walker the pedlar (he that writes the stories of the sufferers and has had them printed), went to look for the Aughty; but, though Patrick Walker had hidden in it for four nights when pursued by the Highland Host, he could never find it again.

"And why did you come here, and what were you doing, Silver Sand?" I asked, as we stood in the flickering light of the wood fire.

"Will you have it bit by bit or all at once?"said Silver Sand.

"I'll wait,"said I.

"And that's for the best." he answered, curtly. The Aughty was a spacious shelter, most of which was man-made. It had a little platform in front of it, twelve feet wide, which in the summer was green with grass; but above and below this, the steep face of the mountain was scarred and sheer. It was, in fact, set on the face of the hill that looked towards the Dungeon, and one turned into it by a sudden and unexpected twist among the rocks. Inside, it had been roughly floored with small logs, and arched above with the same, and at its highest, was only about five feet in high. It resembled the inside of a very small ordinary cottar's house, more spacious than I would think was possible in a mere hill shelter. There was a fire at one end, the smoke of which found its way up through the matted heather in such a way that little of it could be seen from the outside, seeping out unnoticed along the face of the cliff. It was the custom of the wanderers, however, to half-burn their wood at night, and then when cooking was needed during the day to make a clean fire from the charcoal – an excellent idea, and one I which I would never have thought of myself.

I had not been long in the Aughty before Silver Sand gave me something to eat and drink, which indeed, stood ready in a goblet, only needing to be heated on the red embers – a kind of stew, very like that which Eggface had made on Craignairny, but richer.

"How have you kept the secret of this place so long?" I asked Silver Sand.

"Very simple," he said. "I never told a woman. But it won't stay secret for long now, as you'll tell your May, as sure as eggs are eggs."

I had a retort at the tip of my tongue, but it was struck away by a thought which suddenly came to me and made me feel a heartless brute.

"What about the little girl?" I asked, for speaking of my own lass had reminded me of her."What's to happen to Marion Tamson?"

"Save us!" said Silver Sand. "I'm a stupid, idiotic fool to forget about her."

Outside the storm burst just at this moment with exceeding fury. We had to get closer to hear ourselves speaking above the roar of the elements.

"It's a pity that we didn't think about that sooner. It'll be a much more difficult job now, I'm sure," said Silver Sand.

I asked where she was.

"She's in the clay house of Craignairny," said Silver Sand.

I did not like the sound of that – to leave the warmth and safety of the Aughty to go to house of Black Murder, which I remembered with good cause, in the face of a terrible storm.

"And the sooner the better," said Silver Sand," for long before the morning we shall be corked up as tight as if we were in a sealed bottle."

I thrust my hand through the matted covering which formed the door, and found the storm was driving so fiercely, that it felt as if I had thrust my arm into a solid bank of snow.

"Is there no other option?" I said, for indeed I just about had enough.

"No," said Silver Sand. "By the morning it will be too late. She's with evil and unprepared people, and the Lord's arm can reach further than we think."

Which seemed to me then as an inadequate way of describing the character of the inhabitants of the House of Craignairny.

In a moment we were out facing the storm. But after one step we had lost one another. We were blinded, deafened, blown away. I stood and shouted my loudest. When I got my eyes open I saw a fearsome sight. The darkness was white – above, around, beneath – all was a furious, solid, white darkness. So fierce were the flakes, driven by the wind, that neither the black of the earth nor the grey of the sky shone through. I shouted my best, standing with outstretched arms.

My call was blown back in my mouth. It never even reached my own ears. Although I was standing, I was neither able to go back nor forward. A hand reached out for me out of the white barrage. Stooping low, Silver Sand and I then went down the hill, Quharrie no doubt in front, though it was impossible to see him. I heard afterwards that as soon as Silver Sand had stepped out of the cave, he had fallen headlong into a great drift of snow which had risen like magic in front of the door in only a few minutes.

We went blindly forward through the storm – yet with a good sense of direction, for after descending into the valley we saw, through a partial break, the eastern end of Loch Enoch with the snowstorm hurtling across it. The black ice, swept clean by the fierce wind, showed dark in bars and streaks. We came to smooth hollows which we crawled over on our faces, for we did not know how far down they went. We stumbled blindly into great drifts, and rolled through them. In a while we had crossed the top of the ridge of Craignairny.

"We're on to it now!" yelled Silver Sand, putting hand to my ear.

A great heap of snow was in front of me, and I was preparing to jump through it when Silver Sand stopped me. We had suddenly found ourselves beside the cottage of Craignairny – the House of Death itself. Eggface and all her crew lay within – under my nose, as it were.

Leaving me where I was, Silver Sand went round the house to reconnoitre. I stood, reasonably sheltered from the snow, on the side at which the shieling was built against the rock. There was a swirl in the wind, but it was relatively comfortable where I stood, and I had time to think.

In a little while Silver Sand came back. He signed to me to give him a lift onto the roof. Up he went till he reached the window from which I had leapt on that terrible night in the summer. Above it was the skylight through which May had followed me. We had now come for the little one who had been left behind – which I had regretted ever since.

The skylight was barred with snow, but Silver Sand cautiously cleaned it away, pulled it open, and slid back down.

"If there's anybody sleeping there, they'll think its blown open and they'll rise to shut it," I could hear him say in my ear.

The window did not shut. We could hear the wind whistling on the iron edge of it, as though it were playing a tune.

Silver Sand climbed up again. This time he put a knife between his teeth, and, raising himself on his hands, dropped lightly inside. Then I waited anxiously for a few minutes. The wind was so loud that had Silver Sand been murdered inside, I would not have heard a sound. I would then be in a precarious position and, as I leaned against the end of the clay hut, I thought what a fool I was.

To my relief, in a little while Silver Sand put his head out of the window and beckoned me up. I mounted the roof, my knee sinking into the waterlogged, evil-smelling thatch. When I reached the skylight Silver Sand suddenly thrust something out to me wrapped in a woollen shawl. It was heavy, warm and soft. The child, Marion Tamson herself, was in my arms, but she was wasted and thin. She was certainly underweight for a seven year old. We were out and down in a trice. The skylight was closed behind us, and we returned to the ground, and all the time the snowstorm was shrieking and blinding us. Now, I could just make out Quharrie. He had been sitting on the thatched roof of the house, looking into the skylight all the time that Silver Sand was inside, like a statue carved from the granite of the hills with his wild wolflike coat that was shaggy with driven and frozen snow.

Down among the drifts we stumbled – up again over the hill, with not a word spoken. We took turns to lead, the hindmost man carrying the little lamb that was too frightened to cry in the wild of the storm and the darkness of the corner of the shawl. But she was held by loving arms, and I think she knew it.

Quharrie led us straight to the mouth of the Aughty. Without ceremony he shoved his sharp nose under the covering of matted heather and sprang in. Before we could take off our coats, loosen a button or even take our little stolen lamb out of her cosy nook, Quharrie had curled himself about upon the hearth and gone to sleep, as though it was a fine night and he had just come in from a friendly chase on the hill after the rabbits.

Then, from the shawl in which she was wrapped, which were as clean as everything about Eggface was (to give the devil his due), we got little Marion out. I took her on my knee and talked to her, for I always had a way with children, as even May admits. As first the child watched with eyes full of terror; yet it was not long before I won her heart, and she began talking cheerily of brighter days. But in the midst of it all, even whilst she was laughing merrily, her head would fall on my shoulder and she would start crying as though her little heart was broken.

I could not understand this, because I thought we were past the worst, but I had sense enough not to ask any questions, but only to rock her on my knee and hush her to sleep. Silver Sand made up a bed of warm blankets for her in front of the fire, and she rested there very simply and sweetly, though her hands twitched and pulled at her covers, and once or twice she woke out of her sleep with a sharp cry.

Then I cursed those that had caused this innocent child to do that and said to myself, "Wait till you've been with us at the Rathan for a year, Marion, we'll make you forget all of this."

This also came to pass, by the blessing of God. The next day the great storm was still unabated, but nevertheless we stayed in the Aughty in some comfort. We had plenty of good bacon-ham and oatmeal, tons of water outside for melting and loads of peat fuel from Kirreoch moss. We were in no way unhappy – though I was considerate enough to think about those that must be anxious about me. But even then I was too young to think much about that. Hardly any man is thoughtful for others until he is well past thirty. May Maxwell says "Not even then!"

That night, while the maid slept, Silver Sand began to tell me his incredible story.

CHAPTER XLIV.

THE SIXTEEN DRIFTY DAYS

OUTSIDE, the hurricane drove relentlessly from the south.

It was the first of the famous Sixteen Drifty Days which even now are remembered over all the hill country, as the time when dead sheep and cattle far outnumbered the living. The snow drove hissing round the corner of the Aughty and piled against the entrance in a forty foot drift. Looking down in the breaks of the storm we could only see the wild whirl of drifting whiteness in the gulf of the Dungeon of Buchan.

But it was warm and pleasant inside. The fire burned steadily, drawing a gentle draught up the side of the rock, and the makeshift heather couches on the floor were dry and comfortable. Even the House of Rathan could hardly be more homely than this cave called the Aughty, on the eastern face of the precipice of the Star which overlooks the Dungeon.

It was here that Silver Sand, who in reality was John Faa, belted Earl and Gypsy, told his story.

"There was never," he said, "I think, any man who has had such a journey as I have. I who has gypsy blood but who am still an earl of this realm of Scotland; I who am from the outlaw raider families but have ridden with the king's men and worn the dragoon's coat; I that have looked on at many a killing of poor Whig folk, but slept by Peden's side in the caves by the Crichope Water – as a true-blue Whig myself!

"I that was Richard Cameron's man and proscribed by the Government of the Stuarts, have likewise lived under a ban by the Government of the Whigs because of the riding and rustling of my clan. King's man or Hill Whig, Society man or Lag's rider – John Faa has never been far from the end of the hangman's rope; and has never rested soundly in his bed, except when living as poor Silver Sand who makes his simple living by selling red ochre and the scythe sand.

"I was only a young lad when the soldiers began riding, when there was scrambling and chasing after the Whigs all over the West of Scotland. To a gypsy of royal blood all this would have been like the fluttering and quacking of ducks upon a millpond – a matter for themselves. But I was in Dumfries one day, just standing at the end of the Devorgilla bridge, and who should come by up the Vennel but the mad and reckless Laird of Lag.

"'There's a proper lad that isn't a Whig,' he cried, as soon as he saw me standing there; 'I know by the look of his beaver bonnet and the handsome feather in it.'

"The troop that was riding with him, three columns of King's troopers, and some young blades of the country landowners that came themselves with two or three horses to ride with Lag – mostly lads that hated the Kirk for meddling with their lairds' right to free fornication, cried out for me to mount and ride with them.

"'Will you enter service with the King, His Excellent Majesty, and will you curse the Whigs? ' they said.

"I was reluctant to do this; indeed I did not much care for them, for they had held my father's kinfolk down with an iron hand during the thirty years of their power. But to ride with the troopers and bite bread with them, was equally unwelcome to the stomach of a Faa.

"But needs must when the devil drives.

"'Take him to the hillsides at Maxwelltown! ' cried the laird; 'When we get him there he can mount and hunt with us, or he can stay and bleed.'

"So they carried me across until we came to a wide grassy place where broom was growing and the wind blowing. It was fresh and fair, and the innocent birds were singing.

"Lag halted his troop.

"'Now, bonny lad,'says he 'we have little time to waste on the likes of you, but you can have a free choice. Here's a silver mark, to enter the King's service, and here's Sergeant Armstrong's rifle with twelve ounces of the best lead bullets. Three minutes to tell us which one you'll choose.'

"The birds whistled on the yellow gorse bushes, and the wind waved the branches they sat on. The summer airs blew soft. The green leaves laughed drily. They were beech-leaves, and their talk always conveys a sense of malice.

"In three minutes I was mounted on a grey horse belonging to the wild laird. That night they drank me senseless in the old Lag's Tower, where to this day that same laird, whose hand is black with blood, sleeps in his silk bed under safe conduct granted by the Government – while I that have been under a dozen Governments and not done harm to any of them, am a broken man and the King's enemy to this day. But then I am only John Faa and an Egyptian.

"So we rode and rode behind the wicked laird, and as for his ill-doing and ill-speaking there was neither a beginning nor an end to it.

"He would ride up to a farmhouse and knock on the door with the handle of his broadsword.

"'Is the master of the house in?' says he.

"'Indeed, he certainly is!' says the mistress; 'He's eating his porridge.'

"'Hurry him up, then,' says Lag, 'for the Archangel Gabriel' (no less) 'is waiting to take his

afternoon meal with him, and it's a risky thing to keep the likes of him waiting!'

"Then in ten minutes that wife's a widow, and gathering up her man's brains in a napkin!

"Riding under the cover of night to drown out the sound of the psalm with the rattle of musket shot; out on the wide uplands, where there are only bumble bees and snipes, setting up a row of five or six decent moorland men on their knees, as I saw once at Kirkconnel, some with white napkins round their brows, and some looking into the gun muzzle. It was wretched work – wretched work! And the curse of God Almighty has lain on all those who had a hand in it – apart from that devil's knight, Sir Robert himself, whose iniquities the Almighty is most surely reckoning at compound interest, for while he sits snug and hearty to this day in his house at Lag's Tower, in Hell the devil is banking up his fires and heating his irons for him.

"But there was one morning that I had my fill – heathen gypsy though I was. We had stayed all night at Morton Castle and it was daybreak when we mounted and set off. We came across a child at the gully of the Crichope – a lad of ten. When we came up to him, he was sitting on his own in a small den that he had made, whistling like a linnet. He had a can of good sweet milk and a basketful of bannocks. He was close by the mouth of the river Linn. It was suspected, then, that he was taking them to some cave where an outlawed minister was hiding.

"It was just like the laird to get the lad to inform. It was the part of the devil's work that most pleased him, as it did David Graham who had been made Sheriff of Galloway in the place of the Agnews of Lochnaw. They were a fine pair. They scared the little boy, half jesting, half in earnest, until the child was blue with fright.

"Lag seized him by the collar and held him over the Linn and shook him, like a small puppy that you might lift by the scruff of the neck.

"'Tell me,' he says, 'where old Tam Glen is hiding, or over you go.

"The little lad looked down, and – O Patrick! Even as an old man I can see the terror glint in his eye as he saw the great trees at the bottom seeming no bigger than berry bushes. Then he looked up at us that sat on our horses behind the laird and the sheriff.

"'Have none of you any young children at home? Can you watch a child die?'

"He had a voice like a child I once knew and when he spoke, I being but a youngster, and not long from the mother's milk myself, let out in a kind of howl of anger.

"Lag turned quickly, the devil's dead-white thumb marks on each side of his nose.

"'What cursed Whig's that? ' says he, in his death voice.

" Then I cannot tell whether the boy's coat collar tore from his hand, or whether Lag let him drop; but when we looked again Lag's hand was empty, and up from the Linn came a sound like a bairn crying on his own in the dark.

"Lag hesitated for maybe three heartbeats. I don't think he had bargained for that, but then he turns and cries with a wave of his ruffled lace band -----

"'The raven will have sweet pickings off that sprog's bones!'

"But I had had more than enough – I had seen more than I could stomach.

"I was off my horse and down amongst the bushes on the side of the Linn, with a great clatter of stones, as quickly as I could.

"'Who's that!'cries Lag, over his shoulder, for he had turned to ride away.

"'Gypsy Jock,' says one, ' deserted —'

"'Give him a volley, lads. I never thought that rogue was a true man! 'cried Lag.

"But the riders had little stomach for the shooting. The wee laddie had got to them, especially his words, for most of them had children of their own, though some did not admit it. So only a few shot after me, and them mostly Highland men that knew no English except *Present! Fire!*' which they had heard often enough since they began riding with Lag.

"I was down at the lad before the troop had ridden away. But it was over for him. As fair a young lad as you ever saw. I carried him to his mother, stripping off all the regimental clothing as I went, but keeping the sword, the musket, and the brass mounted pistols. His mother met us at the gable end. The bairn still had the empty can clasped in his small hand. O forgive me! Forgive me! Patrick! If I could forget it —"

And Silver Sand laid down his head on the rude shelf in the Aughty and sobbed till I feared he might do himself an injury.

"And his mother took him out of my arms, and she never said a word, nor did any tear run down her cheek, but she asked me to come inside as politely as if I had been a minister. She set the table for me to eat, but you can guess how I felt about food. I just moaned and wept, but she put her hand on my shoulder, and hushed me as if I was the mourner.

Then she laid him on the bed.

"'My wee Willie,' says she, as she smoothed his bonny brow and combed his long, yellow hair that fell on the sheet in wavy ringlets.

"'Even so,' she said, 'Lord, I had thought you might have spared this small boy for me as company seeing he was the last of my family. But it's not to be. One at Drumclog, one at Kirkconnel, and one by the bonny links of the Cluden. I thought the Lord would have spared a widow's youngest child. But the will of the Lord be done.'

"She turned sharply to me.

"'How did he die?'she asked, as calm as she might ask 'What is the time?'

"I tried to tell her, between the sobs – with her waiting till I came to myself and giving me a little pat on my shoulder – as if I had been her own child and not the sinful man that I am.

"' Now now – now now,' says she, by way of encouragement to me.

"O woe is me! Woe is me!" Silver Sand cried, sinking his head on the table board. "May the Lord forgive the sins of my youth."

I was weeping too by this time, and I think the King himself would have wept if he had heard the tale.

Silver Sand went on.

"She stood over him a good while, arranging him and touching him and stroking him.

"'He was a careful boy,' she said, 'and so good to his mother, was my Willie! You helped her every day, and you slept in her bosom ever since her own good man went away. Yes, Willie, my son, you shall sleep this one night in your mother's arms, for they shall never hold anything that she loves again. Tonight you shall lie in the arms of her that gave birth to you, close to her side, where she carried you the black year she lost her man.'

"She turned to me with a kind of anger.

"'And why not? ' she said, as if I had forbidden her.'And why not, I would like to know? Put your hand on him, man; he's warm and bonny – not a mark on him that the yellow hair cannot cover, or that I can wash. Why shouldn't he sleep beside his own mother? He will sleep soundly. I'll not waken him if he is tired. This morning I tiptoed on my bare feet so that he would get a longer lie and a sound sleep – yes, and a sound sleep he's got now, my laddie, O my laddie!'

"'And you were a kind boy to your mother, Willie – a kind, kind boy – and I have no more; it's a sin to mourn for them that the Lord has taken. But he was a careful boy, Willie, and most considerate to his mother. Look man, look – he has even brought his mother's can safe home in his hand —'

"O, sorrow! sorrow!" wailed Silver Sand, rocking himself to and fro, so that little Marion woke, and seeing us weeping, wept too, as a young child might do without knowing why.

Then there was a long pause, and the fire flickered and the wild storm raged outside the Aughty. And the storm within our bosoms sobbed itself out, and we watched little Marion silently till she slept again, our right hands being clasped each in the other.

CHAPTER XLV.

ALIEN AND OUTLAW

"SO that day," continued Silver Sand," turned me into a believer – that is, as far as a gypsy and a Faa can be a believing man.

"But it was a long time before I was trusted by the moormen who could only praise the Lord from deep in the hills, because I was known to be a gypsy and working for their chief persecutor. I was like Paul at Damascus to them; yet in time they believed me, and treated me not as a spy but as a soul plucked from the fire. But it was my destiny to be cast among the more extreme sect, those who were the followers of Richard Cameron.

" As you may have heard, they received scant justice at the Revolution, so that when it was all over, and I returned to what home I had, I found that my own clan had been outlawed, and were under worse condemnation than ever, because of their lawless deeds whilst I had been away.

"It was unlikely that I could stay with them, for the order of the King's council made them become worse outlaws and reivers than ever – although, I think, they were not murderers.

"So I could not live with them; nor, being a Faa, and their chief, could I betray them. What is more, for the sake of the name of my forefathers, I could not be seen to benefit from any leniency that might not be extended to them as well. So I took to the hills and to the trade of selling scythe sand and the red ochre for the sheep.

"And though I have nowhere to lay my head, I am a better and happier man, than the one who witnessed that sight by the Linn of Crichope ever deserved to be. But I have dwelt with my Maker and humbled myself before Him in secret woods and lonely fells.

"The men of the hills ceased hiding in the mosses and moors nearly forty years ago – all except one, and he was a persecutor, a heathen man, and one whose hand was stained by the blood of God's saints. For forty years I have lived where God's folk lived, and struggled with the devil and the flesh in many strange places – often unsure whether indeed I was succeeding.

"And I fear that in these recent troubles I have become too concerned with earthly matters, for which I must be constantly pray for the Lord's forgiveness – and I an unworthy old man. But I have avoided being involved in bloodshed; and, as far as I have been able, I have both been faithful to my friends and to those who share my name. But the task has not been easy, and sometimes I have lost the trust of both."

I stretched out my hand, and humbly asked him to forgive me my unjust words and unworthy suspicions.

"And I cannot call you anything but Silver Sand, and will you still come and camp by the Water of Rathan?" I said.

Silver Sand assented with a sweet smile, and took my hands and kissed them; for a gypsy has strange ways.

But there were many things that I wanted to have explained.

"Why did you, being the man you are," I said,"issue threats like a warlock to the men down there the other night?"

Silver Sand smiled.

"In Rome I must do as the Romans," he said; which, however, I did not think was a very sound explanation or justification.

"But could you in fact perform these things?" I asked, still in doubt.

"They believed I could, which is the same thing. You see," he went on," I have been forced to practise simple ploys to keep myself safe from a wild clan on one side and an unjust law on the other. There are many things I can do easily yet they seem impossible to others. For instance, my arms which were twisted in the torture of the Star Chamber in front of James, Duke of York, have served me well in that I look like a beast when I run, and when we hunt as the Loathly Dogs, Quharrie and I frighten foolish folk out of their wits."

"Indeed, I think you are a little strange myself," I said, my face showing some astonishment.

"Well," said Silver Sand, "I don't doubt that if some of the landward presbyteries caught me, even today I could be burned, just like Major Thomas Weir. But all my magic is simple and very childish – just as simple as red ochre and scythe sand."

I asked if he had ever applied for grace from Government.

He told me no; for that there were none in any Government who would believe that a Faa could be other than a thief and a scoundrel. The doctrine of the Government is that grapes do not grow on thorns nor figs on thistles.

"And to tell the truth," said John Faa, "I was not keen to, since I am a man that has been treated like a criminal for so long, that I would not be happy if I found myself in cahoots with soldiers and lawyers. I love best the fowl of the air that cackle and cry on the moorland, the spotted eggs of the peewit and the great marbled eggs o' the curlew, the fish from the burn and the haddock from the salt sea flats. All these and the taking of them are what mean most to the life of Silver Sand.

I asked him later (for we had plenty of time for our conversations during the sixteen days and nights of the great storm) among other things, what he thought of the Freetraders. He gave me a strange look.

"I think very much like your father did," said he, "in his latter days. I didn't meddle with the stuff myself, but I would not provide information on those that do. I have nothing, for instance, to say about your friends the Maxwells – only (a word in your ear) if I was you I would put my foot down against them using the cellars of Rathan for cargo storage."

He nodded significantly.

"You don't mean to say that they have done that!" I said, with indignation.

"And what else? "said Silver Sand. " They are packed as full as they can be of French brandy, and Valenciennes lace; and if any of Agnew's men were to go sniffing around, it might cause misunderstandings between those in power and you that's such a grand man for the King."

"And are you quite content as you are, Silver Sand?" I said to him even later, to pass the time. Little Marion, to whom the quiet of the cave was heaven, sat at our feet and played with the quaint toys which Silver Sand had made her.

"Content!"said Silver Sand; "why should I not be content? I don't know anyone that has more cause to be. I look over the vastness of God's work all day under His wide, high ceiling, and often all night provided the storms stay away. I have God's Word under my armpit as well – see here!"

He pulled out two dumpy little red covered Bibles, with the Old Testament divided at Isaiah, and the Psalms of David in metre at the end; very clean, but thumbed yellowish like a banknote.

"What more could a man want?" he said.

"But selling sand and red ochre can only take a small part of your time – what do you do with the rest of it when you are not at the Rathan?"

Silver Sand smiled and made a curious little noise in his throat, as May does when she calls the hens for their meal of dough.

"I play games with the lasses," he said, "shouting for them from behind the cornstacks."

I looked at him, and was silent with surprise. He had just been telling me that his aim was to be a godly man as far as possible.

"Did you never hear of the Brownie?" he said, seeing my surprise.

"Yes," said I; "but I don't believe in superstitions. There's no such thing." As being young I knew no better.

"I'll show you on the first starlight night after we are back at the Rathan," said he.

"Tell me now," I said,"Goodness knows, there's plenty of time in this old Aughty."

"Tell on," said Marion, who was wakening quickly from her sleep, and beginning to take an interest in everything.

If it were not for thinking about the great rambling house where the women-folk were waiting – May and Eppie and the Lady Grizel – these days in the Aughty, with the wild men and the wild nature alike shut out, and the danger past (or so I thought), were as happy and memorable as any in my life.

Even today, whenever the winds howl and the shutters clatter, I remember our time in the Aughty. I think we were all happy there, and certainly little Marion gained in beauty and fearlessness every day. At first it was sad to see her shrinking when anyone moved suddenly near her. But this also gradually ceased.

I can hear the soft whish of the snow against the flap of the heather curtain, the roaring of the wind above and the crackle of the heather roots and broom branches on the fire to this day. I can see the red glow of the peats at the back – indeed I can remember everything precisely as they were on these sixteen days of storm when the winds drifted the snow, till in many of the hollows the drifts lay a hundred feet deep, and in over half of Scotland one sheep out of every two died – as well as many shepherds and travellers. Once we heard a great roar as though the mountains were falling, and we all instinctively cowered and prayed that the Destroying Angel might pass over our heads.

"That's a most mighty fall of stones somewhere," said Silver Sand.

"I hope the Star Hill is not coming down on our heads," said I. But it was not the Star Hill. It was further off somewhere about the Hill of the Dungeon.

We waited for a long time, but we could hear no more of it. From the doorway we could only see the great tide of snow-flakes running steadily up the Dungeon of Buchan far below, and occasional swirls entering into the sheltered bend in which the mouth of the Aughty lay. The snow was not falling now, but blowing uninterruptedly north with the mighty wind, as straight as ruled lines in a copybook.

So we closed the flap, after having taken Marion to the door so that she might marvel at the white driving world of snow.

"I think I could float in it like a feather," she said – a feeling I had myself.

It is one thing to read these strange tales, or even to write about them in the comfort of one's own home; but it was quite another to hear them told in the slow, level voice of Silver Sand himself, Johnny Faa, the bloody persecutor and Cameronian gypsy – and nothing like this had ever been heard of before in Scotland. All this, too, while the greatest storm of the century raged outside, and the winds of the Sixteen Drifty Days sped past outside like fiends that rode to the yelling of the damned.

It was satisfying too at meal-times to hear the bacon sizzling in the pan, and smell the pleasant smell of the oatmeal fried with it. Sometimes Quharrie would rise from one side of the fireplace and walk solemnly round to the other, and Marion would follow him, and lie down beside him with her head on his mighty flank. Then he would lift his head and look at her like a great kindly wolf; and because he loved her down in his rough-husked heart somewhere, he licked her on the point of her nose, which seemed to turn up a little in response.

Then at night it was pleasant to draw close to the fire while Silver Sand read from his book – often from John's Gospel, but most often from the Revelation, which somehow appealed strongly to him. Then with all of us kneeling at the hearth, he poured out his soul in prayer – prayers like those he had heard from Renwick and Shields in the last days of the persecutions when John Faa was still on his probation. He would often encourage me to take part in these, but though I was tempted, I never could pray out loud unless I was in my own house.

CHAPTER XLVI.

THE BROWNIE

"You want to hear more about the Brownie?" said Silver Sand. "Well, you probably think that I'm getting too old to play such tricks and pranks. You think, no doubt, that my life hasn't been a very useful one. I am of a different opinion."

I had no such thought, and said so.

"Well, do you remember the year before last? Who was it, do you think, that cut and stacked most of the Maxwells corn late on in the year, when the lads had to go away to the Isle of Man for the first cargo for my Lord Stair? "

"I heard some word of it being the fairies," said I.

"And there you show your gullibility, Patrick, maybe you didn't suspect, you who is so farseeing, that it was Silver Sand with his scythe and his long twisted arms. And who was it that gathered all your sheep into the pens the night before the great storm of February last year? "

"I always thought it was the Maxwells, but they never owned up to it, but I thought nothing of that, for Kennedy thinks no more of telling a lie than of slapping a horsefly that bites him on the hip-bone."

"That he doesn't!" said Silver Sand, with conviction."But," he continued, "he told the truth that time I suppose by accident, for it was just me and Quharrie that penned the Rathan ewes, and dipped them the next night, rubbing tar and butter in their wool to make it grow flossy and long."

And Silver Sand went on to tell us of nights out on the fells and in the green parks about the farm-towns. How he dug the old wives' cabbage patches, as he said, for the pleasure of going round the next morning to hear their speculations.

"'You'll not be wanting any sand for your sickle, Betty?" he would say to some old dame at her cottage door.

"No, not today, Silver Sand," says Betty.

"What's new, Betty? "he would say.

"New!" she exclaimed—"New! Have you heard about some kind people who were in my garden yesterday, came and went, and left it all dug, leaving not so much as a footprint!"

"And that," said Silver Sand," was because of the trouble I took to take the footmarks out with an iron-teethed rake."

"It's most wonderful indeed, Betty; but what would Mister Forbes, that honest man, say to your having such dealings with the fairies? Do you think that's wise, Betty, my woman?"

"Wise here, wise there, as long as I get my garden dug and my potatoes lifted for nothing, I won't look to Mister Forbes! Mister Forbes, indeed! It is a long time since he lifted even a row of my potatoes. He's more suited to eating them, great lazy worthless character that he is!'"'

In this way Silver Sand carried us through the storm with a wealth of tales. I listened eagerly, my toes towards the fire on the hearthstone (for there was a good hearthstone in the Aughty), with one ear on the turmoil of the storm outside, as I lay in front of the fire on my right and left sides in turn.

"Then," continued the story-teller, "there were nights on the corn fields when the sheep shearing was at its height, and the farms lay sleeping under the cool, clean air – nights when it was just heaven to work among the sheaves, and hear the *crap, crap!* of the sickle driving through the corn. Every sheaf was like a friend. Every stook added another member to what looked like a well ordered army. That both raised up the heart and exercised the brain of the farmer, when he came out in the morning and went doddering about the outhouses, and then came sauntering down the field to plan the work for the day.

"'Hi, Rab! ' he would cry to the farm labourer, as he saw my handiwork,'come you here.'

"Then Rab would come out of the barn, wiping his nose, as if he had been tasting the sweet milk-can, or perhaps the mouth of the byre lass, who knows – but looking very sheepish and shamefaced.

"' Rab! Do you see that?' his master would say (with me up in a great tree listening all the time).

"Rab looks. Rab looks again. The look on his face changes.

"' The Lord preserve us,' he cries, as he catches sight of a dozen more fields cut, past the mark where he had finished in the twilight of the previous night —' the midnight fairies have been here. I'm going home. I wont work with a Brownie.'

"'You great heifer,' says his master, 'be thankful that Brownie thinks so much of the place as to work on it. Where a Brownie works the lads will have a light heart and legs that are not tired. He'll need a hearty meal, the poor fellow! '

"So the next day in the evening there's a large basin of porridge and a great bowl of milk set out at the barn-end.

"Then I wrap my great sheepskin coat around me, the one that keeps me warm on the coldest night in a hedgerow, if needs be, and I go off up the lane. There is be some large yokel of a half-grown lout that wants to get favour from the girls. He's watching for Brownie. I can hear his knees knocking at the back of the hedge.

"'BooHoo!' says I, braying like a bullock.

"Up gets Hobbledehoy, and runs with shouting and roaring up to the farmhouse, where the lasses are grouped in threes at the back, fair wet with fear.

"'Never was there such a thing!' Yokel declares. He has seen Brownie. He can describe him. He is

as big as the barn, and covered with a curly hide. He has horns as long as my leg. Then on the morning there is a buzz all round the countryside. From far and near they come to hear Rob Yokel tell about the Brownie that brayed at him from the hedge. Rab tells the tale, and tells it over again. And every time he tells it there's two yards added to the length of the beast, and at least one to the horns. It's a fearsome beast before everything is over."

Silver Sand laughed his silent chuckling laugh, and went on.

"Then there are the trysts of the lads and lasses. There was the time a wicked untrustworthy rogue that had left two lasses in the lurch already, and he came to the church-gate to speak to little Margaret Lauder who is as innocent as a lamb. I saw her flush and look coy. And my bold vain fellow saw it too, for he arranged with the dainty little lass to meet him at the Myrestane gate at the back of the wood. But he never got there to this day. Brownie met him as he came stepping so smugly across the dry stones at Sandy's Ford. There Brownie stood and shook his horns at the great scoundrel from side to side like an angry beast, with a kind of ghostly howl that nearly frightened myself when I made it.

"He fell face down into the burn, because evil-doers always fear evil. Seeing Brownie coming even closer, he got to his feet and ran home to his stable-loft with the ice cold water dripping off him.

"Then who but Silver Sand (and not Brownie at all) saw the little lass home to her mother, and took the opportunity to describe the rogue's character on the way. I'll warrant he gets a flea in his ear the next time he goes to that farm! "said Silver Sand, triumphantly.

"Goodness, man, Silver Sand, but that was good!" cried I, hitting my thigh in my delight. It was the way he told the tale that brought the whole business to light.

"But there's better than that," says he, blinking kindly at me across the red glow of the Aughty fire.

"Many is the time," he went on, " in the old days when Craigdarroch fireplace glowed warmly, and the lads of the countryside got together in the twilight, I have played peep-bo there and seen many unusual things. There was a lass (I won't tell you her name, so don't ask) that I have seen with my own eyes, coming slipping so daintily to the door, and going down by the rustling grey willows that seemed to turn their white undersides to look at her in the gloom of twilight as she passed the three thorns, rushing as if she was going to a love tryst."

It began to dawn on me, yet I so loved my lass that I had no fear of what I might hear from this recording angel of the night and the fields.

"And who do you think came to see her – this bonny lass that left the finest wooers behind with her daddy to talk about the heifers?"

I shook my head.

"She stood by the side of the Solway, with the tide washing up to her feet, and she looked over at the old House of Rathan, where there was a light at the high window, and sometimes a little fire down on the shore. That was the camp of Silver Sand. Maybe it was at the camp she looked, and maybe it was for the sake of Silver Sand that she went down there – but perhaps not!

"At any rate it wasn't the safest place to go, with Freetraders and Yawkins and things like cattle about; so Quharrie and me made it our business to see that she wasn't troubled.

"But what kind of simpleton was the lad that she liked to remain in the Rathan when the bonniest lass in the countryside came down to keep a tryst with nothing but the light from a farthing candle in the House of Rathan?"

"But I never suspected – how was I to know?" I say, for I did feel ashamed.

"Get away, man! You surely must have your eyes in the tail of your coat! You might have known by the way she chided you!"

"O man, Silver Sand, you should have told me,"says I.

"No, no, Laird Rathan, Silver Sand is no tell-tale. It would be a fine thing if a young lass trusted me and the stars that night to the secrets of her heart, if I would then run to tell a great hulk that hadn't the gumption to find the way to her heart by himself."

Silver Sand shook his head at the thought, but I took no offence for all the ill names he gave me. On the contrary, I was exceptionally glad;

because I wanted to believe that her heart was mine before the night of the Dungeon and the fight by the Murder Hole.

"There's one thing more," said he, "that for your peace I may tell you, though you don't deserve it. It was the day you were so ill with the brain injury when it turned to a raging fever, from the scratch you got up by the Neldricken. The doctor that had been brought from Dumfries, had given you up and had seemingly gone away to order your coffin. It was woeful to hear you. They say that they could hear your cries at the Orraland through the open windows that night.

"Well, man, I was there by the water edge, and what think you I saw? I saw a young lass that had been wearing herself out to help you, come out into the night air, and before I had time to get away, she fell down on her knees close by me, and by chance (because I couldn't help it) I heard a prayer for you she thought only the Almighty could hear. She prayed long and hard for you, Patrick, my lad. You hardly deserve the likes of her. She asked that the Lord might take her and leave you a little while bit longer, 'for he's still young,' she said, ' and hasn't had time to be himself.' "

The God of Jacob bless her!" I said solemnly, for I could hardly speak. And small wonder Silver Sand said "Amen!"

But a thought struck me.

"And what," I said, " might you be doing down by the shore at that time of night? Were you not praying as well?"

"Oh. no," said Silver Sand, lightly, " I was just throwing pebbles in the water!"

CHAPTER XLVII

THE LAST OF THE OUTLAWS

On the morning of the seventeenth day, when we were becoming increasingly anxious for those waiting for us although we tried not to think about it, we looked out, and wonder of wonders, the great blast – the greatest of a century – had blown itself out. We gazed out on the face of the world, and the sight made us both fear and tremble in astonishment.

It was a clear, bright morning when we put aside the mat and looked out. The brightness was like the kingdom of heaven. There was a chill thin air blowing, and the snow was already hard bound with frost. We looked down into the Dungeon of Buchan.

Its mighty cauldron with the three lochs at the bottom of it, was nearly full of snow. The lochs were not visible. Neither was the Wolf's Slock. The night before we had only seen a whirling, white, chaos of flakes. The morning showed us the great valley almost levelled up with snow, from Breesha and the Snibe across to the Range of Kells.

We stepped from the door onto the first drift. It rose in a grand sweep which curved round the angle of the hill. We set foot on it, and it was strong enough to bear us. The snowflakes had been driven so hard by the force of the wind, that as soon as the pressure was removed, the frost bound the whole mass together as hard as ice and as smooth as ivory.

Then when we stood on the top there was a wonderful sight to be seen. A wide expanse of drifted snow in all directions. There was no Loch Enoch to be discerned. A dazzling curve of blown snow ran clear up the side of the great Merrick Hill. There was no Loch-in-loch. There was no Outlaws' Island. The same frost-bound whiteness covered everything. The old world was completely drowned in snow.

"God help them that are under that! ' said Silver Sand.

But we could tell at a glance that everyone without the shelter of a roof during the great storm would be long past our help.

Only on the Dungeon Hill opposite could any of the surface be seen. Under the hanging brow of Craignairny there was a great gash like a stone quarry, red and grey in colour – the granite showing its unhealed edges, and with snow surrounding it. We had not seen this landslip before.

Asking Marion to stay in the Aughty till we returned, we set out to explore. We bound kerchiefs about our brogues to keep the loose snow particles from balling; but, both of us being light on our feet, we hardly sank into the snow at all. And Quharrie did not sink at all, but passed over it lightly, and so went in front.

He was a thoughtful though not a morose dog and his manner was usually dignified. But this morning the snow seemed to excite him. He whirled about after the stump of his short tail, so that as he turned, he could only see it disappearing, never seeming to get closer. His chase was not only a long one but a perfectly hopeless one. Yet he spun round nevertheless. He overturned himself in the snow. He slid on his back down the great snow drifts – in fact he did everything except bark. Then suddenly he stood still and erect, as one may see an upright magistrate when involved in light-hearted amusement, suddenly looks about to see whether any one has noticed him, and then walks off with an air as though he was taken aback by the levity of the walk and conversation of the man next to him. That was Quharrie on these great snowdrifts that filled up the valley of the Star Hill.

Before going out we checked our weapons, although Silver Sand sighed and said, "I think that all the weapons we will need today are picks and shovels."

The snowdrifts were bewildering and of exquisite beauty, rosy where the sun touched them – a pale faint blue in the shadow, and with such a delicious play of wavering light where the sun and shade met that it was like the sun shining through deep leaves and flickering in the clearness of a shaded mountain pool.

As we went we probed ahead with our long iron tipped poles. Silver Sand went first, because I knew little about snow; since at the edge of the Solway it seldom lies and, when it does, is never deep. Sometimes we stepped on a snow bridge between two stones – and fell in and had to pull one another out. Sometimes we would start a rush of snow sliding downhill, which always made Silver Sand very grave, knowing how dangerous that was.

We went towards the Isle of Enoch first, from where we had set out the night we came to the Aughty. The snow on the buried loch was so level that it was only by very carefully observing the landmarks that we could tell when frozen water lay beneath us. The side of the Merrick above us was clear in patches, where it rises too steeply to hold the snow.

Soon we came to where we thought the Isle of Loch-in-loch was, but we saw no evidence of human activity underneath the surface of the snow. Looking westward to the side of the Merrick from the highest part of the snow, we saw what seemed to be an oval shaped excavation of some kind.

"There!" said Silver Sand, pointing with his iron-shod pole.

So he went upward and I followed him, till we came to the edge. I shall never forget what I saw, though I only wish to describe it briefly. It was a great pit in the snow, nearly circular, built up high on all sides, but highest towards the south. The lower tiers of it were constructed of the dead bodies of a great multitude of sheep piled one on top of the other, forming frozen fleecy ramparts. But the snow had swept over and blown in, providing a way down to the bottom by walking along the edge of a drift. Looking in, we saw objects protruding from the snow – here the arm of a man and there the horn of a bullock.

I understood at once. We were standing above the white grave of the outlaws of the Dungeon.

They had died in their hillside shelter. With only our poles we could do little to dig them out, and could not give them a permanent burial. It was better that they should lie there until the snow melted off the hill. But we managed to uncovered many of the faces. As each white frozen face came in view Silver Sand said briefly, " Miller!" or "Macaterick!" or "Marshall!" as soon as he saw them.

But there were no Faas among them.

"The Faas have done what I asked," he said,"and at least they have a chance to save their lives."

Quharrie marked the spots where the dead were to be found by digging with his forepaws, throwing the snow through the wide space between his hind legs, and blowing through his nose like a terrier does at a rabbit hole.

We found seventeen, all under the great south wall of sheep, which the starving wretches had built to keep them from the icy blast of the blizzard. I wondered why they had not stayed in their little shelters and clay huts; but Silver Sand said in times of storms, it was their custom to gather into great camps with their cattle, and collect materials for a vast fire in the centre. But the Sixteen Drifty Days had been too much for them.

It was a mighty storm, and the like has never been seen in Galloway to this day. Afterwards when men came to bury the dead, they found good proof that they had endured it out till the tenth day, when their food and their fire both gave out. Then here and there they had lain down to sleep, to wake no more. That is how we found them, poor wretches, and how we left them.

They looked strangely happy, for the whiteness of the snow set their faces as if in a portrait. I found the rascal that would have killed me in the cottage of Craignairny. In death, he looked quite a respectable man. Which made me suppose that some evil spirit had, perhaps, possessed and harried an innocent man against his will. It may be so. The good God knows. The Day of Judgment is not my business.

Then we went towards the House of Craignairny itself. But when we got there we did not find the house, nor any landmarks that we knew. The great gash on the Dungeon brow, which we had seen from the Aughty, had been formed by an inconceivable quantity of rock which had fallen, crushing its way down the hillside, followed by a multitude of smaller stones mixed with snow. The crevice of the hill in which the ill-omened House of Death once stood, was covered fathoms deep in rock, as though the very mountain had hanged itself, like Judas, so that all its bowels gushed out. Could this be the judgment of God made plain and manifest? It was the roar of that great landslide which we had heard when we were in the Aughty, and thought that the Star Hill was about to fall upon our heads.

No-one ever saw hide nor hair of Eggface or her sons, nor of anyone else that had been seen in that evil house, except for the man that would have knifed me who we found in the great Pit of Sheep under the lee of the Merrick. The place is now all overgrown with heather and rough brown grass; but it is still plain to be seen, and the shepherds call it the Landfall of Craignairny. They say that no sheep will feed there to this day, although I do not know whether that is true.

We had, however, seen enough. So we went back to the Aughty till the night, as even on that keen December day the sun was rendering the snow too soft to make travelling easy.

CHAPTER XLVIII.

THE EARL'S GREAT CHAIR ONCE MORE

AFTER considering our options we decided that we should wait till night fell and the new moon rose. Then we would march when the frost had hardened the snow. We found Marion very contentedly playing with a doll which she had made out of a piece of wood and some rags which she had found in a corner. It was touching to watch her hushing it to sleep.

Silver Sand spent the most part of that day in putting the Aughty to rights, stacking what was left of the fuel, and making the shelter as habitable and tidy as when we entered it. "Otherwise," he said, "I would not look forward to returning to it."

It was nearly six in the evening before we started on our way. Silver Sand said that we would go by the Wolf's Slock and the Links of the Cooran, but I did not liked not the sound of this.

The Wolf's Slock will be like a coach road tonight," he said. I did not know what he meant until we came to its edge; then I saw and fully understood.

The gale from the south had swept the snow into the wide Wolf's Throat of Buchan, and from top to bottom a smooth slope descended many hundreds of feet, most beautiful to see in the faint moonlight which shone into it from the east. We had little Marion with us, carrying her most of the way, but letting her run at other times when it was level and there was good going for the feet.

But I was apprehensive, for I did not know how we would manage to descend that great icy precipice safely, taking the child with us. But my companion soon showed me how little I knew. He let me see a trick the outlaws used in the times of snow among the hills.

Silver Sand took a rope from his shoulder and tied it round my middle – then afterwards round his own. Then he took out his great red kerchief and spread it on the snow. Whereupon he sat down on it with a corner fastened to his rope waistband. He told me to do the same, with my legs forked on either side of him. He put little Marion between us, and told her to fasten her hands round his belt and hold tight. Then, with my arms one on either side of her and clasping Silver Sand, we softly slid over the edge. It was a wild ride in the moonlight – slow at first, then speeding up quickly. The snow streamed on either side of us, driving past with a whish like the spray from a boat's nose when she has much seaway. I had a feeling in the pit of my stomach as if I had left all my vital parts sticking to the snow where we left, and I feared that I might be inconvenienced to be without them when we stopped. But despite that it was wildly exhilarating; so much that when we were half-way down little Marion laughed out a rippling, girlish laugh which pleased us.

We slid almost instantly down the steep slope and then glided out in a long, sweeping, downward curve, under which the Cooran lane lay buried. At last, far out on the plain, we came to a halt, and Silver Sand stood up and shook himself.

"What do you think of that, you that lives on the shore and knows everything?" he said, with a calmness that made me admire him even more than I already did, as he dusted the snow from little Marion and then from his own legs.

That was the end of everything worth writing about – at least, all that I have room to write of at the moment; for the carrier has forgotten to bring me my new supply of paper to the Orraland, and for the last twenty pages I have been writing on empty sugar-bags; but my wife is losing patience, because she keeps her garden seeds in them.

But there is a little more to say.

We got horses at the Clattering Shaws, and it was not until the twilight of the following day that we reached the Great House of Earlstoun. I hope never to be so tired again till I lie down and die. It was, by the marvellous providence of God, Eppie Tamson and not my May Maxwell that opened the door to us. Her sister Jen was over at the Rathan, where her tongue could keep the joiners and masons in better order. The men from Dumfries are always a touch wild and unruly. Once they put out a notice on a shop door in Maxwelltown: "Coarse grain only for Dumfries masons." Whereupon the masons crossed Devorgilla's bridge and broke many windows.

I had little Marion in my arms when Eppie opened the door, and I had thought it would be a great surprise just to hand her into Eppie's arms; but Silver Sand pushed me back with his strong elbow, so suddenly that I was winded and could only gasp until I recovered.

"Eppie," he said, "be very quiet. Can you break the news to May – Patrick's lassie? "

"Yes," said Eppie; "are you risen from the dead?"

"Safe and sound," said Silver Sand, "not a ghost among us."

"Come in!" says she.

"Is Sammle in, Eppie?" says he, in a whisper.

"He's in the kitchen with Kennedy and all the Maxwell lads."

"Is he well? Can you take some news to him? Do you think he'll be able to bear some? "said Silver Sand, cunningly.

"What is it?" cried Eppie, gripping him by the lapels of his coat and shaking him so much that Silver Sand vows that she hurt him. But not grievously, I think.

" *This!*" said I, stepping past him and putting Marion into Eppie's arms, still sound asleep, just as she was when she was held by Silver Sand on his horse.

"Hush, woman; don't wake her!"said I, holding up my finger.

Eppie gave me a look of mixed adoration and scorn. I had brought back her life to her – but why would I think that she would waken her treasure!

Silver Sand afterwards said that it was one of the happiest inspirations of my life.

I wanted much to ask about May and where she was; but, of course, there was so much fuss made about the child that I had to go and look for her myself.

I went up to the great room in the tower which Lady Grizel made so comfortable in the winter months. I knocked very gently. The strong voice of My Lady told me to enter. I came into the bright glow of the great wood fire.

The old lady threw up her hands. "The Lord preserve us, Patrick!" she said.

She rose from the chair and came towards me. She took my hand, and I declare but she kissed both it and me, even though she was an Earl's daughter. Then she remembered something, seeing me look around the room.

"Aye, laddie," she said, "what am I thinking of – you have no use for old wives like me."

She stepped to the foot of the stair that led to the tower."May!" she cried, quickly.

There was a stirring above, and then I could hear light footsteps on the stair which made my pulse dance. Lady Grizel slipped out of the room, shutting the outer door with a clang so that I would know that she had gone. She was always a considerate woman – there are few like her.

The stair door opened, and the flicker of the fire shone on a fair lass, pale as a lily flower, who stood framed against the darkness of the turret.

I held out my arms towards her. "May!" I cried, just like the Lady Grizel had done, but in completely different tone.

She put her hand to her breast and came slowly towards me for two or three steps, as if she was dazed and uncertain. Then, suddenly crying out, with light dancing in her eyes, she broke and ran to me. So I gathered my love within my arms.

And now a "Fair-good-evening" to all of you that have come so far with us. I have no more to say, and no more that you need to hear. Mistress May Mischief and I love you for your kind courtesy, and we pray that you, like the dear Lady Grizel, you will close the door behind you as far as it will go, and leave us alone in the firelight, with only the Earl's great chair for company.

THE END.

By the mercy of God this account of our many trials and their happy end is finished at our house of the Rathan, on the first day of April 17–, being the second anniversary of the birth of my son John Faa Heron, my daughter Grizel Maxwell being now in her seventh year, and my dear wife entering her thirty-third—but, as I think, bonnier than ever.

APPENDIX – HISTORICAL CONTEXT

THE KILLING TIMES

Although Crockett makes reference to the Killing Times and the persecution of innocent men in the hills and moorlands, seemingly officially sanctioned, it is perhaps worth elaborating on why this happened. Although peripheral to the main story, these events took place in an earlier time but in the same region as the events described in Crockett's story and clearly had an influence on Silver Sand, and his way of life. I wanted to know more about the events that led up to the Killing Times and undertook some research of this very complex period in Scottish history. If this version of the book does reach wider readership, I felt the inclusion of a brief summary might be helpful. So here goes.

In 1560, the Scottish Reformation Parliament passed legislation which led to the establishment of Scotland as a Protestant nation with its own church, the Church of Scotland. As in England, this was initially a rejection of Roman Catholicism but the governance of the church remained unresolved, leading to a conflict between Presbyterianism and Episcopalianism, which lasted 130 years.

Presbyterianism, with its roots in the teachings of John Calvin, is governed by a General Assembly of ministers, who themselves are elected by their congregations. It commits to defend the Monarchy, but does not require permanently installed bishops nor the Monarch to be head of the church. In this way, it was thought the Church could protect its people from the greed and excesses of the past. Episcopalianism, on the other hand, is governed by bishops, answerable to the monarch, who is assumed to be appointed by God and is head of the church by Divine Right.

The Reformation did not have the support of the Catholic Mary Queen of Scots and her supporters. Following a period of conflict, it did survive although it began to follow the example set in England. Bishops were reintroduced in 1572, for instance.

James VI saw himself as a monarch subordinate to none, even though he was a staunch Protestant and he asserted royal authority over the Church. He ruled in the manner of Elizabeth I in England and encouraged episcopacy against the wishes of the General Assembly. His ultimate objective was to be King of both Scotland and England, and to be head of their Protestant episcopal churches. Following his accession to the throne of England, James, believing that Presbyterianism was incompatible with monarchy, steadily reintroduced episcopacy and by the time of James' death, Presbyterianism was only practised in private by a hard core of intransigents.

Whilst the doctrine of the Church was still rooted in Calvinism, the method by which it was conducted was essentially Anglican. Charles I continued his father's work, but without his father's diplomatic skills. He introduced confession, restored lands to the church and introduced a new Prayer Book, based on the Anglican Book of Common Prayer, in 1637. The people believed this heralded the eventual reintroduction of Catholicism and it unleashed widespread protest and rioting.

The National Covenant, written in 1638 was a declaration of faith, but it was also a political manifesto. Copies were sent for signature all over Scotland and it essentially became a referendum on Charles I's reforms. The General Assembly reversed Charles' changes and deposed the bishops whilst the Scottish Parliament undertook a constitutional revolution. Charles responded using force, but was rebuffed in a series of conflicts know as the Bishops Wars and saw the supporters of the National Covenant, the Covenanters, emerge as a military force.

The Covenanters joined forces with Cromwell's Parliamentarians in the Civil War and Charles surrendered to the Covenanter Army in Newark. They consolidated their position in Scotland and at one stage, a force of 6000 Covenanters from the South West advanced on Edinburgh, with cries of "Whiggamore" thus giving them and their political party a name.

However, the execution of Charles I led to further confusion. Since the Covenant declared that the crown should be protected, the Scots now broke the alliance with Cromwell and declared Charles II king. In return for Scottish support, he agreed to sign the Covenant, which he did when he returned to Scotland in 1650, but the campaign that followed led to defeat for Charles at Dunbar and Worcester. Charles escaped and Scotland was now occupied and subsumed into the Commonwealth for the next 8 years.

Following the Restoration of Charles II, Scotland once again slid towards Episcopacy. All legislation since 1633 was annulled, leading to the restoration of Bishops, the abolition of the Kirk Assembly and the formal rejection of the Covenant. All persons in public office were required to swear an oath, meaning that most Presbyterians were excluded from holding positions of trust.

In May 1662, an Act of Parliament decreed that all ministers required patronage and the approval of the relevant bishop. The Privy Council then enforced this, with the result that over 400 ministers were driven from their homes and parishes, effectively consolidating the supremacy of Episcopalianism over Presbyterianism. Parishioners who did not attend services, largely supporters of the Covenant, were heavily fined, hunted down and beaten, and in some cases executed. The militia were allowed by the bishops to act as both judge and executioner.

Most of the resistance to this came from the South West. Displaced ministers continued to preach, but in the fields and mountains and remote glens. Congregations supported these open air coventicles but eventually they became bitterly persecuted. Dragoons were sent to deal with these gatherings.

The first armed resistance began in 1666 in Dalry, Kirkcudbrightshire when Covenanters overcame some troopers who were assaulting an elderly man. The party marched to Dumfries, growing in strength and captured the local troop commander, Sir James Turner. Not being professional soldiers, their intention was to petition Parliament, their aim being not defiance against the king, but to be relieved from the tyranny of the bishops and secure the restoration of their ministers. However, their resistance came to an end at a massacre of 1000 men at Rullion Green, near Edinburgh. Survivors were tortured, executed or transported. Amnesties were offered in 1669 and 1672 to the dissenting ministers but many refused and their congregations were more determined than ever to support them, although now they attended coventicles armed. Field preaching became punishable by death. In 1678, 4500 highlanders were recruited to support 3000 lowland militia. They repressed the region with much destruction and looting. The lowland lairds appealed against this barbary to no avail and violence again increased.

The bishop of St Andrews, Sharp, was cruelly murdered in 1679 by a group of Covenanters. The perpetrators formed a scratch army which defeated a cavalry of troopers commanded by James Graham of Claverhouse at Drumclog. The army grew to a strength of 5000 but this was defeated at Bothwell Brig by James, Duke of Monmouth, the kings bastard son. Again, this was followed by savage retribution.

Persecution and reprisals continued but the Convenanters were remained defiant but their defeats split the movement into moderates and extremists. In 1680, a field preacher, Richard Cameron, declared war on the King and Government in Sanquhar. Although he was killed in a skirmish shortly after, his followers became known as the Cameronians.

Parliament next introduced an Act requiring all holders of public office to recognise the supremacy of the crown, disown both popery and the Covenant, and to maintain Protestantism. This split the country. Many refused to take the oath and sought exile in Holland. The Cameronians under James Renwick, became more militant declaring, in 1684 in the Apologetical Declaration, that rejected the authority of Charles II and stated that anyone who attempted to harm them, would meet with equal violence.

The King's brother, James, Duke of York was a converted Catholic and believed that he was only answerable to God. He proceeded to relax laws against Roman Catholics, replacing Protestant officials and punishing ministers who preached against Rome.

On May 8th 1685, by order of the Scottish Privy Council, anyone refusing to denounce the Declaration or those attending coventicles, were to be considered treasonous and therefore liable to be executed and their property confiscated. An oath could be put to any suspect and if they refused, they could be executed in the presence of any officer holding a commission from the Privy Council. This began the so called "Killing Times" which was led in the South West by Graham of Claverhouse, supported by Grierson of Lag and upwards of 80 executions were held in 1685. The forces comprised of local conscripted men (including, in the novel, Silver Sand) but was also augmented by a number of highlanders, known as the Highland Host. The latter indulged in much robbery and pillage during their short stay.

The bravery and obstinacy of the Cameronians (which Silver Sand later joined) inspired wider discontent, although this was not sufficient to lead to the overthrow of government or crown.

In 1687, James II relented slightly, and allowed non-conformists to meet in houses or chapels, but coventicles were still punishable by death. This was acceptable to all but the Cameronians. Furthermore, by allowing Catholicism, he angered Episcopalians and this gave prospect to the return of the old Church of Scotland. Exiles began to return. There was widespread discontent across both England and Scotland and James was eventually expelled by William of Orange in 1688.

A Convention in Edinburgh agreed that James had forfeited the throne of Scotland and it could be given to William, provided he protected the laws, religion and liberties of the nation, and specifically to remove the enemies of the Church of Scotland. The remaining Scottish bishops lost influence as they could not swear allegiance to William when James still lived and this left William little choice but to support the Church of

Scotland. Thus Presbyterianism was established as the dominant religion in Scotland with the Church of Scotland in the role of National Church. Richard Cameron's men were pardoned and from being outlawed men, the Cameronians now became an official regiment, and their next action was to defeat the supporters of James, largely Highland clans and who had had success at Killiecrankie, at Dunkeld. The highlanders were led by Graham of Claverhouse, recently created Viscount of Dundee but who had died during the Killiecrankie victory.

Shortly after, the new parliament abolished prelacy and established Presbyterianism, thus ending 140 years of conflict, until the Jacobite rising of 1715.

HISTORICAL CHARACTERS IN "THE RAIDERS"

Covenanters were persecuted all over the Scottish Lowlands but nowhere with such ruthless zeal as the remoter parts of the South West Counties of Dumfries, Kirkcudbright and Wigtown. Nowhere else did the names of the perpetrators – in this region Claverhouse and Lag – appear with such frequency. Most of the deaths associated with them happened in 1684 and 1685, so the appearance of them and their troopers in any community must have been viewed with some dread.

The following characters mentioned by Crockett were real and substantial people; descriptions of them are included here for completeness.

James Graham, Laird of Claverhouse (1648-1689) Already an established soldier in 1678, with the support of the future James II, he was given command of Highland company and tasked with suppressing illegal Presbyterian field meetings. He served under The Duke of Monmouth at the defeat of the Covenanters at Bothwell Brig in June 1679. In January 1681, he became sheriff of the four southwestern counties. Although he married a staunch Covenanter in 1684, he presided over the "Killing Times" notably in 1684-5 when at least 80 executions took place. James II created him Viscount of Dundee in 1688. Following James' overthrow, he led Jacobite resistance but died in 1689 during his successful defeat of Government forces at Killiecrankie. Known as "Bonnie Dundee" in popular song and literature.

Sir Robert Grierson of Lag (1655-1733) – born near Kirkcudbright, became Steward of Kirkcudbright and the member of Parliament for

Dumfriesshire. A Stuart loyalist and an Episcopalian, he assisted Graham of Claverhouse in the policing of Southwest Scotland to suppress illegal conventicles and travelling preachers. As a commissioner for Galloway, he presided over several executions, notably the Wigtown martyrs, two women who were staked out and drowned by the rising tide in 1685. He was loathed and feared across the region, but was rewarded by James II by a baronetcy. On Williams accession he was arrested but bailed and spent the rest of his long life under suspicion of being a Jacobite.

Richard Cameron (1648-1680) – born in Fife, became a field preacher in 1678. In 1679 he was ordained as a Church of Scotland minister in Rotterdam and was encouraged to return to Scotland to inspire the field preachers, who were becoming demoralised by the persecutions they had suffered. He was well received and developed a band of followers. They rode into Sanquhar and read out the Sanquhar Declaration which called for war against Charles II and exclusion of his brother James from the succession and a reward was then issued for his capture. He continued to preach to growing congregations but only one month later was killed in an engagement. However, his followers continued to preach in his name and resist persecution through the Killing Times until the 1688 Revolution.

Rev. John McMillan (1669-1753) – born in Minnigaff, became the first minister of the Cameronians after the settlement of 1688. He preached at Balmaghie, near Lauriston, (Clachanpluck in the novel), from 1700. He was accused of insubordination against church government and was deposed, but he was so popular with his congregation, he managed to keep possession of the church and the manse. The official appointee was left to preach in a barn and was sometimes violently attacked. McMillan voluntarily resigned in 1715. He still used the church but spent time developing support for a new branch of Presbyterianism – the Reformed Presbyterian Church - which ultimately spread worldwide. He left the parish in 1727.

James Renwick (1662-1688) – born in Moniaive, he joined the Cameronians in 1681 and became a prominent member. Largely responsible for the Apologetical Declaration of 1684 which disowned the authority of Charles II. Failure to reject this document could lead to summary execution in the field. Even after concessions were made to Presbyterians in 1687, he continued to defy authority and was captured and executed in Edinburgh in 1688, the last of the Covenanter Martyrs.

Donald Cargill (1619-1681) – a minister who was discharged in 1662 and subsequently held conventicles. He joined Richard Cameron in 1679 and publicly excommunicated the King, amongst others, for which he was pursued and subsequently captured and executed in 1681.

Alexander Peden (1626-1686) – born in Ayrshire, became a minister until he was ejected in 1663 and thereafter became a field preacher, the most celebrated of his time. He Denounced as a rebel and fugitive in 1666, he travelled and preached far and wide until he was captured and imprisoned on the Bass Rock from 1673 till 1678 then sentenced for transportation but was released by the ships captain. Having spent some time in Ireland, he returned to Ayrshire in 1685 where he spent his last days sheltering in a cave.

Patrick Walker (1666-1745) – He was an ardent supporter of the Covenanters in his youth. He was sentenced to transportation but escaped to the South West. In his later life he became a historian and chronicler of the Covenanter era and published a number of detailed, though partisan, pamphlets in the 1720s and 30s and brought the lives of Cameron, Peden, Cargill and others to wider attention than the South West.

Major Thomas Weir (1599-1670) – a Covenanter, he served in the anti royalist army during the Civil War. He became a high ranking public figure in Edinburgh but was later accused of adultery, incest and witchcraft by his unstable sister. Both were executed in 1690. Weir was garrotted and burned.

Billy Marshall (1672-1792) – self-styled "King of the Gypsies" reputedly descended from a group of Roma settlers in Galloway. He rejected the rule of authority and deserted from the Army and Navy on a number of occasions. He was involved in smuggling, highway robbery and petty theft and gained notoriety as a "lovable rogue" but escaped prosecution. Reputedly married 17 times, even fathering 4 children after reaching the age of 100. He is buried in Kirkcudbright Churchard.

A
WOMAN'S
MIND

THE FINAL FRONTIER

Is there a chance for men?

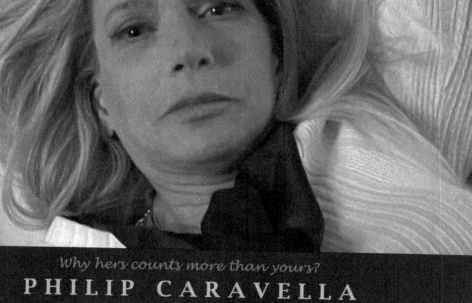

Why hers counts more than yours?

PHILIP CARAVELLA

A
WOMAN'S
MIND

THE FINAL FRONTIER

Is there a chance for men?

Why hers counts more than yours?

PHILIP CARAVELLA, MD, FAAFP, Lt. Col., US Army (Ret.tt)

508 West 26th Street
KEARNEY, NE 68848
402-819-3224
info@medialiteraryexcellence.com

A WOMAN'S MIND: The Final Frontier

ISBN (Paperback): 978-1-958082-70-6
ISBN (Ebook): 978-1-958082-71-3

Printed in the United States of America

TABLE OF CONTENTS

CHAPTER 1

PROMISE, HOPE, LOVE

Passion is sought after by most, in that it is a feeling of an immense need to find a connection, devotion, and love for another person. It is without reason. It occurs between the most connected or bonded of two individuals blending them in a way the confounds many casual observers. When it is perceived by others, they may inwardly tremble in that they have not experienced a similar emotion and may be left wanting.

This book has been written to help couples find a common ground and establish a wonderful life between themselves and their significant others. Upon finding a common ground, we will find love among our relationships. We will bond and blend on most if not all levels. And most importantly we will find the answer and ways to improve our bonds together, forever. I guarantee it.

Men and women think differently in many ways because our brains are wired differently as I will prove to you. Why are the sexes wired differently? God decided that beings that are too much alike would not be as attracted to each other because they would not be different enough to make a union interesting. So, in his wisdom, he chose to have us be quite different on many levels with the hope of increasing the chances of wonder and romance to occur. Also in another vein, a partner may occasionally express different goals and objectives that may likewise be appealing to the other. As they say, "opposites attract." Opposites allow for a more interesting life with another, without necessarily being competitive. There is little place in a romantic relationship for competition. It can "spoil the pie."

Thus, we are wired to help us as individuals achieve our goals in the best way possible. The trick is in finding the right connections and that is what this book is about.

1

Humanity being humane, will always seek the higher ground and for the most part, humanity will succeed in goodness, grace, and living. If that were not true, most of us would not be here.

The future for men and women begins and ends with promise, hope, and love. I acknowledge that my wife Debra, inspired me to write this text in hopes that others who read this will find a similar life and beauty surrounding their lives forever within the framework of each other. They will bond with passion forever.

Disclaimer: The words written on these pages pertain to all people within an intimate, sexual, and loving relationship regardless of their personal preferences.

CHAPTER 2

ARE WOMEN AND MEN REALLY THAT DIFFERENT?

It is fascinating, as I think about how men and women are quite different in the way they react not only to each other but also on how they react to many life-changing events. We often find that we are walking a tight rope throughout our lives, in that life is constantly presenting challenges for us to overcome. How many times has every one of you thought back and wondered? What if I had done that? Maybe I should have married the other one I was in love with? If I had only gone on that one date that I said no to, not realizing that the date I did go on, would be a mistake. We all make a thousand or more mistakes no matter how much time we spend reviewing our options. In this way we are very much alike.

Men and women are different, as you know in many ways, though not in a bad or troublesome way; that is once you get the picture. Our differences are offset by many interesting characteristics that we have as men and women. With clear thinking, maybe it would be challenging and interesting to investigate how we live together, react together, and enjoy life together. How we make a go of it!

Here is an attempt to sort out these mysteries with humor, insight, and hopefully some observations that have a bit of value to all of us. My biggest question to set before all of you, "Is Theere A Chancee Fore Men?" I hope so. And Guess what? There is!!! It will all be revealed as you read on. A great relationship for couples is easy to achieve once you understand the ingredients and how to use them to achieve what both men and women really want; harmony, love, mutual respect, honor, and amazing sex. Let's not leave that out. Sex bonds partners in ways that nothing else will. There are no substitutes for a great sexual relationship with another person. Those that think there are will sooner or later have many other serious problems beyond the scope of this book because they may find that they are looking for sex in the wrong places.

3

Some may contend, that whether there is or not a chance for a perfect union, may be based on from who's perspective one is looking? But I don't think so. In a marriage, you can have your cake and eat it too. You know what I mean kiddos. I truly believe women want men to succeed. And why is that? Because they want the best of all worlds. The best man, the best opportunities, and of course the best life they can possibly muster. We all want the same. So, there you have it. The real question is how to achieve your wants, desires, and an unbreakable relationship. Look no further and read on.

After reviewing the literary research, I have to say the findings on this topic are limited, sketchy, misleading, thoughtless, and almost primitive. In fact, the research is shockingly inadequate. I guess it is too frightening to stare in the face. LOL!

Well men and women are different on so many levels, yet we are alike enough to foster the finest relationships that can occur in society and how is that? You will find out my friends.

Men and women can have the finest relationships because most of our problems should never occur and voting on an outcome will never work unless you both vote alike. It is not about voting. It is about - - - - - - well I wonder now. What is it about?!?

Being a researcher myself, with many publications to my credit has provided a background for my level of expertise and credentials. My medical education and experience in the practice of family medicine has also aided my exploration into the essence of how men and women think alike and how we think differently. Understanding how we think differently and how to make that work for ourselves is the key to a fantastic union.

Why is this question even worthwhile evaluating? Many of us struggle with a variety of problems whether we are single, married, or divorced. Who said life would be easy?

When asked, upon meeting your friend for lunch, we all say. "How are you doing?" Everyone always responds, "I'm fine and how are you?" They of course respond "I'm good. Thanks for asking. What

4

they didn't say is "Janice and I just had a big fight before I came to meet you." Or how about this? "I got a letter from the IRS today and they said I under paid my taxes and owe another $1,569.00." Of course, we always respond with, "I'm fine," no matter how we really feel. And as I turn around to take a seat at the table at the Olive Garden, my buddy sees a knife sticking in my back. Just Joking!

Now let's get real. We all cannot be fine? But we always say we are! Apparently, it is the socially acceptable thing to say. Who wants to listen to anyone else's troubles anyway? We have enough of our own.

Most folks have hills and valleys as they traverse life. But we were never promised that life would be a cakewalk. It is best that it is not, since that might even be on the boring side. Challenges give us character, stamina, and hope for the future.

Now, let's get into the meat of what makes us tick and what also makes are lover tick.

CHAPTER 3

The Decay of Marriage and How It Started

When did problems in marriage really begin to go south? What happened? There are many reasons for this to occur. The decay of many marriages has their roots going back over one hundred years. It is a bit complicated, though not too controversial as you will see once you sink your teeth into the substance of the problem.

Matthew 19:11-12-11-12 MSG
It requires a certain aptitude and grace. Marriage isn't for everyone. Some, from birth seemingly, never give marriage a thought.

As you know, a large percentage of marriages will end up in divorce. If couples have a better and more complete understanding of what makes an ideal marriage and how each could learn from the other, they may be able to incorporate their new knowledge into strengthening their bonds for developing a more loving and sustainable relationship.

I have been married more than once. The first two marriages were poorly thought out and failed as a result. My marriage today is better in many ways when compared to my previous two. As a result, I believe and hope my wife Debbie and I will have a marriage that will last for the rest of our natural lives.

What is a good marriage all about? Do the differences on how a man and woman think influence their decisions and their marriage?

As you read, much of this is conjecture and sheds little if any new information that would provide clues on how men and women think alike much less on how they think differently. In fact, the literature is nearly an embarrassment of incomplete data.

Details in the literature are compiled and composed of facts that many of us are already aware of. The information I have currently found is not of much help in assisting couples on deciding if their bond will be a bond that will last forever. Thus, I decided to leap into the morass and see what I can see.

It is important to look at general Information on how Marriage has evolved in the past two centuries and look at where marriage is heading as an institution and a sacrament. Unfortunately, we must also look at how marriage has often resulted in divorce for a variety of reasons and what may be done to fix this problem that is growing deeper in America.

CHAPTER 4

The Marriage and Divorce Debacle
Is this the End of Marriage as We Know It!

Marriage became an institution in 1549 When the oldest known traditional wedding vows came into play. They can be traced back to the manuals of the English medieval church. In England, there were manuals of the dioceses of Salisbury (Sarum) and York. The compilers of the first Book of Common Prayer, published in 1549 based its marriage service mainly on the Sarum manual. (Wikipedia).

It is now widely agreed that the origin of marriage dates well before recorded history, but the earliest recorded evidence of marriage ceremonies uniting one woman and one-man date from about 2350 B.C. in the Far East.

First, a little history of marriage is in order. The oldest standard wedding vows can be traced back to the Book of Common Prayer, by Thomas Cranmer, Archbishop of Canterbury: "I, ___place a name here___, take thee, ___place a name here___ , to be my wedded Husband, to have and to hold from this day forward, for better for worse, for richer, for poorer, in sickness, and in health, to love, cherish, and to .. (We don't know exactly what was here, but in modern times it has become until death do us part).

Did you know the traditional wedding vows aren't in the Bible, but are based on biblical principles? **This means you are free to interpret those principles and write your own vows.** This becomes important as you will see later in this book. The bible defines marriage as the joining of two into one, according to Genesis 2:24

In the Old Testament we are taught, "Therefore shall a man leave his father and his mother and shall cleave unto his wife: and they shall be one flesh" (**Genesis 2:24**). Married couples are meant to be unified in every possible way.

8

From the earliest days of the Christian faith, Christians have honored holy matrimony (as Christian marriages are referred to) as a divinely blessed, lifelong, monogamous union between a man and a woman.

Matthew 19:11-12-11-12 MSG
It requires a certain aptitude and grace. Marriage isn't for everyone. Some, from birth seemingly, never give marriage a thought.

CHAPTER 5

ARE COUPLES GROWING APART?

There are many reasons for the increasing rates of separation and divorce occurring in America. It does vary from one generation or age group to another. The purpose of detailing the main causes of these problems, is with the hope that couples through knowledge and understanding may be shown how to live a better and more compatible life with the goal of diminishing the huge social stigma of divorce that continues to be a part of American society.

Most currant data indicate the divorce is primarily due to a lack of compatibility and commitment. This is no surprise. The real issue is what are the factors that have the most impact on these problems, which if they worsen will horribly impact the lives of not just the couples but of course their children and grandchildren as well. Society must do better.

The time is long overdue to address the issue of divorce and marital incompatibility. Current research indicates a lack of compatibility affecting 43% of divorces, is related to partners arguing excessively in 56% of marriages leading to the incompatibility and a trip to divorce court.

I believe that with careful thinking, both men and women will be able to have a clearer idea on how both can sit together, discuss their differences, and agree to improve their relationship once everyone is on the same page. That is the hope of this book.

Let's investigate the past. Generations of those who came before us provide clues to where we are today and maybe even more importantly, where we should be tomorrow.

CHAPTER 6

IN MODERN TIMES, HOW HAVE WOMEN'S OPTIONS AFFECTED MARRIAGE?

In 1920 there were just over eight-million women working outside of their home representing twenty percent of the workforce. Women were paid considerably less than men for performing the same work until the Equal Pay Act under President John F. Kennedy was passed evening the playing field. By 2010 more than fifty percent of the workforce was composed of women. By 2018 there were almost seventy-eight million women in the workforce equal to forty-seven percent of the employed. How is that for a change!?

What is not clear in those statistics is whether the men and women in the US military are included in those statistics. I do not believe those statistics were included and if they were, it could change the balance though not likely in a significant way. In any case, that detail may be simply splitting hairs. At the end of the day, there are a lot of married people working and most of them are women.

What effect does all of this have on the divorce rate? Maybe not much? It does of course give women independence as a worker, and thus they are perfectly capable of supporting themselves. If children are involved in a divorce, alimony would be an important aspect of a woman's independence, if she wishes wish to have the primary responsibility to care for their children. This scenario would be based on a very case-by-case determination.

MARRIAGE, SOCIETIES MOST IMPORTANT ARRANGEMENT

Again, let's look at marriages, one of the most important social arrangement any couple could have, given its longevity and potential risk for problems. Before both tie the knot, you had better be sure of what you are doing. Many of us, regardless of our aptitudes will foul this up. And why is that?

11

Marriage is more complicated than it appears to the uninitiated. Men all too often are thinking more about their genitals than about anything else. Women on the other hand are thinking how fine a marriage could be over the alternative and they take a leap of faith into what may become the bowels of hell.

Should couples have any doubt about their impending marriage, a longer courtship will generally answer most of their questions. It is best to be as certain as possible in your hearts and souls before tying the knot. Take your time. Take a break. But no matter, you're still taking a chance.

Marriage is only easy with the best of communication between partners. The most important key to any great relationship is listening. Most of us talk too much and do not listen. Then you wonder why you have issues. Too much talking and not enough listening may be the sign of a narcissist. A woman loves a listener. That is RULE # 1.

Hoping to be able to form a clearer picture for all of us on how men and women interact was my goal. How we love. How we come to appreciate each other on many levels throughout our lives, are critical building blocks we must achieve.

You will not find the answers you are looking for in today's research. In fact, I do not believe it will ever be possible to learn in any effective way how men and women really think about each other since our thought processes and concerns fluctuate from day to day and often from hour to hour. Yet as you know we manage to function well in working out our differences by achieving reasonable and even sometimes even spectacular results.

Therefore, thinking differently as men and women often do about many facets of their lives, may allow for a level of uncertainty for many of us to worry about. However, a remarkably good marriage as many of us desire, is a goal that will often include a level of success well received by both lovers.

Until there is a man/woman species combining us into a single entity, we will never sort it out. Of course, folks, that comment deserves little if any consideration. "Variety is the spice of life." Let us be different, interesting, accommodating, and sexy. If we were identical, we would not be sexy, playful, interesting, attractive, or "human." So toss that idea out of the window.

CHAPTER 7

HOW ARE WE ALIKE AND HOW ARE WE THE SAME?

Let's give this investigation a shot at what makes women and men so special!

I have attempted to dive deeply into the thought processes of men and women on all sorts of subjects and how those thoughts affect our beliefs and actions. As you know, we think alike on many questions. The challenge lies not on how we think alike but more on how we think so differently while deviating from side to side during the process of finding our way down the path of mutual agreement.

Some of my thoughts are conjecture more than anything else. They are also laced with emotions and feelings on how men and women should work together, love together, and play together to form a more perfect union.

Today's research focuses too much on gender biases we are all familiar with, with very little on what really indicates true differences.

Here are a few "differences" that surfaced in my research: comparing women to men. "Men could throw farther, were physically aggressive, masturbated more, and held more positive attitudes about sex in uncommitted relationships." Now, who does not know these things? Can you believe you just read this?

Therefore, because the literature is relatively weak on the topic of mutual thought processes as we cohabitate, it occurred to me to look further by expanding our horizons in searching for the truth.

Any improvements on how men and women could work together on their marriage and living arrangements would be of value for those who may have lost touch on why they married to begin with. On the other hand, marriage will always have its challenges. With love and patience, we will all enjoy many amazing

14

days ahead. The secret is in our thought processes and the ability to accommodate, appreciate, and love our union for the best of all worlds.

In another mind-boggling example of what I would refer to as exposing the obvious, it was determined that men's brains are larger. That is true, if we open our eyes and note that generally men are larger than their mate. Men are larger in general in all aspects of their physical being. That does not mean they have more neurons or convolutions within their brain structure to aid in thinking. Men do not. Women have every bit the same number of neurons and convolutions, as well as mental capacity, though their neurons are in a more compact space. Remember, God wanted man to be somewhat larger than his mate and that's how it has generally always been.

Men and women have the same capacity to learn and to think with the appropriate brain to do so. If we did not have the same capacities, how could we ever be a match for each other in all aspects of living requiring two beings to be nearly identical. Nearly identical is close enough.

Being nearly identical is a far cry from being identical as all of you are aware of. We each have 20,000 genes with only two chromosomes differing between men and women. Men have a "Y" chromosome. Women counter that with an additional "X" chromosome. The Y chromosome gives man his male identity. The X chromosome gives the woman her female identity. It is that simple. Our physical differences are what makes our lives fascinating as we plug away at living life together, bearing children, working, playing, and progressing to the end we will all someday experience.

What about gender bias? Gender bias research has created misleading assumptions about male and female behavior. The research fails to validate discrimination and negative stereotypes. Examples: girls should play with dolls. Boys should play with trucks. Girls should wear pink. Boys should wear blue. What about that baloney? Women are more interested in people, while men are more

15

interested in designing buildings, building cars, and creating machines. We are different.

As you can see, the research is weak and adds nothing to how we should be thinking about real gender differences. How about this? Women are more tender minded. Men have higher self-esteem. Ok, we know these statements are based on gender bias and come from an era of past assumptions. Women, being very much aware of these unconfirmed concepts swept much of them under the rug long ago.

Some researchers believe women are better at multitasking. I believe this is true. Women also have verbal centers in both hemispheres of their brain where men have theirs only on their left side. Thus, it has been said, that women talk more. A woman's description of a vacation or marriage ceremony may be much more detailed while a man may say, 'it was nice.'

A woman tends to revisit old memories sometimes causing fresh feelings of resentment, making her want to vent to her husband when he seems to "care less." In a way I believe that is true, but it also helps to minimize the "after affects" of such interactions between men and women.

When you truly love another person, many of your past disagreements become muted with time. As they say, "Time heals all wounds." Fortunately for all of us it is very true, especially when lovers truly love each other.

Women have a larger limbic system (the part of the brain controlling emotions) which helps them to identify their emotions more clearly. As a result, men need to have somethings spelled out to them in more detail.

Women may be more empathetic having a more active insula portion of their brain. A woman's brain through her insula, conveys the feelings she has for her man, more completely than men can do so in return. Women may brood more on these feelings. To be

16

thorough, women use these God given attributes to help them raise children more effectively than men are usually able to do.

Women have been shown to have a much better memory for facts, dates, names, and faces. Their hippocampus (memory center) is more active than that of a man's. Men do not remember a woman's shoe size, dress size, and other details and only do so when they make a very special effort to do so should they wish to purchase a gift for their lovely lady.

For a woman, her memory of details is automatic. Men usually work to support their family, while a woman with her better memory may work for the same reason, but in addition, she also attempts to prevent familial disasters related to past events.

As you can see, we are different, and we balance each other out for a better union and a calmer family lifestyle. Men's and woman's weaknesses are usually balanced out between them in the name of love.

Men have much more testosterone than a woman has and thus they really require very little to get going. Women look for the mood, the scents, the ambiance, the sounds, and her own emotions to trigger her desire or need for sex. She is much more complicated in that regard, and thus she may shun her man's needs or advances as a result.

Careful planning on the part of men may result in better results. Think about it! Now and then, don't forget the roses for your sweetheart. "A rose in your hand is worth a lady in your bed." Maybe! Women do certainly love a thoughtful lover but let's not forget that above all else, women want their feelings respected. For her, life is not all about sex and romance. It is about bonding, responsibility, longevity, and especially respect. You should be listening to her.

In other scientific observations, men are often better at math and women are better at languages. Most of us are aware of these

17

differences. As a result, men may labor more in industrial science labs while women work in classrooms. We balance each other out based on our mental and intellectual capacities.

Besides, these differences allow for better conversations between the sexes so that we may inform each other easily about our thoughts. Life would be boring if we were more alike than we already are. Our likenesses and differences provide for the best balance between us.

Unfortunately for women, difference in their greater nerve ending density results in a higher sensitivity to pain than have men. My wife Debbie is a vivid example of that. An injury to her neck occurring well over twenty years ago has resulted in chronic pain that she experiences every single day of her life. There is no respite for her. She lives with it daily and so do I. I pray for her, hoping that someday there will be a medication or solution to end this horrible odyssey.

Having a chronic pain problem for any man or woman is unfortunate. Who would want more nerve endings devoted to pain. We are different in that regard. Women have a higher calling in many ways due to their responsibilities required in raising children. Their need to avoid painful experiences may somehow be related in an odd sort of way to allow them to be available to rear their children.

So, there you have it ladies and gents. There are differences of course, but the differences are harder to delineate in real life beyond the obvious. Facts, conjecture, and reality are intriguing and delicate to a degree, but it is here where new light will be shed on how men and women differ, and how they are alike, in the hopes of strengthening every aspect of our interactions and being to improve our bonding. Most people see the value in this topic realizing we are usually better suited for married life rather than single. One important detail that has been proven is that married women live longer with a two-and-one half times lower death rate than that of widows. On top of that, the death rate is lower for divorcees than women who have never married.

Woman should be placed first in any discussion about a man and what he hopes for. Everything a man does is to be attractive and desirable to the woman he finds he is in love with. For most men, it is a natural need to be attracted to a woman for procreation and for nearly all goals in life that would be alluring between two people.

God knew as it pertains to most men, without a woman a man would have little reason for being. God made man to be joined to a woman. He began with men and along came Eve.

A woman gives to her man the gifts of love, compassion, beauty, romance, grace, thoughtfulness, and many other attributes only a woman knows how to really bestow. Men have some of those attributes, but a woman has a side of her that tends to be so lovely she cannot and should not be ignored. A woman can have a sweetness about her that is precious and wonderful. She can be clever, smooth, supportive, giving, interesting, funny, graceful, and a million other things. She has a special way about her.

Even her clothing can give, take, seduce, protect, intrigue, promote, deliver, astound, and provide for, like few other articles are able to do. Her touch is often so light and airy that it whispers upon her man's skin. She loves to give more than she takes. She can be truly angelic when she wishes to be, but ruffle her feathers at times and then you had better watch out.

Biologically she needs to depend upon a man to help provide and protect her flock. Her territory is her territory. Let no one be fooled by that. A woman is everything a man could ever want and sometimes much more than he thinks he may even need. There must be a balance between both men and woman for ideal outcomes.

A woman has boundaries that need to be honored and honed to a fine line for peace and tranquility. There is no greater goodness like a beautiful and wonderful woman for pleasing her partner. Most women have a sense of this and with good taste and civility, a union between a man and woman will flourish. Great communication and an openness that lends itself to an understanding between each other avoids many mistakes. Problems between two individuals often are rooted in poor communication, taking someone for granted, or forgetting which side of the bread is buttered.

Openness on all issues reduces confusion, doubt, and trust and is the foundation of a good and caring long-term relationship between men and women. Men and women are meant to be together and as a rule, few relationships have the meaning and value that has a good marriage.

CHAPTER 8

WHAT IS A MAN?

After completing nearly eight decades of living, first as a son, a boy, a brother, along with a twin sister Phyllis, a cousin, a nephew, a grandson, and later as a car enthusiast, artist, student, man, salesman, physician, soldier, husband, father, writer, researcher, lecturer, and stepfather has provided countless experiences.

With time I have decided that men in general can often be misunderstood by the "Fairer" sex. My hope is to set the record straight. We males have a few short comings that not only remain forever obvious, but we often also exhibit a few hidden and mystifying attributes that may usually be modified or rectified with help from you know who? The "Fairer" sex.

At the end of the day, a trite but generally true concept is, "a happy wife is a happy life". I capitalize "Fairer" out of respect and some humility in giving our women credit for trying to deal with us, but to also recognize that life with each other is not always fair. We must do the best we can to be helpful and congenial to each other. This is also an attempt to clarify who we men are and my goal is to show how we may improve relationships that are not a based-on science, but are rather a labor of love, humility, hope, and even justice.

I have chosen many descriptive words to elaborate upon one man's perspective, since only a woman may appreciate her own needs and how she relates to her man. We men are not privy to such thought processes, and I suspect - that is a good thing. Overall, we both have time on our sides and thus we tend to move slowly while focusing on the same target.

Occasional crossroads, blips, debates, struggles, and various other infinitely trying circumstances will encompass all our lives but that is what gives our lives interest, meaning, reason, and hope for the future. It is in hope and promise that we all live for. For these are the frameworks of all future reasons for being.

Being is a struggle. Promise and hope give us a future to grasp and to cherish. Without those entities, there is little if any reason for being.

Why did I not mention Love?

It is a given that we all require love, and it is in promise and hope we will acquire some semblance of it within our lives. Love is the need that we all search for. We want to see the Almighty who is Love, while peering deep into the eyes of our lover for the presence of God within their soul.

My methodology involves an analysis of many thoughts but without a particular order in each area of consideration since we all face life in completely different patterns and under entirely different circumstances. "Is there a chancee fore Men" in their relationships with the "fairer sex".

There is no room for sarcasm, hate, deception, fear, or disrespectful speech. Kissing and touch are optional yet the best things in life are free. Let's fill our lives with the very best marriage has to offer to all of us. The passionate adaption of all aspects of a good marriage are not only our goal, but our duty as it relates to our loved ones.

We are to be honorable, good, thoughtful, gracious, attractive, fit, clean, adorable, gracious, and always kind. This sounds like too much — but it is not enough. Kindness to each other, rather than course or abrupt words or actions are a duty for both spouses. In fact, it is a requirement to speak to all in a good way. My mother always said to me, "Philip, if you do not have anything nice to say, don't say it at all."

My best friend, Salvatore Torrisi, never spoke badly of anyone. The man was a saint. He unfortunately passed away a few years ago, while under the blade of a surgeon's knife that mistakenly cut through his aorta resulting in "Sam" bleeding to death. Over thirty units of blood could not save him. He was the finest person I have ever known.

We must practice the art of being while always being the best we can be!

Salvatore (Sam) was the best example of graciousness and God like characteristics I have ever known.

CHAPTER 9
TRUTH, RELATIONSHIPS, CHEATING

It is important to briefly review how a relationship between a man and a woman evolves. I will not belabor this point but as you know there are many ways a couple may meet. It may be through a mutual friend, a work associate, a social gathering, a bar, the military, and countless other ways. Maybe in a space capsule!

What is important, is how after meeting do people become involved and fall in love? Initially, there is the physical attractiveness followed by mutual interest related to conversations, intellectual awareness, and whatever it is that most have been through on many occasions while moving forward in a romantic way.

I think early on in a relationship, truthfulness is the most critical aspect one must face. If you do not detect complete truth in someone's behavior, the chance of a secure and a long-lasting relationship is not going to happen.

Truth precedes nearly everything else in life and in nature. In fact, truth is *reality* simply expressed by the honest observer. For it is in the environment of *truth* where we all exist. Truth and reality are the same.

Lies are an attempt to cover up reality though reality will surface given enough time. Lies and deceit do not have staying power and nature by itself represents truth. Truth precedes acceptance and acceptance precedes love.

In a relationship between loving people, the most dangerous and despicable act is that of cheating. Cheating is not only deception but destroys bonding, acceptance, and love. It is the ultimate crime against perfect love. It represents a failure of truth, and with good reason will not be forgiven. God asks us to forgive and maybe cheating can be forgiven, though it cannot be repaired.

Cheating is usually not forgiven by most couples and with good reason. Once a cheater, always a cheater. A cheater is morally corrupt and lacks the character required to change. However as in any case, there are exceptions to any rule though cheating is one that few women will be able to ever accommodate.

Forgiveness is a God given building block between all, though cheating being so reprehensible should not allow for a leap back into love under most circumstances. Cheating tends to happen again and again. Cheaters do not appreciate the concept of true love. They love themselves more than they love anyone else. They are narcissists.

Marriage is predicated on loving your spouse more than you love yourself. If you get that concept, you will understand what marriage demands.

A woman is less likely to cheat, and when she does, it is often from her mate's perspective nearly inconsolable as well.

In the end, truth and honesty are the golden aura for both men and women to honor forever during their eternal bond with one another. A woman expects nothing less. A man is just as demanding. The union of a man and woman combines acceptance, bonding, love, and honor.

All these wonderful attributes are generally within the sphere of marriage and must become the goal of loving couples. Marriage combines the beauty of life, living, and romance in one perfect world known only to every perfect couple. This sounds like magic, though in reality for the blessed that achieve it, it really is magic.

Sometimes magic and pure love are indistinguishable forming a relationship with the flower of peace enhancing their lives. So, let's look at peaceful relationships.

Calmness, tranquility, and easiness are needs we all require, for without them, we would all be frantic beyond description. Peace is the cement within our being that allows us to grow, proceed, and exist without endless headaches and problems. Peace is delivered from those around us.

In a similar vein, pain and suffering are also delivered from those around us, though peace has the upper hand in quality and deliverance. As you peer into your glorious world, no matter where you may be, peace tends to prevail rather than fury. We need to appreciate the gift of peace when we have it and recognize it will prevail over time for most loving couples. Peace and love allow life to flourish.

Peace represents a balance in nature and within our lives. It is the given. It is not the exception. We all will find it within the arms of our lover. When we are cuddling, holding hands, or in a warm embrace, we will find peace and tranquility within that framework. For it is in closeness and intimacy we deliver the love and comfort that carries us into the future while supporting us in the present.

A woman who gives the sensations of touch and caressing to her man will engender the deepest love and affection between them. Men fear loneliness and can become desperate without the touch of a woman and the love that is engendered by it. Men in love, with love returned, will not likely commit crimes of passion.

It is in the passionless and the unloved hopelessness of individuals who are not able to find love that leads to bad behavior.

A woman can hold within her heart and her hands the elements of love and peace so required by her man. With it, men and women will experience harmony and meaning for life that for a few of the fortunate may have no bounds.

Some may think, members of the same sex may have the upper hand when it comes to relationships since they are not as different as they are alike. In the case of gay couples, it is my belief that in reality they are more different than they are alike and thus the mirror what same sex coupes see in their relationships. They see the differences that are attractive to each. I believe all loving couples can understand their partners needs and will support them.

Most of us will thrive in an environment of love, trust, goodness, security, peace, and comfort regardless in which form it takes. What could be better?

Pure love is the best form of love that our lives have to offer to each other. Pure love does not exist outside of the bounds of truth. Pure love is the highest form of love men and women may give to each other. It must be the goal of all men and women or those in a relationship that demands exclusivity and a form of perfect love that may only occur in the presence of honesty, loyalty, trust, and acceptance.

CHAPTER 10
ACCEPTANCE

Acceptance is what we all desire in nearly all stages of our lives and our endeavors. Without acceptance there is little reason for being. Acceptance gives our lives substance and a reason for being. Take away acceptance and you take away even the basic building block of love. Without acceptance there is no way to move on to the higher ground. Acceptance follows understanding and truth.

Acceptance also includes understanding priorities, religious activities, raising children, handling money, working a job, sleeping together, frequent discussions, co-operation, and likely others I have forgotten.

We want our opinions, needs, and desires, respected, and generally accepted. Not all is perfect or legal and therefore some "needs or desires" are either out of reach, immoral, or troublesome in other ways, as would be acknowledged by most sensible people.

Usually "what is good for the goose is good for the gander." In any relationship complete acceptance of each other is required before the goal of bonding is achieved between two lovers. Bonding is the glue of marriage and a life together that will never be broken. With perfect love your relationship will become permanent. You have bonded for life.

CHAPTER 11

BONDING

Bonding is a unity between two lovers that signals a permanent future reserved only for those who will learn what "pure love" is all about. There are many aspects that pertain to how bonding begins and becomes a part of your partnership.

Couples bond in different ways, under different circumstances, and in their own ways. Here you will learn what is required for an unbreakable bond to form between you and your special loved one.

One of the most important ways to begin a bonding process is to learn how to listen. One should listen intently, openly, and non-defensively according to an expert, Sarah Epstein. Sarah noted, if your partner is upset about something, validating their pain strengthens your bond with them. Always ask if there is something you can do to help. Do not assume you can "fix" everything. They want to know that you validate them and that you are both in this together.

Bonding requires working towards common goals, shared dreams, and looking into the future by talking about where your lives could be taking you. Do not count on chance. Sharing your dreams and pacing your future will allow for success, enjoyment, love, and passion in everything you do.

Some activities work best when creating rituals that you work out together. For example, having set times to complete chores, share the work of living together, and having times set aside each day to talk, discuss, and create fun activities are part of bonding process. All these methods will help both of you form emotional connections.

Sometimes, each one of you will have issues that you have not discussed but require attention before they become too engrained. Unresolved issues are the poisons of marriage.

There are a couple of ways to handle these. Each of you should write down the problems that are of bother both to you and set them aside until the time is right for a quiet and sensitive discussion. Then relate your concerns at a convenient meeting that both of you have agreed upon. Meetings are best when attended by both of you at least two or three times a week. Frank and frequent discussions will open the door to solutions that will work for you.

It is easy to solve problems when looking at what is best for your partner while placing yourself in a less important role.

I do not recommend having discussions that may be somewhat stressful before sleeping. Doing so may lead to anxiety issues throughout the night. Nothing is worth that. Plan your meetings for early evening or on weekends. And guess what, should there be no problems to discuss, the time will be ideal to make love together. Frequent love making cements your bond. Bonding, Bonding, Bonding. WOW!

Complicated issues may be more challenging and often are better handled by working with a marriage therapist. Relationship counseling for couples may be worthwhile at times because when working through tough problems. Having an openminded expert may be "Just what the doctor ordered." Real important issues should be handled as soon as possible. Never let them fester.

Remember if it came to that, it is likely that both of you waited a bit too long for resolution. Delaying important solutions to problems complicates the process and thus the weekly meetings are so important. Remember, no issues, more sex. LOL!

Remember the key points about bonding and pure love. Always love your partner more than you love yourself and then solutions are more easily found. Discussions and resolutions are the cement that continues to bond both of you for life.

CHAPTER 12

INTIMACY

What about intimacy? Most great relationships thrive on making love: SEX. Sex is the most powerful source of connecting emotionally, lovingly, and physically. Frequent sex improves a couple's satisfaction on all levels. It is the sauce that makes your love stronger, better, and amazing. The more sauce, the better your bond. Sexual sauce becomes the glue for your love and your lives. Sex is the ultimate bond because it is so personal, intimate, and special. There are no substitutes.

In addition, research confirms that sexual activity provides an 'afterglow' that will last for about two days according to a researcher, Dr. North. Higher relationship satisfaction is a given over time as sexual enjoyment between to loving people becomes the norm.

What about hugging. Dr. Dana C. Avey explains, that studies have shown that hugging for a full six seconds will make you feel closer. The results require a full six seconds. That is enough time for oxytocin within your brain to be released, to achieve a chemical bond that provides a more lasting reunion. Sex, hugging, oxytocin is all good.

There is even a little more to this my friends. What about holding hands? The use of touch is super beneficial for bonding and lends itself daily when out in public. It is a great way to connect, show your love for each other, and brag to others how close you are to each other without saying a word. Sitting on a couch next to each other, while at home watching TV or even when reading a book or magazine is a great way to bond as well. Closeness, touching, whispering "sweet nothings" all go a long way towards romance, love, and sexuality.

Never sleep in separate beds. Always sleep together whenever possible. Physically touching each other with a part of your intimate anatomy will help you to sleep better, longer, and more soundly. Better yet always sleep naked. Cuddle your bottom around her butt (wrap yourself around her posterior) as close as you can. You would be surprised how well both of you will sleep being so close together.

Your body temperature is key on how easily it will be for you to fall asleep. It's part of your circadian rhythm. Your circadian rhythm is a 24-hour cycle that acts as your body's "clock" for sleep. It includes physiological and behavioral rhythms including sleeping. As the night begins; cooling down is so important. Cooling down tells your body that it's time to sleep, so sleeping naked and allowing your body temperature to go down will help you fall asleep faster.

When I sleep naked with Debbie, I cuddle her closely from behind and she falls asleep very quickly. So, there you have it. She's asleep within in minutes. DAMN! "No sex tonight!!!"

Another important aspect of bonding involves close eye contact with your significant other, especially when conversing about important plans or issues. Close eye contact is a big part of bonding by showing that you care, respect, and are sincere about your intentions. It is difficult to fake conversations with good eye contact.

Sincerity is the fruit of bonding, love, and graciousness.

Bonding is the heart, soul, and cement of a unified couple. It is predicated on two people having a very tight and unique relationship that is unbreakable. It is doable even in this era of cheating, divorcing, meddling, and destroying what could have been.

For a few blessed couples like Debbie and I, bonding is immediate, though the way we bonded was unusual if not unheard of.

I wish to tell you our story that is true in every way providing a bonding experience that likely has never happened before at any time in history. I know this sounds crazy, but it happened exactly as portrayed.

About the time we met, neither I nor Debbie had had any recent relationships with any glue or staying power. We had both been searching for that golden fleece without any success.

It is quite difficult to find your perfect partner. Years of failures for both of us had proven that out.

In desperation, I learned of a dating sited; "Plenty of Fish." It had a catchy title and I believed twelve years ago it was safe and worth my time and a gamble or two. So, I was off to the races gambling my future love life and social existence in the dating jungle, arena, or playground, depending on your viewpoint or motives.

After several weeks of exploration, I was not able to find my one true love. Nothing unusual here!!! Finally, after work and dinner, I hit the site for what I said to myself would be the very last time. Frustration was the key word here. Enough is more than enough!

I clicked on the site, submitted my usual search criteria and who popped up???? This gorgeous creature of unspeakable description with blue eyes, sexy figure, wonderful smile, long blond hair, a flight attendant with Delta, and several other attributes of remarkable sex appeal and oomph.

I wondered, "What the hell is she doing here? This must be some mistake. Maybe she is not who she says she is." I thought this is crazy on at least two levels. One, she should not need this web site. Two, she will never return a message to me, so why even bother.

Well, I thought it over and decided, I know I am really messed up in the head to waist even one typewritten word to her but maybe I should. "Forget about it," as we Italians often say. In the past I had written several paragraphs about what a great catch I would be. I even mentioned that I can read and write. I wrote about being a college graduate; about the fact that I wash daily, shower once a week (just kidding) (twice a week- LOL!), can walk and chew gum at the same time. You sort of get where I am coming from? After even further thought, I thought. Okay, I will give this one final shot and after this fiasco, I am trashing this site for good.

But I am not going to write a litany of why she should meet me. This approach failed to bring any fortune and by now I am tired, fed up, and heading for bed. So, I jumped in and wrote these three words, "We must meet." And that was that. I sent it and off it went. I went to bed.

The next day I arrived home from work, grabbed a TV dinner (Stouffers are the "best"), tossed in a tossed salad, grabbed a Diet Coke, turned on the TV news, grabbed a chair, and started chomping on the goods. After that, I rinsed my mouth (always after every meal), brushed my teeth, and headed for the computer. I thought I will see if "the babe" wrote back — I know she didn't — but what the "hell."

I go to "Plenty of Fish", signed in, and pulled up any messages that may have been there. So, what pops up? **The babe I wrote to.** Even to this day it brings tears to my eyes!!! I'm crying right now my dear readers as I write this.

So I say to myself, now this is really, crazy. She was apparently kind enough to leave a message, likely that would go something like this. "Are you kidding me, you loser? Why would I have one second to give to you. Get lost jerk. You are pathetic." She was likely thinking as well, "Now I know why I'm done with this site for good."

That is what I expected to read. Was that there? No! What did she write? She wrote, "And why is that?" Those were her exact words. Not one word more.
WOW! I thought. Well at least she wrote back. That in its own way was huge. She said something. Could this be happening? Hell no! I must be hallucinating!!! There is no way she would write back to me. I need an Alka-Seltzer!

I grabbed the computer and-in-my-shock, and haste, I knocked a glass of ice water off the desk. Who cares, I thought! This babe wrote back to me!!! I quickly wrote back and said, "To take you out for that candlelight dinner that you want."

The next day, she wrote back. We traded cell numbers, and the rest is even greater than what you have already read.

We talked as soon as I received her number for what had to be at least an hour or two or three or four. We lost tract.

I spoke, "Well, Ms. Debbie, where is your choice of places to dine?" She said, "Have you ever heard of Drunken Jacks on the ocean in Myrtle Beach?" I responded, "no, but I live in New York (just kidding)." Deb said, "I will give you the address and location and we can meet at about 7:00 PM on Friday night. Does that work for you?" I said, "It sure does sweetheart! I will see you there my dear."

Friday took forever to arrive, but it finally did. I hopped in my car and drove to Drunken Jacks, about twenty minutes from my home, arriving at about 6:45PM. I saw that the restaurant near the seaside was built on stilts, allowing it to avoid the incoming and outgoing surf.

After parking, I strolled over to the staircase of the restaurant, walked up about twenty steps to the top, stood there and thought. "I had better be at the bottom of the staircase and wait there since the surf is out." So down I went, gazing across the white sandy beach while looking towards the parking lot. The minutes went by painfully slow. And I mean slow! Each one felt like an hour! At about five minutes to seven, I noticed a woman like figure off in the distance walking across the sand.

As she came closer, I noted her long blond hair blowing in the wind. She was well dressed and gorgeous as I hoped she would be. She came closer and closer and closer, walking up to me and without saying a single word, she smiled, placed her lips passionately on mine and kissed me for the longest time. It was unbelievable. Now, who does that? We had never met! After that amazing caress, she said, "I was hoping it was you. Something came over me and I could not help myself." She then said, "I'm Debbie."

That kiss bonded us on the spot! I mean we truly bonded then and there. I bet in the history of mankind, no couple has ever first kissed upon first meeting without saying a single word or without even asking who they are? Is that the craziest thing that could have ever happened? It is one hundred percent true. "The Kiss was our eternal Bond." Right there on the spot. That is exactly what happened. I am still dumbfounded to this day — over ten years ago.

We then walked up the long staircase, entered Drunken Jacks, and we're seated for dinner by the restaurant host. It was an amazing evening. We both ordered a wonderful fish dinner, salads, bread, desserts, and drinks. It was boss! After a couple of hours, I asked if she would like to visit with me at my new home in Myrtle Beach (not New York) and she was happy to do so.

We drove to my home and after arriving, I showed her around. The home was brand new, and she loved it. During our dining experience, she learned that I was a family physician and she noted that she "has been a flight attendant with Delta Airlines for many years." Delta has the finest flight attendants, my friends. What a pair we made!

After becoming more acquainted with each other, the night was growing long and I said, "Well, princess, it is time that I take you back to your car unless, being so late, maybe you should stay the night." She said, "I have never done this with anyone on a first date, but I feel so good about us. Let's do it." We went to bed, made amazing love, and have never been apart since that evening.

Our bond is a bond made in heaven. Debbie is amazing. After almost eleven years it feels like we have always been together, and our love remains more intense than ever. This story is accurate, sounding over the top, but that is how it happened.

36

So, you might say, "Well what does all of this have to do with the last frontier?" I will explain. The "last frontier is not achievable. Landing on Mars is.

The last frontier is intriguing, often misunderstood, and is never within reach. That is what makes the intrigue so amazing, and wonderful. You never want to conquer the "last frontier" because then your life would not be worth living as much. The "last frontier" lives within her mind where it will always be. It is part of her. It is not part of you.

To broach "the last frontier" even just a little bit, begins with listening, caring, paying attention, and giving one hundred percent to her. It is a wonderful one hundred percent commitment. Debbie made the commitment to me with her very first kiss.

The most important part of love is to love your mate more than you love yourself. Period!

If you love yourself more than your significant other, you do not have pure love. You will never experience the deepest possible love with limitless benefits, passion, experiences, goodwill, amazing sexual experiences, and unbelievable times together.

As time goes on in your relationship, your love will become what I refer to as "pure love," Pure love goes well beyond the boundaries of love.

Together, you will both experience all of what is included in true bonding between soulmates. Only soulmates understand pure love. Find your soulmate and you will find a life of remarkable feelings expressed in hundreds of ways on every level.

However, there is much more to finding a soulmate and that is about keeping them.

This book encompasses many but not likely all the parameters that complete a relationship between loving couples. It is my hope, in reviewing these qualities for others to consider and emulate, it will allow for all of us to experience a more complete union with our mates for their duration of our natural lives.

CHAPTER 13

PURE LOVE: THE GREATEST QUALITY OF ALL

The finest and highest form of love I will define, is what I refer to as "pure" love.

Pure love is pure in that it is all good, it is all encompassing, and it is without peer. It is the highest form of love, reserved for our one and only pure relationship, gifted between two pure lovers; the love provided only to a significant lover and to no other.

With this form of love, there is no room for sharing our most intimate thoughts, feelings, and affection with anyone else.

It is not the same as loving one's parents, siblings, friends, business associates, favorite TV show, or favorite dessert; to name a few.

Pure love is a pure love beyond compare, when we look at what is truly important in life and union between the sexes.

Love encompasses feelings that are based on goodness and thus love must prevail in our lives if we are to make a difference and provide a reason for being. Love engenders aspects of peace for it provides a sense of comfort, warmth, and by its nature, generosity. Love must be given to be appreciated.

Love never lives in a vacuum and must be appreciated or known by another human being. Without someone knowing about your feelings, love has no standing. It cannot exist on its own merits because it is in the eyes of others that we become moved and ingratiated.

The only borderline exception I can think of are those who love animals that are special to them. Animals in their own way can provide their own form of love to their friends whether animal or human. Animals know when they are loved. Humans know when an animal loves them. A dog wags its tail.

God is the definition of eternal and pure love. Without the knowledge of eternal existence in the eyes of God, we have no reason to be honest, good, generous, supportive, helpful, lawful, or for that matter any other positive aspects of being that support the concept of love.

For it is in the belief of God that we truly exist and remain good. God is the universe of love. We try to emulate his love by being good and loving to each other.

I have also thought of love within the framework of peace because in many ways they are closely related. Love engenders a sense of value between two that goes well beyond what peace can accomplish. Love is a caring and a desire to join with someone in a close and intimate form of being. Love is the ultimate gift between two people and provides the food for existence. Without love there is little reason for existence.

Nearly everything a man or woman does, is done to accomplish a loving bond with another person of significant value. Usually, a man will drive a clean and interesting car to attract or please a woman rather than to simply show it off to someone else. Men sometimes take pride in showing off a beautiful set of wheels at a weekend car show, though usually our significant other is the primary reason we drive a clean, exciting, and beautiful mode of transportation around town. Some want to impress their friends or fellow workers, but that concern is of lessor importance as compared to impressing their spouse or loved one.

How a man dresses and takes care of himself is driven by his relationships with a woman. He often does things for reasons that seem foolish but deep down inside he's trying to over-the-long-haul, prove that he is worthy to be loved by someone special. Whether it is about how he dresses, speaks, or where he lives, or what he drives, or how he earns a living. In the end, it is about surviving within the realm of a special lady.

Love has no limits, because those who love each other will repeatedly state they love each other beyond the love of yesterday. Love and feelings grow and transform us. For those with love within their sphere of influence, they have found the holy grail of life and living.

Love is not surpassed by any other entity on any other scale. It is our primary need. It is the reason for being. Love is the building block of life as we know it. We cannot live in a vacuum for long. Without the hope of love, we would likely give up and perish.

Eternal love within the arms of God is the final an ultimate love we all require and will strive for when all is said and done. On this earth however, it is the love between a man and a woman or between others who find the same needs that only can be satisfied by two humans who truly understand each other and cannot be happy without being in the arms of the other.

Love supersedes all other needs and gives us a glimpse of what love will be like in heaven. When a woman shows a man the love she can provide for him, she will see a magic the likes of which she could never have imagined.

An amazing woman is about others. They have the highest calling and provide special gifts for those she holds close to her heart. It is possible that a woman can see some of these same characteristics within her man. Men give women most of the credit and it is his reason for being.

When someone perceives there is not a reason for being, they will sometimes take the next step to solve their unbearable pain. Is that solution wrong? In their eyes it becomes the only answer. It becomes the answer when that person was deprived of love, support, and comfort to the degree that they can no longer go on without it. It is related to a miscalculated or sometimes bizarre set of circumstances generated sometimes from another individual even more confused or disassociated then the person they have ignored.

Those who cannot love were usually not given love when they required love, often during the beginning of their lives when their set of values were being developed as a very young child. They were therefore created in a variation of what humanity is, an aberration of sorts.

In fact, the evil of those without love in their hearts are not human on any level. Because humans like God must be loving to be human. Love defines humanity. Evil is not human. The evil were never loved. Their evilness was created after birth by another life form that many in police work refer to often as monsters, after shocked police have witnessed horrible crimes that the "evil" are capable of. Some of these evil beings cannot be honored by humans when only God may understand their horrible actions and the causes for them. God could possibly salvage them for eternity. For God is all good.

A fine woman knows a good man. She relishes in his presence. Women want someone who is open minded, listens to them when they speak, believes in their needs, wants to be appreciated, shown affection, compliments them in how they look, how they dress, their makeup, their body shape, their sexiness, their eyes, their kiss, and everything else that makes a woman a woman.

It must be spoken to them daily; once a month is not enough. Women like men, can be very insecure and need constant reassurance. You cannot tell a woman often enough that you love her, that you believe she is beautiful, funny, caring. She must hear it from you, countless times per day. Women can be just as insecure as men and require constant attention, often in the finest of details. "Sweetheart, your eye lashes are so long, so elegant. You are a dream come true." That is what pure love is all about. It is giving to her an infinite amount of attention, love, and playfulness. You cannot squeeze her sexy butt too often, even in public.

When it comes to her clothing and what she would like to wear, she expects to model before you all her new clothes even

42

before she wears them and especially before going out in public. Period!

You had better say she looks gorgeous!!! And why is that? Above all, she wants "you" to be pleased. Believe me, she has inspected every aspect of that piece of clothing many times before she completed the purchase, especially if it were intended to be worn with you in mind. She loves to impress her friends, but you are even more important on her hierarchy. There is a lot to be said about showing your lover her due respect. It is very important for men to open every single door for his significant other; car doors, entrance doors at home, doors on buildings; all doors, except bathroom doors. LOL!

When was the last time you saw a man open a door for a woman? In our culture, fathers have failed their sons in showing how to respect a woman. I open doors for my wife one hundred percent-of-the-time; not ninety-nine percent, one hundred percent. She will wait for me to arrive at her side of the car for me to pull her door handle and open her door. She will wait at the next door and make it easy for me to grasp the handle by stepping aside. This is what my wife expects of me. I am so happy to oblige her. She is so precious.

Now what do I expect of her? I have one dear request that is ongoing. I would like her to allow me to make love to her at least once or twice a week. In the bible it says that a woman's body belongs to her husband as much as it belongs to her. I think as men, we often misunderstand that passage. It does not mean we can demand for her to give herself to us whenever we want it. She does have the right to say no. It may be that time of month? She may be sickly, tired, hungry, upset, or just not in the mood? However, most of the time, a conscientious woman should try to please her loving mate.

Try to be on the same page with her when "you want it." Pick the best times that make sense. You may precede your request for afternoon or evening fun, by asking her in the morning, "How did you sleep last night?" You may ask, "are you hungry my dear?" "Can I make dinner?" "Should we go and grab a bite?" "Can I pick up the

43

room for you." "Maybe I can vacuum the carpet since you're tired and your back has been bothering you.?" To some men this may seem to be outlandish, however you had better learn on which side to butter your bread if you want happiness.

Bottom line! Check on all the likely reasons why she may say no and then fix those for her before you hint at intimacy. But remember the "rose." She will love you for it and your sex will be the finer for it. A rose is a rose is a rose. Sex is sex is sex. There are no substitutes, as you already know for either one. A rose by any other name is a Rose! Your wife or partner is the rose for you.

Well, Debbie's preference are tulips. Can you believe it! So, she receives tulips. Again, as I said before. A tulip is a tulip is a tulip!!! You better know which side of the bread to butter.

A woman wants respect, love, attention, and intimacy just like you. Pure love is giving to each other and not taking from someone. It is giving. Not taking. Those who give, will receive in return many more times than what they have offered. A good woman will always place you first. But for a good woman to be good, you must also be good to her. Good deserves good and delivers in spades.

Pure love delivers in many ways if it is shown and developed over time. The more years you live together, the more time you must develop understanding, clarity, and wisdom from your experiences together. It is an ongoing evolution. A good marriage is constantly evolving. Let it evolve. Let her evolve. You will evolve. Pure love is the basis of all evolution.

The number 13 is feared by many. I think the foregoing chapter, number 13, at least for love – put the number 13 in its place. Love defeats the intimidation of the number 13.

CHAPTER 14

THE BEAUTY OF SEXUALITY: Sleeping Naked

At the end of the day, why does a man want to be with a woman? What does a woman provide that another man cannot in a heterosexual relationship? Why do men go to whatever lengths it takes to garner the love and possession of a woman to whatever extent it takes to have her in his life?

The cold hard truth is that it is essentially often about sexuality, childbearing, and of course companionship as time goes on. Few men can be happy without a sexually fulfilling relationship. The same may be true for a woman, though her goals must be and will be usually related to childbearing to insure the future of mankind. It is better that we work with each other to obtain the same end.

The end is happiness and fulfillment on many levels beginning often with sexuality for men and ending with your woman's need for companionship, protection, and children.

A woman cannot tolerate any other woman from trespassing on her territory. It is an obligate need that all women require and demand. They use their beauty, sexuality, and seductive abilities to acquire and forever keep the very last drop of their man's nature. They are unrelenting, unforgiving, and never accepting of another woman's attempts at stepping into her domain. On this topic, a woman can be more extreme than any man may care to think about.

As sexuality comes in to play, other needs for a while at least will fall by the wayside. Sexuality has no peer. It is the highest form of bonding between two. And, when people are bonding, stay out of their way. Bonding supersedes all other forms of discourse.

In a more comprehensive way, look at the glory of sexuality. There are so many aspects of sexuality and marriage that can improve your passions beyond what many have ever experienced.

With that in mind, I will offer to all of you a few insightful thoughts that will enhance your sex life in many ways.

First, let's consider the cavemen days of yore that are long behind us. Men and women have entered a new era putting aside the crude aspects of cave people. Some of you have thought of most of the unpleasantries that could be associated with making love, however there may be a couple of things you have overlooked and may not have even considered. Therefore, I wish to go over some of these for you amazing lovers.

First cleanliness is next to Godliness when it comes to being sexually active with your special lover. A good cleansing shower before going on a date or before making love is very important. Body odor on any level is not acceptable and a poison between two lovers.

The same is true of bad breath. To avoid gingivitis or gum disease, the main causes of bad breath, rinse out your mouth after eating each meal. It is surprising what you will see going down the drain as you do so. Do this even at a restaurant before leaving for home by running into the bathroom for a moment. Do not rinse your mouth at the dining table. Brushing your teeth with a paste high in fluorides is the key to great dental hygiene and in preventing gingivitis, halitosis, and tooth decay. The dentists will hate you for following this advice.

Look on the paper/cardboard container holding the tube of toothpaste under the ingredients label to find the highest fluoride concentrations. Compare name brands such as Crest, Colgate, Sensodyne, and several others to each other. By brushing two to three times per day, your visits to the dentist will be dramatically reduced. You will also be far less likely to ever require dentures (often disfiguring in many ways and are nothing like your real teeth). Loss of teeth is primarily due to gum disease, allowing your teeth to loosen, all from a failure of frequent brushing with toothpaste high in fluorides. For some reason, dentists do not review this need as much as they should.

46

One more thing; smoking is very bad for gum disease and other travesties of the mouth including cancer of many forms. Find a way to quit smoking before it "quits you" through death.

A clean mouth is the first objective before making love. Sweetness will carry the day. Even a quick rinse with mouth wash will seal the deal.

Another very important aspect to consider is to be rested and ready to go. Tiredness will put the kibosh to most sexual activities that require a degree of effort. However, in the "heat" of battle, some degree of tiredness is over looked when everything is ticking. On the weekend, maybe a one-hour nap, before your adventure begins, will provide the best outcum (not a misspelling). Debbie and I often nap before making love.

Remember when going to bed, warm up your hands before touching her by either soaking them in warm/hot water in the bathroom sink or warming your hands on your own body parts before touching her. Cold hands are a distinct NO-NO!

Next, make sure you both agree to go to bed naked. Nakedness promotes all the right emotions and triggers all the right hormones when you wish to act on them. Sleeping naked regularly is wise and "productive." It is freeing both physically and psychologically. It also builds trust between the both of you.

Sleeping naked has been scientifically proven to improve health. Sleeping naked increases your brains oxytocin level, making you feel more aroused, lowers your blood pressure, heart rate, and prepares you for sexual activity. Sleeping naked for most of us is very sexy and appealing. There is no substitute for skin-on-skin contact to "get the show on the road." Cuddling while you sleep is very beneficial for your health.

Current research shows that only eight percent of couples reported sleeping naked. We have a long way to go to reverse this trend. Naked sleepers are also more likely to sleep together to keep each other warm. Naked sleepers are more likely to have a happy relationship and to have lower anxiety and stress levels. Most of these details were reported in the journal, **Psychology Today.**

There are other health benefits that may stem from sleeping in the nude. By helping your body to stay cooler overnight, sleeping naked helps your body increase its stores of brown fat. Brown fat will help burn energy reducing the number of calories eaten from being stored as ordinary fat.

Some women love wine, champagne, or a drink before sex to put them in the mood. Of course, men do not care for that. (Just Joking).

The new thing on the block for many is cannabis before sex. It real turns some folks on. Of course, whether it is doable depends on if it is legal or not where you live.

Not all women enjoy the same sexual sensations or touch. Some like Toys and some don't. Some like oral sex and some do not. Women who love oral sex, often will state that it provides the greatest orgasms for them with the ability to continue to orgasm as the process goes on. After a while, she will still not be satisfied without penetration which is the best way to "climax" your bonding activities.

Spend some time with each other discussing what they enjoy the most and make those your initial targets every time you make love. Over time, her needs and yours may change. Often discuss what each of you still prefer or would like to try. Maybe something new and different would be the ticket. Nothing ventured, nothing gained.

Great foreplay is the key to a great sexual adventure. Be sure you are well rested before jumping in. Make sure your room is on the cool side. Cold is even better but cover yourself with sheets and or a blanket of course. Coolness allows for a better experience for many couples.

Some couples like to watch porn and others do not. Men love porn more often than women. I believe it has been shown in studies, that

48

most women no matter how attractive or sexy they feel do not want to compete with the women actors in the video. It is personal preference.

This statement will sound very odd to many readers; however, studies have shown in some cases, a few women enjoy the concept of being taken, in the way of being "raped" by her lover. Other women despise the idea out right and will not have it.

As I have learned in the practice of family medicine, many women have been unfortunately raped in their lifetime and thus for most of them (but not all of them), they could never re-live any experience even remotely reminding them of what happen to them on that ugly day in years gone by. Other women who have been raped, look at it differently over time and would feel comfortable with the idea of her true lover taking her "virginity" so to speak, away from her.

Other women love the idea of being spanked (in a controlled way) during sexual activities. Others do not care for this. Of course, none of these activities should ever involve physical harm to your lover in any way. It is all personal preference.

All sexual partners should have a clear understanding on what is acceptable and what is off limits. It is best to have this discussion early on, once sexual activity begins between to loving partners. If your lover starts pulling your hands away from some parts of her body, that should be a good hint to you that she did not find whatever you were doing to her very pleasing. Maybe a slight change of the behavior would make it acceptable.

No two couples are alike. Fine tuning love making is a desirable goal I make to all practitioners of the art of love making. It is truly an art form if there ever was one. Good art takes practice and in this case respect.
Honor her wishes.

One of the sexual foreplays I enjoy most with Debbie is to kiss her all over her body. I will often start kissing her face, lips, and neck while moving downward to her upper chest, breasts, nipples, and then southward to her abdomen. I love kissing her entire abdomen down towards her pubic area yet skipping that for later. Her inner thighs are kissed from top to bottom. After that I asked her to turn over so I may kiss her entire back and then her buttocks. Many ladies also loved to have their toes and fingers caressed and suckled. Go for it! Sometimes she will even insert her fingers deep inside of her tunnel of love and then place them into your mouth for your enjoyment. All of this takes time, but she may really love it.

And you know the rest. Making love to your special friend is infinitely one of the best parts of life and should be done as often as possible within the frameworks of each other's needs and desires. An orgasm together with intercourse for most couples is the ultimate trip.

What about "petting" my friends. Stroking gently every part of a woman's body is wonderful for both of you. Her nipples may be very sensitive and sometimes her breasts are tender due to the presence of small lumps or nodules within her breasts from fibrocystic disease. She may like them to be suckled but not squeezed. Remember that a little gentle fondling of whatever she enjoys may be a ticket to the golden fleece. That may even be a great nickname for her special part. "Sweetheart my golden fleece is really, really, really in need of attention. Can you help my dear?"

Great sex, will grow your relationship on many levels and is the fruit of loving each other to the max. Great sex goes with a great marriage. If you do not have this going for you, your marriage may be in trouble.

Exceptions apply to all comments you have read. No two couples are alike. I am sure there are those of you with a fine marriage, lacking sex completely due to medical conditions or other disabilities. Bonding between two comes with time and is the supreme end we should all hope for. It goes beyond sex.

As men grow older, in many cases they may lose the ability for multiple orgasms. Most men will usually be able to have orgasms with intercourse though this may diminish also with time. If it does, they may still be able to have orgasms with oral sex. Your significant other may be agreeable to this. She may wish to perform oral sex on you to the point of orgasm and maybe not. Some women and understandably so, do not care for oral sex with her man. She is not into the taste or the "outcum" and that is that.

One more point to consider is to give your private parts a nick name. Nicknames are fun, more casual, and less threatening. The reason for this is to allow for little suggestions to your mate about showing interest in sexual activities later in the day. For example, to her you may say, "Do you think 'Little Pussy' (golden fleece) would like to have some fun after dinner this evening?" She could say to you, "I would really love to kiss 'Little Richard' this evening! What do you think sweetheart?"

Nick names are cool, wonderful, break the ice, and well received by most. They are easier to use then, Dick, Cunt, Pussy, which comparably sound a bit crude and less romantic to many. Think about it.

On many occasions, even out in public, I will gently squeeze Debbie's buttock on one side or the other. Debbie never minds. I think she believes it will make viewers jealous. I bet it does! No one has ever approached us about doing something wrong. However, I think it is best not do this around children.

Guess what "Mr. Hot Pants." You can even under the right circumstances bring 'Little Richard' out of his secret hideout and ask for her to give him a little kiss. It is sweet and sends the right message. She will usually go along for "the ride."

Always remember to ask your lover what they like and do not like. It changes and may go back and forth from time to time. Knowledge is power. Sex is power. Sex is beautiful. Sex is amazing. Go for it. Your marriage will be the better for it since as mentioned much earlier, bonding is enhanced between you and her whenever you have a wonderful sexual experience. DO NOT TAKE IT OUTSIDE OF YOUR MARRIAGE.

CHAPTER 15

The Art of Touching

Touching a significant other has rewards that are inescapable. Everyone loves to be touched. The form of touching that I am referring to is between two loving persons. It is gentle, soft, and not surprising; meaning not out of the blue where it may scare your lover. Touching provides a wonderful sense of goodness that is difficult to describe, yet obvious in its benefits. Placing you hand on someone in a loving and gracious way is a "feel good" sensation that is hard to beat. You know when someone loves to be touched.

THE ART OF THE MASSAGE

Let's now look at massage. My wife Debbie loves to be massaged. For her, part of that is related to the many aches and pains she has related to her neck and back from a former injury early in life. Debbie loves a deep firm massage involving her painful, tender areas primarily of her upper back and lower neck region including both sides of her upper shoulders. Massage tends to relax her and helps her to fall asleep.

For myself, I do not like a deep muscle massage. Once I went to a massage clinic in Las Vegas for what I thought would be a wonderful experience but for me it was like a thirty-minute torture session, the likes of which I will never want to repeat. It was the first "professional" massage session I have ever had and thus I did not know what to expect. It was also the last.

Your significant other may love a massage either when going to bed and just before falling asleep. Sometimes she or he may even enjoy one before sexual activities, to put them in the right mood. Everyone is different, so ask first before diving in.

Ask if they would enjoy a soft and gentle massage or a deep muscle version. Of course, there are degrees of each form and that is where constant feedback may be the order of the day. What parts do they want massaged and the level of firmness must be discussed as well even before starting in.

Debbie likes to have her upper left shoulder area deeply massaged at first while later moving over to her to her right side. She also loves to have her upper back massaged on both sides. She could go on forever with this, though after about five to ten minutes, my left hand grows tired and I must let it recover for a bit before I start over.

For Debbie this form a massage is not associated with sexual activity. So, there you have it. Massage has a real place for those that you love. Go for it as often as you can.

CHAPTER 16

MARRIAGE QUALITIES THAT GIVE BACK

No relationship on Earth is more important, protected, and desirable than that between a man and his wife. It is the union of God between the two of you and then you both become one. For humans it is the ultimate bond.

It only happens with the mutual gift of one to another in the form of a loving unbreakable bond. It cannot be forced, coerced, invoked, demanded, or required on any level other than the true force of mutual love like no other. Love is the cement that binds and remains unbreakable in the best of cases. In a perfect world a man's wife is the most precious gift he can ever experience on any level.

A wife is however much more than a woman and a partner. She is everything he is not. A wife is the cement that holds a family together more than anyone or anything else could ever hope to do. A husband protects this relationship on every level, because without it, he has very little if any useful contributions to make that a woman will appreciate as handsomely.

There is no competition when it comes to any other union in life. A mature and benevolent love has bonded both husband and wife into a single union. They both long to be in each other's arms or better yet, snuggling beside each other at all hours of the day or night9.

More individuals could experience what a true love relationship embodies if they are open to all the senses, responsibilities, and gifts that such a relationship requires.

At the end of the day, those who have the ultimate relationship, experience the goodness and sensuality that only a bond between two can provide. It is a sense of completeness and sophistication beyond any other relationship and unbreakable by any force except for the final solution.

Yes, as a wife you can complete your man in ways that nothing else will ever accomplish. The secret is based on first-rate communication at every level from the bedroom to the workplace.

Men often do not understand their woman. In fact, we are frequently mystified by their simplest behaviors. Women are sometimes a bit complicated for us to always understand. Some of us may require a daily if not an hourly update on what is really intended.

Men are programmed so differently that some things may go above or beyond us. We are not stupid. We are confused. Confusion is just as bad, because we may not know how to appropriately act under every circumstance.

So, ladies that is where we rely on your help. If you're not pleased with our behavior, please let us know what you want and be quite direct about it in a gentle way. You would be surprised how much better, stronger, and wiser your relationship can be when you both understand each other's needs.

Help your man in this capacity and you will reap amazing benefits. As time goes on, in the case of true soul mates, each of you will eventually begin to figure things out. A woman can help her man become a good man by clarifying what he should do to please and reward her on a frequent basis. The more often each of you professes love and shows it by your actions through romantic gestures, the more a relationship will solidify. Love is accentuated by romance.

Romance involves sweet gestures and all things that two lovers desire to show how much love they have for each other. Romance proves a loving relationship between two truly exists. It is an ongoing never-ending gift given to each for the rest of their lives.

Another very important aspect of a marriage is mutual support of the other person in various ways. There is psychological support, emotional support, financial support, and being there for each other. Support is a bond that keeps giving in different ways.

Support can be the backbone of a relationship making for a solid and convincing bond. It is not to be taken lightly but must be a constant quality that holds everything together nearly on the same levels as trust and love. Support is another glue that bonds couples for life. It is a convincing form of love in its own way, and it proves you're there for them. Support is more of a mandatory part of your relationship because it is not optional. Support is not generosity. Support is a function of peace, love, acceptance, and being always there for you.

Generosity is a giving to others to help them either with needs or to gift them for the fun of doing so. Generosity is a level above support. Support implies a limited position where generosity implies a no holds barred gift that was not expected. Generosity becomes a surprise. It goes beyond the norm. It is given by those who can afford to do it and wish to go above and beyond what is ever required. Find a generous spouse and you have a better than normal marriage.

Generosity is not rare though it is nearly mandatory in a "perfect marriage." Support and generosity go hand in hand. Together they provide strength to your bond.

One last quality that is a building block of all marriages is responsibility. It is a two-way street in any man/woman relationship since they share this attribute equally on all levels. Responsibility is never an option but a requirement, for without it, any irregularities are accentuated by fear, deceit, and possibly even rage in the worst of circumstances.

Responsibility is another glue that holds together your relationship just like truth and love. In some ways it may be even the skeleton that binds together everything in your marriage to allow it to flourish.

Acceptance, trust, bonding, marriage, support, responsibility, generosity, and gifting are all part of God's plan to perfect the union of a man and a woman. As you can see, none of this is by chance. It is all about finding that one person you will be devoted to for life. It is complicated but workable by those who love each other beyond reproach. It is perfection.

CHAPTER 17

ROMANCE HER TO PIECES

There is no substitute for romance in a loving relationship. In fact, who would give it up? Romance is the spice of and the glue that holds everything together. There can never be too much of it. It needs to be part of every relationship on a frequent and endless occurrence. When two people are truly in love, romance is the best part of being together.

Love demands caring and giving to each. With every gift of love, a spoken word, a compliment further cements you love for each other. In fact, for those who see your romantic gestures, it becomes the envy of all who may not have been given the same gifts: that certain look, the sweet smile, the soft touch, the wonderful squeeze, the light kiss on the lips, the "I love you" out of the blue, the full hug from head to toe, the stroke of her feminine delights, the scent both can exude, the look, the sexy clothes, the wonderful posturing, the special photos that only two should view, the promise of a special trip, the walk in the woods, the trip to the bark park, the museums, the get-to-gathers, the family bonds, the extra things one does without provocation, the delight to give, the love to accept, the sweet spoken words, the caress of her hair, the touch of his, the kiss upon her neck below her ear, the soft touches that should be endless, everywhere and anywhere, the affection in public, in private, at the in-laws and at the out-laws. It is all good.

It is about maintenance, beauty, wonder, grace, gifts, sweetness, goodness, value, intimacy; it is romance. Romance involves the workings between two wonderful people we call love. Romance cements the love.

CHAPTER 18

TO HAVE OR HAVE NOT: CHILDREN

In your marriage, most would agree that having children is one of the finest, if not the best advantage of being together. Children are the fruit of everything many have ever lived for. They are a blessing and of course your greatest responsibility when all is said and done.

Let's look at the responsibility of having and caring for children. Raising children can be very complicated and difficult at times. What is amazing is that none of us take any classes or college courses in how to do it. Too much is assumed by most meaning that everything will fall into place when it comes to knowing what to do.

Raising a child is not easy, but with love it becomes doable. Having help from a grandmother is a blessing. If you can move her in for a while, life may be a bit easier, assuming she does not become controlling, overbearing, or dictatorial. You know what I mean?

As a couple, it is important to have regular discussions on how to improve the care of your children. Treat your child as you would also like to be treated. Give them lots of attention. Keep your eye on everything they do and everything they can get into.

Frequent discussions concerning all aspects of child rearing must be a regular topic between parents. Children are not hard to raise, if early in their lives, you put their needs ahead of yours.

At some point however, their requirements may not always be primary, and a line may have to be drawn in the sand. You will figure most of this out, when as parents, you put your heads together to help each other do what is best for all concerned.

Here is a bit of advice that I wish to pass on to both parents that may be helpful. Why is it that babies often cry? The key word here is often. Assuming there is no trauma or illness involved, the common reasons that a baby will cry are due to hunger, tiredness, or a soiled diaper. Sometimes they just want to be held. Check all of these out before looking for other possibilities because they are easy to do. You will get it right most of the time.

Raising children is a difficult and time-consuming endeavor that deserves every bit of effort that they require. Reviewing this is very important since it can become a source of many angry and bitter arguments that are usually preventable. It is easier to raise a child properly than it is to fix damaged goods. Believe me about that statement. An ounce of prevention is worth more than a pound of cure. Some children become so engrained with bad behavior, they are not fixable and become a problem to society as time goes on.

I would like to shed a bit of light on what can go right and what can go wrong. If you truly love your children as you should, usually you're on the right track. "Loving you children too much" is just as dangerous as not loving them enough. Children are not adults. They interpret their lives more from a fun and playful point of view and not from a practical or efficient point of view. This has the potential for many unexpected outcomes in rearing children and thereby influencing your marriage and lives in a positive or a negative way.

Some parents go way overboard in giving their children everything they want. Often these parents do not require any effort on their child's part to be accountable, responsible, or work for anything. Everything is given to them in spades. For these children, life is a beach, a miracle, a game, a party.

Is that what your life is about? It's a big party. Buy everything you want. Don't pay your bills. Don't go to work on time. Do to not take care of your home or positions. Don't bother paying taxes. Do not obey the laws of driving. Steal left and right. Cheat on exams.

Children who lie, cheat, steal, and have never had chores or work responsibilities were given everything on a silver platter. They were NOT taught responsibility. They were taught that everything must be given to them. They were catered to excessively. Life is never

61

that way for the rest of us. When you do too much for them, they expect the same from others throughout their lives. You have created a monster who is also a narcissistic. These children will pay a huge price in the future for their lack of their ability to place limits on their behavior. Life is a process of limits, hard work, accountability, and rewards. Life is not a beach party. It is not a game.

Children and adults who have earned their way function at a higher level than those who have not. Children who are properly raised are an asset to society. Your responsibility is to raise good children into adulthood.

Children should not be given everything. It is a better principle to have them understand that many things in life should be earned beginning early in their lives. They must have chores to complete beginning early in life to teach them respect and responsibility. For example, they pick up their room daily, throw away trash, make their beds, help clean, and improve their surroundings on a constant basis.

This is not achieved by threats or punishment but by showing them how they can grow up in a proper way by helping the family as a unit achieve worthwhile goals. They will not make their bed perfectly, but they will improve the art of bed making with time. They will not be cleaning their bathroom sinks early on, but later they will. They will not be cutting the lawn, but by the age of ten or eleven they will. They will learn how to scrub floors, clean up messes, and contribute in every way they should as a family member. They are not slaves. They are your helpers because you are not able to do everything for them.

The more they learn to do, the better they will be accepted by their peers as being helpful and not a problem. Are their college roommates going to make your child's bed in the dorm? Are their roommates going to pick up their messes, fix what they have broken, or cater to every need, and desire they have? I think not. If your child is eventually thrown out of a dorm or loses a roommate, it may be on you, and not on them. Think about it.

Children are a direct reflection of how you live your life. You either did a great job in helping your children become successful or you did not. If they cheat on a test, it is on you. If they steal, it is on you. They become you.

Now, why are we talking about this? Children good or bad, have a lot to do with how your marriage is going to be. Good people have good children. Children learn through osmosis, example, and peer pressure. With good children you have peace and love that goes around to all family members.

Fighting over a child's bad behavior should rarely occur. And why is that? When children do and respect what they should be doing, there is little that parents will fight over in the process of rearing their children. Good children result in a better marriage.

Early on in a child's life, it is somewhat valuable to provide a small allowance to them, for completing their chores. It gives their work a sense of value. An allowance is never free. It is not given for doing nothing. They must earn it.

Children must begin working at jobs that earn money as early as possible; cutting lawns or washing a neighbor's car (not your lawn or car - that is free). They should start their first job by age sixteen, such as working at a store in your neighborhood. As an Example, the money they earn goes into the bank for future college expenses or for a car for transportation. Maybe ten percent would go towards items they want. The rest is banked. It is called responsibility. It is on the job training. It is for their own good.

Kids who are loved and responsible, will hang around similar children, and would be less likely to get into drugs, cheat, or steal. See how easy this is!!!

When your children are on task, your marriage will bear the fruits of having more time with your significant other. A good marriage is a key to having wonderful children. They love to see you hug and kiss each other. Remember the purpose of discussing the proper way to raise children is to reduce the incidence of problems that would otherwise surface at some time, when in fact these problems are largely preventable.

Another big issue that needs to be addressed is when your children become of age to drive, what are some of the issues to think about. Your marriage will be affected by driving issues, should your children get into accidents, speeding citations, and so on. On this matter, as you are likely aware of boys and girls are different. Learning to drive a car is a big deal. Girls have a lower accident rate. Boys have a much higher accident rate, because they take chances. Do not buy a car for them until they have driven a family car for at least one to two years. When and if you do buy them something make sure it is a lower powered vehicle and not a sporty car. When they grow older, they can buy their own sporty car should they chose to do so. Driver's education, as you know is also a good idea. Do you owe your child a car? Absolutely not. You owe them a roof over their head, clothes on their back, food in their tummy until the age of 18, and twelve years of primary education. And that is that. Everything else you provide is a bonus. It is not required. It is not to be taken for granted by your children that you owe them anything else. Period! (I love that word!!!)

Do the right thing. Give your children the chance to become successful and an asset to society. Always guide them in the right direction.

CHAPTER 19

Do Marriages Fail or Do You?

The leading causes of divorce in America begins with infidelity, next financial disagreements, then weight gain, lack of intimacy, lack of equality, lack of preparation (picking the right partner), poor communication, addiction, and very few others.

Infidelity is associated with some of the others including weight gain (someone has lost much of their sexuality as perceived by their mate). In this case, the other partner may look elsewhere for intimacy and sexual pleasures. Financial disagreements may lead to anger, fear, and loss of security within their marriage, leading to infidelity since a spouse's faith may have been lost by careless spending habits by the other. Money is the root of all evil, especially when you do not have it.

Ruining A Marriage

I am somewhat reluctant to review some problems that may creep into a marriage or a relationship that you may have little control of. One of the old standbys to weaponize themselves is a jealous neighbor or an acquaintance that employs the "dirty" trick of gossip. Gossip is not fully understood by men because men do not usually gossip. Men do not care to. Men are secure in their own skin. Men almost never attack the intentions or appearance of another man since they do not have the same need as a woman in protecting their turf.

Gossipers do not have what you have, and due to their own insecurities and misfortune, they gossip about another's status to make themselves look better. Gossip is a poison that generally has no credibility and should be cast aside by the listener. It is generally rubbish, to make the gossiper look better than they are. In fact, it when it happens, it tarnishes their credibility. We can see through them.

65

Woman I believe, due to their procreative needs and protection of their brood will always require full control of her domain and will never yield approvingly to another woman who trespasses. It is for that reason, gossip exists. Gossip exists to destroy other women at the first glimpse of any infraction or even potential infraction on the slightest level that may give another woman a reason for pause when it comes to her man.

There is no safe level when it comes to another woman's intentions. Proof of that is for a huge majority of woman, a man's cheating is never acceptable because it steals from her the requisite security she needs to survive and protect her children. Once that is gone her relationship with that man is over.

Selfishness is another disruptive if not a destructive force that can tear apart any relationship. It is what happens when a person places their own needs first.

The humorous if not interesting thing about selfishness is that a person will receive more than they give if they take care of their partner's needs before the needs of their own. Giving has a way of being returned. Taking, steals from us the opportunity for someone to give back to us because it is perceived as self-centered, thoughtless, and disagreeable. One man's toy is another man's headache. We all need toys. Women call their toys jewelry, handbags, sunglasses, clothing, and of course shoes. Men call their toys sports cars.

For some, their toys become nearly spiritual in nature. With aging I have learned that a relationship with a wonderful woman is where life is at and it is not in the garage, at the lake, in the field, or on a target range. Debbie is my finest toy (no disrespect in any way is intended Sweetheart). "She is boss."

There are a few things, in the interest of being comprehensive I want to touch upon, though for most of us, these are areas that we never should visit. Though it may be becoming more common place, wife swapping is one of those. I suspect women who participate are more independent and do not require the security of one man. For most married folks, this is not appealing nor acceptable. Period!

With the new evolution of women in the workplace, it could very well be that their genetic makeup is somewhat giving way to their own survivor abilities and thus they are able to begin to behave more like men. They become more man like in their sexual behavior as well. It is my observation in reading the literature that usually wife swapping fails and is relegated to broken marriages and ultimate unhappiness.

Marriages are either from the beginning lost through poor preparation and planning; "in the heat of the night", or from so many other circumstances that were not properly thought out from the very beginning, such as an unplanned pregnancy or even an STD. In today's day and age, there are so many ways to prevent pregnancy that it should not happen. Though some do it to trap their partner and then must live with the consequences. Of course, STD's speak for themselves and can be horrible in their outcomes.

Tension over personal finances in more established marriages often leads to significant friction and severe anxiety. Some spouses have different desires when it comes to lifestyle values and or they are not frugal enough. He may want the latest automobile and she loves to purchase endless amounts of clothing, shoes, fragrances, and designer handbags. Too much is spent on expensive trips and vacations. Too much is too much.

All of these unthought out spending habits, may have disastrous affects leading to bankruptcy, debt collectors, and God forbid even homicides. In many marriages the financial disagreements become "the final straw" that "breaks the camel's back."

CHAPTER 20

LET'S LOOK AT THAT UGLY WORD; "DIVORCE!"

What plays a role in divorce? According to a recent survey of 191 CDFA professionals from across North America, the two other leading causes are infidelity in 28%, and money problems in 22%. The other 7% are scattered among many other causes that are variable from time to time.

The divorce rate doubled in from 1910 until 1920 from a rate of 4.5 divorces to 7.7 divorces per one thousand citizens. Some people believed that this "high divorce rate" was related to women seeking alimony from men, however feminists did not appreciate this connotation. In fact, the above rates were relatively small compared to modern times.

What was the divorce rate like in the 1940's? In the 1940's couples rushed to get married before WWII. After the war and during peacetime the divorce rate soared as those couples dealt with the reality or post-war living. They realized they were not compatible as time went on. In 1946 the divorce rate reached an all-time high of 43 percent. However newer statistics looking at our younger generations in America now indicate a rate as high as 50%. That begs the question, why even marry to begin with unless you truly have your feet on the ground and know what you are getting into. This is another reason to consider Marital Insurance going forward. Now what is that you may wonder? You will find out.

What factors are affected by race when it comes to our high divorce rates?

The black divorce rates that were studied years ago indicated they had the highest divorce rate at about thirty-one percent, followed by the Hispanic rate at eighteen and one-half percent, with the white divorce rate being closer to fifteen percent. The Asian rate was lowest at about twelve percent. Even though the total number of people divorcing in modern times is high, the overall percentages between races may be remaining roughly the same. There are no current statistics at this time that clearly spells this out, however the important issue is not the exact statistics, but the issue primarily revolves around what must be done to solve these problems.

Now let's dig a bit deeper into other contributing factors that are huge problems in the divorce debacle. In 1830, historians have found that drinking alcohol was heaviest in the early 1800's. It was found that in 1830, the average US adult downed the equivalent of seven gallons per year of alcohol. Please remember there are lies, damn lies, and there are statistics. This is an example of a statistic, and one of the worst "statistics" when it comes to accurately portraying the truth. I would call it sloppy research. Let's get real! I suspect most of the over-the-top drinking involved primarily men with a much lower percentage attributed to women. It could be for example men drank far greater than seven gallons per year with women drinking far less.

In 1849 the term alcoholism was first used by a Swedish physician, Dr. Magnus Huss to describe the adverse effects of alcohol on the human body.

The American Medical Association (AMA), first recognized alcoholism as an illness in 1956 based on the theory that excess drinking is a disease that affects the structure and function of the brain though it appears that Dr. Huss caught onto this idea much earlier. There is no question about the validity of that statement and to take it a bit further, it is likely due to a genetic quirk that many people have been endowed with.

Of course, the internet was not available as it is today for people to know what other people were studying in their day which has resulted in a lack of knowledge from one society to another.

WHAT ABOUT DRUG ADDICTION and ITS RELATIONSHIP TO DIVORCE?

Drug addiction has been prevalent in American society since the mid 1880's, when narcotics like morphine and laudanum were marketed to consumers as a cure-all for all their problems. These substances were found in all types of products, from asthma medications to (if you can believe this) teething syrup for infants. **You can't make this up!!!**

What are the top three factors of addiction? Genetics plays an important role as recognized in alcohol addiction. Knowing this should place everyone on notice when they know that alcoholism runs in their family. Under those cases, family members must be very cautious about using alcohol or any known addicting substance of any kind especially heroin, cocaine, fentanyl, and other similar substances. If you want problems, sample one of those and see how much trouble you will be in.

In the 1960's "hippies" smoked marijuana which today is recognized by thinkers and most authorities as being helpful medicinally for many, and not necessarily a "gateway drug" to addicting substances such as heroin and other narcotics. Kids in the ghettos pushed heroin, a very dangerous drug as we all known.

A Harvard professor, Dr. Timothy Leary "urged the world to try LSD, of all things. If that isn't the craziest thing I have ever read. In popular beliefs of that era, the 1960's were believed to be the heyday of illegal drug use, but the newest data indicates that was not the case. We still have many fish to fry before we solve this drug abuse issue. Drug abuse in my mind seems to be the most difficult problem of modern society. It is all about good education, starting with our youngest members of society and moving forward. For the older adolescents it may be too late. Once an addict, often always an addict. It is a brutal and tough problem that has been mismanaged for decades leading us to where we are today.

Another key problem associated with drug abuse is a lack of parental supervision when it comes to their children resulting in future drug abuse, addiction, and ultimately crimes against society and future partners. Parenting, at the end of the day, likely has the most significant effect on how your children will turn out. Will they be an asset to society or a drag on society. How your children ultimately turn out is a function primarily on how you nurtured and raised them. If you were too overly protective, too forgiving, and too accommodating, your children will take too much for granted. They will believe society owes them a living and thus they will be less productive. They may likely get into criminal activity after they have run out of ideas on how to work their parents, the system. They will not be able to stand on their own two feet often resulting in criminal activities to support their drug habits, their lack of money, and their lack of a sufficient education as they romped through the jungle of laziness and believing everyone owes them a living. Worse of course than the above, is in the case of children being horribly abused by parents and older siblings, which also ultimately for some children, allows them to become horrid citizens and monsters in the worst-case scenario. Husbands, wives, and parents have their work cut out for them. Good judgement on how to think about raising your children and respecting their needs would minimize problems that children, adolescents, and young adults will face with time. Parenting classes should be mandatory. Will it ever happen? Of course not! That sounds too much like "big government;" somewhat like what goes on in China to a degree. Remember their one child per family rule form the last century, which has cursed them with not having enough young adults to support their aging population. They are in hot water. All of these issues may lead to mental health problems among family members that will remain in some cases a problem as time goes on. Let's hope these issues are all amenable with time.

CHAPTER 21

AFFAIRS AND CHEATING

Marital affairs have long been known to contribute to higher divorce rates though not as much as most would believe. Over the past twenty years, marital affairs or cheating as most would call it, has been the cause of a divorce twenty to twenty-five percent of the time. Husbands are caught cheating twenty to twenty-five percent of the time and their wives are involved in cheating about ten to fifteen percent of the time.

Why do affairs happen? As they say in crime, it is related to opportunity, and motive, though usually not money (as in crime). Office affairs at the workplace are a large portion of these misdeeds. The gym, bars, social clubs, and even neighborhood gatherings may contribute substantially as well.

The greatest temptation is related to dating sites on the internet. Remember, other than workplace temptations, the other opportunities were few and far between in the days of yore. If your marriage is on a bit of shaky ground, your spouse may be easily temped by a sexy, hot, number at work. A wife may have also been putting on a few too many pounds in the first five years of her marriage which has been shown to be a contributing factor for men to shop around. When men gain weight during marriage, it has less of an adverse effect on their wives concerns. Much more about this will be considered later.

Surprisingly church has been shown to be another place of temptation. Who would have "thunk" that? Lack of communication plays a role in that a new friend at work or elsewhere may be more "fun" and "interesting" to talk to.

A drop off in marital sexual relations and sessions of intimacy may also play a significant role in setting up the temptations for cheating. Sexual desires and needs play a bigger role in the breakup of marriages, I believe, though research does not hit that as hard for a divorce as one would think. It could be that spouses do not want to admit that they have failed each other in the bedroom; falling asleep too soon, watching too much television, spending too much time on the internet, and of course too caught up in taking care of children, and their needs, which often will interfere with a good sex life.

How long do extramarital affairs last? About fifty percent of them tend to last between one month to one year. Long term affairs may last for about fifteen to twenty-four months and sometimes beyond. When one of the two marital partners recognizes the affair is occurring, it generally results in a divorce. But not always. Sometimes couples get involved in "threesomes" or other arrangements though those experiences are not common.

Violence is another major cause of divorce and is likely the most dangerous of all, sometimes leading to death of one spouse or the other. In fact, police will say, that racing to a home with potential marital violence occurring is the second most dangerous intersession they become involved in during their careers. The first of course is criminal behavior known to be involving firearms at the time of a 911 call.

Well, you may wonder what the chief causes of most of the violence are, that may occur in marriage. You do not have to wonder long. Drug abuse, addiction from narcotics, alcohol, "uppers", and other psychotropic drugs are the primary cause. Since the 1900's and before, many addicting drugs have been associated with endless crime sprees to support habits and have resulted in horrendous criminal activities both within society and the sacrament of marriage. The only good news is that far more criminals are being captured and jailed due to modern use of DNA and related sciences. These amazing new tactics have resulted in the overall rate of serious crime decreasing substantially in the past thirty years. If you do a crime, you will likely be serving time. It is as simple as that. Very few serious crimes involve people who have no known connection with each other. Therefore, random crimes are the unusual forms of crime though as

73

you know, mass shootings with automatic weapons appear to be on the rise but likely are not up ticking the crime rate.

We happen to hear about every mass shooting that is occurring often in real time, and this gives the impression that they are on the rise. The statistics are not in. Automatic weapons should have very limited access to most civilians. When our constitution was written, the "right to bear arms" did not have automatic weapons available to take into consideration. It is time to think this over again. Most people would be able to protect their homes and businesses with a shotgun, automatic 9mm, or a revolver, and do not need to have a fully automatic weapon at their side for general home or business defense.

COMING FULL CIRCLE

Times have changed. Big time! Society is not recognizable, compared to even two hundred years ago. Over the past several hundred years, enough issues regarding marriage have changed, that it's now time to rethink on how men and women should unify love affairs and relationships. While it is established that about half of all marriages end in divorce, it is equally poignant that some would be led to believe that breakups are initiated by both genders equally. That is not true. In fact, it is surprising to some, that most breakups are a result of women ending a marriage in seventy percent of all marriages.

As of 2022, what is very interesting according to the Pew Research Center, thirty percent of U.S. adults are neither married, living with a partner nor "engaged in a committed relationship." Nearly half of all young adults are single — thirty-four percent of women and an amazing sixty-three percent of men are not attached.

My hope is that with more complete information, couples will improve their chances of living long-term relationships with a much lower chance of breakups. Breakups are not inevitable. They are clearly related to preventable problems that each adult should be able to look at when thinking on how relationships may go wrong.

An insurance program, that I will propose much later in this book, will offer an interesting angle on how to improve the union between women and men allowing for a longer, improved, and more durable marriage. Is this really an insurance program? Not really, but my suggestions will likely insure a more lasting relationship than what marriage has achieved in recent decades.

(I thank **Wikipedia** and **Google Search Engines** for factual details included in much of this work. It gives my beliefs credibility, for only the truth will stand the test of time.)

CHAPTER 22

EXCESS WEIGHT GAIN IS OFTEN A FACTOR

Other very significant problems that often effect a marriage is one partner or the other gaining significant amounts of weight. This is especially true of women in their first to fifth years of marriage.

Women, obesity, and marriage are somewhat closely related to each other though not in a positive way. Are obese women less likely to marry? They are much less likely to marry than normal weight women and are more likely to earn less money and remain poor. In the case of men. Very overweight men are less likely to marry though they seem to be as well off financially as normal weight men.

In the case of men, obesity leads to an increase in sex-hormone-binding globulin which results in lower levels of testosterone within their bodies. Lower testosterone levels are linked to smaller male genitalia; smaller testicles and shorter penis. Along with that misfortune, they often have a drop in sexual desires and a drastically reduced libido.

About sixty percent of people with an overweight spouse claim that they are unhappy in their marriage due to their spouse's excess weight and lack of sexual attractiveness. In the other forty percent, spouses do not consider weight as being an issue. It could be because they are often overweight as well.

High school women are more concerned about their weight than are men.
The findings from an eight-year study of 10,039 randomly selected people who were 16 to 24 years old, when the research began, documented the profound social and economic consequences of obesity by following a population for years.

Women are more willing to date an overweight man than the reverse. Once married, obese husbands are less happy with their marriages than other men. Men who have lost weight have fewer marital problems than those that have gained weight during their marriage.

Obese wives that marry are happier with their marriages than normal weight wives. Some believe these women feel fortunate to be married in a market that decreases their value and thus they are happy and feel fortunate to have a husband. This theory is more hypothetical and may not be true. Apparently, each partner knows what they are getting into and therefore are satisfied from the get-go.

Newly married women gain more weight than other wives. In their first year they gain about seventeen pounds. By the fifth year of marriage many have gained up to twenty-four pounds. Some cultures value "round bodies" though not in America.

In the U.S., the higher one's socioeconomic status, the thinner a person is likely to be. Parents weigh more than nonparents. Married people weigh more than unmarried people. Whites tend to weigh less than Hispanics and African Americans. People are growing fatter as time goes on. Most admit that slimness is a more ideal state to be in.

Society tends to reject the obese and as a result they are often subjected to discrimination and stigmatization in areas of work, education, marriage, health care, and social areas. Obese men may have more marital problems because their wives could be pressuring them to lose weight.

After a divorce, over sixty percent of men were more likely to gain weight than men who remained married. Women's risk of weight gain after a divorce was much less probably because they were more often than not the ones to initiate the divorce.

In college-age students, overweight individuals are at a disadvantage in dating and developing relationships with the opposite sex as compared to thinner students.

A huge concern today in America is that the obesity trend is not abating. Obesity is a life-threatening problem related to many preventable diseases including cancers, heart disease, and type 2 diabetes. Obesity is erasing any health gains made by Americans who have given up smoking resulting in vast increases in other forms of disease. Over the past fifty years in America, the obesity rate has nearly tripled with more than fifty percent of our population being overweight or obese.

And why is that? My research at the Cleveland Clinic and while working in the private practice of medicine conclusively has proven that the primary cause of obesity among Americans is due to a sedentary lifestyle not seen in the 1800's and the first part of the 1900's. Most "experts" believe it is due to diet irregularities and increased consumption of calories, though my research indicates that is not the case.

In the past one hundred and fifty years we are eating fewer calories, consuming healthier foods, and yet we continue to gain weight. Genetic changes cannot account for obesity problems over such a short period of time. Genetic variations take thousands of years to evolve, if not longer.

In the 1850's, nearly all Americans were normal weight except for bankers and accountants? It is not about calorie intake. Over the past 150 years we have become much more sedentary resulting in excess weight and obesity.

Weight gain is also a creeping problem that gradually happens but when it reaches a level that a partner is found to be less attractive and sexually unappealing, it will sometimes lead to infidelity at worst or the loss of intimacy at best. That said, some people like larger spouses and are not influenced by their weight.

A good marriage is predicated on keeping your hand on the pulse of your marriage. Always see what you can do to improve your relationship on every level with your spouse.

Exercise daily together. Walking, biking, treadmill, swimming, tennis, are all great ways to spend time with each other while maintaining normal weight and a high level of physical conditioning.

CHAPTER 23

TIME OUT
Time With Friends

Everyone needs some time to themselves. It could be meeting with others, belonging to a club, going to a library, or for a woman spending time with the ladies. Everyone has different needs. The hope is that your needs do not subtract from your marriage and relationship. Your marriage must always be the most important component of your life. If it is not. You should probably not be married.

Many women love to meet with their lady friends to shop, play sports, attend workshops, and any number of other activities. How often this should happen is negotiable but should not occur too often if it causes significant problems related to your responsibilities as a mother or between you and your significant other.

In the same vein, your spouse could also meet with their friends for similar activities. Golfing, fishing, or hunting are often high on the list for men. Going out to a tavern three or more times a week is usually a sign of other problems in a relationship.

Under ideal circumstances, both of you could be gone about the same time, unless of course there are children to consider.

Everyone is different. Debbie and I chose to spend nearly all our time together. I do not go out for evening or weekend get-togethers with others. Many folks do, but we love being together above all else.

If you're spending too much time apart, (only you and your spouse knows) maybe you need to sit down and discuss what is appropriate. Some time away is often a good to focus on personal needs and desires. Do not go overboard!

WORKING OUT

On a regular basis, daily is best, either at home on your own equipment, outside, or at a gym. Workouts are very important for good health, living longer, and living better. I spend forty-five minutes daily, usually in the early morning for brisk walking, jogging, biking, or combinations of those to maintain good health. Daily exercise will lengthen your life by slowing down your aging process, as proven by research at the Cleveland Clinic by Dr. Michael F. Roizen, an expert on aging.

Please allow your spouse to indulge in these activities so you and her can have the best and healthiest life together.

Not everyone will exercise. However daily exercise is in the best interest of everyone for a longer, healthier, and better life. Most women who develop breast, uterine, and ovarian cancers in their fifties and over have been overweight and failed to exercise on a regular basis.

A woman stores estrogen in her fatty tissues. The more fatty tissue that you have, the greater amounts of estrogen you are storing within your body. The excess estrogen over stimulates your breast tissue, uterine lining (endometrial cancer), and ovaries. As you reach age forty-five and older, gaining excess weight may lead to colon and pancreatic cancer as well as the others.

The more you exercise, the less you will weigh, and the lower will be your chances of death from most chronic and serious illnesses. You will live longer and better.

Diet is important as well and all should follow appropriate guidelines, especially by reducing the intake of processed foods.

CHAPTER 24

SURPRISING YOUR SPOUSE

Now here is something you men should consider on a regular basis. Your wife will be wild with desire when you do amazing things for her that will mean so much to her. It means to her that you really care and that you truly love her.

Do you really want to please your wife? Ask her which room in your home can you paint, to freshen things up. She will choose the color of course. You can choose the time when you're able to begin. One room may lead to another and soon your entire home may be freshened up, however that is not the goal. The goal is to gift her your time and your pleasure in pleasing her. You will be rewarded. Now let's face it! What is more fun, golfing or painting a room? Gentlemen, you KNOW it is pleasing your wonderful wife. That is the most fun.

Fixing something that is broken is also a great idea. There are always a few things that need to be addressed. Your wife will love you for it. "Is Theree a Placee Fore Men?" Fix a few things and your place in her life will be cemented. Women love surprises. Add another project to the "gimish" and see how even better things will be. Your wife will love and treat you so fine.

The more you do for her, the more she will return the favor in so many ways. Bonding together forever requires the gift of giving to each other in many ways. For her and her home, it may be home improvements. Her home is her "highest love" after you and your children. Plus, she will have bragging rights with her lady friends. Think about that! Bragging rights!!!

GIFTING

Now let's talk about gifting. Your wife will never tire of surprises. Remember the main topic of this book is, **The Last Frontier: A Woman's Mind.** We are getting closer to exploring and fulfilling her needs, though we may never fully complete all of them. Because you and I (unless you're a woman) will never fully understand what are all her needs?

We can challenge ourselves into getting as close to her needs and desires as we are able to within our limited knowledge of her intimate mind set. Her mind set will always keep you guessing. But that is what makes your marriage interesting, wonderful, and challenging. Marriage in Latin means, "Confusing your man." Now that was a lie if there ever was one. LOL!

A few additional suggestions are in order here my friends. All women love flowers as you already know. There is something about flowers to a woman that has no pier. Flowers, being one of God's greatest creations, are beset with beauty that men cannot duplicate with his own hands. Flowers are a proof of God's existence, just as is a good dog. They only compare to each other in their level of perfection. When you give your special lady flowers, it says to her that she is perfect. It is that simple.

Another wonderful gift for her, that will take her by surprise is a new bottle of her favorite fragrance. Do not forget that fragrances are made from flowers and a lot of them. That is why they are so pricey; pricey-smicy-who cares? It is for that hot tomato at your side. I bet a wonderful bottle of her favorite perfume (maybe a Kardashian version) will do the trick!

A new designer handbag to be given to her out of the blue, is another explosion of love and passion. She will tear her clothes off for you – before nightfall. *I hope!!! If not, tear up this book!!!*

Maybe a special trinket; a new watch, a belt, sexy underwear, or a hot, hot night gown falling from her shoulders will do nicely.

Of course, you know where I am going with this ---- a new pair of shoes. Now that will be mind-blowing for her. They must be designer shoes and what currently is in vogue. In fact, maybe check out the magazine, **Vogue**. Shoes are to a woman what sex is to a

83

man. I hope you get my gist. Shoes/sex --- shoes/sex --- Shoes/sex. Okay I am obsessed with sex! If you met Debbie, you would know why.

Also, a little online research may open a few doors for other surprises. There can never be too many surprises. Believe me. Do NOT ask you male friends. They will not have a clue. They need to read this book as well. In fact, buy them a copy or pass yours on to them.

A great surprise for her proves your unending love and devotion for her. Treat your lady like you would love to be treated yourself and see what happens.

In fact, I'm taking a break soon from writing to hop in bed with Debbie. She loves me to be at her side whenever she is there (in bed). She loves cuddling. She loves contact. She loves romance. She loves everything. She loves me.

Let's Talk about Movies

Movies could be another great idea. She gets to choose. Not you. No exceptions, that is unless she returns the favor someday and has you choose.

In the same vein. Let her pick out the television programs you watch together at least fifty percent of the time. Do not concentrate on sports too often. Women are not like most men. Sports can drive some ladies crazy. If that happens, you're going backwards.

Remember your rewards will be greater when she gets to choose. Who ever said marriage is a peach? Well, in the South it can be.

TIME TO HERSELF

If there is one thing most of us wish for, it is having more time to ourselves in doing what we believe is fun. It can be anything that she believes is entertaining, picking strawberries, taking a nap, biking, reading a book, shopping for shrubs, staring at the sky. Whatever she wants. Rest and relaxation are helpful for everyone.

Give your special person time to themselves. They will love you for it. Even better, bring them a drink, a treat, a picture of yourself. Never be afraid to romance them. A special kiss, a wonderful hug, a back rub, will all add to their experience. Love should have no boundaries. Invent ways to please her. She will reinvent your marriage; a goal we should all pursue.

CHAPTER 25

In-laws or Outlaws; which are they?

Ok, here is another touchy subject. In-laws have the knack to create more problems than they solve. And why is that? It is because they are in-laws: period. In fact, in-laws can be more like out-laws in some ways. All people are different and thus they have their own ideas of what is good or bad for their children. Essentially, they have their children's best interest at heart, just like you and I. How can they possibly know what is best in anyone else's marriage since they likely do not even know what is best for theirs.

They are not part of your intimate marriage. Intimate in this case refers to the inner workings of your marriage from top to bottom.

Both sets of in-laws can cause an amazing number of problems for married couples. Now, I apologize to all of you wonderful readers who beg to differ. There are many in-laws that are not out-laws. Some are amazing and know when to keep their business to themselves and know when to lend an open hand (money). These in-laws are not a problem, though I suspect they are in the minority.

However, many in-laws do not get it and they often never will. On some occasions in-laws are fabulous when they take you out to dinner (if you get to choose where to go), when they take you out on a fabulous vacation (if you get to choose where to go), if they buy you a new car (you get to choose which model), and if they babysit when asked to (if you get to choose when). Otherwise, they may be a pain in the butt. Both sides of the "in-laws" can be challenging depending on one's perspective.

Try to work out with your wife or husband when in-laws can become involved within your life in the most benign of ways. Decide between the two of you when your in-laws should mind their own business. It takes a lot of experience, love, trust, and closeness to

know what to say and how to say it. It can be very, very, very tricky.
Good luck with this topic folks.

"I am heading for cover!"

CHAPTER 26

WHAT ABOUT WORKING

Working is tricky, but generally this problem has already been favorably "worked" out by the time you are reading this book. Everyone's situation is different and the need to work is so variable and unique that I dare not with any real enthusiasm wish to tackle this subject. If you want help with this, consult your bank account, your debts, your uncle (just joking), or your lawyer.

"Leave me out of this."

SHOULD MEN HELP WITH THE CHORES?

YOU'ER darn straight men should help with the chores! Are you kidding me? Men usually do the outside stuff, cutting lawns, sweeping out the garage, painting the back door, throwing the junk out, taking out the trash, fixing the gutter, raking the leaves, killing the weeds, washing the cars, repairing the cars, cleaning out the basement, fixing the light switches, stopping the leaky faucet, fixing the toilet when it plugs up; you get the picture. Men, that is what we do! But there maybe something else she wishes you to do, and your answer is "Of course my dear. Absolutely."

Also, "sweetcakes," before I leave for work, can I do anything for you that cannot wait? Anything my dearest! How about a sweet kiss? I love you so much baby! I can hardly wait to return home and sweep you off your feet." **"What do you mean, you would rather have me sweep the floor."**

One more thing sir, and this is a very big thing that will ingratiate your life with your wife forever. Remember to be thoughtful. Before you leave for work, ask her daily, "Sweetheart, how about if I pick up something or stop for something to bring home to you before I return from work? What could you use?"

At lunch time when you call her (you better) also ask her, "Baby, can I pick up dinner for us on my way home this evening. You have been so busy. You need a break. How about Italian, Chinese, or Mexican. Whatever babe? You name it."

"Life in marriage gets better, the better you get it. **Get it?**"

CHAPTER 27

EVENING PRAYERS

Putting your children to bed at night is enhanced by having them kneel at the side of their bed to thank the Lord for a good day and a good home. My parents taught that to all of us. As we grew older, we continued to remember God at the end of the day, however in our own ways.

Before falling asleep, prayers are a great way to help most of us relax and settle down. Prayers are unique to each person and usually are best said by yourself. Sometimes when Deb and I go to bed, I will ask her a question and she will say, "Not now honey. I am saying my prayers." She and I pray every night. Prayers help us fall asleep. Prayers are a good faith way of showing your connection with God and with your spouse. This is not for everyone, as you know. But it may be for you.

In my prayers I remember the day's events and thank God for wonderful food, fun, and the many accomplishments of my spouse and myself. Life is not always rosy. In that case, I ask God to help me be a better man and do the best I can to help others in every way.

Things that go wrong are all too often due to our own negligence and not handling problems or tasks in a better way. Every day I learn. I am getting better with time. As an example, Debbie and I rarely have important disagreements. We continue to hone our marital skills daily, with ever increasing love for each other.

It is all about listening to your spouse and complimenting them about everything that goes well. They will love you for it. Do not take for granted a person's life. Life is and will always be a struggle for everyone. Our struggles are more related to not paying attention and in taking someone for granted. Everyone is precious. Your significant other is far more important than your next vacation, television, car, or home. Make your life a journey of successes on all levels. It is easy to do this as soon as you take selfishness out of the equation.

Both men and women on average will fall asleep with in seven minutes or less of placing our heads on a pillow. If it takes longer, anxiety may be a cause and seeking medical attention for this is a good plan. Check with your family physician.

CHAPTER 28

A GOAL IS A GOAL IS A GOAL

It is a good idea to review your goals at least twice a year. Goals and needs will change due to so many interwoven struggles and changes in your life that are never predictable. That is why regular meetings and discussions in a pleasant environment is a good avenue to follow. Sometimes it is best over a glass of wine and at a restaurant you both enjoy.

Bringing along some notes might be helpful. Goals will change. The way you reach your goals will change. The art of negotiations will always be important. Look at all aspects of what you are choosing based on your finances, health, children's needs, work objectives, and long-term retirement plans. It is not difficult for those who love each other. Always keep in mind your spouse's needs more than that of your own.

CHAPTER 29

Lovers for Life

The premise of this undertaking has been to open our eyes on how men and women think differently and how they think alike. As we grow to understand the relationships between the sexes, we learn how to develop a long, beautiful, and loving marriage. There is a lot to be said for knowledge. A good relationship focuses on 'perfect love,' that only one man and one woman may have for each other. There are many facets that each of us must consider when hoping to develop that one and only bond for someone special.

Men may do things for reasons that seem foolish to others, but deep down inside he's trying to prove that he is worthy to be loved by his special lady. Whether it is about how he dresses and speaks, his neighborhood, the car he drives, or how he earns a living, it is about living within the boundaries his lady expects.

A woman likewise has the same goal in mind when it comes to her choice in a partner. She wants to please, excite, and attract the best man she can. We are all different. What is right for one person is not the same as what is right for another. Thank God for that or we would all be after the same person. That is the beauty of being different. Since we are all different, we all look for a different person that is our perfect match. No one else will do.

Love has no limits. That is because those who love each other, will repeatedly state they love each other beyond the love of yesterday. Love and feelings grow and transform us. For those who love someone within their sphere of influence, then they have found the holy grail of life and living.

Love is not surpassed by any other entity on any other scale. It is 'the primary need.' It is the reason for being. Love is the building block of life as we know it. We cannot live in a vacuum for long. Without the hope of love, we would likely give up and perish. True love will only be satisfied by those who understand each other, and they will not be happy without being in the arms of the other. Love supersedes all other needs and gives us a glimpse of what love will be like in the next life.

Show a man or a woman the love they can provide for the other, and you will see magic the likes of which you could never have imagined.

An amazing woman is about others. She may have the highest calling because she will provide special gifts for those, she holds close to her heart.

Men often give women most of the credit for a great relationship. It is unfortunate for the many that are unable to find their one and only love. After many false starts, most of us will learn what we really treasure in a relationship and with persistence we will likely succeed.

Those who cannot love and were not given love as a child when their values were developing, will struggle the most. Their values are tarnished by distrust and abuse. I have known those poor folks on different levels. They will always struggle in relationships because they were mistreated, and the meaning of real love escapes them. They have serious trust issues. Childhood abuse is all about fear and a lack of trust on all levels.

Given time, most of these folks, as they grow up will form a love for another person after decades of efforts. Unfortunately, their love for that person will be speckled with periods of doubt because real trust was never a part of their formative years. Their idea of love will not likely be of the same intensity as that of others, unless they are able to find a partner who is good, trusting, and with a beautiful soul. Trust is the key in all successful relationships and between all beings.

Your treasure is out there. Never give up. But when you find that one person you so desire, you will cling to them almost to a fault.

Give them some space. Trust and love for you and them will evolve with time. You will be able to have the 'perfect love' you deserve.

Love in a perfect union is what these writings are all about. It is about achieving perfection through listening, hearing, and seeking the love for another person that must supersede you own needs. Perfect love is what all people crave whether they realize it or not.

We all have needs, hope, and a plan. We learn to appreciate someone on many levels to achieve what we all really want; it is not a new dress, a new home, or a fancy sports car. What we wish for is to be fully accepted and loved by an amazing individual who is not judgmental, critical, or derogatory. That person desires the same in their life as you wish for in yours. It is a perfect love that has no bounds.

In a good marriage there is no room for sarcasm, hate, controlling speech, yelling, screaming, deception, fear, or violence. If these things are occurring on any level, then marital counseling is a must or the possibility of a separation or a divorce must be considered.

Not all marriages are a perfect match as you are aware of. Most are unable to make a go of a marriage that is linked to alcohol, drug abuse, physical abuse, crazy spending, or cheating. There is no room for these problems in marriage. When it occurs, you have chosen the wrong person.

With a long enough dating period, these problems should be detected before most couples have tied the knot. Do not rush into marriage. Take your time. If you do not feel a true bond early on, likely you were not meant for each other. Bonding usually occurs early in a relationship, because when it is there, it is there. It is a feeling of magic that you have not experienced before. Bonding is not a question of luck or chance. It is a chemistry that you both have for each other whenever you're together. Either you have it, or you don't. Look for the chemistry or keep looking for the right formula. It is better to be safe than to be sorry.

My wife and I had an instant bond with our very first kiss. It is rare but it happened to us. Our bonding occurred even before we formally introduced ourselves to each other. We hadn't said a single word to each other, not a word. It was all in the kiss. It was God given.

There are a couple of other attributes worth noting. Judgement is one of them. It is a measure of purity that varies from moment to moment when struggling to perfect a relationship. It is interesting because it may be consistently good in your marriage, but sometimes foolish activities blow up the entire concept that we continually look for in each other.

Judgement refines our activities in a positive way when properly applied to all circumstances. Your woman will watch for this attribute just like a hawk watches its prey.

Another quality a woman may look for, realizing it is somewhat unrealistic, is the quality of perfection. Perfection is a utopian paradise not within reach of any of us and will never be, yet it is the prerogative of a woman to look for that quality in every man, the perfect father, brother, nephew, and alas the perfect husband.

This is not to be.

We are flawed and always will be. We say stupid things. We do stupid things. We act stupidly. And why is that? Because sooner or later, the Ides of March will encompass even the best of us, and we will fowl something up. To our spouse, bad behavior appears to be careless, foolish, silly, thoughtless, lazy, meaningless, crazy, or just downright stupid.

Guess what? They are often right. But guess what men? Our women are very forgiving, understanding and do not expect perfection. What they want is a good effort. You did the best you could. Not every challenge works out. Perfection is not what she wants. A really great day is one in which everything goes well. Well, is fine. Forget perfection. She will be happy.

CHAPTER 30

THE LAST FRONTIER

So, we start at the beginning!

The last frontier is not what you may surmise. Rather it is untouchable, unseen, uninhabitable, often confusing, sometimes distorted, often agreeable, just as often not, protective, easily ruffled, difficult to mend, easily hurt, often disrupted, very consuming, ultimately desirable, inelastic, forgiving, unforgiving, demanding, expecting, but always full of love. That is the Final Frontier! It is your wife. She is the Final Frontier! She is LOVE!

The LAST FRONTIER: A WOMAN'S MIND

Is it definable:	NO
Is it understandable by men:	NO
Does she understand:	BETTER THAN US

She will not always be understood or definable by her man and that is a good thing. The same can apply to us. In attempting to understand her, it helps for us to move in the right direction when thinking, from experience, her needs and hopes.

Under the best of circumstances, we may achieve our goals in our marriage with time and compromise. The wonderful woman we met so long ago always deserves our best efforts. Going forward, we will likely achieve the highest level of love for her over any other person.

We hope to acquire an understanding and an intellectual handle on how our woman thinks. Even if it is to just keep up with her. We men operate sometimes in a relative vacuum and should not assume too much. Like us, a woman's thoughts and needs will fluctuate. That is normal. Constantly listening to her and truly paying attention to her wishes, in time will allow both of you to live a wonderful life together. Life is complicated for all of us but careful attention to the details of mutual love will fulfill our needs. She is worth it. I am thankful that I found Debbie.

Men will not grasp many of the idiosyncrasies of the last frontier. But it is in that reality, that greatness and wonder persist.

For the unknown will remain intriguing, desirable, and hopeful but never obtainable. The unknown allows for an unending journey to pursue and hopefully to win over the controlling facet of a woman's mind as well as her wonderful body as it exists for us men to enjoy.

My cousin through marriage, recently lost her husband due to unfortunate surgical accident. He was 76 years old. She has been beside herself and will likely be struggling with her loss for the rest of her life. I feel for her, though on the other hand she had many glorious years with him, that gave their lives together so much value. With time they both became more and more acquainted with each other. They slowly and likely completely discovered most if not all the smallest innuendos of "The Last Frontier."

"My hat is off to them. They made it!"

A WOMAN'S MIND

The final frontier is final for a reason. It is the end of the road. It is the last stand. It is the boundary that will never be crossed successfully by your man. And is that a good thing? I suppose it is! And why is that? Because once you conquer the final frontier, there is nothing left. There is no mystery, no challenge, no worthwhile target to achieve. You do not want to understand her anyway, but if you could, (don't worry you won't) the let-down may be crushing and would likely result in a boring existence that neither a man nor a woman would ever want. It is just like sex. You never will achieve everything you want and that is why you keep coming back for more.

Peer into her eyes. Look for a clue as to what she is thinking. Don't spend too much time doing this. You won't find it. What she truly wants is endless love shown by your ability to listen, forgive, forget, cherish, own, support, give, and show up. That's all there is to it my friends.

Do not buck the final frontier. Leave it alone!

Your woman knows what she wants.

She will find a way to achieve it.

Get out of her way.

AS INTENDED

Wonder Wisdom Worship: Marriage

"As Intended!
I think of time.
Of eternity.
Man & wife are one.
They become others.
Others become one.
Love cycles between all.
Hand in hand.
Heart in Heart.
For Eternity.
As Intended! "

(I thank **Wikipedia** and **Google Search Engines** for factual details included in much of this work. It gives my beliefs credibility, for only the truth will stand the test of time

For men, an increase in body weight can lead to an increase in sex-hormone-binding globulin, which causes the sex hormone testosterone to fall. Due to a drop in the sex hormone, sexual desires and libido may decrease drastically, which can in turn impact your sex drive. Obese men and some overweight men are also

Does obesity affect romantic relationships? The data about weight is particularly striking, with **60 percent of people saying they are unhappy in their relationships if their partners are also significantly overweight.** However, in the case of the other 40 percent, the weight issue is not a problem, and some prefer it to being a normal weight. Everyone is different and it is best to discuss any potential challenges that may affect your marriage on a regular basis. No issue is too insignificant and even the big ones are solvable if people love each other.

What causes obesity & overweight? (EXERCISE DIMINISHES THESE)

In my research, I have found that for most overweight people both men and women, the primary cause of obesity is a sedentary lifestyle. Proper nutrition is next in Importance. Genetics plays less of a role than you may think. Yes, you may see several members in a single-family similarly overweight and you thus may believe there is a genetic component, however the answer is this. In the same family, people eat the same when growing up into early adulthood, and they tend to follow the same exercise programs as well. We learn through example; good and bad.

- Some believe that the environment plays a role. I believe that is true. In parts of the country such as California with a more balanced climate, people have more opportunities for outside exercise. The world around us influences our ability to maintain a healthy weight. However, people in Florida, though having warm weather most of the year still may be on the obese side unless they live near a beach and swim often.
- Genetics in general is less important than most would believe. Even if one tends to be overweight based on their perception of genetics. A Good exercise program will offset that connection most of the time when people workout with a cardio type daily walking or cycling program.

100

- Health Conditions and Medications may be a contributing factor and should be discussed with your primary care physician or your nurse practitioner.
- Some people wish to incriminate stress, emotional factors, and poor sleep however most of us have many of these issues and still retain normal weight by exercising daily and eating a nutritious diet. You may consider reading my book, "Weight No Longer" for further help about improving your weight and over-all health.

Although high school women are more concerned about their weight than men are, women are more willing than men to date an overweight person.

Once married, obese husbands are less happy with their marriages than other men, but men who have lost weight report fewer marital problems then men who have gained weight during marriage.

Obese wives, on the other hand, are happier with their marriages than average-weight wives. While newly married women gain more weight than other wives and often more than their men, few will gain a lot in their first year of marriage.

Some cultures value big round bodies, though not the United States. In this country, the higher one's socioeconomic status, the thinner a person is likely to be.

Married people weigh more than unmarried, parents weigh more than nonparents, and whites tend to value lower weight, and thus weigh less than Hispanics or African Americans. In the first year of marriage, women gain on average seventeen pounds.

While the population of America and even the rest of the world is getting fatter, ideals about body weight increasingly emphasize slimness.

Society tends to reject obese individuals. They may be subjected to discrimination and stigmatization in many areas including education, employment, marriage, housing, health care, and also many social areas.

Research has also found that women in high school are more likely to date overweight men than the reverse. Women are more likely to consider themselves overweight and have more stringent body weight ideals than men have.

One theory about obese women being happier with their marriages is related to recognizing their decreased value in the marriage market when a society stigmatizes obesity.

Obese men may be more likely to have marital problems because their wives could be pressuring them to lose weight, resulting in hostility and conflict.

Obese men had the lowest likelihood of being married when looking at other men.

At the end of the day, overweight and obese people are more likely to eventually wind up in divorce court.

Significantly overweight women are less likely to marry than women of normal weight. They are also more likely to be poor and to earn far less.

In surveys looking at college-age participants, overweight individuals are often less likely to be chosen as sexual partners when compared with those who are thinner.

In the early 1960's only about fourteen percent of people had a body mass index (BMI) of over 30 which is indicative of obesity. Today about forty percent of adults have a BMI of over 30 and thus are obese. Many more are overweight. We have a big problem.

Why has America become more obese?

Most "experts" believe the increase is primarily the result of **consuming more calories.**

This is NOT TRUE. My research at the Cleveland Clinic clearly proves that weight gain is chiefly due to a more sedentary lifestyle than calorie consumption unless the consumption is way above normal. You can prove this to yourself, by beginning a first-rate daily exercise program, and watch your weight decrease without cutting calories. However, reducing man-made carbohydrates in your diet such as candy, pastries, cakes, pies, cookies, and the like will change your world in amazing ways.

The rate of obesity has nearly tripled in the United States over the last fifty years. Again, our calories have not increased by a staggering triple amount though our activity level has nearly completely bottomed out. That is the cause. That is the issue. It is time to face reality.

.dipsomania

By the late 19th Century, **dipsomania**, or alcoholism, was being treated as a disease. The first arrest for driving under the influence of alcohol was in 1897. In 1955 the first breathalyzer was patented. Americans drink an average of 2.3 gallons of pure alcohol a year compared to 7.1 gallons in 1830.
Did people drink more in the 1960s? Some of those stats are counterintuitive -- for instance, **people in the 1960s don't seem to have consumed more alcohol on a per capita basis than we do now.** Apparently, it was the 1970s that were the peak of booziness in America.

Which is a reason that divorce rates increased during the 1960s and 1970s?
Why, then, did divorce increase during the 1960s and 1970s? One reason is the increasing economic independence of women. As women entered the labor force in the 1960s and 1970s, they became more

economically independent of their husbands, even if their jobs typically paid less than their husbands' jobs.

How does drug addiction affect divorce?

Similar to how substance abuse affects property division, **addiction is most likely to affect alimony when an addicted spouse has harmed the couple's finances.** In most states, a judge could decide to award additional alimony to the spouse of an addict if the addict drained the couple's finances fueling the addiction. Of course a judge can dictate whatever they wish, however for practical purposes that does not mean much when it comes to collecting.

Why did divorce increase so dramatically in the 1970s?

The 1970s marked the period when, for many Americans, a more institutional model of marriage gave way to the "soul-mate model" of marriage. Of course, the soul-mate model was much more likely to lead couples to divorce court than was the earlier institutional model of marriage.

What did the divorce rate do between 1960 and 1980?

In the US, divorce rates more than doubled from 2.2 per 1,000 in 1960 to **over 5 per 1,000** in the 1980s. How does addiction affect a marriage?

As drinking or drug use gets worse, it starts to take more and more time away from the couple, taking its toll by **creating an emotional distance between the partners that is difficult to overcome.** These couples also report that they fight and argue a great deal, which sometimes can become violent.

Printed in the USA
CPSIA information can be obtained
at www.ICGtesting.com
LVHW052252210224
772452LV00009B/207

9 781958 082706